Synchronized Breathing

By
Tara Ellison

TWCS
PUBLISHING HOUSE

First published by The Writer's Coffee Shop, 2013

The Writer's Coffee Shop
(Australia)   PO Box 447 Cherrybrook NSW 2126
(USA)   PO Box 2116 Waxahachie TX 75168

Paperback ISBN- 978-1-61213-189-4
E-book ISBN- 978-1-61213-190-0

A CIP catalogue record for this book is available from the US Congress Library.

Cover Illustration: Nina Hunter

www.thewriterscoffeeshop.com/tellison

This book is dedicated to late bloomers.

Chapter One
The Lemon Marriage

Having to move back in with my mother and teenage brother at the ripe old age of thirty-five seemed to loudly announce my failure as an adult. Ugly thoughts rattled around inside my head as I packed up the car and put Oliver into his car seat for the drive over the hill to my mother's apartment in Beverly Hills.

As we wound our way up through the canyons, the wretched nagging voice that keeps a running tally of my missteps had a field day. *Congratulations on yet another screwup, Scarlett. What's this now—a stalled career and a failed marriage? You're on quite a roll!*

That voice was happy to throw a virtual catalogue of prior lapses in good judgment back in my face, as if it thought I needed reminding. Despite those missteps, this time I knew I was doing the right thing.

Sometimes it's difficult to pinpoint the exact moment when a marriage goes from merely unraveling to unsalvageable. It can be an insidious process; you don't necessarily feel the cords fraying as it's happening. But sometimes a sequence of events can clobber you over the head as in, 'take that, stupid' and you know that fighting for the marriage isn't going to be worth it. The outcome isn't going to be good, in fact, it has become terminal and it is no longer a matter of *if* but *when.*

That's how I felt when I found the photos.

My mother was over, visiting. Oliver was napping and she wanted to show me an article on the Internet about the benefits of extended breastfeeding. She followed me over to the computer and took a seat beside me. As I turned the computer on, a new file in the corner of the desktop titled *homework* caught my eye. As my husband was chronically underemployed, the folder became instantly intriguing. What homework could he possibly have and why wouldn't he have said anything about it? Curiosity got the better of me. I clicked on it and then gasped as we were greeted by the contents of his private photo collection.

"Oh, my," my mother said and didn't bother to mask her pitying tone. "Let me put on my glasses."

I was speechless. But that didn't stop me from frantically clicking on all the files. My husband had been busy. There were literally hundreds of photos showcasing his member in various artistic poses—Naked Erect Penis in the garden catching some rays, Erect Penis proudly emerging from a sea of bubbles in the bath. Sleepy, Flaccid Penis lying in repose on the couch. He had lovingly documented his dick in all facets of its daily life.

My mother let out a long sigh and shook her head.

"Well, that's a very time-consuming hobby. No wonder he doesn't have time for a real job, he's already got one."

I couldn't argue with that.

But that wasn't the end of the union. We limped along for months after that, somehow managing to survive our fights—that was until today.

Dragging an oversized suitcase behind me, a well-worn diaper bag slung over my shoulder and balancing Oliver on my hip, I hauled us into the elevator. I let Oliver press all the buttons, purely because he loved to. Besides, it delayed the inevitable.

Here I was—returning to the womb after the collapse of my marriage. It was official: I was a mess. I was a walking advertisement for the utter mismanagement of my life. If there had been a management team responsible for this succession of lousy choices, heads would be rolling. But sadly, the only rolling head was my own.

The one person who was positively *ecstatic* at this news was my mother. Oliver had barely touched the doorbell when she flung the door wide open, as if greeting a spring feast after a winter of famine.

"Darlings!"

Her face dropped when she saw my tear-stained visage, and then again at the box of animal cookies that had exploded out of the overstuffed diaper bag and onto the floor in the hallway.

Oliver darted past us in a mad dash to get to the fish tank, which was the center of the universe as far as he was concerned.

"Oh, Scarlett. Come in, darling" she said, and gave a dismissive wave of her manicured hand. "Don't worry. *Everybody* has a crappy first marriage. Husbands are left by placing one foot in front of the other and not looking back. It's time to pick yourself up and move on."

She stepped out of the way as I lugged our belongings and shards of animal cookies over her threshold.

My mother—or CeCe, as she preferred to be called—had three marriages under her belt, so leaving a husband was a subject she knew quite a bit about.

"You're are still young, Scarlett. Well, okay, maybe not exactly *young*, but young enough, and you don't look *too* worse for wear! Plus, you have darling little Oliver's welfare to consider now, so you simply cannot indulge your taste in *subpar* men any longer."

My questionable taste in men had long been a favorite subject of CeCe's to revisit whenever the opportunity presented itself. And as her newly minted roommate and captive audience, this was a good one.

"Darling," she said, "the only surprise in any of this is that you lasted as long as you did in that lemon of a marriage. This is the best bloody decision you've made in years!"

To say that CeCe was not fond of my soon-to-be ex-husband was an understatement.

That man couldn't lure me out of a burning building was the nicest thing she had to say about him.

Immune to his charms from the very beginning, her naked loathing was hard to miss. She could send an unmistakable chill through the room on a sweltering day merely by laying eyes on the man.

He didn't exactly strive to alter her low assessment of him, either. Despite my urging, he wouldn't so much as lift a finger for her or clean a dish after a holiday dinner. Blessed with good looks, he was the sort of Los Angeles fellow who expected to be catered to. Unaccustomed to women rebuffing his charm, he wasn't used to having to *earn* anyone's favors. The sheer gift of his presence was supposed to be enough. Until, of course, it wasn't—which was how I ended up on her doorstep.

Seeking refuge with my mother made about as much sense as leaping from the frying pan into the fire but I didn't have any other options. Planning ahead was never something I was good at, and sometimes one has no idea that this will be the day one leaves their husband.

"Well, I do think we should pop open some champagne and celebrate the end of that lemon marriage! It's about time." CeCe headed purposefully to the kitchen, taking time to do a little victory jig on the way.

"Oh . . . no, I'm not quite up to celebrating yet." I sank into the couch wearily, watching Oliver smacking the side of CeCe's oversized fish tank, sending terrified goldfish darting in every direction.

"Look, Mama! Make them *go*!" He watched with pride at this accomplishment.

"Don't whack the glass, Ollie. That scares them," I said with more than a reasonable note of irritation. Each loud thwack felt like a new crack forming in my skull.

"Oliver, the fish are a bit tired, darling. They've been swimming all day," CeCe called out from the kitchen. "Let them have a rest. Come here, love. I saved some lovely big chocolate strawberries just for you. Look!"

Oliver obediently heeded the call and joined CeCe in the kitchen.

CeCe was very good at anticipating when I was about to lose it. She relied on distraction to diffuse tense situations, often employing chocolate or booze—ideally both. This was one of her greatest attributes, as far as I was concerned.

CeCe set the elegant, slender glasses on the coffee table and proceeded to open the bottle of Dom she kept cold for precisely these sorts of occasions.

"No, CeCe, I don't want to drink. It will only make me feel worse."

"Nonsense," she insisted, and handed me a glass. "We have to mark the occasion. Thank God you're finally off-loading that dropkick. Cheers!"

As the newly appointed hostess of my divorce party, CeCe was a hard person to say no to.

"Cheers." I lifted my glass to take an obligatory sip of the annoyingly happy bubbly.

Oliver was preoccupied with two large chocolate strawberries and began taking turns nibbling on them while pink juice streamed down his chin.

CeCe made a preemptive dive at him with a cloth napkin and then took a seat beside me. "Here's to the end of that awful chapter with the miserable X!"

We had dubbed my husband 'X,' so Oliver wouldn't know whom we were talking about. It was about the only non-expletive laced, child-friendly name CeCe could come up with for him. Wanker, asshole, and shithead weren't going to cut it.

"Now, I blame myself for this travesty of a marriage," CeCe said. "Clearly, I made some sort of colossal screwup somewhere in your upbringing that you resorted to marrying him in the first place. Exactly how you became so wretched and desperate that you thought he was your last option is anyone's guess. If only I'd sent you to that Swiss finishing school, you would have learned to make better choices. You would have been exposed to a better class of men . . . and *this* would never have happened."

This was a tired old joke between us and translated to 'if I'd sent you away, you might have done well and married *rich* instead of an underemployed musician without a pot to piss in.'

"I doubt a Swiss finishing school would have saved me from myself, CeCe." I was tired of beating a dead horse.

"Well, at least we could have tried!" CeCe gave an exasperated exhale.

CeCe had her own plan of action regarding romance: Find—and sometimes marry—a man, leave said man, and then move to a different country. Rinse and then repeat, sometimes in dizzying succession. By comparison, I was a rank amateur. But if there was one thing I learned from leaving our native Australia and traveling the globe with CeCe, bouncing from man to man, it was that no matter how hard you try to leave it behind, shit travels.

Leaving my own marriage had been a fantasy for quite some time. In fact, from within an hour of Oliver's birth, I had been aware of the clock ticking down on our union. There was an unshakable sense of *what the fuck have I done?* I tried to dismiss it as postpartum malaise but instead of clouding my thinking, it was as if things suddenly became crystal clear. I felt as if a veil was snatched away and what I was left with was an unsustainable situation.

The sole power X held over me was Oliver, a fact not lost on either of us. When we argued, X would race over to Oliver and hold him up out of my reach, taunting me. When these fights would drag on and become unbearable, I dared to suggest separation, and held my breath to see how he would take it. He would laugh at the suggestion and throw my past in my face. "You can't support him. You're a loser, Scarlett. What have you ever done with your life? If you wanna go there, I'll make sure that no judge in the world will give you Oliver."

That threat was enough to keep me contained, at least for a while. Part of me was scared he might be right. It was no secret that I had never been good at making sound financial choices in life, and hadn't had a steady job in years. In my darkest moments, I did feel like a loser. It was painful to think that I was so transparent, but that was how I had always been. I'd never developed much of an exterior barrier against the world. Despite disappointments in life that might serve to toughen others, I remained very much a soft-shell crab.

"So, that's it then? *C'est fini?*" CeCe snapped me back to attention.

"Yes, that's it."

"What happened this time?" CeCe inquired with a hint of excitement.

"Our same dysfunctional dance . . . and then he said the magic words . . ."

I paused and watched Oliver dancing in front of the television. Blissfully ignorant of the significance of the day, he was sucking on his strawberry and bouncing in time with the music from a peanut butter jingle.

"He said 'Take all of your shit and take *your* baby and get out,' " I said quietly.

"Ah, yes. Well, we've heard that refrain before." CeCe reached for a chocolate.

"Yes, but this time I didn't wait for him to calm down. I suppose I'd had enough. I did just what he told me to do . . . and here we are."

"Well, it's about time. I can't imagine what you ever saw in him. And to think of all the other eligible men you've met . . ."

"He cast some sort of spell on me, I guess, that caused all logic and reason to disappear. Whatever it was, it's worn off now so let's not dwell on it, shall we? Moving on . . ." I said with faux cheeriness.

Oliver darted around the living room searching for the items he'd stashed during our last visit a week ago: his tiny silver airplane with the chipped red paint, the well-worn SpongeBob SquarePants blanket, and his blue rubber ball with white stars on it. He set out his recovered items on the antique Chinese table in front of CeCe, next to his stack of favorite books.

"Read a story, CeCe." Oliver plucked one from the pile and set it on her lap.

CeCe had cleverly trained Oliver from the beginning to refer to her as *CeCe*, and never *Grandmother*. *Grandmother* was *très gauche* in CeCe's book—not to mention sexually repellent—and therefore forbidden. Come to think of it, calling her *Mother* didn't rate much higher.

With Oliver and CeCe occupied for a moment, I excused myself. All I wanted to do was crawl into a hole and hide, but with a toddler, one was never afforded that luxury. A nervous breakdown was out of the question, so a moment of solitude in the loo would have to suffice.

I fished my cell phone out of my purse. I needed to call my best friend, Emma, and give her the news.

As I walked down the long corridor to the guest bathroom, I passed CeCe's wall of family photos and was struck by the lone photograph from my wedding. It was as if I was seeing it clearly for the first time. X was smiling with his arms clasped around me territorially and I was staring into the camera, wearing a vacant gaze. Despite the frozen smile, a sort of resignation registered in my eyes. On some level, I knew what I was in for, and somehow accepted it.

I checked my reflection in the bathroom mirror. Was there anybody in there anymore? Sometimes it was hard to tell. I used to have a lot more life in me. I used to have a bit of spark, a bit of game going on. What happened?

CeCe had been quick to share that one of her dear friends had expressed concern over how sad I looked in recent photos. I believe she used the words *beaten down* and it was hard to argue against that sentiment. Still, CeCe's genes were putting up a good fight. I could still be considered somewhat attractive—at least in good lighting—but I had looked unhappy for a long time and it would take a while to undo that. There was now a deep worry crease etched between my eyebrows that I'd have to live with and my dirty-blond hair hung shapelessly around my face, in dire need of a trim. I was hardly in go-out-and-set-the-world-on-fire shape, but exactly who is when they've just left a marriage? Most people looked like shit on a day like this unless they were having an affair and enjoying tons of sex. I should be so lucky.

I called Emma.

"I've finally done it," I said when she answered. "I've left him. Oliver and I are at CeCe's."

"Holy shit. Are you okay?"

"I don't know. It's too soon to tell. I feel a bit wobbly. One moment I'm excited, and the next I want to throw up."

"Listen, this split has been coming for a long time." Emma's voice could always calm me when I was in a state. "It was bound to happen. The only thing you had in common with him was that you wanted to start a family."

"I blame that damn *Newsweek* article that told me my eggs were getting old and that if I didn't hurry, I'd have to flush the dream of being a mother down the toilet, too, along with all the other dreams I didn't quite live up to . . . so I grabbed the nearest penis in a mad panic, and look where it got me."

"It got you a beautiful son."

"That's true. He is the best thing that ever happened to me, so from that perspective it was a brilliant move. But I have this sinking feeling that the undoing of this marriage is going to be a lot harder than the getting into it was. I've no idea what I'm going to do now."

"You don't have to figure it all out today. Just deal with one day at a time right now. Get some sleep. Let's talk in the morning. This is a big step. I'm proud of you."

"Thanks."

Unlike other dreams I'd let go of, motherhood was not going to pass me by. And that's where X came in. Timing was the key element in our union. My lifelong dream of being an actress had died a slow and painful death and it seemed that creating my own family was the only dream I had left that was attainable.

I splashed cold water on my face and willed myself to pull it together.

Oliver was sitting on CeCe's lap listening enraptured to her racy version of *Little Red Riding Hood* when I returned.

"Yes . . . he was a very, *very* naughty wolf, up to all sorts of tricks that put him in bad standing with the young ladies in his village." She bounced Oliver wildly up and down on her lap to emphasize the naughty bits, while he giggled uncontrollably. CeCe's wicked sense of humor was another asset I was counting on to get me through the next uncertain months.

"Come on, Ollie," I said. "It's time for your bath."

"No, you relax. I'll give him a bath." CeCe swept him up into her arms.

"Thanks, CeCe." I was thrilled at having a rare moment with nothing to do. That specific aspect of domesticity with CeCe was something I could get used to. She was very helpful with Oliver and it was a stark contrast to life with X. He never helped me bathe Oliver. He was a fastidious house cleaner but did little in terms of helping with childcare. If I left them together briefly to go to the market, when I returned, Oliver would be crying and X would be whining about it. It was hardly worth the bother. Oliver and I developed our routines and X became less and less a part of the equation. In a way, it seemed Oliver and I had been in rehearsal for this separation for ages and by now, we had it down.

I surrendered into the comfort of one of CeCe's oversized chairs and swung my legs over the arm of it as if I were a child. Here we were, safe in my mother's apartment. The thought both soothed and repelled me in equal measures.

Then I had the joyful realization that I could turn the television on—and watch any program I wanted—without X berating me for it. Television was for simpletons, he reasoned, but it was merely another form of control.

CeCe's apartment had been acquired in a settlement with her third husband and she lived there with my nineteen-year-old brother, Sam. A nicely appointed apartment, it sat on a palm tree lined street and was filled with her beloved Chinese antiques. It was spacious and offered a dazzling view of the Hollywood Hills but there were only two bedrooms—and both were very much taken. CeCe already had a crib in her bedroom for Oliver for whenever we visited, and she graciously offered me her day bed to sleep in. Living in a dorm room setup with my mother was hardly anybody's idea of a good time but it would cover us for the time being. I was counting on some miraculous twist of fate to occur and facilitate us finding a place of our own, although I had to admit the idea terrified me.

A few days later, as news of the split spread, three of my closest girlfriends—Autumn, Susan and Emma—came over after Oliver's bedtime to lend their support. With Oliver sound asleep in the next room, we were free to say whatever we wanted without having to edit or use delicate, boring language.

The four of us had come to Los Angeles in our twenties to make our mark. Emma and I were studying to become actresses, Susan was driven to be a top talent agent and Autumn . . . well, nobody was really sure what her original goal was, but her biggest claim to fame was as a voracious man-eater. Here we were, over ten years later and Susan was a partner at her agency, Emma enjoyed success as a working actress, and Autumn was in demand as a stylist as well as a world class consumer of men.

CeCe had left for a date, but ever the hostess, she set out a wine and cheese platter for us with a side of chocolate truffles. It was classic CeCe—a first-aid kit for the senses. We sat around the fireplace and I began to fill everyone in on the split.

Autumn spoke with characteristic candor. "Oh, come on, Scarlett, it was time to move on. What were you doing with him anyway? He was always talking about how '*evolved*' he was. What a fucking bore! Anyone who feels the need to tell you how 'evolved' they are obviously isn't. You're in your sexual prime. I say we throw you a divorce party and get you back out there! You need to get back on the horse!"

"I couldn't even find a horse in this funk, let alone remember what to do with one if I did," I said flatly.

It was a sad fact that I didn't fantasize anymore. I had trouble conjuring anything remotely sexy in my head. It was as if my former sexy self had closed up shop entirely and moved on. *And that used to be my very favorite part.*

"Oh, I'm pretty sure you'd remember how to ride one . . ." Autumn gave one of her trademark snickers.

"I don't recall the last time I had sex that wasn't . . . perfunctory," I said, and searched my memory bank for a highlight.

"There's a big hint right there. Who needs perfunctory sex?" Autumn recoiled at the thought. "I would have been long gone."

"Yes, but that's what any relationship becomes. At least you're free now to start over," said Susan. She may have become the very picture of married stability, but I knew her back in the single, chandelier-swinging days.

Emma opened the Cabernet and poured four glasses. "I feel so guilty that I didn't try and stop you from marrying him. He wasn't the right man for you. We should have staged an intervention or something."

"I felt that way, too, but you wouldn't have listened." Susan accepted a glass of wine.

"You're right. That's the scary part. I had a terrible feeling it wasn't going to work but I felt compelled to do it anyway. How screwed up is that? I leapt into this marriage with my fingers crossed, so I have no business being surprised that it didn't work out."

"Look," Susan said, "you have Oliver out of the deal. That makes it all worthwhile, doesn't it?"

"Absolutely," I said, cheered by the thought. "My only defense is that I thought it was what I was supposed to do. I was at *that age* with absolutely nothing happening in life, so it seemed like the logical next step. I just had no idea how much work being married to the wrong person can be. It was misery."

"Every marriage is work, but the trick is to pick someone you actually want to be married to." Susan smiled at me.

Susan was my opposite in almost every way. Logical and levelheaded, her pragmatic view of life was so foreign to me that I often thought she was speaking another language.

"I'll try to remember that for next time," I said. "If there ever is a next time."

"You gave it your best shot," she said. "Personally, I thought you should have bailed right after you found all those nude photos. You've been very tolerant, as far as I'm concerned."

"What photos are you talking about?" Autumn asked. "Why I don't know about this?"

"You've been away on location. Tell her." Emma nudged me.

"One day, while I was using the computer, I stumbled upon his extensive nude photo collection."

"Of other women?" Autumn shrieked.

"No . . . that would actually make a certain amount of sense. They were all nude pictures of *him*, but mostly just of his dick."

I got up and put another log in the fire, as Autumn scrambled to reclaim her jaw from the floor.

Stunned silence followed, so I pressed on. "His penis obsession was hardly a new thing. After all, it was his most prized possession, but seeing the photos en masse was a bit much. There were hundreds of pictures of his penis—chilling out in the garden, lathering himself in the bath, erect penis checking the mailbox. It was nuts. It was like that traveling Gnome series of photos—but each one featuring his dick in a new pose. Even his winking asshole made some artistic cameos!"

"Jeez . . . how on earth did he manage that?" asked Autumn, instantly intrigued.

"See . . . all that yoga pays off." Susan's quip sent Emma into hysterics.

"Hey, I'm not saying the guy isn't creative! It's amazing how creative you can be when you have nothing to do all day but play with yourself." I squeezed myself back on the couch in between Emma and Autumn.

"Wow . . . I had no idea. I guess he's not the total bore I thought he was after all," Autumn said with awe.

"I just had less and less respect for him and that's a very difficult thing to overcome in a marriage, especially with all of our other issues."

"So, what did you say to him?" Autumn was now almost bouncing out of her seat with excitement.

"I said *what's with all the dick photos*? He laughed and said he was 'just having some fun'. He even turned one of the photos into his screensaver so that twelve gleaming images of his penis greeted me every time I used the computer. It felt like I was living with a teenage boy who'd just discovered the pleasures of wanking and not a forty-year-old man. CeCe caught an eyeful too. She was there when I found them."

"What did she say?" asked Emma.

"She said she was *underwhelmed*."

"And let's face it, CeCe would know!" Susan said, sending Emma into another fit of giggles.

"Wow. I had no idea." Autumn continued to grapple with the news. "He just looks so . . . *vanilla* to me."

"That's what all the gay guys do," said Emma. "They send each other pictures of their dicks! Do you think he flipped to the other team?"

"Who knows what he was up to? All I could think was '*What am I doing here?*' I'm exhausted from nursing and caring for the baby all day and night while my unemployed husband blasts music and dances around naked in the garden taking pictures of his cock, like some demented elf."

"Do you think he was having affairs?" Autumn asked the question everyone was wondering.

"I don't know . . . maybe . . . probably. But in the end I didn't want to know. I didn't need confirmation. I just wanted out. I wasn't winning any awards in the doting wife department, either. We had this resentment toward each other that lay just under the surface and counseling didn't help. I wasn't up for all that cock worshipping. It got to the point where I couldn't stand to sleep with him—so yes, he probably did go and find someone else. It was beginning to look that way. I couldn't fight for the marriage anymore. What was the point?"

"But you did try to make it work. I watched you struggle," Emma said softly.

"I did try to make the best of it but it became so exhausting. All that cooking I did, trying to be Martha fucking Stewart. I tried to conform to his crazy diets. It drove me nuts. Every week a new one: vegan, raw, macrobiotic and then cycle back to steak and martinis. I mean, come on! He was always trying to *find* himself by trying on different jobs, different diets and fitness routines, and all those yoga retreats."

"Oh, my God . . ." Emma rolled her eyes dramatically. "Forget the yoga! Do you remember that crazy cycling phase he went through? That was the worst! He was always pedaling somewhere on his bike, like a mad cycling fool in his colorful spandex shorts with his weird little helmet." Emma leapt up and acted out furious pedaling around the living room, eliciting riotous laughter from the group.

"He didn't know who he was, and that was part of the problem," I explained after we'd all calmed down. "But he also didn't have a clue who *I* was. Just because he met me in a yoga class he assumed that I was this 'Yoga-Girl' and ultra health-conscious, when anyone who actually knows me can tell you I eat far too much sugar, I can't live without my caffeine and television, and I can get bloody lazy if I don't watch out."

"Well, you are Australian. That should have been his first clue that there'd be some bad behavior," Susan said.

"He despised all those things about me. And trying to be something or someone I wasn't just to make him happy, wasn't working. He had this fantasy of me that I could never live up to." I drained the last of my wine.

"Remember how he used to get mad if your hair didn't look perfect? That always bothered me." Emma quickly topped off my glass.

"Yes, he made me do the 'hair check' all the time. If we were going out and he didn't like the way my hair looked, he'd wait in the car and send me back inside to fix it." I cringed at the memory.

"Okay, that's just weird," Susan said with authority. "What guy cares what your hair looks like? Usually they want to mess it up, not fix it. That's creepy."

"I always felt like I was disappointing him in one way or another." I felt that familiar knot forming in my stomach.

"I think you've got that backward." Susan commented and took a sip of wine.

"I kept thinking, '*Is this what I've waited my whole life for?*' Is this what I came all the way to America for? It just felt like some heavy karmic debt I had to pay. There wasn't anything joyful or redeeming about our marriage —other than Oliver—and that's a big burden for a child to bear."

"Next time, don't marry the stalker!" Susan warned.

"That's true," I said. "He was terribly hard to shake."

"Before you get serious with anyone again, he's going to have to pass a committee," said Emma, reaching for a slice of Brie.

"The good news is it can only get better!" Susan said.

The acid began churning in my stomach again. I got up to fetch the antacid tablets from my purse.

"And by the way," Emma called after me, "where is the fabulous Miss CeCe tonight? She would hate to be missing out on any X bashing."

"Naturally, Miss CeCe has a date." I looked around for where I'd thrown my purse and tossed a few of the colorful tablets into my mouth and began to chew them, followed by a swig of wine for good measure.

"Why is it that your mother has more dates than anyone I know?" asked Emma.

"That's an easy one," Autumn said. "It's because CeCe's one lusty broad! The last time I saw her she gave me a lesson on the importance of giving a proper prostate massage! She even demonstrated with a gyrating finger!"

Autumn lifted her pinkie in the air and showed us her best twirling technique.

"Yep . . . that's my mother for you," I sighed, and took another swig of wine to dispense with the unpleasant chalky aftertaste.

"Where does she meet all these men? I'd like to meet more men," stated Autumn with surprising enthusiasm coming from someone already in a relationship. Autumn was famously allergic to monogamy.

"Mostly through Internet dating sites, but sometimes other sources," I said, and flopped into the armchair facing Susan. "All she has to do is step out of the apartment and they seem to trail her all over town."

"I love your mother," Emma said with enthusiasm. "She's hysterical. We once had an entire conversation about vibrators and lubrication—which ones are organic and don't have all the silicone and crap in them. She's a wealth of information, that woman. She shares sex tips as if she were sharing a soufflé recipe. Maybe she should write a sex blog for seniors or something—"

"Well, that's all very entertaining, but not when it's coming from your own *mother*!" I groaned.

"Come on, it's still funny."

"The other day, she was extolling the virtues of anal sex while tying Oliver's shoelaces, and I just about lost it! I got really pissed off. She can't get away with that forever . . . he's a two-year-old now but he won't stay two forever! She honestly sees nothing wrong with sharing all of this info and has no regard for whose little ears she might be polluting—mostly mine. Besides, I really don't need those images dancing in my head." I shuddered at the thought.

"Well, what did she have to say about it?" Autumn's interest was suddenly piqued.

"Oh, I don't know. She was going on and on . . . something about trying to avoid it while you have hemorrhoids." I sighed, exasperated.

"I would think that wouldn't need to be stated." Susan gave a snort.

"God bless her! I'm sure she's having hotter sex than all of us put together," said Emma.

"Speak for yourself," Autumn said with a hint of indignation.

Autumn fancied herself an expert on sex and the idea that someone might have anything over her, let alone a sixty-year-old woman, likely didn't sit very well.

"Who's having hot sex?" Sam, my brother, asked appearing out of nowhere and startling us into an awkward silence. He'd been so quiet in his room that I'd forgotten he was home.

He took the gum out of his mouth and launched it into the fireplace.

"Believe me, you don't want to know." I grimaced.

"Fair enough. So how is everyone this evening?" He popped a white chocolate truffle into his mouth.

"Sam . . . tell me, how old are you?" asked Autumn while giving him an appraising once-over that made me slightly uncomfortable.

"Nineteen." Sam gave a halfhearted tug at his low-riding jeans. A very healthy portion of his teenage ass was hanging out in the terribly offensive style all the kids his age seemed to favor.

"You're turning into quite the fox, Sam. Are you still with your same girlfriend? What was her name again?" Autumn continued to grill him playfully.

"Mikki. I'm on my way to pick her up now. We're going to a movie." He ran his hand through his hair, which was stiff from all the hair products he regularly plied it with.

"Sam takes after CeCe. I'm the only one in this family that tanks in the love department." I waved my wine in the air in the defeatist fashion I'd resorted to a lot recently.

"Have fun. Say hi to Mikki for us." Autumn craned her neck to watch him walk to the door.

"Good-night, ladies." Sam waved and disappeared into the night.

"He is going to be quite a lothario. I can smell it." Autumn nodded approvingly.

"Autumn! You've known him since he was a little kid." I felt protective all of a sudden.

"I didn't say I wanted to date him!" Autumn chuckled. "I was just acknowledging what a fine young man he's growing into."

"Well, I don't like to think of him that way. He's my baby brother."

We heard the key in the lock, and CeCe appeared.

"CeCe . . . come and join us," I called out to her.

CeCe walked in and immediately cheered at the sight of us. "Oh, I'm glad you're all still here!" she said, and took off her jacket.

"How was your date?" Emma asked.

"Ah, my date . . . well, he was a crashing bore and he lives in Simi Valley." She laid her jacket down over the back of my armchair. "I can't decide which is worse."

"Simi Valley?" Autumn scoffed at this bit of news.

"Isn't that a bit *geographically undesirable* for you, CeCe?" Susan offered diplomatically.

"Yes, among other things." CeCe sighed. "Of course, he didn't *tell* me he lived in Simi Bloody Valley, which was clever since I would have instantly dismissed him if he had. He was smart enough to meet me halfway, but the statistical likelihood of me finding my match hiding away in the boondocks of Simi Valley is about twenty million to one."

"Forget that clown. Come and have some wine with us," Emma said as she opened another bottle of wine. "We were just talking about you!"

Emma poured a glass and handed it to CeCe.

"Thank you, darling." CeCe gladly accepted it, and perched on the arm of the couch.

"You're looking ultraconservative tonight, CeCe," said Susan.

It was true. CeCe was unusually subdued in a black silk pantsuit with a single strand of generously proportioned pearls.

"I don't think I've ever seen you in pearls before, CeCe." Emma agreed.

"Ah, well . . . it might *look* conservative." CeCe slowly fingered the pearls. "But you haven't a clue where these pearls have *been,* now have you, darling?"

"That's right, we don't," I said quickly. "And let's leave it that way, shall we?"

"I can assure you that they've led a very full and well-traveled life," CeCe said while everyone erupted into laughter.

"Thank you for that lovely visual, CeCe. How about a toast?" I attempted to steer the conversation in another direction.

"All right, then, Scarlett. I'll make a toast. Here's to exploring new fellows and new adventures!" CeCe said with renewed enthusiasm.

"Hear, hear," said Autumn with vigor.

"I'll happily take a new man, but I'm not sure my husband would approve," said Emma with a wicked laugh.

"Yeah, sometimes I'd like to trade mine in, too," said Susan.

"Don't despair, ladies," said CeCe, warming to another of her favorite subjects. "No need to ditch the old ones. Contrary to popular belief, you can teach an old man a few new tricks. It's all in the presentation. They are generally quite willing to learn. You really can get them to do just about anything."

"No, CeCe, *you* can get them to do just about anything," I said. "We've decided you should teach a class or write a saucy blog or something!"

"Well, I'll drink to that, too. Bottoms up, ladies!" CeCe lifted her glass.

With the twinkling lights of the Hollywood Hills in the background, the five of us toasted to new beginnings while I attempted to squash my growing apprehension along with my burgeoning ulcer.

Chapter Two
Men for CeCe

CeCe had been puttering about in the closet when she stuck her head out the door, looked over to where Oliver and I were reading on her bed and said, "Darling, are these your knickers or are they mine?"

She held up the tiniest pair of apricot-colored Cosabella G-string panties and waved them at me.

"Um . . . they're yours." I acknowledged the fact after a totally unnecessary inspection.

My sixty-year-old mother had sexier underwear than I did, a depressing fact I chose not to dwell on. CeCe had sought to remedy this situation for years and bought me flimsy, barely-there lingerie that I hid in a drawer and had no occasion to wear. Whose mother buys their grown daughter knickers with naughty little peepholes in the back?

Living in cramped quarters with one's mother was not without its challenges, the least of which being the delicate laundry issues. Having to share a bedroom as if we were college roommates and not presumably mature women quickly grew tiresome. CeCe often made unusual moans and called names out in her sleep, which she confessed often got her into trouble with her lovers. Unlike Oliver, who slept like a log, I had a hard time quieting my thoughts as it was, and didn't need to hear CeCe barking orders at lovers in her sleep.

There are few secrets in a two-bedroom apartment spilling over with occupants. It was quickly apparent that even my baby brother enjoyed a better sex life than I did, which was admittedly a low bar.

CeCe went back to her lingerie and Ollie and I went back to reading *Goodnight Moon*.

Just as I got Ollie settled down again, Sam and his steady girlfriend—a dark-haired minx named Mikki—darted by the bedroom door talking and laughing loudly on their way to the kitchen.

Ollie bolted up and made a mad scramble to get off the bed and out the door to them.

"Ollie, come back!" It was impossible to compete with the allure of a teenage uncle.

Mikki was a near-constant presence in the apartment and stayed over most nights. She was so skinny that if she stood sideways, she nearly disappeared. Severe looking with pale skin, she wore her jet-black hair in an asymmetrical bob which she straightened every day with a flatiron. She may have been from Beverly Hills but her wardrobe screamed Las Vegas and consisted of very revealing, low-cut T-shirts that always showed a flash of a leopard-print or fuchsia bra underneath, and barely-there nylon miniskirts. Black ankle boots coupled with white bobby socks completed her look. Despite her flamboyant wardrobe choices, the most fascinating thing about her was her extraordinary confidence. An unusually opinionated girl for nineteen, Mikki was a force to be reckoned with. It was not unusual for her to tell a roomful of adults that they were *misinformed* about politics, religion, or any other topic that came up during dinner conversation. My little brother had his hands full.

As soon as Ollie made it out to the kitchen, Mikki and Sam darted back past him, tousling his hair in the process, and retreated to Sam's room, locking the door behind them.

Ollie trailed after them and wailed his displeasure at the closed door.

"Sam . . . open door, now! *Please* . . ." Ollie cried while taking his disappointment out on the indifferent door and thumping at it.

"Not now, Ollie. I'm taking a nap."

"But, you're not sleeping. I can hear you! Saaaaammmmm!"

"*Not now, Ollie!*" Sam said in a tone that Ollie knew not to challenge.

Ollie leaned his head against the door in defeat.

I watched this familiar scene play out and waited.

Oliver reluctantly dragged himself back to me, and sank heavily into my arms. "Mama, I'm pissed out!" His cheeks flushed with frustration.

"I know *just* how you feel, sweetheart," I said and tried not to laugh. CeCe and I were both guilty of saying we were 'pissed off' about something from time to time, and this was his version.

Before long, strange noises began to emanate from the bedroom, squeaking sounds that landed somewhere between a bleat and a meow.

Ollie's face scrunched up as he strained to decipher what the noise was. He turned his attention in the direction of Sam's closed door again.

I started singing in an attempt to drown out the feral noises. "The wheels on the bus go round and round, round and round, round and round . . ."

"Wait . . . Mama, stop! Stop singing!" Ollie tried to cover my mouth with his hand. "Is that a *cat*?"

"No, there are no cats in there, Ollie," I said.

"Shhh . . ." He paused, listening intently. "What is that?"

"They're playing a game called 'Old McDonald had a farm' and they make funny animal sounds!" I said, pleased with my ingenuity.

"I want to play, too." He tugged at the leg of my sweatpants.

"They're playing the teenage version," I said, and whisked him away from the bedroom door and the mysteries it contained.

Sometimes the fact that I had anything left of my sanity felt like quite an achievement.

CeCe preferred to turn a blind eye—or blind ear—to whatever Sam was up to in the apartment. While Sam and Mikki were content to frolic in his bedroom making animal noises, CeCe was actively baiting her hooks and trolling the Internet for eligible men. The moment she got home from work, she grabbed a glass of wine and made a beeline to the computer to check the day's haul. With the giddiness of a teenager, she couldn't wait to share her 'Catch of the Day'.

"Oh, darling, come and have a look at this fellow," CeCe said, tapping a perfect red nail at a profile picture on her computer screen. "This one says he likes sailing . . . and traveling . . . and Indian food! And he has a full head of hair!"

"A trifecta," I said, unsure of what else to say.

"You're not really looking at him . . . have a *good* look," she said ignoring my lack of enthusiasm.

I leaned over her shoulder to get a better look at the fellow in question. They all looked the same to me. "That's nice, CeCe. He looks . . . *nice*," I said, straining to come up with something. "At least he's not wearing a wedding ring in the picture on the boat. That's a good start."

Historically, many of her Internet prospects turned out to be married and looking for a little fun on the side.

"Here, what about this other one . . . let me find him again. He really is a bit naughty with his innuendo!" She chuckled. "But a bad boy now and then can be a good thing! Oh, this chap here, he *loves* his limericks. He sends me one every day. Listen to this:

There was an old boy from Philly,
Who had a wonderful way with his willie,
The women would tease and strip, he took his pick,
Jiggling his hips, he fucked their lips,
He was an expert at diddling those fillies!"

"Wow. That's talent for you. I'm really tired, CeCe. I need to go to bed." I was desperate for an escape.

"Darling, this is how it's done these days . . . it's a virtual carousel of fellows. This whole world of available men comes right to you, right in your own home," she said, relishing the concept. "It's like shooting fish in a barrel!"

"I can hardly wait," I said, flatly.

I felt a panic attack brewing, and briefly entertained an urge to run away until I remembered that I had nowhere else to run.

"This is what you'll be doing shortly, too, darling. It's so much fun!"

I nodded and started picking again at my already raw cuticles.

"We just need to get you back out there. I'm really excited about your future, Scarlett, and you should be, too!"

The Victoria's Secret sweatpants that Sam and Mikki had given me for my birthday were a little less snug around the bum these days thanks to my 'divorce diet,' and that discovery was about as close to excited as I got about anything. A carousel of men was something I felt quite certain I could do without.

"I'm going to go and check on Oliver," I said, and left her to her own amusement.

"All right, darling," she said.

Observing my mother at close range again was illuminating. She'd always had a way with men but now I was viewing her through experienced adult eyes. CeCe was a champion dater with more energy than most women half her age—including me—and she maintained an air of detachment that bewitched men in droves. A curious mix of allure and indifference, they couldn't figure her out. She was not only beautiful—with piercing ice blue eyes, light brown hair and a slender, yet voluptuous frame—but more impressively, CeCe was smart as a whip. She loved nothing more than a good game of verbal volleyball and could intellectually wipe the floor with most of her opponents if she felt so inclined. However, that keen intellect became totally disabled when choosing men. My father, her first husband, decided when I was a baby that fatherhood was not for him. Theirs was a torrid love affair that wasn't built to survive the rigors of child rearing, so he took himself out of the picture, and hadn't been heard from since. CeCe's choices in men often defied explanation, much like many of my own choices. Living with her was a painful reminder that the apple fell very close to the tree.

No matter what mistakes I had made in the past, Oliver was living proof that at least I had done one thing right. Having this little person to love and care for gave my life a much-needed purpose. Sunny little Ollie had the ability to pierce whatever funk I was in momentarily, but he wasn't used to having me in such a distracted state. He would cup my face in his tiny hands and say, "Don't make the sad face. Just make the Mama face!"

Oliver was adjusting well to our new living situation. CeCe had been Oliver's primary babysitter since birth and hence they shared a close bond. In the mornings, CeCe often made tea and pancakes with him before she went to work. On the weekends, she would take him on the veranda to do some gardening or to lunch at Neiman Marcus. This was a routine that had been in place for quite some time and now there was even more time for activities.

Oliver never asked when we would be going home. I wondered how he was processing this huge change.

"We're going to be staying here with CeCe and Sam for a while," I told him. "Mama and Daddy are going to be living in two different places but you will still see both of us."

"Okay, Mama" was all he said about the subject.

X and I communicated mostly via e-mails and Oliver started having regular visits with his dad three times a week. One morning, when I dropped Oliver at X's, I noticed that every photo I was in on the refrigerator collage now had a monster magnet placed directly over my face. I was a vampire in one, a scary green dragon in another, and Frankenstein's monster in yet another. This represented a lot of effort. The precise placement in areas that Ollie couldn't reach indicated a rather tall suspect. I gave X a look and said, "Nice."

X grumbled something inaudible.

He didn't look like he was faring very well. His blond hair was uncharacteristically unkempt and his brown eyes seemed perpetually bloodshot. He was furious with me for leaving, and despite what I said, he seemed to prefer to believe that this was merely a phase I was going through and that I was coming back.

"You've gone crazy. This isn't you," X insisted as he followed me down the driveway out to the car, leaving Oliver unattended in the house. "You're having a really bad postpartum reaction."

"What are you talking about? Oliver is two!" I said, incredulously.

"You just need to come to your senses and love me again," he said, grabbing my wrists unexpectedly and trying to pull me into an embrace.

"What are you doing?" I struggled to get free of him.

"I can make you love me again."

"Stop it." I pushed him off. "Ollie's in the house alone . . . *please* watch him." I hurried down the path to my car. I looked around to see if any of the neighbors had caught any of this madness.

"Stop this nonsense and come home!" He hovered behind me as I got into my car, and draped himself over the open door, making it difficult for me to close it. "I *know* you still love me . . . you just need to come to your senses." He began to sob, making it almost unbearable.

I cringed. What hold he once had over me was long gone. "Are you listening? I don't want to keep going through this with you. *Please* go and check on Oliver." I firmly closed the door. His persistence rattled me. He wasn't hearing anything I said.

"You're having a breakdown, Scarlett . . . but we'll get through this," he shouted through the crack in the window. "I still love you!"

Still shaking, I drove off leaving him standing on the street in his bathrobe.

—✕—

Most husbands would prefer to think their wives had gone mad when they wanted a divorce. I had my share of moments of madness but I was not mad. At least, I hoped not.

Later that day, Dr. Goldberg, my longstanding ob-gyn called out of the blue.

"Your husband called me," he said. "He seems to think you've lost your mind and are suffering from postpartum depression—even though I pointed out the extreme unlikelihood of that scenario at this late stage."

"What did he want from you?" I was completely bewildered.

"He made some disturbing allegations, Scarlett. I've known you for a long time, so I didn't buy it, but other people might. I don't know how to say this but . . . watch your back."

"What do you mean? What is he planning to do?" My whole body began to tremble.

"I have no idea but it doesn't sound good. Take care of yourself, Scarlett."

"Thanks for letting me know." I was seething. I hung up and instantly burst into great floods of tears.

When things weren't going as he planned, X always had a few tricks up his sleeve. I'd seen this behavior from him before, but it had never been aimed specifically at me. It was deeply unsettling.

"How dare he?" CeCe shrieked when I told her. "He's got some bloody nerve. If anyone's loony it's him."

"You and I know that but some people don't see through him. He can be creepily convincing."

"You have the creepy part right but I have to believe that people aren't going to buy anything he says. He's hardly an impartial player in all of this."

I hoped that she was right.

I worked to avoid awkward exchanges by making them brief or by bringing someone with me. But even when I didn't have to see him, he called every day to speak with Oliver and we would go around and around again.

"When are you coming home?"

"I'm not coming home."

"Let's talk about this—"

"There's nothing to salvage here. This separation has been a long time in the making. It's not a snap decision." I didn't want to meet with him or give him any false hope. We'd already been to counseling. Twice. There was no point in dragging it out further.

"I didn't think you really meant it." He sounded surprised when I maintained my position.

"But I did mean it. We don't work together. You know that."

"I want my family back."

"You love the *idea* of us, of having a family, but you don't love me." I was quiet but firm.

X was invested in how we looked, the portrait of an attractive, young family—but none of it had ever felt real to me. It was as if we became illuminated only when people were watching.

"Are you having an affair?" he asked.

"No, of course not," I replied.

There had been no affair, but I had certainly been ripe for one if the opportunity had presented itself.

"You must be seeing someone or why else would you leave?" he insisted.

"No, I'm not leaving you *for* anybody . . . I'm leaving you for me."

Seeing no progress, he swiftly changed tactics. "Your mother is making you do this."

"What's CeCe got to do with anything?"

"This is all her fault." His voice trembled with anger.

It was true that CeCe was never a fan of his but she had never actively campaigned for this outcome.

"This separation is all my doing, I'm afraid. No co-conspirators here."

"Sure it is," he grumbled.

The cleaving process was exhausting. X refused to take any responsibility for problems in our marriage and that was one of the many reasons I was leaving him.

In the beginning of our relationship, X had won me over with charm and persistence. He was fun and *available*—quite unlike other men I'd dated. In hindsight, perhaps he was a little *too* available and I should have questioned why other elements in his life were lacking that he had so much free time for me. Unfortunately, one never thinks of those things in the throes of a blossoming romance. X hated his job selling advertising for a radio station and preferred to sit around, strumming on his guitar, composing love songs. How those traits in my mind translated into *husband* and *father* cannot be easily explained. He was more like the fun college boyfriend that you have a fling with but never consider marrying. Unfulfilled by our careers and desperately seeking to fill that emptiness, our static-cling relationship propelled us forward into domesticity. Before long we were living together, then married and then pregnant, in quick succession.

We were both to blame in the collapse of the marriage but X preferred to let his anger bleed out onto CeCe any chance he got. She was an easy target. If she made the mistake of answering the phone, he would say, "I know what you're doing CeCe . . . you're on a mission to get rid of all dads," or some variation on that tired theme, but his wrath wasn't limited to CeCe. If Sam answered the phone, X would bellow, "You're not Oliver's father! I know what you're trying to do . . . you're never going to replace me!"

Sam would hand me the phone and whisper, "Look out . . . X forgot to take his meds today!"

X's next move was to cut off my cell phone and family credit card. Although I was expecting he would do it at some point, it upped my anxiety considerably. I felt unmoored, as the last vestiges of marital security were being stripped away.

When these dark, emotional storms were looming, Sam would often say,

"Hey, Ollie, why don't we go down to the park?" Then he would scoop Oliver up with one arm and turn him upside down until Oliver was laughing hysterically. Sam was a big kid himself, so he was a great help buffering Ollie from any fallout. Happily, he had a lot more tolerance for mind-numbing kid activities than I did—especially in my current state—and he would sit on the floor with Ollie and build with his blocks, play cars, or make Lego towers.

While Sam was happy to swoop in and help, Mikki was less predictable. Sometimes she was an angel, but then other times, having a two-year-old boy taking attention away from her left her hurling expletives in Sam's direction. Another argument between them would lead to further audible rounds of makeup sex.

During Ollie's visits with his father, there was the strange new burden of free time. So accustomed to having a toddler with me 24/7, I felt bereft without Oliver bouncing on my hip, sharing his sweet, bubbling commentary on the world. There was no Ollie to sing in the car with and no Ollie to snuggle up with to take a much-needed nap.

It seemed I had forgotten how to conduct myself as a separate person. Mommy-mode was all I knew. Trips to the market became futile. Sometimes the point of my mission—find something to eat—seemed beyond my capabilities. It was as if the aisles were filled with items in a foreign language. Everything looked familiar but I was lost.

The sunny Southern California climate seemed to mock my despair. The weather was perfect. There were annoyingly perfect-looking people everywhere living perfect-looking lives in perfect-looking houses. It was dreadfully oppressive, not to mention lonely. Looks must be deceiving. Could I really be the only person making a mess of their life in this perfect-looking town?

The nights were the worst. While Oliver slept peacefully, I would often sit in the living room in the dark and watch the goldfish in the fish tank, as if waiting for them to tell me what to do next. Their swollen bodies danced and sashayed confidently before me with tiny flecks of gold catching the light in the most mesmerizing fashion.

"Oh for God's sake, Scarlett, stop staring at the bloody fish and go get yourself a man." CeCe flicked at me with her tea towel. "At least get your hair done or a manicure or *something*. Your hair is looking very drab and you've been picking at your fingers a lot lately, darling. You'll feel much better if you get out and do something for yourself."

"She's right. Do one thing right now to make yourself feel better," said Emma during a call while on a break from shooting a television commercial. "Go to a movie, go for a walk or go down to the mall and have a wander around."

"That sounds very sensible, but I have no idea what I even like anymore. I just feel numb," I said, aware of how strange that sounded. "I expected to feel a bit better by now, that's all. It's been a month and the vast relief I was expecting hasn't arrived. I couldn't wait to leave and now . . . everything feels so black to me."

"It's still early in the process. You knew this wasn't going to be a picnic. He wasn't going to make this easy for you."

"You're right. He was going to fight this no matter what. I have no regrets about leaving. It's just been a bit glum, that's all—"

"It's called divorce and there's a reason it has such a bad rap. It sucks but you'll get through it. I'll call you later. Love you!"

"Thanks. Love you, too."

I sought comfort in another cup of tea. When in doubt, have some more tea, as my grandmother always said, which CeCe later amended to wine.

Exchanges with X became cool, but mostly cordial. We existed beneath the thin veneer of civility, circling each other, unsure of what the other was going to do next. Who would make the next move? I suspected he was up to something. He was a little *too* quiet. Friends referred me to several attorneys but I hadn't made a move before X surprised me and served me with divorce papers. I hired the first available lawyer and put the retainer on my credit card. Then everything deteriorated from bad to worse.

"There is nothing lousier than a Christmas divorce," I said to Emma as we walked through The Grove, dodging Santa's elves and carolers. "A Christmas divorce announces that all pretenses of civility have been stripped away and the parties couldn't wait one minute longer to tear into each other."

"Maybe courts should shut down for the whole month of December."

"What could be more miserable than being fought over by pit-bull attorneys while having happy Christmas music blasted at you at every turn like some sort of warped soundtrack?"

"Yes, it's hideous," Emma said. "But you have to do it sooner or later, so you may as well dive in now. There's no reason to delay it."

"You're right."

I watched a young mother smoothing her son's hair into compliance before taking his turn on Santa's knee. Having to watch other people's holiday merriment without my son felt like cruel and unusual punishment. What was the point of any of it without Ollie?

With Oliver as our sole marital asset, we embarked on a nasty custody fight. Several times a week, legal-sized envelopes arrived from my new divorce attorney and sat ominously on the kitchen counter. My stomach would wrench at the sight of them. They were exploding bombs of emotional shrapnel designed to inflict as much anguish as possible. I would leave the hate-filled envelopes sitting unopened for days.

"CeCe! I cannot believe these papers!" I shrieked after finally reading the contents of one of them. "It seems that anyone I've ever met—including his *entire* family—has written a declaration stating what a terrible mother I am. This part here says I'm a bad influence on Oliver because I do not respect animals. *Respect animals*? Do you know what he's referring to? He's told them I couldn't stand the stinking blackbirds in the yard that wreaked havoc and ruined my vegetable patch. I threw a stick at the bloody things once! That's my 'big danger to animals moment'. Call PETA immediately!"

"Well, why can't you put in there that he used to masturbate with the kitchen utensils?" CeCe retorted. "And tell them that it traumatized you and that's why you don't like to cook anymore. You should put that in there! Now *that's* cruel and unusual punishment!"

"I can't put that in there. The judge doesn't want to hear that. I can't even believe I told you about that."

"Well, he's a vengeful bastard. He's doing exactly what he said he would. He's trying to take Oliver from you. There'll be a line around the block with people ready to declare what a loon he is. Don't you worry, it's all nonsense."

An assortment of betrayals flowed thick and fast on the divorce track, including documents chronicling our marriage—and my behavior—in twisted detail with startling declarations from people I had formerly counted as friends or in-laws who now assailed my character. Bizarrely, this process even extended to include near strangers, people whose random interactions with me somehow confirmed my husband's low opinion of me as a mother and qualified as fodder for X's case.

I was completely unprepared for this vile aspect of divorce.

"Nobody warned me to expect that every silly thing I'd ever said or done, or every irritable exchange I'd ever had would be trotted out, taken out of context, or spun to make me look like the worst human being on the planet." I complained bitterly to my lawyer who, much to my chagrin preferred to let some of the silly accusations stand. He didn't want to waste time with what he saw as insignificant blather. His calm demeanor soothed me on the phone until I remembered what it cost me to actually get him on the phone. Invariably, when we hung up, the sense of panic resumed.

I was in way over my head. X had been vastly more productive with his free time, soliciting people and cataloguing damaging declarations. The absurdity didn't end there. I was required to read each ridiculous accusation and give my version of events. It was madness with a price tag to match. It was a complete waste of time, energy, and resources. I only had one credit card and this legal battle was going to suck it dry.

"You naively assumed that nasty divorces were reserved for celebrities or people with lots of money. You're finding out that isn't the case," Emma said.

"I'm getting a crash course in all of it now."

Aside from the regular searing pain in my chest, the divorce was leaving what I feared was an indelible stain on my psyche.

There were physical tolls to be paid, too.

"Darling . . . you're getting very skinny and not in a good way. For God's sake, have a sandwich." CeCe would reprimand me but I could barely eat. Or sleep. I dropped twelve pounds in a month—startling on a small frame. I hadn't looked thirty-five before all the shit hit the fan, but the stress and incredible fatigue made me feel seventy-five.

"Here you go, I got you a present." CeCe presented me with a big plastic bag containing new paints, a set of brushes and canvases. "Why don't you start painting again? You used to love it. And if you do that, you'll get more therapy out of it than talking to the fish at night."

"CeCe! Thank you! I guess that's better than drowning myself in large amounts of alcohol, which was sort of the direction I was thinking about taking."

From that point on, my sleepless nights became more productive. The paintings were predictably dark and raw. They were portraits of women, often naked and looking wounded, some standing at the edge of a steep cliff, looking out. Others featured frail women sitting alone in oversized chairs, their faces hollow and sunken-looking. It was how I felt—naked, vulnerable, broken. I hid them away in the hall closet and couldn't bear for anyone to see them. They were so starkly personal that I couldn't risk feeling any more exposed than I already did.

I still had no idea what I was going to do next. When people asked me what my plan was, I would smile and say 'I'm working on that' or if I was feeling surly, I might say 'I'm thinking of joining the *Cirque Du Soleil*.'

After witnessing a few rounds of pummeling, courtesy of divorce court, CeCe stepped up with her cattle prod. "This is enough now, Scarlett. Stop moping. Go find yourself a bit of fun before you shrivel into a bitter old prune! Go on a date! Oliver deserves a mother who's happy. You can't allow this to define your life. Get cracking! Shake the cobwebs off!"

"Okay, but I'm *not* ready to do the Internet dating thing."

"Well, you need to do something, and that much is abundantly clear."

After Oliver was in bed, CeCe and I often had conversations over a glass of wine or a cup of tea in front of the fireplace. These were the prime moments in which CeCe loved to revisit my lost romantic opportunities.

"Oh, Scarlett . . . you should never have let that fabulous Francesco get away."

"CeCe, that was fifteen years ago."

"Yes, but you would have had a very good life with him. He was an excellent provider . . . a true Alpha male. He loved the best of everything in life."

"Yes, Francisco was loaded, but don't you remember how difficult he was? His nit-picking drove me nuts. Who cares how much money he had? I never would have been able to live with all that scrutiny. He would stare at me and I'd think he was going to say something nice like how much he loved me and then he would say, 'Oh, sweetie, your skin looks like shit. You *really* need to get a facial' or 'Are you sure you need to eat *another* piece of chocolate? It'll go straight to your bottom, right where you don't need it!' I was never skinny or fit enough for him. He hated my clothes, too. The criticism was relentless."

CeCe was unconvinced. "Nah . . . he was a fabulous catch. You never should have let him get away."

Irritated by her lack of support, I decided to share the final deal-breaker.

"Well, he might have been a 'fabulous catch' but he was a little weird, sexually."

This got her attention.

"Weird? In what way exactly?"

"He wanted me to pee on him while we were having sex . . . but I couldn't stop laughing long enough to perform. So I guess I managed to screw that up, too. Yes, for some skinny bitch with perfect skin who likes to piss on her rich man he was 'the perfect catch' but he wasn't for me."

She let out a long sigh. "Is that all? For God's sake, Scarlett, the world could have been your oyster and you threw it away! You pissed away a *golden opportunity*!" She chortled loudly, enjoying her own joke. "Scarlett, you and your delicate sensibilities . . . I can't imagine where you inherited those from! You know, I had a lover once, his name was Herbert . . . or was it Garry? He was very fond of that sort of thing . . . I think it's perfectly acceptable, as long as you're the piss-*er* and not the piss-*ee*!"

Sharing details with CeCe always backfired. Not only would it titillate her, but it would also highlight another arena in which I was somehow deficient. Then it would prompt her to divulge a memory of a past lover's predilections, and disclosures of that nature from one's mother were best kept to a minimum.

CeCe's robust sexual appetites and proclivities were topics I preferred to steer clear of but this was virtually impossible. Even the most innocent topic—or a news story on television about Homeland Security—would remind her of a tale about her traveling through airport security from Mexico with her vibrators, or somehow linked to another memory of a raunchy encounter she felt compelled to share.

Still chuckling at the memory of Herbert, she said, "What you need is a bit of romance. Put some color in your cheeks! Recycling might be a quicker option at this point. There must be somebody from the past you want to dig up."

"All right." I surrendered. "Let me give it some thought . . ."

Chapter Three
The Ex-Files

It was time to get the ball rolling. If I kept focusing on the divorce, on how long it was taking, and how little control over any of it I had, it made me nuts. I needed some male company. I needed a distraction. Precisely one candidate unfurled himself from the recesses of my mind—the surly old Malibu Pirate, Dominick.

"I've thought about what you said. I suppose I could give Dominick a call and do a bit of recycling," I told CeCe the next day.

"Oh yes, darling Dominick!" she said, getting excited. "Now that's a stellar idea!"

Dominick had been the last man I dated before I married X and was now about to be the first person I looked up post-marriage; my marital bookend. There was a certain pleasing symmetry to this decision—and it signified movement—although I wasn't certain in which direction.

Dominick and I had plenty of history. Ruggedly handsome and masculine in a way that weakened the knees of any female in his vicinity, if he was available, he would fit the bill. Dominick could be counted on for exactly two things: witty repartee and a rollicking good lay. We dated over a number of years before I got married, but had never sustained anything resembling a conventional relationship. That wasn't his style. Dominick kept it casual. He enjoyed his position as a privileged bachelor far too much to compromise the myriad of opportunities with the Malibu babes who would literally stroll down the beach and offer themselves to him.

Besides his sexual prowess, I also craved his wicked wit. Dominick's sense of humor rivaled CeCe's in terms of its blatant political incorrectness. He could almost be considered an Australian male in terms of bawdiness. He could be charming if it suited him, or if he was in a foul mood he could be a total asshole. It was a roll of the dice. He could turn that wicked tongue-lashing in my direction—and not always in a good way.

I indulged myself in my own highlight reel of old memories with

Dominick. I imagined what it might be like to be with him again. Possibly naked. I had a fondness for him that survived despite questionable behavior on his part, and a marriage on mine.

Our sordid history had started ten years earlier, when we were introduced by a guy named Teddy from my acting class.

"You need to meet Dominick B. He's having a birthday party this weekend in Malibu—you *have* to come. His parties are really fun." Teddy scrawled the address on a piece of paper and handed it to me.

I wasn't in the habit of turning down invitations to parties in Malibu.

'Dominick B' turned out to be from a prominent Hollywood family and his birthday party was populated with celebrities, hip children of celebrities, and women who mastered that chic tawny Malibu beach look effortlessly. Emma and I had tried unsuccessfully to blend in. I remember feeling very self-conscious in my new a-little-too-snug lime green pants—which could not have been less Malibu chic—and was seriously rethinking that purchase when Dominick appeared and introduced himself. He had a great smile. I liked him immediately.

After securing two glasses of white wine for us, he was dragged away by a tanned, midriff-baring six-foot blonde who tossed her artfully shaggy mane and whispered suggestively in his ear. He turned, looked me in the eye and said, "I'll see *you* later," as if he meant it.

Dominick's house was standard bachelor fare, except for its location right on the Malibu sand, which elevated it to spectacular. There was a large deck overlooking the Pacific Ocean and a hot tub filled to capacity with bikini-clad lovelies. The living room featured a pool table, a huge television and a large dining table filled with delicacies from Marmalade Café—a local Malibu restaurant. Emma and I wandered around and helped ourselves to some glorious coconut cupcakes. While Emma was chatting with a music executive, I noticed that the six-foot blonde was now happily seated on someone else's lap.

Dominick appeared behind me, touched my elbow lightly, and said, "Come take a walk with me."

I leapt at the bait.

He gave me a brief tour of the rest of the house—including the master bedroom, which showcased large photographs of his famous family. This family presence loomed large, like a shadow over the room. There was a glossy magazine that featured one of his sisters on the cover displayed right next to the bed. It was a curious choice. Did the women he bedded need additional prompting? It was hard to imagine he needed help getting anybody's knickers off. Did coming from a Hollywood dynasty guarantee you were a better lay? As if reading my thoughts, he suddenly seemed embarrassed by the memorabilia and abruptly concluded the bedroom tour. We then made our way down the side steps and onto the beach.

"And this is my backyard," he said and gestured out to the ocean.

"Lucky you."

I studied his face in the moonlight. He was distinctly male. There was nothing feminine about him. He had a strong jaw and light green eyes that sparkled mischievously. I liked the way he moved. He had a lingering, leisurely gait, which suggested he'd just finished doing something naughty and you'd just have to wait until it was your turn. His dark hair was thick and wavy and casually swept down over his eyes. I resisted the urge to run my fingers through it.

"Where are you from?"

"I'm from Sydney, originally."

"I love Sydney! I've spent a bit of time there over the years."

Although the conversation was innocent, he held my gaze in a way that made me blush.

Teddy called out to us from the balcony and broke the spell. Apparently, there was an urgent matter that required Dominick's immediate attention, so we headed back to the house.

Once inside, I ran into Emma. "There you are! I was looking for you— where did you disappear to?"

"I went for a walk with Dominick. He's really sexy!"

"What the hell's on your face?"

"What?"

"On your eye . . . what is that?"

"What are you talking about?"

"Come in here." She pulled me into the nearest bathroom and examined me in its harsh, unforgiving light.

I looked in the mirror and was horrified to find that there were remnants of the coconut cupcake stuck to my eyelashes. I must have wiped my face and inadvertently smeared on the crumbs, which were now clinging like crusty little snowflakes to my eyelashes. It looked like I was in the throes of a nasty bout of conjunctivitis.

"Oh, great. How did I not realize that was there?"

Emma dissolved unhelpfully into a fit of giggles.

What a fool. There I was thinking we were having a 'moment' on the beach together and that he couldn't take his eyes off me, while in reality he was probably wondering if I had a contagious infection. How utterly mortifying.

"Let's get out of here," I whispered.

I was too embarrassed to face Dominick, even *sans* crumbs, so we left without saying good-bye.

When I saw Teddy the next week in class, he didn't mention Dominick but invited me to another party the following weekend in Santa Monica.

Dominick was there when I arrived at the party. He seemed a little drunk. Teddy made sure to mention that Dominick was now courting a girl with a Hollywood pedigree, and had been sending her flowers all week. I wasn't sure why he needed me to know this important detail but I immediately felt deflated.

I wondered what type of flowers a man like Dominick might send. Roses would be too predictable. Lilies wouldn't be enough of a statement. Maybe peonies?

Disheartened by this news, I avoided Dominick all night until he cornered me in the kitchen.

"There you are! Where are those lovely green pants?"

"I gave them the night off. In fact, I may be sending them on a permanent vacation to Goodwill."

"Don't say that! I'm in love with them! I could keep track of you all night in those things, neon green in a sea of beige. They were perfect. Like a green flag waving at me from across the room!" He gave me an exaggerated wave to illustrate the effect. "Men start wars over asses like yours. You should be proud of that booty. Don't hide it, for God's sake! Flaunt it!"

I couldn't help but laugh. He was cute and funny—but courting someone else. What lousy timing.

"Well, nice to see you but I have to go," I said and headed for the door.

"Let me walk you out." He didn't wait for a response and ushered me out the back door, which led into the alley. Once outside, he made an awkward lunge for me, pressed me up against an oversized garbage can, and sloppily attempted to stick his tongue down my throat. I had been dying to kiss him but not in his current state and not like this.

"Come home with me." His voice was slurred.

"What?"

"You heard me . . . come home with me. I've been thinking about you all week."

"Oh, is that right? I can't imagine you had the time between sending flower arrangements to what's her name?"

He looked completely floored.

"Oh . . . that . . . well, I was trying to make a good impression . . ."

"What kind of impression do you think you're making trying to mount me on the garbage can? Who's getting the better deal here?"

"You're the better deal, Scarlett."

Why was it men only said this to me when they were drunk or committed to someone else? Why couldn't I be someone's *better deal* when they were sober and single?

I pushed him off. "Good-night, Romeo!"

I crossed the street to my car.

"You know where to find me if you change your mind!" he shouted after me.

He stood at the side of the road, a sexy unavailable drunken mess.

He was precisely my type.

The next time I ran into Dominick, it was eight months later at a coffee shop on Montana Avenue. He and what's her name had broken up and he wasted no time in finally asking me out on a real date. One date turned into several. We had romantic dinners in Malibu and went for long walks on the beach with his dog. Things were going well between us but as soon as I started to relax a bit, I felt him pulling away.

Luckily, work was keeping me busy and I didn't have time to dwell on Dominick. I landed a plum makeup job for a press junket promoting a blockbuster action film with a big film star—the devastatingly handsome Garrison Lee. Having a glamorous all-expenses-paid week in New York with a big movie star does wonders for a girl's spirits. Garrison's good looks were exceeded only by his grace and charm. He had a good sense of humor about the silliness attached to being a movie star and was easy to work with. A job with him was a dream gig. Had he not been married, I would have flung myself at him. Garrison's New York hair-stylist GiGi turned out to be tons of fun so we ran around Manhattan together shopping or just hanging out, and had a ball. It was just what I needed.

Job done and flush with cash, I treated myself to a yoga retreat in Santa Barbara. By the time I came home, Dominick had been looking for me.

I didn't pretend to resist. Curiosity got the better of me. I raced out to Malibu to see him. He looked happy to see me. Even his dog seemed happy to see me.

"Oh, no . . . you've caught the too-much-yoga disease. All you girls catch that. You're getting too skinny. What happened to the ass I was so enchanted with? Where did it go?" he asked while trying to lift my skirt with his barbecue tongs. He pulled me onto his lap and kissed me.

"I've missed you," he said while kissing my exposed shoulder. "Can you believe I'm saying that? I'm usually impervious to that gooey shit. It doesn't happen often, let me tell you."

Dominick prepared a wonderful lobster dinner for us and we ate it on his deck at sunset. While he concentrated on his lobster, I drank in every detail about him. His face was tan from an afternoon in the sun. His five o'clock shadow highlighted his undeniable scruffy appeal, while his linen shirt was loose and falling open to expose a map of baby-fine hair on his chest. As I watched him struggle earnestly with his lobster, I was overcome with such a bubbling desire for him that I couldn't contain it. I had to have him. I stepped away from my lobster, walked over to him, and planted a buttery kiss on his lips as I ran my hand down his shirt and unzipped his pants. We made love right there on the wooden deck.

Things went well for a while but then without notice, the scales tipped and he bailed. I started seeing someone else, and he started dating someone else, but that didn't stop him from calling to check the temperature.

The phone calls typically went like this:

"Hello my saucy Scarlett. What are you doing?"

"Nothing in particular."

"Why don't you come over and sit on my face?"

"Why, that's the most charming invitation I've had all day."

It would all depend on the timing. If he managed to catch me when I was bored enough with no real boyfriend prospects in sight, we might be on again. Sometimes I would summon the strength to sit one round out and tell him to piss off, but the key to his extraordinary success was his timing. He would wait long enough between calls that I couldn't possibly have managed to sustain my irritation with him. We would drift back together like this until I had the audacity 'to go and get married', which he took as a personal insult. When I ran into him at yoga—married and six months' pregnant—he looked utterly betrayed. For once, I was the unavailable one.

Now, I was available again.

The devil you know is better than the devil you don't, as CeCe says. So why not give him a call? I had nothing to lose.

Chapter Four
The Return of the Malibu Pirate

While I was married, I heard a rumor that the old pirate was living with a masseuse named Lisa. The thought of Dominick allowing a woman to move in with him boggled my mind. I was fascinated to know how she had accomplished this feat. Back in the old days, sometimes in the mornings after a tryst, he would leave before me but glance back and say in a hopeful tone, "Will you be here when I get home?" I always had things to do and lying about his house all day—without a key—simply waiting for him to return struck me as not the right choice. But maybe this masseuse woman had decided to dig in her heels and not leave.

It was time to find out.

I rang his office and his secretary dutifully took my message. I hung up wondering if he would bother to return my call but within minutes my phone was ringing.

"Scarlett, you *saucy* slut! How the hell are you?"

"Oh, hi . . . that was quick, I *just* called you." I was unprepared for the immediacy of his response. I had assumed it would be days before I heard from him, if at all.

"Well, I just checked my messages. How would I know what time you called?" He feigned indifference.

"In any case, it's nice to hear from you. So . . . how are you? I heard you have a girlfriend . . . and you're living together. Good for you!"

"Yes . . . she's great. We're . . . having a great time"—his voice trailed off —"And how are you? How's your kid? What's his name, again, Opie?"

"No, it's Oliver. He's amazing. I'm so grateful to have him but other than that, the marriage was a complete disaster. We're in the process of divorcing," I said, mincing no words.

"That's great news!" Suddenly springing back to life. "I was hoping you were calling to say that. He wasn't for you, Scarlett. Everyone could see that. Lisa and I broke up a month ago. It's still hush, hush. I haven't announced it yet. But I *need* to see you," he said, dropping all former pretenses.

"Oh . . . wow. . . I'd like to see you, too. When?"

"How about tonight? Can you come over?"

"I can't do it tonight," I said, exhausted at the prospect of all the grooming rituals I would need to accomplish to get ready for an impromptu roll in the hay. I didn't have my game on. The old swashbuckler would have to battle a recalcitrant bush overgrowth before claiming his prize, and if I recalled, he didn't have much patience for obstacles.

"Then how about next Tuesday at eight? Come over and we'll get dinner," he said, switching gears.

"Great," I said. "See you then."

It was that simple.

Reuniting with Dominick was as easy as falling off a horse, which was about as much good as it would do me.

CeCe was beside herself at this news.

Her approval of men was often in direct proportion to the size of their bank accounts. Wealthy equaled desirable. Not wealthy equaled bloody waste of time, and required a dropkick back into the pond. If a man had considerable means, almost anything he did was worth putting up with. Dominick was sexy, plus he was wealthy *and* kinky—it was as good as it gets in her book.

CeCe had been crushed when I had stopped seeing Dominick and began dating X. Her anguish was compounded several months into my marriage when she caught me trying to hide shampoo bottles from my husband so that he didn't berate me for 'unnecessary extravagances'. CeCe was appalled that I had to account for any unexplained fifteen-dollar purchases on the family credit card and was reduced to hiding them. X didn't subscribe to the idea of discretionary funds.

"This is not how you should be living. I didn't bring you up to live like this, Scarlett. Dominick would never have treated you this way."

To be stuck in an unsatisfying marriage, and then to be broke and miserable on top of it, was inconceivable to CeCe. If one had to be miserable and married, there ought to be sufficient funds in which to drown one's sorrows, thus ameliorating further impact.

Tuesday rolled around and it was time to see Dominick. I made pasta for Oliver and got him ready for bed early. Throwing on a simple but flattering black dress, one of the few acceptable relics from my single days, with sling-back heels, I prepared to make the all-too-familiar trek out to Malibu. I'd made that trek so many times over the years that my car could almost get there on its own without my assistance.

CeCe eyed my outfit approvingly. The dress wasn't tight anymore but it was tight enough in the right places.

"Oh, it will be *so* good for you to see him again!" She clapped her hands together for emphasis. "I always liked him."

"Maybe. But he's still an asshole . . . let's not forget that part."

"There's something special about him," CeCe said, dreamily.

"Yes. He's a *special* asshole. See you later. I won't be late."

I drove down to the 10 Freeway and then headed out west to the Pacific Coast Highway. I drove with the windows down to breathe in the crisp sea air, happy for the January chill it brought to my flesh, reminding me that I was alive.

Dominick swung the heavy wooden gate open to greet me.

Damn he looked good.

"Hello, Sexy Cat!" He whipped me into his arms.

Fresh out of the shower, he smelled even better.

He didn't say another word and just held me. His lightweight cashmere sweater felt exquisite to the touch and I let my hands explore the breadth of his back. I melted in the presence of his masculinity. He had gained a good ten pounds since I'd last seen him, which I found to be a turn-on. His body felt so strong, so deliciously potent pressed tightly against mine. This new girth only served to excite me—all the more to penetrate me with. Forceful electrical currents shot down my spine, culminating into a fine buzz between my legs. I had forgotten the latent power of being held. Our chemistry, after all this time, was undeniably strong.

Unnerved by my body's immediate Pavlovian response, I questioned what I was doing. Now that I was a *mother*, I couldn't very well keep running around and dropping my knickers at the drop of a hat. I barely managed my affairs before I had a kid, what would happen now? Should I surrender to this old dance of ours and start having sex again? My libido had been quietly contained for years, and now I was about to let it out of the box. I was afraid of what might happen next.

I pulled at my dress as it was inching itself up toward my stomach in compliance with my body's primal response to him. *Yes! Yes! Yes!*

We walked through the courtyard to the house. Barely recognizable, the courtyard had undergone a complete transformation. It used to be a graveyard of hardy neglected plants, empty pots, and cacti that weathered his abuse nicely. This new incarnation was filled with night-blooming jasmine, exotic-looking trees and plants in seriously shiny brass pots. Someone new had been in charge of things around here. I noticed that he hadn't bothered to take down the Christmas lights that were still winking good-naturedly at us.

"So, how is your mother? Now there's a *real* woman! I bet she really knows how to enjoy herself in the sack," he said with his trademark wickedness. True to form, he liked to say something offensive to break the ice.

"You're probably right. But that's an image I'd prefer not to think about. She's fine, thank you."

Pushing the envelope even further, he continued. "You know I *love* Australian women . . . I was going to ask her out. Maybe you could leave me her number?"

"I hate to break it to you, but you're not man enough for her," I said, evening the score.

"*That's* for sure!" he said, and we both laughed.

I followed him into the kitchen where he proceeded to pour me a glass of Cabernet. He had taken the liberty of ordering my favorite lamb chops and salad from Marmalade Café, and two plates sat on the kitchen counter awaiting our attention. It felt like old times.

"You know, it occurs to me that my current predicament could be *entirely* your fault," I said, teasing him. "If you hadn't been such a jerk, I might not have run out and married the very next man I met."

"Yes. It's all my fault. I'm terrible at that boyfriend business, but you already know that." He handed me the elegant stem glass, hoping to distract me and change the subject. No such luck.

"Yes, that's right!" I said, rising to the theme. "And the deal breaker was that you were terrified of the whole kid thing . . ."

"*No*, I said I'd have a kid with you," he said, very slowly, measuring his words carefully. "As long as you promised to go away after you delivered it to me!"

And with that he scored the knockout blow.

"That's not how it works." I sniffed. Unfortunately, he was much better at this sparring game than I was. "Anyway, I seem to recall there was some question about your sperm count. So you would have been excluded as a potential candidate, anyway. All those years of pot smoking, you probably haven't got any boys left!"

"Oh, I bet I have one left and I bet he's a *really* good swimmer!" He squeezed my ass for emphasis.

We both knew what I was there for but this sudden blatant gesture ratcheted my nerves up a notch.

I sipped the wine and walked around the house pretending to appraise his recent acquisitions, in an attempt to delay the inevitable. The new furniture was another vestige of the missing masseuse. Large, intricately carved dark wooden mirrors adorned the walls and gold statues of Indian deities sat serenely around the house, coolly impervious to the neighboring pool table and huge flat screen television. It was a collision of two worlds.

We sat down to dinner and discussed his recent romantic failure and my own fine mess. What a pair of misfits we were.

"You must have *really* wanted a kid because anyone could tell from a mile off that guy wasn't right for you," he said while carefully slicing into his lamb.

I sighed. "I didn't think it through very well, did I?"

"I run into him on the Westside a lot. I watch him closely when he's with the kid. I look out for the little guy."

"Thanks. I appreciate that," I said. It was the closest thing to concern I'd ever seen from Dominick. It was most becoming on him.

"What are you going to do? Divorce is one thing, but you have a kid now. A lot of guys aren't going to want to deal with that . . . *complication* . . . you know?"

And there it was again. Whenever he said something nice, he was compelled by the need to say something shitty to restore the balance he preferred.

"I'm not worried about that." I lied and feigned a casual tone. "I'll figure it all out in due time."

I rapidly lost my appetite. "Excuse me, I'm going to the loo." I slipped off the barstool and made a quick exit. I didn't like the direction the conversation was heading in and the last thing I needed was his negative perception of my life. What he was really saying was that *he* wasn't interested in my complicated situation. Fuck him. He was such a pussy when it came to dealing with anything requiring an adult perspective. What he didn't understand was that all people came with some sort of baggage, including the little tarts he found on the beach. People, by nature, *are* complicated.

Inside the bathroom, I surveyed the numerous beauty products scattered around the counter—pricey La Mer moisturizers, assorted facial scrubs and lip glosses. His recently departed lady had chosen to leave these little reminders that she had laid claim to the premises—and him. I opened the jar of lotion and smeared on a gloriously hefty amount. It didn't look like she'd been gone twenty-four hours—but more notably—it looked like she planned to be back. Women might abandon cheap makeup but not two-hundred-dollar face cream. I wondered if she imagined he'd be screwing women again so quickly. She probably knew. Ugh. Was this a wise move? I didn't want to step into someone else's drama. I had enough of my own.

I peed and weighed the option of leaving without sleeping with him. He was already annoying me and we hadn't even gotten to bed. In the old days, he used to have the decency to wait until *after* the fact.

There was no sign of Dominick in the living room when I returned. There were freshly lit candles lighting the path back to his bedroom and Bryan Ferry playing softly throughout the house. He had refilled my glass of wine and was now probably in his office smoking pot. He always smoked before sex. Pot provoked a violently unsexy response in me and made me want to hurl, so Dominick knew better than to offer me any.

My favorite perch beckoned out on the deck. I nursed my Cabernet in the moonlight and watched the surf crashing angrily at the shore while Dominick fortified himself for intimacy.

Then suddenly, he was behind me, and began kissing my neck.

"I see you lost your baby weight. You were looking pretty round last time I ran into you. You don't look half bad for somebody's mother," he said while slipping his hands under my skirt.

I moved away from his hands but they adeptly slid back into position and into my panties. "Fuck you." I moaned as he quickly began working his fingers into me.

"Well, I *was* hoping . . ." Turning me back swiftly into him, he kissed me hard. "Isn't this what you came for?" He placed my hand over his crotch. He was instantly erect. I gasped.

He lifted me up and I wrapped my legs around his waist.

He carried me into the bedroom to give me one of his trademark poundings. This was not a discovery expedition that demanded careful or romantic navigation—this was re-entry to a friendly land on a well-used visa, and he set about claiming me. He removed my dress and panties and I unbuckled his jeans. We kissed and quickly found our rhythm. Smooth and sleek, his body was familiar under my touch. I had spent many hours studying the broadness of his back, the slender narrowing of his waist that gave way to his small, sweet ass. It was always startlingly white compared to the rest of his tan body. I knew his penis and what it craved. It was primed and ready to reclaim its swashbuckling adventures back into my willing and neglected pussy. He was alert to all the signals my body gave, and responded in kind. In bed—and only in bed—we were good together. Like a good game of tennis with a frequent partner, I knew the strokes he liked to play, I knew his drive and I knew the final score—one all, or if my nerves got the better of me, one, love.

This time it seemed I couldn't score if my life depended on it.

Once the game was over, I didn't want to linger. It was time to get home to Oliver and my *complicated* situation.

"You didn't come," he said with annoyance, breaking the brief post-coital calm.

"No. Perhaps I've forgotten how." I felt around the bed in the dark for my discarded dress.

"No. You didn't want to. I can tell when you want to. You open your legs really wide," he stated matter-of-factly.

"Is *that* what I do?" I laughed. It seemed the only appropriate response. "I'm out of practice, I guess."

"Come back here." He leaned over to me, opened one large arm, and swept me into his chest and back down on the bed. He wrapped himself over me like a blanket and held me for a minute. I tried to relax into him, to breathe with him again and enjoy the fleeting comfort he was trying to offer. It was a rare moment of tenderness from Dominick but I couldn't allow myself to surrender to it. *It wasn't real.*

"Let's have another go! I think I can go again." He rubbed at his crotch. "You need to have an orgasm before I let you leave. It's bad for my reputation."

"I applaud your enthusiasm, but I do have to get home." I wriggled out of his hold and slipped into my shoes.

"Fine. But I owe you one."

"Fine."

He got up, walked me to the door and then hesitated for a moment. "It hasn't been too long since I split with Lisa. I think it's best if we are discreet."

"You know me better than to count on my discretion!" I threw one of Dominick's famous old lines back at him.

His face dropped suddenly.

"I'm kidding," I said. "*Of course,* I'll be discreet. I'm going through a divorce. I don't want anyone knowing my business either."

I kissed him and squeezed his body against mine for the last time.

"Good-night, Scarlett. Drive safely."

"Good-night."

I turned the car around and zipped back down Pacific Coast Highway.

The possibility of reigniting an affair with Dominick had been intriguing. I longed to feel the spark of a fun connection again and the comfort in familiarity but nothing felt satisfying about this reunion. It was an empty fuck. It was like eating a whole chocolate cake and then realizing that you didn't even enjoy it. It doesn't matter that you didn't enjoy it because you're still stuck with the tab. My heart sank and I felt worse as I skirted back along the coastline.

Was this what post-divorce life was going to consist of? Random shags here and there whenever the opportunity arose. The prospect seemed awfully grim. The idea of being in sync with someone was what I longed for. I wasn't about to give up but it needed to be the *right* person.

Oliver was sleeping soundly on CeCe's bed with pillows on either side of him when I got home. He was wearing new orange pajamas with monkeys on them that CeCe had bought him. Instantly, I felt better. I cradled my little monkey man as I moved him into his own bed and tucked him in. His cheeks were flushed and he looked like a little sweaty blond cherub.

CeCe had nodded off in front of the television still clutching her empty glass of red wine. I carefully removed the wineglass from her hand and set it on the table. It seemed like I had taken a giant step backward in time— still seeing Dominick and living with my mother again. I didn't know whether to laugh or cry.

Instead, I pulled out my paints and started a new painting of another broken woman. It felt like my insides spilled out onto the page, taking flesh and guts with them. When I was done, I would likely paint right over it. It would be too painful to look at again in the daylight.

CeCe eyed me closely in the morning, barely containing her glee. "So . . . how is our Dominick?"

"He's about the same, I'd say. He asked about you, though."

"What a charmer that boy is!"

"Yeah, that's one word for him. Or 'pervert' works, too," I mumbled.

I made myself a cup of English Breakfast tea. At least there were some things you could count on to make you feel better. I threw some extra sugar in for good measure.

"Are you going to see him again?" She reached across me for the jam.

"I don't know. Maybe. Maybe not." I avoided looking at her.

"You should definitely see him again. It would be silly not to." She spooned a large heap of raspberry jam onto her toast.

Oliver came into the kitchen, and out of the corner of my eye I saw CeCe slip him something.

"CeCe, did you just give him chocolate again?"

Oliver erupted into guilty giggles and darted back into the living room.

"I might have," she answered.

"I've asked you not to give him chocolate in the morning. It winds him up and then I have to deal with the aftermath all day. Please don't."

"I can tell you didn't have enough of a visit with Dominick. Maybe you should schedule another one. Soon."

I could tell CeCe's head was already filling with Dominick fantasies. I had to make a preemptive strike and squash them or she would be driving me mad, and let's face it, that was a short trip.

"Look, CeCe, just to be clear, Dominick is *not* riding in on a white horse to save me—or anyone else for that matter. He can't even save himself! He's still stuck in the same rut in his life, doing the same things and avoiding anything that would require a real commitment from him. He's still doing the same bullshit dating routine. It doesn't make him happy but that's all he knows. He's not into overcoming any of it. He's a one-trick pony. He has his own problems to deal with. I have to do this on my own. I have to create a life for Ollie and me *on our own*! And you perpetuating this idea that someone will come along and fix it for me isn't helpful."

"Oh, that's rubbish. You haven't given it enough time to know that yet," she said, refusing to take anything I said seriously, as usual.

"Well, I can tell you that he isn't interested in anybody with a little kid." I stirred the pot of oatmeal for Oliver. "He made that *abundantly* clear."

"Oh, darling, he's just saying that. Don't believe him."

Arguing with CeCe was an exercise in futility. She could say whatever she wanted, but I knew he meant it.

Chapter Five
Shag-less And Penniless

There exists inside the mind of every female, a tiny spot—or perhaps, as in my case, an exceedingly large and annoyingly vocal spot—that remains impervious to logic or reason. This silly spot is wretchedly self-sabotaging and is the part responsible for those nagging thoughts of *I wish that rat bastard would pick up the phone and call me*—even when you absolutely know this is the worst thing possible. It's also the part that thinks it's a good idea to go over to his house late at night for a meaningless shag in the first place. I did my best to ignore that grumbling little voice that demanded to know why he wasn't swept up in whatever charms I might have left and wasn't calling me—even when the answer was absurdly obvious.

Even more pressing than any emotional rewiring issues was my very own impending financial crisis. Leaving one's husband was one thing, but leaving without any money was quite another. My credit cards were nearing their limits and the legal bills had numbers so large that the only way I could function was to think it was a crude joke. They couldn't possibly mean ten-thousand dollars? Ha, ha, ha, that's hilarious. Where in hell was I going to get ten-thousand dollars? I couldn't begin to comprehend what to do with the bills, so I added them to the ever-growing pile of hateful legal mail in the corner of the kitchen, safely obscured from view under some handy Chinese takeout menus.

As much as I longed to distract myself, sticking my head in the sand and having romps with deadbeat ex-boyfriends weren't going to cut it. Being flat broke and getting divorced was a wake-up call of the worst kind. I scrambled to resuscitate some sort of work.

Makeup artistry was the vocation I'd turned to after I realized that an acting career wasn't going to pan out. I lacked the fortitude and thick skin needed to survive as an actress. It was a natural extension of my love for painting. In many ways, it fit well. I found I was quite good at a particular niche—natural beauty. I specialized in barely-there makeup, using minimal product for maximum effect.

Dusting off my resume, I began the hunt. My entertainment industry connections were stale but that didn't stop me. I called everyone, fellow artists, publicists and managers, and feigned cheeriness in the hopes that someone might want to hire me again.

Finding work would have to coexist somehow with Oliver's schedule and the ongoing court dates. That was the tricky part. Having Oliver for less time and then having to sacrifice some of that precious time with him for work was almost unbearable. Freelance jobs had to provide enough to cover babysitting fees or were an exercise in futility. I couldn't always rely on Sam or CeCe to be available to watch Oliver when I had a job. I had to come up with a workable arrangement. It was like a giant puzzle that needed to be sorted out and I had no idea how to maneuver all these complicated pieces.

It was safe to say that I sucked at puzzles. Pretty much nothing had gone as planned in my life, so why should marriage or divorce have been any different? The great irony was I had been so determined to give Oliver a different experience than my own fragmented childhood. I had all these ideals of what motherhood was and wasn't going to be. I had been so determined *not* to be CeCe, diving into relationships with men and dragging a wayward child or two behind me. I wasn't going to work. I was going to be a stay-at-home mother and be present and involved with every aspect of my child's life. I would be available to go on fieldtrips or work in the classroom. I couldn't recall CeCe stepping foot in any of my classrooms. But all of those fantasies of perfect motherhood had imploded with the marriage. Now all I could do was scrounge around for the salvageable pieces. It seemed the harder I tried to make different choices than CeCe, the more similar we became.

I had way too much time to ponder my poor choices. I needed a job. It seemed that a hefty part of the prescription for moving past one's shitty divorce was to lose oneself in one's work—which becomes an even greater challenge if one isn't employed. It was time to remedy that.

A posting for a makeup artist on craigslist led me to 'The World Renowned Enchanté Beauty Retreat' located in Beverly Hills. Enchanté was a salon specializing in custom makeup and beauty services for 'The World's Most Glamorous Women'—as it proudly proclaimed on the website. The salon environment was new to me. A freelance schedule was more conducive to my time with Oliver, but that only held up if I had actual bookings. From experience, I knew that when work was slow it could mean a few scary weeks without employment and I needed consistent work. The puzzle was starting to look somewhat manageable. Oliver would be with X half the week, and childcare could be worked out for any additional days. Susan had suggested someone she knew might be available to watch him. Perhaps this could be the opportunity I'd been waiting for.

I called and spoke to Freddy, the salon manager. He informed me that I would have to pass a scheduled interview with Priscilla herself and a makeup application demo to determine if the salon and I would be a good match.

"Priscilla is very picky about her *artistes*. Only the very best survive here," he said in a tone that struck me as a bit ominous.

"That's fine. I'm good at what I do." I surprised myself with a new burst of confidence. Screw this Priscilla woman. I wasn't going to let her intimidate me. Oliver and I needed stability and some crotchety old broad wasn't going to scare me away from what could potentially be a great gig.

I arrived at the appointed hour of one o'clock in the afternoon in a simple but stylish black skirt and cream silk blouse. The salon featured a pastel candy-colored theme and was decidedly girly. Over the front door hung a large plaque that said 'Through these Portals pass the World's Most Glamorous Women.' Sitting throughout the salon were white oversized couches accented with pink and peach beaded pillows, and there were two large vats of dyed-white peacock feathers beside the front door. Perhaps it was a nod to all the preening that went on in there? Did someone have a sense of humor? The thought cheered me, as I watched the makeup artists applying products to their patrons at a furious pace.

I mingled among the women trying on makeup and looked for someone in charge. They were clearly understaffed and the lone guy manning the counter was working up a sweat while keeping pace with the steady stream of Beverly Hills women demanding their custom makeup. I waited my turn and as soon as I mentioned I was there for my interview with Priscilla, the previously harried man's disposition changed instantly. He greeted me with a huge sigh of relief and gave me an enthusiastic but sweaty handshake.

"Oh, thank God you're here. I'm Freddy. We spoke on the phone. Come with me." He ushered me over to an armchair and whispered, "I'm having the hardest time with our staffing. The last four candidates haven't survived their first day. The last one left in tears . . . the poor girl!"

"Oh, really?" My new confidence was flagging.

"Priscilla is with a client but she'll be with you in a minute." He gestured toward the back of the salon.

"Okay, then," I said, not taking my eyes off Priscilla, the petite whirling dervish in the corner who left teary makeup artists in her wake. Tiny and teetering on her wickedly high Louboutins, she had an overpowering mass of immaculately blown caramel-colored hair and sported ample cleavage. She didn't look all that menacing as she twirled in and out of her customer's face, dabbing colors on her brush and painting her maquillage masterpiece, but I was on guard.

I waited an hour for an audience with her, during which time I closely observed the makeup applications being turned out by her three employees. Heavy, spackled on makeup paraded past me. My standard 'understated natural beauty' look wasn't going to cut it with this crowd.

Finally, I was presented to her eminence. Priscilla looked me up and down and gave me a nod as if to say 'you'll do.'

"So, honey, tell me . . . who have you worked with?" She fired this at me in a thick New Jersey accent.

I rattled off what I hoped was an impressive list of the celebrity clients I'd worked with. Some of the credits were very old and the precise usage of my talents somewhat dubious—I'd once applied lip gloss to Eva Longoria at a photo shoot, which may not be exactly the same as actually *doing* her makeup, but I didn't bother to point that out.

"Let's see what you can do." She tossed her caramel mane as she turned her back and dismissed me.

Freddy escorted me to a vacant makeup station then went over to the only available artist and gave her the bad news that she was to be today's guinea pig. My guinea pig was petite and voluptuous with a raven-hued pixie haircut and a pretty face that dropped at the news. She looked over at me with the enthusiasm of one who had just been informed it was their turn to scrub the toilet.

"Scarlett, this is Tori!" Freddy said and ignored Tori's exasperated sigh. "And she'll be your model today!" Freddy attempted to will her into compliance with his phony good cheer. When that didn't seem to be working, he said, "Oh, come on now, Tori. You're usually such a good sport! Okay, Scarlett . . . work your magic, girl!"

I hadn't done anyone's makeup in years. I hoped that I still had some magic to be conjured.

Tori reluctantly eased her bottom onto the stool in front of me and began to smear her face with makeup remover. I memorized the theatrical makeup she wore as the large sweeps began to erase it. Heavy, dramatic black-cat eyeliner stubbornly began to lift off. Relieved of the clever distraction of liner, her blue eyes were bloodshot.

"I was out clubbing last night and got two hours of sleep," Tori said, studying the damage in the mirror.

Devoid of the porn-star makeup, Tori was a very pretty girl. Instinct urged me to preserve her natural beauty and not replicate the look she had been sporting, but I knew that was not what the task required.

I rolled up my sleeves and went to work slapping on the foundation. I made sure to use a lot more products than I normally would in my former minimalist style. More products used translated into more products to sell to clients, and Priscilla—as a keen businesswoman—would be watching for that.

Playing up Tori's blue eyes with smoky gray-blue eye shadow, I topped them off with tons of thick black eyeliner and applied fake eyelashes. Freddy told me that false lashes were *de rigueur* in this joint—even for daytime—and I had better know how to do them well. Loading her lips up with gloss, I had to admit that the new look was comparable to what she had been wearing before, although still somewhat pared down. No matter how I slapped it on, my hand could not quite achieve the heaviness that had been there before.

Tori snapped her pink bubble gum to punctuate her boredom and gave me a wan smile. She looked like she was maybe twenty and I thought about how different our lives must be. She was a hard-partying young girl just starting out in life, and I was a much older, divorced single mother.

"Get some of the glitter shit," said Tori, pointing at a row of tall, sparkly powder shakers. "Priscilla *loves* when you use that stuff."

"Thanks." I swept on a good measure of the glittery powder stuff that smelled like vanilla cupcakes.

Tori was getting restless, so I signaled Freddy to come over.

"I think we're done here."

"Okay. Yes! Yes! Good." He inspected Tori's face closely. "I'll tell Priscilla!" He then waltzed off in Madam Priscilla's direction.

Tori sat there checking her text messages and giggling, and I wondered what was so amusing.

"Do you like working here?" I asked her, for lack of anything else to say.

"Yeah . . . it's fine. You can make decent money," she answered while her fingers pecked furiously away at her phone.

My glance drifted over to the artist at the opposite station. I had been aware of him staring at me while I was applying Tori's makeup. Intuitively, I knew it was not my technique he was evaluating. He had long, thinning dark hair, tanned skin, and small brown eyes. He looked over at me and raised his eyebrows in a sort of exaggerated acknowledgement. He was a Latin Fabio—all brawn and flowing hair—a living version of the cover of a romance novel. Our eyes met again and this time he held my gaze in the most overtly sexual way. It was wildly inappropriate in a business setting and I looked away. When I thought it was safe, I darted my eyes back again for confirmation. Was I imagining it or did his tongue really just whip around his lips? It was the visual equivalent of being slimed. I felt like I needed to take a shower. I mentally christened him 'Labio'. He looked like he belonged on a *Saturday Night Live* skit—an over-the-top comical Latin lothario trying to get a leg-up on his clients. He was too outrageous to be real. Most men I encountered in the beauty business were gay and usually great fun. Labio, with his intense, dark energy, didn't seem to qualify in either category.

Freddy came back and summoned us excitedly over to Priscilla.

Priscilla sported delicate gold-rimmed glasses and examined every pore on Tori's face while I held my breath.

"Honey . . . you can't do lashes for shit . . . but we can work on that. The rest of her face is fine."

I stepped in to inspect the errant lashes, and indeed the edge of her right lashes had sprung free and was now waving enthusiastically from the corner. She was right. They looked like shit. At least she had pronounced the rest of her face as 'fine'. Not exactly a ringing endorsement, but they were desperate and it would serve to get me in the door.

"Wait over there." Priscilla pointed a freshly manicured French-tipped nail over to a sofa in the corner where I was to await further instructions. I collapsed onto the sofa with a large exhale and watched Priscilla and Freddy discussing my fate. My stomach was feeling the effects of the stress of the audition and I didn't care what happened next. Tori went back to her station where she checked her new makeup in the magnifying mirror and made her adjustments. I decided not to take it personally and watched, fascinated, as she applied more eyeliner and darker shadow in the crease. I avoided looking anywhere in Labio's direction.

Freddy came bouncing over excitedly. "Priscilla would like you to start on Tuesday. *Only* for a trial at first—you understand—but hopefully it will go well and we'll get to keep you!" Then he became suddenly very serious. "Now, Priscilla demands absolute professionalism from every *artiste*. You must be one hundred percent committed to Priscilla and to this salon. We will not tolerate slackers. Beauty is a serious business. There will be no vacations before one year of employment and sick leave is to be avoided at all cost. Oh, you don't have any children or a pesky husband or anything do you? No, of course you don't. You're too smart for that! Now, we can go over the manual later, but I wanted you to know that this position is strictly for serious *artistes*."

If I heard the word *artiste* one more time, I thought I might vomit.

"Yes, of course. But . . . um . . . I should mention that I actually *do* have a child. I managed to get rid of the pesky husband but luckily I get to keep the child!" I was joking but he wasn't amused. "Not that my having a child should become an issue or anything, but I thought it was worth mentioning." I held my breath and waited to see how this bombshell would land. He cocked his head to the side as if it were a great strain and grimaced.

"Oh, fine, but whatever you do, don't tell Priscilla you have a kid. And don't let it get sick or interfere with anything," he whispered to me.

"No problem," I said, forcing a smile. Freelance work was so much less complicated. I could feel an ulcer coming on and I hadn't even started yet.

Chapter Six
The Beauty Shop of Horrors

On Tuesday, wearing a navy wrap dress I'd borrowed from Emma, I arrived fifteen minutes early and cooled my heels outside, drinking my latte and watching Beverly Hills waking up. Freddy ran up, out of breath and struggling with multiple large shopping bags at two minutes to ten.

"Hi. You didn't hear the phone ringing, did you?" He didn't attempt to mask the panic in his voice.

"No." I relieved him of some of the shopping bags he was toting.

"Oh, *thank God*. Priscilla rings at ten-to almost every day and if I don't answer . . . well, let's just say it's *not* good," he said, fumbling with the keys.

"I didn't hear any ringing."

"Good. Come in," he said. "Start familiarizing yourself with the merchandise." He waved at the display units. "I'll get you some product info to read. Mostly you'll be following the other *artistes* today and watching how it works. You'll get the hang of it quickly."

Freddy whipped around the salon and brought it to life—lights, music, and action!

Tori ambled in at ten minutes past ten looking like she'd just finished her round at the clubs.

"Tori . . . tut, tut!" Freddy admonished her. "Ten ten is not ten o'clock."

Tori ignored him. She wore a black nylon mini-dress with what CeCe refers to as 'hooker shoes'—perilously high black plastic slip-on wedges. She leaned over her mirror and lethargically began to put her face on.

"Remember, we're all going to have to help train Scarlett today," Freddy announced.

"Good morning, Tori," I said, brightly.

She looked startled and managed a grunt in my direction, clearly not ready to deal with my caffeine-fueled enthusiasm.

The morning was quiet, which gave Tori plenty of time for her obsessive primping. I watched, riveted, as she did her makeup, and then kept redoing parts of it over and over, as if stuck in a groove. More mascara, more lash curling then repeat. It was a wonder she had any lashes left. The task of training me fell on her shoulders but it was far less of a priority than pruning her eyebrows. And so I waited. After a taxing round with her brows, she turned her attention to me.

She studied my face for a moment. "You're going to have to wear more makeup. Ya gotta sell this shit and you can't do it wearing that 'natural' makeup," Tori said with clear disdain. She thrust a large blush brush into my hand and nodded toward the unit displaying sparkly pink and peach blushes, and bronzer.

"Right . . . 'the glitter shit.' I forgot!" I walked over to the unit, made a mad swirl over all the colors, and swept it on my face with wild abandon.

But Tori wasn't done. "*And* ya gotta wear something that looks like ya got something going on. Ya know? Ya need some game. Something trendier, more *happening*, you need to look hipper."

I laughed at her brazen assessment. "Okay . . . I'll see what I can do." Silly cow. This was a Diane von Furstenberg dress, and belonged to Emma —a bona fide working actress who oozed game. If she thought this ensemble lacked zest then she would go absolutely apeshit if she saw my 'mommy' wardrobe. This was as hip as I was conceivably going to get without a big, fat influx of cash.

"Cool," she said and then refocused her scrutiny on my face. "Today we need to do something about those brows. Sit down and I'll fix them."

Leery after watching her attack her brows with something nearing an obsessive-compulsive disorder, I shook my head and declined. "Um . . . not today."

"Why? Trust me. You need it," she persisted, coming toward me armed with her tweezers.

I checked my offending brows in the mirror. They were a bit untended, but hardly a disaster. It was true that I was guilty of letting myself go a bit since having Oliver and would have to make more of an effort to fit in here. I enjoyed the transformation of makeup, but I didn't live and breathe it like some people. It wasn't my life. I, personally, couldn't give a flying fuck about the hottest new mascara or compulsive brow pruning. This new environment was going to require a bit of a stretch.

"I usually prefer this one guy I know to do it." I tried to put her off but who was I kidding? Nobody had come anywhere near them in years and that much was obvious. "Okay, if you really think I need it . . ."

She nodded and pointed to the chair.

I surrendered into it. "Knock yourself out."

Tori had finished with one brow when her twelve o'clock client arrived and she booted me out of the chair. A look of panic flitted across my face as she dispatched me. One brow was sculpted and filled in while the other one was left looking overgrown and bushy in comparison. I tried to sweep the offending brow back into compliance but that seemed to make it worse.

"Don't worry, I'll fix the other one after this," she said, noting my despair.

I surveyed the damage. Now I had dramatically uneven brows—a before and after brow on the same face! How could I possibly dispense beauty advice in this lopsided state? Who would take me seriously?

Five minutes later, Labio sauntered in. I pretended to be engrossed in Tori's makeover appointment so he wouldn't try to engage me in conversation, but no such luck.

"Hey! New girl! Neeeew Girl!" he squealed.

I ignored him until Tori stopped applying violet eyeliner to her client and giggled at me. "*Someone's* calling you."

Labio half walked, half glided over to me, hips thrust forward in a way that made the top of his body look disconnected from the bottom. A cloud of heavy cologne arrived before him. He gave me a sly, appraising smile that started at my shoes and meandered its way up.

"Hey, new girl . . . whassup?"

"Not much. Just learning the ropes." I instantly regretted my choice of words.

"Stick with me, New Girl. I'll show you the ropes," he said with a wink.

He busied himself setting up his station but then turned his attention back to me.

"Hey, what's up with your brows, baby?" he asked, looking quizzically at my one errant brow.

"Oh," I said feeling my cheeks flush with embarrassment. I had forgotten about them. "Tori was doing them when her client arrived. She said she'd fix them."

"Sit down. I'll fix them," he said, and gestured to the chair in front of him.

"That's okay, Tori will do it," I said and looked over to Tori to save me.

"Oh, I have another client right after this so ya better let him do it." She was of no help at all.

It was clear I wasn't going to win this round. I sat in his chair and hoped it would be over quickly. Labio leering inches from my face was the very last thing I needed.

He put on a good show of combing, trimming, waxing and plucking, while thrusting his pelvis forward in time with the music in a distracting fashion. And in case my attention wasn't drawn down toward his bobbing assets, his tight black leather pants—worn to highlight his seemingly considerable girth—sported a silver lion's-head belt buckle that kept dancing in front of me, making it impossible to miss.

I wondered just how much I had screwed up in a past life to earn this humiliating position. Wasn't my stinking divorce enough?

"So, New Girl . . . what's your deal?" he leaned in and said in a hushed, intimate tone.

"I'm a divorced single mother with lots of bills. That's my deal." I answered sweetly but with enough bite to hopefully repel him. I'd forgotten that Freddy told me not to talk about my kid.

He laughed heartily at this. "Single mothers still like to have some fun. They need it the most. Yeah, I know some *fun* single mothers . . ."

"I'm not one of the fun ones," I stated definitively.

"Well, I can take you in the back room and we can find out for ourselves. You might surprise even yourself," he said loud enough to be heard.

Tori looked over at Labio and smiled knowingly.

"Is that an initiation rite around here?" I said after catching the exchange.

"Yeah . . . maybe it is." He laughed and ignored my tone. "I've had most of the girls here."

Labio had sexual harassment lawsuit written all over him.

"No, thanks. I'll pass." I felt queasy.

He took his time with my brows, making sure I got plenty of exposure to his thrusting nether regions. Labio turned out to be a brow wizard. He filled them in at the ends where they were sparse and wimpy, shaped them and gave me the illusion of a lush supermodel brow. I hated to admit it but he was talented. He'd made a huge difference in the way they framed my face. I hadn't realized how scruffy they'd looked before.

Released from Labio's clutches, I thanked him, scuttled away to recover on the other side of the store and occupied myself cleaning the eye shadow display units, lest Freddy think I wasn't busy enough and send me back into the fray.

Freddy came over to admire Labio's handiwork.

"Let's see. Oh, yes! Fantastic! Today I want you to watch him work. Stick with him as much as you can. He is the most talented *artiste* here and the one you need to learn from."

"He seems a bit . . . forward." My stomach roiled at the thought of spending a whole day with him.

"Oh, he's a flirt but all the ladies *love* him!"

Not this lady.

We watched as Labio helped a cute young thing into his chair.

"He's starting with a client right now . . . go watch," he said and gave me a shove in Labio's direction.

Labio's client looked to be in her early twenties. She was pretty with short, chestnut-colored hair and a body of generous proportions on display in a tight low-cut T-shirt. There was something sweet and innocent about her demeanor, despite her provocative attire. She was not representative of the typical clientele—the older, established, well married Beverly Hills women.

Labio introduced me to his client, Jodi.

"I'm 'training' the new girl," he said with an exaggerated wink to Jodi.

He groomed her brows while they chatted about people they were dating. Their familiarity indicated they had known each other for a while. They carried on an intimate conversation, unperturbed by my presence, and included me in pieces of it. Jodi was filling him in on her new boyfriend, yet despite said boyfriend, it was obvious she was enchanted with Labio.

"Well, I bet this new guy isn't full-service like me," Labio said, enjoying the exchange. "Bet he doesn't 'go downtown' like I do! I can 'go downtown' and eat it like a vulture!"

Jodi laughed. "He's a *good* boyfriend! Not like you!" She looked over at me and said, "We used to date."

"Oh? You're much too young and cute for him!" I said, truth in jest.

"He dumped me because I didn't 'represent Detroit,' " she said sheepishly.

"You didn't what?" I was clueless.

"I didn't 'represent Detroit,' " she repeated, eliciting another blank look from me.

"I didn't let him do me in the booty," she said, and they both started giggling.

"Yeah, you gotta 'represent Detroit', baby. That's part of the deal! You gotta represent the backend!" he said, nodding affirmatively.

"Oh, no you don't," I said to Jodi, my protective mothering instinct kicking in. "You don't have to do anything *you* don't want to do."

She smiled but wasn't listening to a word I said.

"So he broke up with me . . ." Her eyes stayed locked on Labio.

"Yeah, but she still wants me . . . and whenever you're ready to change your mind, girl . . . I'll be here!" he said, thrusting his hips back and forth, which sent them both into another giggling fit.

Priscilla arrived, and I took it as my cue to look like I was doing something and left Labio and Jodi. Freddy sprang into action. Like a bee swarming about her head, he trailed her throughout the salon, buzzing about the day's events.

Priscilla's arrival put everyone on alert. Postures were more erect; conversations with clients became more discreet. Priscilla wore expensive, well-cut black pants and a lightweight cream cashmere sweater with lots of gold chains bearing baubles and trinkets. Her oversized Jackie Kennedy glasses shielded her from unwanted eye contact as she strode purposefully through the salon. The Queen had arrived.

It wasn't long before I was summoned to her quarters.

"Nice brows," she said, noticing instantly. "He did a beautiful job. He can teach you a lot, you know."

"So he's told me," I said dryly.

"What I care about is your selling ability. I want to know that you can sell any product in this place. Now go and try everything . . . get a feel for the line."

"Yes, Priscilla." I went to help Teddy put lip glosses into the dispenser.

The day dragged on and I sold barely anything. It was not a good first day. I felt useless, made worse by the fact that I was acutely aware Priscilla was evaluating my performance. But the more I tried, the worse it got. It was exhausting to pretend that I put great importance on lip gloss and blusher, when clearly I didn't. I suddenly knew what it was like to be a clock-watcher as I willed the day to end.

Finally, six o'clock arrived but before I could leave, Priscilla wanted to see me.

"Your sales are sluggish, to say the least. Let's get it going, girl! You need to produce numbers. We don't carry any dead weight around here."

"My sales will be better tomorrow," I promised.

"Study the catalogues tonight. Go do your homework," she said, and handed me an additional stack of catalogues.

Having a job was supposed to be a good distraction from my divorce malaise, not deepen it. There was not an ounce of spring in my step as I walked the four blocks back to the only cheap parking I could find.

Freddy was there when I arrived the next morning and was busy sprucing up the salon for the day ahead. He was placing glass bowls of fresh gardenias on the counters, and was a highly caffeinated nervous wreck.

"Everything must go smoothly today. Priscilla has a *very* important client coming in today and everything must be puurrfect!"

Tori came bouncing in with uncharacteristic energy in her gait.

"Hello, everybody!" she said gaily.

"You're in a good mood," I said in shock.

"I got up early this morning and went out to the stables for a ride."

"Oh, God, Tori . . . did you shower?" Freddy asked with more than a touch of irritation.

"No . . . why?" She giggled.

"Tori . . . you know why."

"Okay, okay. Keep your pants on. I'll go wash off . . ." She headed toward the employee bathroom in the back.

"She comes in after her 'ride' at the stable smelling like horses and sex, and I can't deal with that today," said Freddy. "I hope she gives that coochie a good old wash." He began sniffing at the air, pulled out a can of Lysol and darted around the salon spraying at invisible targets.

"Oh, fuck!" Freddy shrieked from the back of the store. "Priscilla's fish has died! Tori, get out here! You're going to have to run to the pet store and buy another one. Maybe she won't notice."

"He probably died from all that shit you spray in here," Tori said, lifting her miniskirt as she wiped the back of her thighs with paper towels.

The three of us stood glumly around the small fish bowl and gave Paulie, the purple fighting fish, his last rites before Freddy flushed him down the toilet.

"Was she very attached to Paulie?" I asked, watching the purple swirl disappear down the bowl.

"She named him after her ex-husband—the one she liked," Freddy said, and dispatched Tori to the pet store to buy another purple fish.

She strolled back in an hour later with a blue fighting fish.

"Oh, that's not going to work. He's not even the same color!" Freddy shrieked.

"Well, that's all they had," Tori said, snapping her gum at him pointedly.

"Put him in there. I'll go find a replacement after work tonight. Hopefully, we'll be so busy today that she won't notice."

Priscilla arrived at noon on the dot. We held our breath as she walked to the back to put away her purse, there was a slight pause, and then she turned right around and stormed back out.

"What the *fuck* happened to Paulie?" she asked, glaring directly at Freddy.

"What do you mean? He's in there, isn't he?" Freddy answered, quivering slightly.

"Why is he turning blue? He was purple yesterday. What have you done to him?"

Freddy froze on the spot and didn't dare say anything, so I jumped in.

"I heard somewhere that changes in the water or different acidity levels can make them change color. I'm sure it's temporary." I had no idea what I was talking about but it sounded good.

"Really?" Priscilla turned to me. "How do you know so much about fish?"

"I have a younger brother. He buys a lot of pets," I said, which was a true statement.

"Hmm . . . he better be back to normal by tomorrow."

We stood frozen until she snapped us out of it. "Well, stop standing around and get back to work. We've got makeup to sell."

"Thank you . . . that was a great save!" Freddy whispered to me after she was out of earshot.

"Anytime," I said, mortified that I was now willing to lie about fish in order to fit in.

—∿—

Sales were easier on the second day. After studying the catalogues, I knew a lot more of the product names. Freddy threw me a few easy clients who liked to buy everything, which helped boost my confidence.

Priscilla's presence in the salon kept everyone on edge and the staff quaked in anticipation of a correction—everyone except Labio. They had worked together for years and he seemed to have an agreement to do as he pleased. I wondered if she'd been intimately exposed to those gyrating nether regions.

There were unspoken rules for the rest of us that I quickly picked up— never leave the store if Priscilla was present, personal errands were a no-no, and lunch breaks didn't exist. Running out to buy lunch was frowned upon and was viewed as a lack of commitment. Time away from the salon meant lost potential sales. If I *insisted* on eating during the day, it was suggested that I bring a packed lunch and scarf it in the back room.

A very dim view was taken on any personal errands—this much I knew—but I desperately needed to run to the bank one block away to deposit a check. If I didn't deposit this new check to cover the ones I'd already mailed, then some would bounce. I felt like such a loser having to beg Freddy's permission to run out for a measly ten minutes. How had my life deteriorated to this point?

Finally, he agreed to let me go to the bank as long as I promised not to do it again. To prove what a valuable employee I was, I ran myself ragged for the rest of the day servicing as many clients as I could and meticulously scrubbing all the tester display units. I became a furious flurry of productivity and didn't even take two minutes to eat my protein snack bar. The rest of the day went by in a blur of brow-taming, lash-dying and makeup applications.

By comparison, the freelance world was much simpler. It could be feast or famine but I didn't have to twist myself into a pretzel to be accepted, or lie about dead fish. How I longed for another dreamy job with Garrison Lee. It would take at least three weeks of salon work to equal what I could make in one day working with a movie star like him, but I didn't have any high-paying jobs on the horizon, so I'd have to stick it out and make this work. I put the most pleasing version of myself forward and tried harder to fit in. It was almost like dating.

On my third day at the salon, as fate would have it, Oliver came down with a cold. It was a perfect storm of shitty circumstances. Oliver had been up a lot of the night. CeCe had an early meeting and was gone before seven in the morning, and Sam had stayed over at Mikki's, so there was nobody around to help. Oliver was in a foul mood and did not want to be put down for a second, so it was impossible to get ready. Exhausted and clingy, he did not want to go to the babysitter. It was a nightmare. It was heart wrenching to leave him when he wasn't feeling well and all he wanted was Mommy. Oliver was feverish and distraught—the worst possible time to introduce a new sitter. I didn't dare tell Freddy my child was sick but I had to do something. I was going to be late. I called the salon.

"Enchanté Beauty Retreat." Freddy answered in his usual singsong fashion.

"Hi, Freddy, I'm running a few minutes late," I said, and braced for the impending freak-out.

"Get in here ASAP!" He dropped the faux sweetness and screeched at me.

By the time I arrived, I was over an hour late. Harried and out of breath, I was dismayed to discover that Priscilla was already there, which could only mean bad news for me. The salon looked as if a cyclone had just blown through with products and makeup brushes scattered across the counters.

Priscilla stayed in the back but broadcast her displeasure with a few stony stares thrown in my direction.

Freddy solemnly gave me the news.

"Scarlett, you've disappointed us and let us down," he said, fingering an envelope in his hands.

"I'm sorry. It couldn't be avoided. It won't happen again, I—"

"No, it won't happen again. We had a huge rush in here this morning. A busload of Japanese tourists descended upon us, and Tori and I couldn't keep up. Priscilla called during the madness, and because *you* weren't here she was forced to cancel her doctor's appointment and come in early."

"Oh, no. That's terrible timing . . . it's usually so quiet in the mornings . . ." I struggled to think of something to say that didn't sound lame but came up with nothing. He'd already shared his dim view of sick children with me. I looked over at Tori, who wouldn't make eye contact with me. It felt like the ground beneath me was giving way and there was nothing to hold on to.

"Sorry, Scarlett," he said, in a tone that told me he was well versed in this sort of farewell speech. "But this 'trial period' isn't going to work out." With his lips pursed up like a cat's arse, he handed me the envelope.

My head was spinning with the speed of my demise. I hadn't even lasted three days. That one would earn me another mention in the loser handbook.

"I'm sure you read in the employee manual that this was only a trial and we are in no way obligated to you. We need someone more *reliable* and *committed*. It's too bad. I really liked you." He gave one final sniff before retreating to relative safety behind the counter.

"That seems a little extreme. Aren't I supposed to get a warning or something?"

"No. Read the employee manual. We've seen enough to know that you have your attention elsewhere. We don't give personal errand breaks and we don't give warnings."

"Don't you want me to cover my shift for the day? You're shorthanded," I asked, unable to absorb the finality of this breakup.

"No. You don't need to see out the day. You can leave now." He took out the Windex and started cleaning the counter. Gone was any trace of camaraderie or anything I thought I might have gained by conspiring to cover for him with dead fish. He had his firing face on and nothing was going to penetrate it.

I looked over at Priscilla, who was watching it all go down from her perch in the corner.

I stalked over to her. If I was on my way out, I may as well go out in flames. "Are you serious? That's it? I wasn't even here a week!"

"Don't worry, kid," she said coolly. "It's a big town. You'll find something else."

Frustration flamed under my skin. Unable to think of a good comeback line, I turned and headed out.

Labio passed me as I was leaving the salon and said, "So long, *chica,*" as if he had already heard the news.

It was a true measure of my own dysfunction that I felt a stab of regret as I walked the four blocks to my car. It was another place I didn't fit in, another thing I had failed at. My self-esteem was at an all-time low. I picked up some chicken noodle soup from Bristol Farms and raced home to Oliver.

Oliver was napping when I got home. Marta the babysitter was paid her day rate and released early—it wasn't her fault I'd been fired. She was counting on the income, too. I licked my wounds, made tea, and lay on the couch all day cuddling with Oliver. We had a marathon of all his favorite television shows: *Maggie and the Ferocious Beast, Bob the Builder* and of course, *SpongeBob SquarePants.*

Oliver perked up and by evening was feeling much better. He puttered about the apartment, playing with his toys and Lego blocks. The same could not be said for me.

Emma called. She had been at an audition at CBS and was in the neighborhood. I gave her the news.

"Oh, screw them! That was only supposed to be a temporary gig anyway."

"I hadn't realized just how temporary . . ."

"Forget them. I'm coming over to cheer you up. I'll bring dinner!"

"You are a saint," I said, brightening at the thought of a well-timed visit with Emma. CeCe had a date set up for after work and the apartment was feeling a little too quiet.

"Have you considered doing commercials again?" Emma asked as we sat in front of the television and shared an order of spaghetti bolognese and buffalo mozzarella salad.

I laughed at the suggestion. "I haven't done a commercial in years."

"So what?"

Emma had been my cheerleader since we'd met in acting class twelve years earlier. We'd clicked instantly and worked with each other on all our audition scenes. Emma was undeniably the hotshot in our class and it hadn't taken long for casting directors to take notice of her and launch her career. Since then, Emma had worked steadily in the business and had made a killing in commercials. Acting jobs came relatively effortlessly to her but I had never had the same luck. In fact, in the circle of actress girlfriends I'd started out with, I was the only one who hadn't achieved any measure of success in the business—a fact that was not lost on me.

I lured Oliver over with a mouthful of pasta and did my best to aim for his mouth as he slowed down briefly before he did another lap around the living room.

"It's time for you to get out there. You made some money doing them before, why not have another go?" Emma made it sound seductively easy.

"That one Tylenol spot I did ran for ages . . . that was a godsend, " I said, and savored the idea for a brief moment. I had been lucky to land a few before; maybe I could do it again.

"Look at this spot," she said, and gestured at a commercial playing. An attractive yet generic looking blond woman was dancing about her kitchen enthusiastically cleaning her floors with a Swiffer mop. "You *totally* could have done that one!" she said with growing conviction.

"I guess it couldn't hurt to try it again. It's not like I have anything else going on," I said as I watched the woman dance around the screen. I could feel myself being reeled back in.

"I'll talk to my agent about you," Emma said. "I'll pitch you as a fabulous Australian import she has to meet!"

"Ha. *That's* a bit of a stretch . . . but it would be great if she'd meet with me. Thank you."

"No problem. I'll call her."

Emma was the rare actress who rooted for other people's success. She was a true gem. No matter what state I was in—dumpy and pregnant, depressed and unemployed, or unhappily married—she always insisted that things could turn around dramatically. It was true. In Hollywood, one audition could literally change your life. I had seen it happen to people all around me. It was the hook that kept me from freeing myself completely from my old dreams of an acting career. If I kept one toe in the business, that one audition *might* just happen.

"I think we should be celebrating," she said, throwing one jean-clad leg over the couch. "That lame job was for the birds. Who wants to be stuck there all day with those nuts? You'd lose it!"

"I know but I needed the job. Do you have any idea what my bills are at the moment? I can't bear to think about it."

"I get it. You're stressed. But don't waste any energy on that place. You can make more with one good commercial than a year of work in that shitty salon. Besides, it sounded awful. What a loony bin!"

"It probably wasn't the right place but being fired by the loons in the loony bin has an especially bitter ring to it," I said, and poured Emma a glass of chardonnay. "It was my first attempt back into the working world and I crashed and burned."

"Think about getting back in the game. It can't hurt to shake things up a bit."

"Let me give it some thought."

I spent the rest of the evening watching commercials and studying what the actresses were wearing and doing in the ads. I had to admit that there was a flicker of excitement at the thought of being in that world again. Despite years of rejection, I could still be lured back. Such was my addiction to the entertainment business. Some actors looked down their noses at commercials and deemed them lowbrow, but I suffered from none of those airs. If someone would hire me for a commercial—any commercial

—I'd be ecstatic. Emma's enthusiasm made it all seem possible, and that sense of possibility was the elixir I needed more than anything at that moment.

Chapter Seven
Return of the Hee Haw Honey

Spurred on by Emma's enthusiasm, I picked six commercial agencies to approach and mailed them each a cover letter with a headshot.

Not a single one responded.

It appeared that nothing had changed in that game; still a lot of doors slamming in my face and yet somehow I felt different. If I could just get in the door with one of these agencies, maybe I could make something happen.

After X picked up Oliver, I dashed over to meet Emma at Urth Caffé on Melrose Avenue for a coffee and some brainstorming. Melrose Avenue is famous for its fashionable stores and trendy, colorful hipsters. It was good for me to get out of the house. In Los Angeles, simply being out and about and running into people often created opportunities. It was the way business operated and networking was often the quickest route to employment. Sometimes all it took was running into a publicist or manager and work materialized as a result.

Urth Caffé had been one of my favorite spots before I was married and moved over the hill to virtual oblivion in the valley. Not much had changed in the years since I'd frequented the café. It was still popular with the 'in' crowd and the frenetic energy still gave me a buzz, as well as their lattes.

From our table on the patio, under our emerald-green umbrella, we watched as the hip, beautiful LA people paraded by us on their way to secure their treats. It was a mix of unemployed actors and models mingling with young students and a handful of professionals in business attire. As usual, I wasn't sure what category I fit into, if any.

"This place looks like a film set," I said, looking around. "Only in LA do you find such freakishly good-looking people. When you live here and marinate in this weird environment you forget that it's completely abnormal! Everybody's a size two. Look! Even the palm trees are anorexic!"

Emma laughed. "Oh, it's absurd, isn't it? There's nowhere in the world like it. It's a different breed out here."

Like clockwork, truckloads of would-be actors and models were deposited daily in Los Angeles and everyone was pursuing *something.* And I was no different—just older and more jaded.

We watched as a striking model in ultra-low-slung jeans clutched her teacup Pomeranian and argued with her boyfriend about how to order her nonfat cappuccino correctly.

"I have no business being out having coffee. It's an extravagance." I suddenly felt a pang of guilt. "You should see the bills I have piling up. I have no idea how I'm going to pay them."

"Well, pay them off slowly if you have to. Staying home and getting more depressed doesn't help much either," Emma said, always the sensible one.

"I need to dust off my makeup kit and get back in the freelance market again. Screw Priscilla and her minions. I've ordered some business cards and have been calling and e-mailing everyone I know to let them know I'm still alive and to put the word out there. My contacts are a bit stale but I'm working on it." I spooned the froth from around the rim of the honey vanilla latte into my mouth.

"That's all good but we're going to get you a commercial agent as well. Almost everybody has two careers in this town. There is so much work in the young-mom category you'd be right for. There's nothing to lose by checking it out." Emma made it sound so simple.

"I submitted to half a dozen agencies and didn't get a single bite."

"Let's call Darcy right now!" She reached into her new Marc Jacobs purse, purchased off the set of one of her commercial shoots.

I listened as Emma dialed her agency and engaged in light chitchat with the assistant. Emma carried a lot of clout and was one of their favorite clients. After a moment, she hung up. "Darcy's going to call me back and I'll set up a meeting for you. This is what you need to get going."

The prospect of acting again both thrilled and terrified me. Unlike Emma's natural success, booking commercials had never been that easy for me. Years of acting classes had done little to take the edge off my audition anxiety. The times I actually booked jobs were if I was hungover, sick, or had a hot date waiting for me. An altered state or distraction seemed to override my nerves. Some successful actors I knew drank before auditions or popped pills to quell their anxiety but I couldn't bring myself to do it. Maybe I didn't want it badly enough.

"What's happening with Dominick? Have you had any secret trysts lately?" Emma said, as she watched a young Brad Pitt look-alike walk by with his bulldog.

"No. I'm avoiding him—or he's avoiding me—I forget which. That's a dead end and if I hang out with him, I'll get used to him and his nonsense again and I can't afford that."

A lanky man in an ill-fitting suit with disheveled hair came over and thrust a piece of paper in front of me.

I stared at him blankly, thinking he might be a process server.

"Sign this for me." He set a ballpoint pen on top of the paper and nudged it in my direction again. His energy was so frenetic that he made me uneasy.

"What for?" I asked him, completely lost as to what he could possibly want.

"Aren't you Naomi Watts? I've seen *all* your movies," he said, as if expecting to be thanked for this loyalty.

I laughed nervously, relieved he wasn't trying to serve me legal papers.

"Oh, no, that's very flattering but I'm not Naomi. You've got the wrong Aussie," I said and pushed the paper back toward him, unsigned.

"Yes, you are," he said with growing irritation, and shoved it back. "I've seen all your films. Why won't you just sign it?"

"I would but I'm *not* Naomi," I said and pushed the paper back. This was becoming a silly game.

"Yes, you are. I've been watching you for twenty minutes," he said, becoming increasingly agitated.

"Dude . . . don't you get it? She's *not* Naomi!" said Emma definitively.

The man snatched up his paper and pen, shouted "*Fuck you!*" at us, and left.

"That was charming," I said as we watched him storm down the stairs and out onto the street. "Maybe I should have just signed it."

"See, you've already got a stalker!" said Emma, gleefully. "It's a sign! You're back in the business!"

Emma set up an appointment for me later in the week with her agent, Darcy Hobbs. This was a town built on connections. Sometimes all it took was getting a foot in the right door. Now, what was I going to wear?

"Just go in there and knock 'em dead!" said the divine Miss Em, calling from the set of her latest endorsement—a yogurt campaign—to give me the requisite pre-interview pep talk.

"Remember: You have *tons* of potential and could be earning them a *lot* of money—so go in there like you own the place!"

"Ha! You're a riot!" I said, aware that if I were the sort of creature who could convincingly pull that off, I wouldn't be in this predicament in the first place. That being said, having nothing left to lose felt like a strangely liberating place to be. Life was literally wide open. Who knew what avenues I might pursue? I was tied to no career whatsoever. No man, other than Oliver. Another round of rejection would not be the end of the world. Divorce was making a hardier creature out of me, whether I liked it or not.

Sam agreed to leave his video game post to watch Oliver for my meeting with Darcy. I gave him some cash and they headed down to the park. Sam was an excellent babysitter on most counts but he drew the line at changing a 'dirty' diaper. He could handle a wet one, but a dirty one was out of the question. "It's just too *nasty!*" he would say and shake his head. This meant he was suitable for the briefest of absences. The clock was ticking down from the time I left.

I brought my old audition look out of retirement for the interview: tousled hair and light makeup, which I hoped made me appear 'naturally appealing.' Jeans with a simple blue button-down shirt conveyed the right amount of California Casual but stopped short of being sloppy mom. Juxtaposed unhappily with this carefree California look was the deep furrow etched in my forehead that was getting deeper by the day. I could hide the dark circles under my eyes but makeup couldn't camouflage that particular divorce damage. Maybe it wouldn't matter. Maybe there was a commercial market niche for harried-looking, stressed-out divorced mothers.

Darcy Hobbs's agency was located in an office building on Sunset Boulevard, on the tenth floor that offered an incredible view of the city. I took a deep breath and opened the door, which put me immediately facing the receptionist sitting safely behind the barrier of a dark wooden desk. She looked like she was moonlighting from her real job as a model. She had creamy, perfect skin and her long, dark curls were draped provocatively over one shoulder.

"Can I help you?" she asked, while her eyes danced over me, completing a quick scan of my entire outfit.

"Hi. I'm Scarlett Spencer. I have a three o'clock meeting with Darcy."

"Just a moment," she said, picking up the phone to announce me. "Have a seat. Someone will be with you in a minute."

I took a seat on the black leather couch and pretended not to notice her continuing to size me up from behind her desk. The walls were lined with the headshots of their premier clients. There was one of Emma in one of the stills from her lucrative dishwashing soap campaign.

Rummaging through my oversized handbag, past the diaper wipes and long-forgotten bags of cookies for Oliver, I dug out a legal-sized envelope containing all my old headshots. I needed to weed some old, unflattering ones out. The envelope hadn't been opened in years. It was a trip down memory lane to scan through the various footprints of my life revisited through a series of headshots. A frightful selection of hairdos and over-the-top makeup represented different phases and incarnations of my twenties: classic-looking short blond bob, short pixie Mia Farrow hair, and then there was a long bob à la Faye Dunaway in *Bonnie and Clyde* with sultry makeup. The pièce de résistance was my winged homage to Charlie's Angel, Farrah Fawcett. The catalogue of bad hairdos and quest for reinvention made me think of the man responsible for a lot of them—my ex-boyfriend, Grant.

Grant was a tortured soap opera actor, obsessed with the movie and theater worlds he felt he missed out on by toiling away in the slums. An avid movie buff, he saw everything in life as a wardrobe experiment with me cast as his eager mannequin. Life was lived like an extended acting class, preparing for roles that never materialized. Life with Grant gave me entree into a world I'd dreamt of for years. Sitting around listening to his friends analyzing great acting performances until the wee hours of the morning felt like a privilege to me. It was a world I longed to be a part of and I soaked it all up.

I was deep in nostalgic revelry when Darcy's assistant came to fetch me. His name was Nick and he looked like a young Irish schoolboy—tall, skinny, and fair with pink cheeks. He was amiable but stopped short of being too friendly. I hurriedly shoved the photographs back into the envelope and followed him through a series of rooms until we came to the large corner office.

A booming voice called out to me from behind a large oak desk.

Just breathe, I reminded myself.

"Come on in! Emma tells me I have to meet you."

I was happy to see that, in sharp contrast to her receptionist, Darcy had the market cornered in the 'normal-looking' department. She appeared to be in her fifties, heavyset and had shoulder-length, ash blond hair. Behind large red-framed glasses, she scrutinized me up and down while I discreetly did the same.

Darcy eyed the envelope in my hands and said, "So . . . what did you bring to show me? Come and sit down."

I handed her the envelope and took a seat opposite her, trying very hard to exude an air of calm while she flicked through the headshots.

Darcy visibly recoiled in her seat. "Jesus, honey . . . do you have anything more recent? These are archaic."

"Oh, yes, the most recent ones are in the back." I bolted up, mortified, snatched the envelope out of her hands and hurriedly produced the least offensive-looking ones. My cheeks felt flush with embarrassment.

"Emma tells me you have a kid," she said as she scanned quickly through the headshots.

"Yes, I have a little boy and his name is—"

"Uh-huh, that's nice, honey . . . but are you serious about working?" She paused and peered at me over the rim of her red frames.

"Well, yes. I have to because I'm a single mother now and I—"

"Don't care about the sob story, sweetheart. Just need to know if you can make it to auditions," she said with a faux smile.

"Oh, absolutely!" I said, nodding for emphasis.

"We have to do something about that hair," she said, tilting from side to side as she assessed my bobbing head.

"Oh . . . really? What do I need to do?" I started pulling at strands of it, trying to identify the offense.

"The length is *okay,* I guess . . . but the color? It's all kinds of wrong. You're too blonde! Jeez, are we doing a *Hee-Haw Honey* revival? Much too *Beverly Hillbilly*! Nobody will take you seriously. Tone it down. How are you going to sell fabric softener with that hair?"

So much for the expensive 'Malibu Beach Blonde' look in which I'd recently invested nearly three hundred dollars that I couldn't spare.

"Maybe I could put a rinse on it?" I asked, completely horrified by the suggestion. What was she talking about? I'd *never* considered going darker. What would be the point? Wherever my hair shade was, my mood inevitably followed.

"I don't care what you do with it. That's your problem," she said as she flipped the packet of headshots onto her desk. "Get me some copies of your most recent headshot and I'll start sending you out and we'll see what happens. Let's do some new headshots, but in the meantime, take care of that hair! Less *Hee-Haw Honey*. Think more cute soccer mom."

Darcy stood and maneuvered her considerable girth around the desk to shake my hand.

I swept the headshots off her desk and into my purse before she could rethink her decision.

"Cute soccer mom . . . got it. Thank you, Darcy! I'll get right on it."

"Okay, sweetheart, bye-bye. Nick will show you out."

And with that she closed the door on me.

Nick was decidedly nicer to me on the way out but it barely registered.

I floated back to my car. If I wasn't mistaken, I'd just landed an agent.

Chapter Eight
Back in the Game

The next week, Darcy sent me out on a milk commercial, and I waded back into the audition pool.

I left Oliver with Sam and put on my best representation of what a young*ish* television mom might wear: khaki pants, a pink T-shirt and flats. It was an unofficial uniform and needed to straddle the line between casual but still put-together because, let's face it, nobody wants to see the tatty sweatpants that we real moms run around in.

The casting office was running behind and the waiting room was packed with every kind of perfect-looking housewife imaginable. Feisty redheads, subdued brunettes, and perky-looking blondes lined the hallways.

I took a deep breath and tried to pretend that this wasn't my first audition back and that my stomach wasn't doing flips.

I did a quick scan and guessed that none of them was a bona-fide mom. Not a single one looked like they'd had a day dealing with potty training or wrangling children. They were far too calm looking or maybe it was just a surfeit of Wellbutrin beaming back at me.

These phony moms came ready to do battle with their made-up, powdered faces, focusing on the task at hand—booking the commercial. I noticed a pretty brunette whom I had seen in a number of commercials. She had the right combination of elements. She was attractive but had a quirky edge which made her stand out. I studied her as she was checking her face in her compact. This woman showed up with her A-game on. Watch and learn, I thought. Following her lead, I fluffed the damp hair that clung limply to my sticky forehead and rummaged around in my bag to find some powder.

The line was moving very slowly. The dirty diaper clock was ticking. I needed to get back to Oliver before the turd fairy visited.

Finally, my name was called and I walked into the audition, headshot in hand. The room was sparsely furnished with harsh lighting—standard for the audition process. The bored guy behind the camera, a moonlighting actor himself, flatly instructed me to step in front of the camera, stand on the mark, and state my name. There was no dialogue in the commercial. We were simply required to look happy while involved in activities with our pretend television children—not exactly a huge demand to place on rusty acting chops.

"Imagine you're walking on the beach with your kid," he said. "High energy! Happy times in the sun! Okay . . . *action!*"

I stated my name and gave him my best happy, TV-land smiles. I threw my imaginary child into the air and twirled him around. As it turned out, I probably could have brought Oliver to the audition.

And then it was over.

"Okay, thanks for coming," he said, opened the door and called out, "Next."

'Thanks for coming' was the official kiss of death. Roughly translated it meant: 'I think your audition sucked but I'm obligated to be nice, anyway, in case you're related to somebody important.'

I shrugged it off and hurried back to my car. Who cares what he thought? I was back on the audition circuit.

I did have some callbacks where producers were afforded a closer look but I was ultimately turned down for soccer-mom roles for Pizza Hut, Wonder Bread, Visa Card, Palmolive soap and a host of others.

I wondered when Darcy was going to yell at me for not changing my hair. I had been successful at avoiding her and the subject of hair color altogether. I made sure I washed it a lot, which would help minimize the brassiness, or so I'd hoped. With all the changes happening in my life, changing my hair color was one more than I could handle.

Between auditions, I looked online for work and submitted myself for whatever freelance makeup jobs I could—weddings, photo shoots or any event that came along. I noticed that there were regular ads for Priscilla's, the *Beauty Shop of Horrors* as I dubbed it. It looked like other *artistes* didn't last long, either, which made me feel a tiny bit better.

In our considerable downtime, Oliver and I became masters of the cheap date. We went down to Santa Monica beach and played in the sand, went to various parks and spent time at The Grove shopping mall.

With Oliver not yet in preschool, I was obliged to provide some sort of stimulation but it was probably more for me than for him. I needed to escape the emptiness of a life without a schedule, without steady work and with nothing to cling to. I needed to escape that feeling of failure. I should have been able to get some traction and make something happen by now.

We forged our own routine of going to the park in Benedict Canyon to look for wildlife. We would hunt for ladybugs, frogs or ducks that I would often sketch. When we got home, we would get out some paints for an impromptu art class. Oliver and I would then reproduce some of the day's wildlife stars—a ladybug, a sleepy turtle or a vibrant green frog.

Happily, it turned out that CeCe was surprisingly skilled in the potty-training department. "Oh, darling. You know I'm exceedingly good at the *trousers-off* parts!" she said, her face aglow at the thought.

Before long, she had Oliver sitting comfortably on the potty, looking at his books, singing potty songs and waiting patiently for the turd fairy.

The woman worked miracles.

"Okay, darling, let me see what you have there," she cooed sweetly at Oliver, when he'd finished his business. Oliver was delighted to show her a pot with a few gleaming turds smiling back at her.

From her reaction, you'd think he'd produced three gargantuan diamonds out of his ass.

"Oh, darling! What a good boy you are! What a wonderful job you've done! Yay for you! Yay!" she said, and clapped excitedly.

Oliver beamed with pride.

And in that instant, the key to CeCe's extraordinary success with men became crystal clear to me.

When Oliver was with X, I was forced to focus on my life, whether I liked it or not. It was achingly quiet without Oliver's laughter. Not being able to give him a bath, put him to bed and read him stories as I had always done made my heart heavy in a way I had never known. Even driving wasn't the same without singing nursery rhymes together or listening to Oliver grappling with the complicated Alanis Morissette lyrics, belting out the words he recognized here and there: "*I'm not the doctor!*" and "Eight easy steps . . . la la la . . . *out is in* . . ." His joy infused everything and thus his absence created a huge void.

—∽—

"It's a dirty little secret that divorced parents *love* their downtime," Susan kept telling me. "Just wait. You'll see. Instead of agonizing over it, you'll learn to enjoy it. My divorced friends now say they can't live without it."

"That might well be true but I'm not there yet."

One step at a time.

I wasn't supposed to be thinking about men but I found that I was.

That tryst with Dominick—however unsatisfying—had woken something up again. I wondered what it might be like to have a real date again but I had no idea where to find one.

I found myself checking out sweaty men at yoga, wondering what they were like in bed. I wasn't particularly attracted to any of them but at least I was looking.

Nobody else around me seemed to have a problem getting a date.

I started looking for other single moms, to ask them what was in the handbook that I was clearly missing. The only problem was I didn't know any.

Georgina was a single mother who I often ran into at yoga. As we walked to our cars one morning after class, I took the opportunity to ask her how she met men.

"Oh, I don't have any trouble meeting men," she said patiently.

Duh. Of course she didn't have any trouble meeting men. Georgina was gorgeous with long auburn locks and a killer body. She might as well have said, '*You dumb fuck, look at me! Do you think that's an issue?*' She probably had to beat them off with a stick.

"People try to set me up on blind dates all the time," she said. "But, ugh, those are the worst. Friends will call me up and say, 'Oh, you have to meet so and so' and then they rave about this person they know who turns out to be a nightmare!"

Now, aside from her physical assets, Georgina's independently wealthy, so she has zero tolerance for troglodytes. From looking at her, you would assume she could have her pick of any man. It was fascinating to learn that even for someone like Georgina, dating successfully in Los Angeles wasn't that easy.

"These guys would come to pick me up and I'd think, 'Oh, *you're* being fixed up with me? But *I* can't possibly be fixed up with *you!*' Really, what are these people thinking? Do they think I'm *that* hard up? What am I supposed to do with these bozos?"

"I can't imagine what they're thinking," I said as I hurried to keep up with her long-legged stride. It took two of my steps for every one of hers, and she wasn't about to slow down.

I hoped that it would be a lot easier for me because clearly I wasn't as picky.

Casual dating didn't seem that hard but what if you wanted something more substantial?

My friend Autumn had no trouble finding dates, either—even though she was technically already in a relationship, albeit an unconventional one. Monogamy was not a viable option for her and she didn't apologize for it.

Autumn called me on her way home from spinning. "Meet me in the Palisades and we can grab a hike before lunch. I have a shoot in Palm Springs this week, so I'll be leaving in the morning."

If I attempted a spinning class *and* a hike, I would likely be dead.

"Okay, I'm on my way."

Autumn had been a successful model for years and now worked as a stylist for fashion shoots and commercials. We'd met at a commercial audition years ago. Not content to sit still, she was always jetting off somewhere exciting, doing a photo shoot in Bermuda, or leaving to live for a month in India. She had a voracious appetite for life—and men. Autumn operated without the nuisance of an internal editor—much like CeCe—and didn't have a conventional bone in her body. She functioned rather like a man. She took lovers as she pleased and discarded them like used tissues.

Back in the old days, we would go for hikes and she would fill me in on her latest conquests.

Now with time on my hands for such things, I wasted no time in tagging along for hikes again.

We met at our designated spot and started at a leisurely pace that Autumn quickly accelerated.

"This guy I've been seeing is starting to bore me." She turned and waited for me to catch up.

"Why is that?" I panted. Boring her was the kiss of death.

"He's okay in bed, nothing outstanding. He's in commercial real estate, so I meet him downtown in these lofts and we fuck but then he insists on going to cheap shitty restaurants so we don't run into anyone he knows."

"Is he married?"

"I think so. We don't discuss our primary relationships."

"Well, that explains that behavior. Why can't you date someone single?"

"All the best ones are taken," she said and laughed.

After our grueling hike up Temescal Canyon—well, grueling only for me —we rewarded ourselves with a couple of chai lattes from Starbucks. She started telling me about another man who was squiring her, a starving artist type who would likely only hold her attention for five minutes.

"How do you meet all of these men?" I asked her as we found a table outside.

"Oh, God, Scarlett. Men are everywhere. You get dressed and leave the house—that's what you do. You need to get back out there. You need to be having sex again. You need to start living again. That clown of an ex-husband of yours isn't wasting any time."

I did a quick scan of the neighboring tables, in case the clown ex-husband was in the vicinity.

"The less said about that, the better," I said quietly. "I'm sure he's not wasting time but he had a head start back when we were still married. So that's not exactly *fair*. I'm trying to get out there. I'm fighting the good fight. I did a bit of recycling. What else am I supposed to do? Run into the street and wave a sign? *Single-mom here ready to dust off the cobwebs and have another go?*"

"It doesn't matter how you do it but you have to get back on the horse," she said calmly as if it were the easiest thing in the world to do, and for her, it was.

As if on cue, Dominick rounded the corner carrying his yoga mat and chatting with a very buxom yoga babe.

"Hi, Scarlett." He gave me a wave and kept going.

I nodded in his direction. "There goes my recycling bin."

Autumn laughed. "Hey, I wasn't sure if I should tell you, but I ran into X the other night at this Indian restaurant. He was with a girl."

"Great. How nice for him."

"She was kind of . . . young."

"Perfect. I know I shouldn't care—especially since I instigated this whole divorce—but hearing about my ex-husband dating is still . . . weird."

"It'll be easier when you find somebody and are having fun."

Much to my chagrin, X did seem to be faring well in the date department. One evening, at one of our designated drop-off points midway between homes, he met me to hand over Oliver and instead of his usual 'I don't give a shit' uniform of jeans and a T-shirt, he was dressed up in dark jeans and a black dress-shirt. I recognized the shirt as one that I'd bought him for his birthday. He tossed the diaper bag at my feet and announced gaily, "See you guys later . . . I have a date!"

He looked thrilled about this news and seemed to be moving forward so rapidly that it completely threw me. I was shocked to realize tears were sliding down my cheeks. It was okay to go home and have a good cry about the general state of matters but not in front of *him*.

I was mortified by this unexpected response. He was just as stunned and stood transfixed, looking at me for a moment.

I felt compelled to explain this odd occurrence. "Oh, ignore me! I've had a bad day and I just got a sixty dollar parking ticket!" Which was in fact true, but it still didn't explain my reaction.

"Have a nice time." I feigned good cheer and gave him a wave.

"Good-night, daddy," Oliver said and waved, too.

X walked away and Oliver and I headed back to our car.

"What do you say we go get some ice cream, Ollie?" Emotions were bubbling up that required an immediate pint of ice cream to squelch.

Wretched uncoupling! If only it took half as much work to get into a marriage as it did to undo it, a lot more thought would go into the whole damn thing. Nothing about getting divorced was simple.

The legal process, which should have been straightforward, was dragging on. There seemed to be small hearings and appearances in which nothing much happened except wasting everyone's time and running up the hideous legal fees. I didn't understand any of it. All I knew was that it felt like there was a price to be paid, a pound of flesh to be exacted and I was being punished in every conceivable way for escaping my marriage.

Other than Oliver, there were no assets to divide. X's modest inheritance and our marital home came from his late uncle and were therefore untouchable. His actual income—as he declared it—was very little and left me with a monthly pittance that was laughable and would barely cover two weeks' worth of groceries and diapers.

The courts were going to have to decide our custody agreement if we were incapable of reaching one on our own. X and I couldn't agree on what day of the week it was, let alone on a permanent schedule for Oliver. Of course, the lawyers whipped everyone into a frenzy so that a peaceful resolution was next to impossible. It was a giant mess. A trial would be insanely expensive, and the only way to avoid one was to make a deal with X.

The thought of more intense negotiations with X was almost more painful than the legal process. I wasn't sure how it would all pan out. *Just keep moving forward*, I reminded myself. I didn't have to have all the answers right this very minute.

Darcy's office phoned with a callback for a young mom role for AT&T. Oliver was with X all day until 4:00 p.m. which meant I had time for a quick trip to the pawnshop to sell off the last of my jewelry before the audition.

The pawnshop owner was getting used to seeing me. I had made this sad little pilgrimage before with anything I had that was remotely worth something. He was in his late sixties, with very fine, white hair he combed over his balding pate. From his unique pawnshop perspective, he'd probably seen the decline of a lot of relationships. On this particular visit, I was pawning my engagement ring. I had held on to it as long as I could, but my legal bills demanded I put any remaining sentimentality aside. Really, what was I saving it for? The irony of selling the engagement ring to help pay for the divorce was not lost on me.

"I'm down to the wire . . . this is the last piece of jewelry I own," I announced for no particular reason. "I'm pawning the engagement ring to pay the divorce attorney—if you can believe that!"

He smiled and said nothing, but at the end of our exchange, he surprised me by producing a box containing an impressively large engagement ring from a cabinet in the back.

"Have a look at this one . . . try it on," he said and watched my expression transform entirely.

It was a stunningly large, gleaming princess-cut diamond on a simple platinum band. I gawked when I saw the sixty-thousand-dollar price tag tethered delicately to the band, as if that might lessen the impact. I had never seen a ring that cost that much, let alone tried one on.

"Oh my God! That is an outrageous rock!" I said with awe.

"I want you to have a little hope for your future, dear," he said, sliding the black velvet box closer to me. "Try it on."

"Really?" I gingerly slipped it onto my finger. My eyes filled with tears. It was mesmerizing to behold. I held my hand out in every direction to admire it catching the light. "Wow . . . I can't imagine owning such a beautiful thing!" I said with amazement.

"That's why I wanted you to try it on. I wanted you to *know* what it feels like. Life has a way of working things out, dear, even if you can't see it right now," he said.

I must have looked as downtrodden as I felt. No wonder no one had booked me for a Tide commercial. Who wants a sad sack trying to sell you things?

I inhaled deeply, wanting to capture that feeling of excitement and be able to call it back at will.

"Thank you," I said sliding it back to him. "That was a very sweet gesture."

"It was my pleasure, dear."

The casting call was crammed with young mom types when I arrived. Some of the moms had brought their own children to the audition, which made me miss Oliver. Several were chasing their offspring around the room, attempting to wrangle and subdue them. Bringing kids was risky. If your kid has a meltdown and annoys everyone, even if they like you, you're probably not going to get the job.

My name was called along with another blond pony-tailed mom. We said our names in front of the camera, answered some goofy questions about what Halloween candy we liked. I liked Snickers bars, she liked candy corn. The producers, agency people and the young director observed us from a safe distance and gave nothing away, saying only 'thank you,' as we left.

As I headed out the door to the street, a strong gust of wind swept a number of the size-card sheets out onto the street with me, creating a scattered mess on the pavement. As I struggled to collect them, I noticed that the director had walked outside to smoke a cigarette. He looked like an artsy professor. He was stocky with thick well-groomed gray hair, had an English accent, and was exactly CeCe's type.

He leaned against the wall and watched me as I scrambled to snatch up the fliers, looking terribly uncool in the process. Our eyes met. I smiled and shrugged, acknowledging the awkwardness of the moment. His face broke into a warm smile, and in that instant—although I couldn't explain it—I had a feeling that the commercial was mine.

I left the callback to pick up Oliver from X's feeling strangely elated, fueled in part by the fourteen-hundred dollars I had in my purse from my trip to the pawnshop.

The engagement ring must have transferred a little good luck to me; the next morning my phone rang.

"You booked it, sweetie! Congratulations! You booked the AT&T commercial!" Darcy's gravelly voice waxed enthusiastically over the phone.

"That's fantastic news! Thank you!"

"It's a great beginning, Scarlett. Go get 'em!"

I hung up and called Emma immediately.

"See, I told you this was going to happen!" she said excitedly. "Well done. This is just the beginning. We have to celebrate!"

I told Oliver that we were celebrating Mommy getting a "fun job" and he could select any restaurant he liked, and we would go buy a new toy. Oliver picked his favorite restaurant, Johnny Rockets, and the two of us had a celebratory dinner of chocolate shakes, fries and cheeseburgers.

It had taken a bit of work running around to auditions but finally it was paying off. The commercial would film the following week and pay several thousand dollars with the potential to keep making more in residual payments if it stayed on the air. While it wasn't going to put a dent in my daunting legal bills, it was a step in the right direction.

The shoot was short and simple. I played a busy soccer mom and I hadn't even had to dye my hair. The filming included shots of me with my phony television family interacting on our cell phones. I couldn't believe how easy it was or how much money they were paying me to do it.

As a treat for booking the commercial, Emma and I went shopping for a little present for me as well, nothing too outrageous, but a little something to commemorate the moment. It had been a long time since I had bought myself anything and Emma insisted.

We drove out to the Malibu Country Mart and looked around in all the chic and fabulous boutiques. We sat on the benches and had ice-blended mochas from Coffee Bean & Tea Leaf, and watched the Malibu natives in the playground frolicking with their kids.

"Do you notice anything funny?" Emma asked.

"What?"

"All these Malibu Mamas are wearing the same uniform—jeans and loose, colorful flowery shirts—and look! They all have long flowing hair. The only ones with their hair pulled back are the nannies."

I looked around and she was right. The domestic nannies had their hair back but *all* of the other women had long, unrestrained locks and sported a sexy-hippie, Earth-Mama look.

"That is funny! What do you think it means?" I asked, mystified that they could all coordinate on a grand scale. "Did they send out a mass e-mail? Tuesdays are for jeans and boho tops, Thursdays are for long flowy dresses?"

"I think it's a condition of employment," she said watching the decidedly less attractive nannies wrangling toddlers. "Thou shalt not flaunt thy hair nor thy tits in front of my husband, damn it woman! And while we're at it, thou shalt wear dowdy clothes and hopefully be on the chubby side!"

We walked over to Blue Haven, my favorite boutique, which had the most divine clothes—luxurious cashmere sweaters, vixen dresses and trendy accessories. All the clothes were bright and colorful because black just doesn't cut it in Malibu. The salesgirls were local young lovelies, the daughters of music moguls and celebrities, and often had less than the tiniest hint of interest in assisting anyone.

I walked around the racks, looking at the clothes, and admiring the way the salesgirls threw together looks that were striking but seemed casual and effortless. Chic dresses paired with chunky boots that looked fabulous together, worn with an assortment of long necklaces. Maybe you needed to be twenty to pull it off, but I took notes anyway.

I spotted an actress who was married to a famous director stocking up on tawny cashmere sweaters, jeans, and high-heeled boots to keep warm on the chilly Malibu nights. Her teenage daughter piled garment over colorful garment on the counter for the salesgirl to ring up. That must be fun, I thought, not to be burdened by anything as mundane as a budget.

"Look at these beautiful cocktail dresses." Emma held up an emerald green silk halter for my approval. "Why don't you try one of these on?"

"I never go anywhere to warrant that sort of a dress. You try it, it's more your color."

"If you buy it . . . the occasion will present itself!"

While Emma was trying on flirty party dresses, I discovered a lovely necklace that I instantly fell in love with. Two delicate gold hearts looped through each other and hung on a dainty gold chain in the jewelry case. It was darling, and the best part was that it was only one hundred and twenty dollars—dirt cheap for Malibu. I liked the idea of buying myself a simple piece of jewelry after recently parting with the last of my old collection. The hearts represented Oliver and I, and our new beginning. I paid the salesgirl and slipped the necklace over my head, feeling certain it would bring me even more luck.

After nearly a year of crap, it felt like I was back in the stream of life again.

Chapter Nine
Mr. Hollywood

The lucky streak continued when I ran into Sara Seeley—a high-level publicist—at yoga. We had worked together years earlier on Garrison Lee, and her client list had only flourished since then. The last time she had tried to book me for a job, Oliver was a newborn and flying to New York was not an option but now the timing was fortuitous. Garrison had a new film coming out called *Freud* that had Oscar written all over it.

"Come and do Garrison's grooming," she said casually, as if these words couldn't potentially transform someone's livelihood. "This is an easy junket, it's here in town. And then we'll have a chance to catch up!"

"Thanks, Sara. That would be wonderful!" I tried to maintain my cool and match her casual tone as we walked to our cars but my insides were doing somersaults. It was *Garrison fucking Lee*, for God's sake, a man who left trembling women in his wake. This was great news, and I was so happy I'd dragged myself to yoga or I would have missed out entirely. In LA, it was remarkable how much depended on being in the right place at the right time. It was as if the entire town ran on serendipity.

I held my breath to see if she'd call the next day and sure enough, she sent me an e-mail confirming the gig.

I hadn't worked with Garrison in five years and was beyond thrilled. Junkets with someone of Garrison's stature were plum gigs. They paid very well, were usually held in luxury hotels, and with Garrison I could be assured it would be fun. And this would mean another two thousand in the kitty. *Holy shit!*

CeCe and I did a victory dance together in the kitchen, much to Oliver's amusement. I grabbed Oliver, hoisted him onto my hip and waltzed around the dining room with him, singing, "Mama's making money! Ca-ching!"

He giggled and kept chanting, "Ca-ching! Ca-ching!"

The day of Garrison's press junket arrived and my nerves were a wreck. I had not worked with any handsome movie stars in five years, let alone

Garrison Lee! There had to be some sort of monumental shift occurring in the universe.

Garrison was as lively as ever and gave me a cheeky smooch on the lips when he first saw me that sent a ripple through the phalanx of studio publicists who kept a close eye on us. Garrison was in high spirits. The advanced word on his performance in *Freud* was great and award buzz was building.

Garrison was eager to catch up on our five-year gap. He liked to grill me about my love life and held a very dim view of divorce, so I gave scant details and showed him a picture of Oliver before changing the subject. I didn't relish the idea of a lecture on divorce from a movie star. Garrison's own marriage seemed to be surviving his celebrity condition nicely. They had three kids to show for their fifteen years together and from all accounts were very happy with each other, which was a complete rarity in the entertainment business.

I prepped Garrison with the minimum of fuss, as he didn't tolerate the makeup process well. He considered it unmanly and cringed whenever I came after him with concealer and powder. It was a delicate balance between keeping him happy with minimal makeup and putting enough on to satisfy his publicists. After torturing him with additional grooming rituals for a few minutes, I took a seat out of the way with Sara and watched Garrison charm the steady stream of foreign journalists. The older female reporters were the most fun to watch with him—he charmed the pants off them—and many of the younger ones were overtly flirtatious.

Garrison amiably tolerated the palaver but it was an exhausting process.

"I'm wilting like a fucking daffodil in here!" he joked as I powdered him between interviews. "It's like a gang-bang. How many more do we have to go?"

"It's better if you don't know, Garrison," Sara said.

"You know . . . you could have my tickets for tonight," Sara said to me while we watched a young Japanese reporter in a very tight miniskirt sitting across from Garrison cross and uncross her legs a few times while the sound man adjusted her microphone. "I have to escort Garrison through the press gauntlet," she said, keeping a watchful eye on the Japanese vixen shuffling in her seat. "But I have a hot date tonight, so I won't be going to the movie or the after-party. I've already seen the movie. You should go."

"Thanks, I'd love to!" I said, thrilled to have an invitation to something. I texted Emma on a break and she was onboard for a night out.

I raced to pick up Oliver from X and then the tickets from the publicity office. Oliver fell asleep in the car, so I carried him half a block on my shoulder to the building and up the stairs, battling searing back pain from high heels and the extra weight of Oliver.

The receptionist behind the stainless steel desk insisted that I show her identification in order to collect the premiere tickets. She watched me struggle with my one free hand to produce my wallet. Balancing Oliver's bottom on a raised knee, I resorted to dumping the contents of my handbag out on the desk in front of her. What did I need ID for? Did I look like a fucking terrorist? Did I look like a blond, harried, high-heeled terrorist toting a sleeping toddler, plotting to wreak havoc at a Hollywood movie premiere? What were the odds? Eventually, I uncovered my wallet and presented my driver's license, and with tickets in hand, we headed home.

CeCe was home from the office early and sorting through the mail when we arrived. I watched as she separated the ominous legal envelopes from the rest of the innocuous mail and set them in my growing pile on the kitchen counter. I sighed. They would have to wait.

I made spaghetti and meatballs for Oliver while he watched an episode of *Bob the Builder* and hurried to pull myself together before Emma arrived to collect me.

When Emma rang the doorbell, I was still digging in the closet trying to find something to wear. She was stylish in one of the fabulous Diane von Furstenberg dresses from her collection. She followed me into the kitchen, bouncing Oliver on her hip.

"I love that dress on you. Is it new?" I asked.

"Yes, the stylist got it for me from that commercial I did last week. It's cute, isn't it?"

"It's darling. The red and black pattern looks really sharp. It's put-together but not too dressy—very chic."

"Thanks," said Emma and turned her attention to Oliver. "I'm borrowing your mommy for a little while and taking her to a movie, but then I'll bring her right back. Okay?"

"Okay, Auntie Emma. You can see Mama," he said, enchanted with her. Emma could get Oliver to agree to just about anything. He was fascinated by the secret powers she possessed that enabled her magically to appear on the television.

"Can you believe we're going to a premiere together?" I said, handing her a glass of chardonnay. "How many years has it been?"

"Too many. Hey, why don't you wear those Catwoman boots? You were so excited to get them and I've never seen you wear them. Break those puppies out!"

"Really? Is it time?" I said and laughed. They had been tucked away indefinitely.

"Hell, yes!"

I dug around in the closet and produced the notorious Catwoman boots. I pulled them out of their slumber in the protective black bag and held them up for admiration.

"Ooohhh . . ." Emma and I collectively sighed at the sight of them.

They were the one truly fabulous wardrobe item I owned. Bewitched by them at first sight at Barney's, I kept going back to check on them. The salesman had seen me coveting them and whispered seductively, "These boots will change your life! You *must* try them on."

Of course, he was right. Once I tried them on, I couldn't bear to part with them. Svelte black leather that hugged my calf with a killer heel, they felt powerful and slightly dangerous. The leather was impossibly smooth as I zipped them behind my calf all the way up to the knee. They were so sexy I wanted to live in them. I had paid for them with cash and two separate credit cards in order to hide the purchase from X.

All of that effort to claim them and yet I'd never even worn them out of the house. I turned them over and looked at the soles with not a mark on them. They were magnificently preserved.

"My life-changing boots . . . I bought them and left my husband. Maybe they should come with a warning label!"

"Put them on. Let's shake things up a bit!"

I sat on the edge of the bed and zipped them up. It was a rush to wear them out. I took a deep breath and felt my energy shifting out of work mode.

Emma touched up her makeup while I threw on a cream sweater and a black suede skirt that I'd owned since I was twenty but now fit again thanks to my shitty divorce diet.

Oliver decided my going out for the evening with Emma was not such a great deal after all. He grabbed me around the neck and started to howl when we were leaving.

"Don't go, Mama," he said, as his eyes filled with tears. The tears clung obstinately to his thick lashes, then surrendered and cascaded down his cheeks.

"I'll be back very soon, my love." I kissed his wet cheeks and smoothed the hair off his forehead.

CeCe peeled his little hands away and said, "Let's go wave to Mama out the window. Let's go! Bye-bye, Mama!" CeCe quickly slammed the door on us before Oliver could fuss more or I could change my mind about leaving.

I paused by the door, listening to him wail inside. My heart was heavy at the thought of leaving him again so soon.

"Come on. He'll be fine. It makes you a better mother if you take time to do stuff for yourself," said Emma and looped her arm through mine. "And we haven't been out to one of these things in years!"

We drove in Emma's groovy Prius to Westwood for the premiere. My functional, beat-up SUV was less flash than the occasion called for.

"I just know you're going to meet someone tonight. I can feel it!" Emma said as we inched our way toward Westwood in the rush-hour traffic.

"I doubt it. I don't meet people at premieres." I threw on some lip gloss anyway for good measure.

We arrived in Westwood, parked the car in one of the lots, and made our way up the street to the Mann Village Theater, which was illuminated up by huge Klieg lights. Westwood Village sat next to the UCLA campus and the streets were buzzing with a mix of young students and Hollywood insiders heading to the premiere. The students looked so fresh, so young and brimming with potential. They looked miraculously untouched by life and disappointment. I found it startling. When had this great divide taken place? When had I slipped into the distinctly older, cynical and divorced category? It felt like it had happened overnight. Where had all those years gone?

My stomach dropped as we approached the red carpet. Nothing so blatantly announced your status in Hollywood. Either the photographers wanted to take your picture or they didn't. You were important or you weren't. They wanted Emma's picture and they weren't interested in mine. I stepped out of the way and watched her have her moment in the limelight.

"Emma! This way! Emma, smile!" they shouted.

Emma smiled like a pro and turned, giving them different angles to cover.

While not yet a household name, Emma was in a category where she was recognizable. She had worked so much as an actress but wasn't identifiable with any particular role. Her myriad of theatrical roles were diverse and yet she'd had so much success as a commercial and voice-over actress that sometimes she was literally all over the airwaves.

I waited in the foyer for Emma to finish.

"Emma! Hi, honey. How are you?" Emma was grabbed into a bear hug by a woman with long blond hair extensions. "Where is that handsome husband of yours?"

"Chris's at home, having a beer with the dog. He doesn't like to come to these unless it's one of his own projects—or one of mine."

"Awww . . . I love that guy! Such a talent. Tell him I want to be in any movie he writes or directs. I don't care what it is, I'm in!"

"I'll tell him."

The woman had gone overboard with her bronzer. I resisted the urge to dig a makeup brush out of my purse and tone it down for her.

"Gotta run. Take care, honey."

They exchanged air kisses and she disappeared back into the sea of people in the lobby.

"Who was that?" I asked.

"I have no idea!" Emma said, and we both burst out laughing.

"It's so funny to be doing this again. I feel like I've lived a lifetime since the old days when we used to run around and crash premieres and parties."

"You have. You have a kid now. That's pretty epic."

"But here we are again and it feels exactly the same. Like I dropped back in without skipping a beat."

"Except this time, we've been invited! Let's make the most of it tonight. It's my job to make sure we have a blast."

"You didn't turn into a hausfrau as soon as Chris put that ring on your finger. You're still as much fun as you ever were. I love that about you."

"You weren't a hausfrau either. Come on, let's load up on free popcorn and soda."

I waited in the foyer for Emma to finish posing for the photographers. The crowd filtered in and collected free treats from the attendants. The stars of the movie were dressed to the nines, as were other actresses working the red carpet, but most of the other people looked like they'd come from the office—stylish but all about business.

As we made our way to find our seats, Garrison was ushered through the lobby with his posse of handlers and bodyguards in front of us. He looked over and gave me a wink as he passed. My entire body felt flush. Any time Garrison showed me attention it made my knees weak, which made doing his makeup very challenging. He was drop-dead handsome.

"God, he's a sexy fucker!" Emma said admirably. "He just winked at you! Those boots are working."

"Don't make me laugh. These heels are so high I need to concentrate on not tripping over!"

The theater went dark and the credits rolled. We clapped enthusiastically when Garrison's name appeared on the screen. One thing that had never gotten old for me was going to the movies. I loved being transported out of my own life and into someone else's.

Freud turned out to be a finely crafted, small movie and was just the sort of film the Academy loved to recognize. Garrison was fabulous in it. It was primed to make a big splash on the awards circuit.

The post-screening party was located at the Armand Hammer Museum down the road from the theater in Westwood. The reception was held in a large courtyard with a sprinkling of white-dressed tables around the edges and a swarm of people mingling in the middle. Emma and I made good use of the dessert buffet and found the last available table—right next to the restroom. We were content from our perch to enjoy the mini crème brûlée and watch the world parading by. The benefit to sitting near the restroom is that sooner or later everyone makes an appearance.

We watched as a couple of tipsy starlets staggered past us on the way back from the ladies' room with their dresses askew. One of them was the starlet Shelby Scott.

"There goes the latest rehab effort . . ." said Emma.

The girls laughed loudly and leaned into each other for support.

"It's too bad," Emma said as she watched them walk away. "I worked with Shelby on a show once and she was really sweet."

I texted CeCe quickly to check in, and she said that Oliver was sound asleep. Everything was fine. I put the phone back in my purse and relaxed.

"Oh my God . . . I had a blind date with that guy once." Emma gestured to a nerdy-looking guy in an expensive suit awkwardly balancing an overladen dinner plate and a glass of wine. He was wandering around looking for somewhere to sit.

"He works at one of the studios. We went out to dinner and he wouldn't let me order anything to eat! Can you imagine? The waitress came over and he said, 'That's okay, she's not hungry.' Cheap fucker! Look how full his plate is! Bet he hasn't missed a meal since!"

Emma and I gave the guy dirty looks until he looked up and caught Emma's disapproving glare head-on. He stood frozen for a second, managed an awkward smile, and then started to walk toward us.

"He better not even *think* about sitting with us," Emma muttered.

The cheap fucker thought better of it. He aborted his course and moved down the line to try his luck in friendlier waters.

"Thank God." Emma sighed. She called over a sitcom writer she had worked with to join our table and then invited a young comic she knew from The Groundlings Theatre. The empty seats at our table began to fill.

A publicist Emma and I had known for years named Randall stopped by with a handsome young man trailing behind him. I assumed it was his hot young boyfriend.

"Scarlett, this is Jeremy Plume," he said.

After chatting for a moment, Randall went off to work the room, leaving Jeremy adrift. He asked if he could join us.

"Please do. We're dying of boredom over here!" Emma waved him over.

Jeremy found the last empty seat next to me. He was tall with scruffy sandy-colored hair and a nicely tailored slate-gray suit. He was possibly a little *too* good-looking for my taste and I didn't pay much attention to him. In my experience—and my marriage—good-looking men are often more energy than they're worth, and there's always a line of women behind you.

Emma and Jeremy entered into a lively conversation about New York, and how much they missed the theater life. They carried on their conversation while I watched the parade of well-wishers make their way to Garrison. Garrison had recovered from his journalist gang-bang and was now graciously receiving his doting public. I watched the Hollywood elite wait their turn to buss his cheeks and gush over his performance.

Jeremy turned to me while Emma was chatting with her neighbor. "Did I see you in the movie?" he asked, cautiously.

I laughed. "No. I'm not in the movie."

"Well, I thought you *could* have been in the movie . . . you look familiar," he said, his voice trailing off slightly. "Did you work on the movie?"

"No, I did Garrison's grooming for the press junket today," I stated, unsure what he was angling for.

"Garrison is a friend of mine," Jeremy said, seizing on some common ground.

I smiled but said nothing.

"I've known him for years. I'm producing a project that we're hoping to do together."

I smiled and nodded. I was terribly out of practice making small talk with Hollywood people and didn't feel like I needed to, despite his attempts to get something going.

Emma returned to the table with a fresh glass of Cabernet, took a sip, and then set it down next to me.

"Hey, I've done a poll this evening," Jeremy said, leaning forward conspiratorially. "And I can tell you that we are sitting in a museum and not a single person I've spoken to tonight has *ever* set foot in here. This would never happen in New York! What typical, uncultured LA people we are!" he announced with pronounced glee.

"You're right," I said. "We are a pathetic lot."

"Let's drink to our lameness!" said Emma, and gave a toast to the table.

Jeremy's face clouded over. "I've had a traumatic evening," he confided. "I was over at another table saying 'hi' to some people I knew and this actress sitting with them totally chewed me out for not recognizing her! I've never been so embarrassed. She's on some cable show, Carly Dingle? Do you know who she is? She yelled at me in front of people I've known for years. I'm completely mortified."

Emma and I laughed but he looked so injured by the experience that I felt obligated to say something. "I've never heard of her, either, if it makes you feel better."

"Nah," said Emma. "Carly Dingle? Sounds like a porn star name to me!"

"She's a pretty brazen porn star, then. She chewed me out in front of the whole table!"

"Oh, forget about her!" I told him. "Don't let one silly cow ruin your evening."

No wonder he had asked me so gingerly if I was in the movie. He didn't want to risk getting his head chopped off again by another surly actress. But he needn't have worried. I only had an AT&T commercial under my belt and that wasn't nearly enough to embolden me to behave like a bitch.

Garrison's agent spotted me and called me over, so I excused myself to go and say hello. When I returned, Jeremy had disappeared.

Emma and I stayed for another thirty minutes, laughing and enjoying ourselves like old times. It felt good to be out. I started to relax a little. Being out in the world and chatting to people was fun. When we'd finished our drinks and had grown tired of rubbing elbows with the Hollywood elite, she dropped me off. I was happy to get back to real life—and a delicious little boy who didn't care what my outfit looked like or if I was a successful Hollywood *anything,* or what movies I had or hadn't been in. Oliver couldn't care less. The Hollywood nonsense was much more palatable with my sweet little fellow at home to put things in perspective.

Chapter Ten
Dating for Beginners

I didn't give Jeremy another thought until I got a call from Randall a few days later on his behalf, to inquire if he could call me for a date. We hadn't engaged much at the premiere but it was precisely this cocktail of aloof disinterest that guys like Jeremy thrived on. Next time I'm attracted to a man, I have to remember to ignore him. It works wonders!

Jeremy had gone to the trouble of tracking me down. Nobody had bothered to work that hard for me in years. It was a bold, sexy move. I felt a wave of excitement and called Susan—who knows *everybody* in town—to get her opinion of this Jeremy character.

"Yeah, I've met him. He's cute. He's done a bunch of indie films. What do you have to lose? You could use a date!"

That neon sign flashing *Needs a Date* over my head hopefully wouldn't be quite as obvious to Jeremy. I kept reliving the night we met, trying to trace even a glimmer of attraction or interest from him. It's usually not that hard to gauge a man's interest. I was out of practice, but this guy flew under the radar. Like a stealth scout of potential dates, he achieved his covert mission and then slipped into the night. I hadn't been aware I'd left an impression. It must have been the boots.

The next day there was a message on my voice mail.

"Hi. It's Jeremy Plume. It was nice to meet you the other night. I'm in San Francisco doing a film. Call me back. I'd love to talk to you."

I replayed his message. He had a lovely, deep voice. I wanted to call him back immediately but couldn't decide what I was supposed to divulge about my situation. Where was the single-mom's handbook when you needed it? Did I dare lead with 'I'm in the middle of a messy divorce and I have a three-year-old son. And if that doesn't scare the shit out of you, then yes, I'd love to have dinner with you'? Or was it smarter to dole out this information one nugget at a time to try to lessen the impact? Who knew what the protocol was?

After pondering my options for several minutes, I took a deep breath and called him back. We chatted for a while. He had a casual, easy manner and laughed a lot, as he did the night we met, and he mentioned that he had heard from Randall that I was divorcing and had a child. The 'dirty work' had been done for me! I felt myself exhale with relief.

"I've never dated anyone with a child before," he said. "But I don't have any problem with it. I'm not afraid of kids . . . but I am afraid of marriage! That marriage thing terrifies me!"

I laughed and said, "Me, too!"

"I'll be back in LA next week, so what about dinner on Friday?"

Oliver would be with his dad. "Perfect!"

And it was done. Finally, a hot date! The excitement of having a date was followed quickly by the realization that I had no date clothes. Nothing I owned was suitable for a date with a hot, young movie producer. The one remotely cute outfit I had—a black skirt and sweater—was what I'd been wearing the night I met him and I couldn't very well recycle that again so soon.

Emma was thrilled at the development and let me rummage around in her closet.

"See! I told you something was going to happen! I just knew you were going to meet someone. He was cute . . . and at least you know this guy's got a job."

"That's going to be a prerequisite from now on," I said, and dug around for something sexy. I wanted to feel sexy again.

I tried on a few more of Emma's wrap dresses but nothing felt right. Emma was busty and I was dealing with the sad aftermath of a lengthy stint of breastfeeding. I stood in front of the mirror in my underwear and tried to give them a shove together and upward so that they looked less . . . *withered.*

"God, I can't wear *anything* low-cut. My boobs look scary!"

"They're fine!"

"They're fine if you're into the stretched-out gas-pump look. Do you think young movie producers are into that? Maybe I should stick to a turtleneck," I said with exasperation.

"Well, think of it this way, post-breastfeeding boobs are something he definitely hasn't seen before!" she said, giggling at the thought.

"The object isn't to terrify the guy. Besides, I'm not sure that I like him or that he's worthy of all this effort . . . but I do feel excited at the prospect. I'm ready for the drought to be over."

Inexplicably, for this important first date, I settled on a leopard-print sweater that I bought from a tiny boutique on Beverly Boulevard. After I purchased it, it struck me as garish but at least it covered the boobs. It must have been some sort of postdivorce identity crisis purchase. What message was I trying to convey? Wild divorcée? Did I need to assure him that just because I was a single mother, I wasn't a boring soccer mom, even if I did occasionally play one in a commercial?

I paired the ugly sweater with the black skirt he'd seen at the premiere. It was the best I could do. I looked at it in the mirror from all angles. It looked like a cheap unwashed thrift store purchase, which wasn't all that far from the truth. After a furious scramble through my closet revealed no suitable last-minute alternatives, I resigned myself to it.

As I was on my way out the door, CeCe stuck her head out of the kitchen and did a double take. "You're not actually going to wear *that,* are you?"

I stopped dead in my tracks and thought about another furious hunt through my closet, but since Jeremy was already downstairs waiting for me, I shrugged and closed the door behind me.

Jeremy was on his BlackBerry when I got downstairs. He unlocked the car door and signaled apologetically that he'd just be a minute.

I was thankful to have a moment to catch my breath and not be expected to converse with him. He was wearing a charcoal-gray suit with a light blue shirt, and was more handsome than I'd remembered. My palms began to perspire.

"So sorry about that," he said, placing his BlackBerry on the seat next to him. "I'm dealing with lawyers on this project I'm doing. Do you like sushi? I know a great place on the Westside. It's a hole in the wall but the food is amazing."

"That sounds fine," I said, and we headed west on Santa Monica Boulevard.

Jeremy's rental car was littered with passes granting him entry to various studio lots around town, indicating he'd either been on a lot of meetings or was just terribly messy.

He asked me about the status of my divorce, and I sighed. Better to sort the men from the boys. If he was going to be scared off, it may as well be sooner rather than later.

"It's been quite contentious but hopefully the worst is behind me." I blurted it out.

"Oh, I'm sorry to hear that," he said, unprepared for the frankness of my answer. "My parents divorced when I was five, so I have some idea of what you're going through." After that he wisely steered the conversation to safer waters.

We arrived at the sushi restaurant, which was located in a shopping mall. Jeremy swung his door open with such gusto that he sent it crashing into the pole right next to the parking space. If he noticed, it didn't register and he bounded over to ring for the elevator to take us up to the restaurant.

The sushi place had very little ambiance. Cheery yellow walls and unadorned plastic tables made it look like not much more than a cafeteria. He definitely wasn't out to impress me. But Jeremy promised the food would compensate for the unassuming décor. Still, it was an interesting choice.

Jeremy's lack of Hollywood slickness appealed to me. He was nothing like many of the men I met in the film business who seemed to be intoxicated with their own success. He was charming in an unrehearsed, slightly awkward way and had a boyish exuberance that I found endearing. The latter was something I had zero experience with since I'd never dated 'boyish' anything, unless you counted 'boyishly unemployed.'

The hostess showed us to a table by the window.

"They don't have any menus here. Hope that's okay. They serve you a set dinner of sushi. It's delicious. You'll love it."

"Do they have any cooked food?" I asked, and scanned the walls for any listing of specials.

"No. It's all raw. It's the real deal."

Since my pregnancy and abstinence from sushi, I had been unable to go back to eating raw fish. I always stuck with something safe from the cooked selection on the menu, but on this occasion I wasn't sure what to do.

"Do they have any edamame?"

"I don't think so. They don't even have miso soup."

Dish after dish arrived of raw fish in various configurations. My stomach lurched just by looking at it.

Not wanting to appear disagreeable by objecting at this late stage, I slapped on a ton of soy sauce and struggled as best I could. I did a lot of pushing soggy fish around on my plate and not a lot of eating. He watched me with a sly smile and probably assessed me as another Hollywood girl who didn't eat.

He then proceeded to devour every morsel that was placed in front of him.

"Where did you grow up?" I asked him, wanting to get ahead of the questions.

"On the east coast, mostly. I went to one of those highbrow schools for wankers. The whole Ivy league experience."

I laughed. "I appreciate how familiar you are with the term *wanker*. You don't often hear Americans tossing it about."

"Oh, yeah. I have some English friends who say it all the time. I like the sound of it. *W-a-n-k-e-r*. It sounds so much more offensive than just calling someone an asshole."

"I completely agree." I laughed again. "Anyway, carry on."

"While toiling away at the wanky school, I wanted to be an actor but then I sort of fell into producing and loved it. One gig led to another, and here I am. Right now I'm mostly doing smaller films but we have a few bigger ones in the works . . ."

The waitress kept replacing our dishes with new ones but they were still all raw.

"Now I make movies and put all my friends in them."

"You must be very popular."

"Enough about me. I want to hear about you." He held eye contact when he spoke. His eyes were an unusual mélange of amber. They reminded me of a tortoiseshell pattern. I kept waiting for him to look away but he didn't. I didn't look away either.

"What would you like to know?"

"Everything. Tell me about your son."

I told him all about Oliver and how things had been going at CeCe's.

Jeremy held eye contact when he spoke and listened to me in a way that reminded me how sexy it is to have someone interested in what you have to say.

"I couldn't live with my mother again. That would not end well." He laughed at the suggestion. "I can barely tolerate her once a year."

"It's less than ideal but there are some benefits. She's pretty good with Oliver—other than giving him chocolate for breakfast."

"Show me some photos of Oliver."

I showed him some shots on my phone.

"He's really cute. He looks a lot like you." He handed the phone back to me.

"Thank you. That makes me happy to hear."

"I don't have any kids. I've made movies instead."

Jeremy told me tales from the sets of his movies and how he liked to come up with creative solutions to problems. It was clear how much he relished his job as a producer. He seemed confident when talking about his work and much less so when talking about other subjects, making him seem alternately mature and then quite young. I couldn't determine his age.

"How old are you?" I finally got up the nerve to ask.

"I'm thirty-four . . . how old are *you*?"

"I'm . . . in that vicinity." I replied, relieved that there were only a couple of years between us. "You're a bit young for me," I said with considerable cheek.

He raised an eyebrow at this news.

"Really? Why? Are you into geriatrics?"

"I guess that depends on the geriatric." I laughed.

"So you think I'm *young*?" He grappled with this news.

"Young-*ish*. I've just always gone in the other direction."

Older men had always been more my type. Life experience was something that turned me on. X was five years older, Dominick was ten years older . . . maybe it was time to start over.

"You might want to revise that thinking," he said, reading my mind.

Jeremy started telling me about one of the first movies he produced and all of the obstacles he had to conquer along the way.

"And then we ran out of money and didn't think we'd be able to finish shooting. We were just kids out of school . . . but at the last minute, I was able to talk a money guy into giving us a loan and it saved the whole production. Then we ended up becoming a festival hit!" He was gesticulating wildly with his hands. His passion was contagious.

It was impossible not to smile.

I found myself wondering what it might be like to kiss him. He had beautiful, full lips. It required concentrated effort to focus on what he was saying. I had made the decision not to have any alcohol on our date. Starved for affection, I couldn't be trusted in this state of deprivation. After a couple of drinks, I might have to be pried off his face—or other parts of his body—and so I stuck to green tea. But it was such a delicious feeling longing to kiss someone again, and I wanted to savor it. Tonight I was to be the very model of decorum and restraint—if not verbally.

Jeremy was smart and funny and the conversation flowed easily. We covered everything from our dysfunctional parents, to religion and even politics, making a complete circle of the very topics you're not supposed to tackle on a first date. We laughed so much during dinner that my cheeks ached.

"When I saw you sitting at your table, I wanted to meet you. I asked to be introduced."

"Really?" I felt my whole body tingle as Jeremy upped the ante and took the conversation to a sexier level.

"Yes." He was looking into my eyes again, not breaking the gaze. I could feel my skin flush under the heat we were producing.

"Don't you drink?" he asked, watching me sip my green tea.

"Yes, on occasion."

"Were you drinking the night we met?"

"I might have had some wine," I said, wondering what behavior prompted that query. I strained to remember any obvious transgressions that night and couldn't come up with any obvious faux pas, which didn't exactly mean there *hadn't* been any. "Why? Did I do something embarrassing?"

"No. I was just curious." He chuckled.

With neither of us drinking, the evening was over much too soon. The restaurant turned their tables over quickly and before I knew it our server had dropped our check. Jeremy grabbed it and paid it.

We drove back toward Beverly Hills and I happened to glance over at his hands, resting casually on the steering wheel. They were large, with thick, beautifully formed fingers that he tapped lightly on the wheel in time to the stereo. I felt a tingle run down my spine and then an overwhelming urge to climb into his lap.

"I don't really eat sushi," I said, as if it needed announcing.

"Yeah. I kind of noticed." He laughed. "Why didn't you tell me? I would have taken you somewhere else."

"I don't know. You seemed excited about it. I always just order something cooked at a sushi place, so it's not usually an issue."

"I feel bad that I didn't give you dinner. You're going to tell your mother I was a lousy date."

"No, I'm not! It was the best non-dinner date I've had. How's that?"

"That'll have to do. For now."

It was only nine thirty, surely too early to be going home on a Friday night? Didn't he want to go somewhere for a coffee or dessert or *something*? I didn't want it to end.

I kept my hopes up right until he turned left onto my street and did a U-turn so that he was depositing me directly at my door.

There was an awkward silence, which I broke by thanking him for a lovely evening. He said he had fun, and leaned in toward me. I had no idea where he was aiming for, and in response I clumsily landed a kiss on his cheek.

I fished around in my purse for my keys.

"Okay, then. Good-night, Jeremy!"

"Good-night, Scarlett."

I opened the door and stepped onto the grass where my heel sunk a little too smoothly into what I could only presume was dog shit. I ignored the dog shit, gave him a little wave, and then he was off.

CeCe took one look at my crestfallen face when I walked in the door and gasped, "Why are you home so early? Was it a dud?"

"No. He was great. He's smart and funny. It was the most fun I've had in years. But it's only nine thirty-seven. I don't remember ever being home this early from a bad date, let alone a *good* one. I guess I was having more fun than he was. If memory serves, men go to great lengths to prolong the evening and keep you out as long as they can—if it's going well."

"Just as well. You did say you thought he might be a bit young," said CeCe, returning her attention to her merlot and her beloved Bill Maher.

"I guess . . ."

"Oh, look . . . that politician's on . . . the one that had an affair and left his wife. Would you look at that twinkle in his eye! He can hardly sit still. You can tell that new woman's been giving him a bit of the old prostate tickle. Look at him! *Oh, yes!* She's been twirling in the magic pot! Tickle, tickle, tickle!" CeCe giggled and crooked her finger a few times to demonstrate her technique.

"Thanks, CeCe. If I ever have sex again, I'll have to remember that."

I took off my makeup, changed into pajamas and was preparing to face the unsavory task of removing the remaining dog shit from my shoe, when my cell phone rang.

"Hi." It was Jeremy. "I just got home and I wanted to tell you I had a great time."

"Oh . . . me, too! It was really fun." I was thrilled to be hearing from him so soon.

"Give me an e-mail address . . . I'm going to put you into my phone, *right now.*"

The way he said it made it sound naughty and I was dying to explore the concept of naughty with him.

I gave him my e-mail address and home phone number, as directed.

"I'm flying back tomorrow but I'll call you next week."

"Great."

I shrieked at CeCe as soon as I'd hung up. "That was him! He just called! He wanted to make sure he had all my info . . ."

"As well he should," CeCe said without taking her eyes off the telly.

"Well, this puts a new complexion on things!" I did a victory jig around the living room for good measure.

This was a fine beginning.

Chapter Eleven
A Kissing Spree

Romance is a drug with many benefits. The mere suggestion of it can cast the happiest shade of pink over everything. Suddenly ex-husbands are less annoying, teenagers playing loud video games all night don't provoke ire, and the future feels brighter somehow. I was constantly in a good mood and had new reserves of energy. Life was becoming a teeny bit fun again.

Jeremy left to go back to Northern California but kept in touch.

My phone kept chirping regularly with texts. Who knew a cell phone could be so entertaining?

I'm sending you a sushi platter. Just want to make sure you're home.

He made me laugh. Unaccustomed to the attention, I blossomed like jasmine in the spring.

Oliver immediately noticed this new upbeat attitude. "Mama, you have the smiley face on today!"

"Yes, I do, don't I?"

"I like the smiley face," he said, offering me his own smiley face to kiss.

"Me, too, sweetheart," I said and covered his face with kisses.

Oliver and I went about our daily adventures and I went on auditions but I had a happy new bounce in my gait. Thanksgiving was coming up and I didn't know when I would see Jeremy again but the anticipation was divine.

Jeremy called while we were grocery shopping.

"I've canceled my plans to go back east, and I'll be at my aunt's ranch near Santa Barbara over the Thanksgiving holiday," he said with that deeply masculine voice. "What are you doing? Will you be in town?"

"Yes. Oliver will be with his dad this Thanksgiving, but I'll be around," I said trying to exude calm while balancing the phone and attempting to silently thwart Oliver from dislodging the entire apple pyramid display.

"Good, I'd love to see you again. You could come up on Friday. The ranch is beautiful. We could hike around the property and—if you felt comfortable—you could stay in one of the guest rooms. There's plenty of room."

"That sounds great. I'd love to."

I jumped at the chance. My first Thanksgiving without Oliver would be too painful to contemplate. I'd never enjoyed holidays before Oliver arrived; they only highlighted what I felt was missing in my life. But now, holidays as a divorced parent—when it wasn't your custody turn—*really sucked*. The only way to survive them was to keep as busy as possible. Now Jeremy had swept in unexpectedly and given me something to look forward to again.

Oliver was with me until noon on Thanksgiving Day. We bundled up and went for a walk in the ducky park. The ducky park was nestled high in the mountains above Beverly Hills and you had to travel through winding steep roads to get there, but once there, it was worth it. You were transported to a different place.

It was serene and lovely but Oliver seemed subdued.

"Hey, Ollie, look at those squirrels. Do you think they're playing a game of tag?"

I tried to cheer him by pointing out the squirrels chasing each other but he stood quietly, kicking his boot back and forth in the dirt.

"Daddy says if I cry then I won't get to see Mama again," he said finally, his lips quivering slightly.

I dropped to my knees and held him, swallowing hard to prevent the lump in my throat from getting bigger.

"My love, don't you worry about that. We will *always* come back together again. Nothing will change that," I reassured him. "*Mommy always comes back*."

Oliver rested his head on my shoulder for a moment until a large duck marching out of the water in front of us distracted him. He chased after it, leaving me to compose myself and follow him.

While we were walking back to the car, we saw a mother deer with her young grazing at the side of the hill. We stopped in our tracks.

"Look, Oliver . . . how beautiful! That must be a lucky sign. You don't see deer every day in Beverly Hills!"

Oliver had brightened by the time we got back in the car. I put on one of his favorite songs, the old Herman's Hermits' song, "Henry the Eighth."

"I'm Hen-er-y the eighth, I am, Hen-er-y the eighth I am, I am," Oliver sang at the top of his lungs. We belted it out together as we drove out of the park and headed over to the valley to X's house, where Oliver would stay for the next two days.

"Bye, Mama," he said, hanging tightly around my neck as I got him out of his car seat.

"Bye, sweetheart. Have fun with Daddy. I'll see you in two days."

X came out to meet us. "There's my boy!" he said and took Oliver from me.

"Hi, Daddy," said Oliver softly.

"Hey, Ollie . . . show Daddy the new dinosaur we got!" I said in an attempt to lighten the mood.

X set Oliver down and he started digging in his backpack to extract the buried dinosaur, leaving X and I to face each other. X was dressed up in black linen jeans and a dark blue shirt with delicate Indian embroidery on the chest—another one that I had bought him during the marriage. They were going somewhere but I knew better than to ask where. The judge presiding over our divorce case had ordered us to go to co-parenting classes as part of a pilot program in California. In the workshops, we were instructed to maintain a *strictly business* relationship with former spouses— as in none-of-your-fucking business—and refrain from asking personal questions. We were also not allowed to ask Oliver questions about his time with the other parent. Oliver now had an existence with X that I knew nothing about and was excluded from. Oliver would be spending his holiday with people I didn't know. It was so alien to feel so removed from your own child's life.

X looked at me and said dryly, "Happy Thanksgiving."

"Happy Thanksgiving to you, too." I affected what I hoped sounded like a jovial tone.

Oliver produced the new red T. rex we'd gotten from the toy store and waved it at X.

"Very nice," said X. "Let's go inside now and play with it."

"Bye, Oliver . . . I love you!" I said and waved as I got back into the car.

Oliver looked over and waved as he walked up the steps into the house with X, hand in hand.

Driving away, I stopped fighting the sadness and let it pour out. I pulled over and gave into the huge, heaving sobs. We'd been doing this dance for nearly a year but it still felt peculiar to drop him to X, at our old home and leave knowing it would be two whole days until I saw him again. Nothing felt natural about divorce. I wondered if Oliver would ever get used to this dual existence. Sometimes he seemed okay with it, and other times he had to be peeled off me, screaming and clinging for dear life. The exchanges were often harrowing experiences that took a long time to shake off, and who really knew what toll it was taking on Oliver?

It wasn't his fault that I married a man I couldn't live with anymore. I had gotten away but I couldn't shake the feeling of having left Oliver stuck with the tab.

Before going home, I stopped back at the park and sat on our favorite bench by the pond. I watched as the turtles and ducks circled over to me expectantly. There was something remarkably soothing about being out in nature, watching the animals going about their business. They weren't lamenting that it was Thanksgiving and they were getting divorced. They just got on with it.

When I got back to the apartment, CeCe was playing Eartha Kitt at full blast, bouncing around the kitchen, glass of chardonnay in hand, preparing her typical hormone-laden turkey with all the fattening trimmings, candied yams and apple crumble. It was pure American comfort food and I couldn't wait. We were celebrating a big American holiday, and yet Mikki was the only American. CeCe, Sam and I were Australian, but as grateful immigrants, we wholeheartedly embraced the tradition.

"Perfect timing, we're almost done."

"Great." I glanced over at the pile of unopened legal correspondence.

"You look glum. When are you seeing that Jeremy person again?"

"I'll drive up and see him tomorrow."

"Good. Here . . . put this on the table," she said, and handed me an oven mitt and a bowl of marshmallow-covered yams.

Mikki, clad in her usual micro-mini and high-heeled booties, was busy setting the table.

"Hi," she muttered to me as I passed her at the table.

"Hi, Mikki."

"Okay, we're ready to start now," said CeCe. "Mikki, tell Sam to stop playing those wretched video games and come and sit down."

I poured myself a glass of wine and helped CeCe bring the rest of the dishes out to the table. Sam reluctantly tore himself away from playing *Grand Theft Auto* and joined us.

"Start everybody! Oh, Sam, darling . . . that is a very lovely rump but do we really need to see it *all* the time? Can you please pull your pants up?"

Sam gave a lethargic tug at the low-riding jeans that left his Calvin Klein briefs almost fully exposed. He poured two mimosas, handed one to Mikki, and they took their seats.

"If Oliver were here, this would be a perfect day," said CeCe, heaping great servings of turkey onto our plates.

"I know. It sucks, but we have to get used to it. This is the way it will be from now on—one year on, one year off. At least we get Christmas this year."

"It's bloody nonsense. I'm still waiting for the Hand of God to reach down and smite that man for the way he's treated you!"

Sam laughed so hard he started to choke on a mouthful of turkey.

"CeCe, it's one thing to think that way, but you aren't supposed to say it out loud," I said with exasperation. "You know I'm hardly X's biggest fan, but like it or not, he's still Oliver's father and we have to watch what we say. Oliver's sharp—he knows what's going on—and soon we won't be able to get away with spelling out words anymore. Those hideous parenting classes rammed down our throat how detrimental it is to bash the other parent."

"Well, he's not here, is he? I'm careful when he's here. If Oliver's listening, I'm careful to never mention what a complete arsehole his father is . . ."

"Thank you for your restraint, CeCe. I know it doesn't come naturally to you."

"You told me he has pictures of you on his fridge with devil magnets over your face!"

"Yes, he does. I saw them and he's a royal prick, but there's nothing I can do about any of it."

"Mikki has decided to go to makeup school!" said CeCe, abruptly changing the subject as she always did when I pissed her off. "That's the news of the day. Tell her, Mikki."

I looked over at Mikki in her raccoon-like black eye shadow with a thick layer of glitter smacked on top for effect. I'd long entertained the fantasy of wiping all that makeup off her. She had delicate features and pale skin and would have benefited from a minimal approach but minimal wasn't her style. Maybe she would gravitate toward special effects.

"That's great, Mikki." I smiled. "Let me know if I can do anything."

I noticed CeCe had barely touched her plate.

"CeCe, why aren't you eating?"

"I can't dally. I'm meeting a new fellow for a drink," CeCe said cheerfully.

"What? Right now? It's Thanksgiving. We just sat down." I said, surprised at my own irritation.

"Yes, I'm meeting him in the bar at the Montage in half an hour."

"Who is he?" I asked, quite certain that I was better off not knowing.

"He's some sort of secret spy for the government!" she said, giddy with excitement.

"Yeah, I bet that's what they all say." Sam laughed.

"No, really, he is. It's all very hush-hush. He's *fascinating*!" CeCe insisted.

"Why doesn't he have plans for Thanksgiving?" I asked.

"Maybe spies don't do Thanksgiving." Sam snickered.

"How will we find you if he kidnaps you and ferries you away to the Middle East or somewhere?" I sounded like *her* mother.

"I'll be sure to send up a smoke signal," she said, darting off into the bedroom, leaving us sitting at the table.

She came out dressed in black pants, high-heeled sandals and a charcoal silk blouse.

"You look beautiful, CeCe," I said. "Make sure you mention you have a strapping young son who's got a black belt in jujitsu!"

Sam puffed himself up, flailed his arms in the air and gave his best impression of a ninja assassin.

"Cheerio, chaps!" she said, hesitating slightly at the table before leaving.

It was a moment that in normal families might have elicited a hug good-bye or some token display of affection—after all, it was Thanksgiving and she was bailing on us. But CeCe didn't do hugs. Maybe once a year she might attempt an awkward embrace and that was usually at Christmas—

which ranks higher than Thanksgiving in the holiday order—and only after a few drinks.

The next day, I made the drive up to meet Jeremy at his family's ranch. Liberated from having to make sensible mom food choices, I fortified myself with a breakfast of chocolate ice cream and leftover apple crumble.

The ranch was located in the most picture-perfect farmland imaginable. Movies and commercials were shot there for precisely that reason. Large picturesque parcels of green land, with big houses and perfect white picket fences wrapped like gift ribbons around them. It almost didn't look real, with each one lovelier than the last.

I paused at the gate of a rambling estate and pressed the buzzer. A man's voice answered. "Yes?"

"Hi, this is Scarlett. I'm here to see Jeremy."

"Yes, come in and drive up to the main house," the male voice instructed me.

The huge wrought-iron gates opened slowly and I drove in. Once inside, there were a number of houses to choose from, making it difficult to distinguish the 'main house'—they all looked like viable candidates. Focusing on the 'drive up' part of the instructions, I followed a small road past three of the potential candidates on its way winding up the side of the hill. It was the most beautiful farm I'd ever seen, with supremely manicured lawns and paddocks populated with free-roaming horses. I arrived at a large white house distinguished from the others by an impressive stretch of lawn and a row of golf carts lined up neatly in front of it. Opposite the golf carts were a fleet of black cars with what I guessed could only be Jeremy's beige rental car standing out like a sore thumb. I pulled in next to a Land Rover and caught a glimpse of Jeremy bounding across the lawn to greet me.

Once he reached me, he stopped a little abruptly and seemed unsure as to whether he should hug me. I wondered if he was nervous, too.

"It's nice to see you. Thanks for coming," he said, kissing me quickly on the cheek.

Perhaps he thought that was all I liked. That brief contact was long enough for me to catch a whiff of residue from his shaving cream. It was such a distinctly pleasing aroma.

He introduced me to his uncle, Isaac, who was following a few steps behind him. It was a good sign that Jeremy felt comfortable introducing me to his family this early in the game. It was a risky move. What if I turned out to be a complete nut?

We said good-bye to Isaac and set out for a walk around the property. It was an idyllic retreat. Time slowed down as we watched the horses grazing on the emerald green grass. Who knew that grass came in such a vibrant color? It was almost fluorescent. Oliver would have been beside himself.

"I'm so glad you came. I was worried that I wasn't going to get to see you this trip."

"I'm happy you felt comfortable inviting me. I wouldn't have wanted to miss any of this," I said, and gestured to the dreamy surroundings. I wasn't brave enough to tell him that I had been counting the minutes until I could see him again.

"I love coming here. It's a shame they're selling it," Jeremy said wistfully.

"They're selling it? If I lived here, I would never leave."

"Well, if you like it, you could live here. It could be yours for twenty million." He laughed. "That's the listing price."

"I should have brought my checkbook."

Jeremy gave me a tour of the stables, making a particular point of the mating stables.

"And this is where all the dirty business happens," he said, admiring the mounting apparatus.

"Aha . . . so that's why you lured me out here."

"Absolutely!" he said, smiling as a slight flush turned his cheeks pink.

"Let's take the ATVs up the mountain," Jeremy said, and walked toward a row of large off-road vehicles sitting by the barn. The bikes looked complex to operate and, not being the most mechanically coordinated individual, I thought I would likely do myself serious harm. Jeremy caught my look of apprehension and seized the opportunity it presented. He straddled one of the four-wheelers.

"Strictly for safety, I *have* to insist that you ride with me!" He smiled and patted the seat behind him.

"You've heard about my driving, then!" I laughed.

I put my hand on his shoulder and climbed on behind him, then quickly moved my hands to the side handles. Jeremy peeled them away from the handles and wrapped them tightly around his waist instead, forcing our bodies to be in direct contact for the first time.

"This is much better!" he said, and squeezed my hands under his.

He felt warm and firm. My thighs were wrapped tightly against the outside of his and my stomach was pressed into his back. My body instantly started to stir from the arousal it produced. He waited for me to settle in and then hit the gas. My heart started to race along with the bike.

After one lap around the property at a terrifying pace, we started to wind our way up the side of the mountain. The landscape was very rocky in parts that required careful negotiation, and then the path would open up into wider spaces, which Jeremy would embrace with great speed. The wind whipped my hair around and the brisk air put me in such a good mood that I didn't mind the frequent assaults from the branches of overgrown shrubs we passed at breakneck speeds. I nestled my head against his warm back and tried not to look down the side of the hill.

Jeremy took peculiar delight in running over any young trees that had the misfortune to grow near his path. The game appeared to be to shear as many young trees as he could, leaving a swath behind him. He crushed them under the ATV and cheered. It was curious behavior for someone who claimed to be such a devout Democrat.

We continued our climb toward the top of the mountain and I started to relax a bit.

"This is the most fun I've had in years!" I pressed my mouth against his ear so he could hear me.

He turned and smiled at this news. "I'm really glad you're here," he said and rubbed my thigh.

When we reached the top, we got off and stretched our legs. The sky was a glorious mélange of pinks as the sun started to slide into the coastline in the distance. There were horses and cows on farms surrounding us grazing on zigzag patchwork quilts of grass. It was a world away from LA. I felt calm and serene. I took a moment to exhale and revel in this idyllic post on top of the world.

The sun was going down and it was getting cold. I was still savoring the view when he turned to me and said apropos of nothing, "Do you think we should have our first kiss now?"

"I guess we're sort of obligated to with this view."

I held my breath as he moved in closer and gave me a slow, gentle kiss. He brushed over my lips lightly, giving me just a brief taste of those exquisite lips. I could feel my balance slipping away. I wanted to lean into him and fully consume him but he broke away.

"Come on, let's go." He turned and grabbed my hand. "I'll show you some more highlights on the way down."

Downhill was slower going and required intense negotiation between the bike and the rocks. These sudden lurches caused me to slam into him in a wildly erotic fashion.

We rode along the edge of the mountain and down to another scenic spot. This time, we paused on a plateau facing the other direction. All you could see were big green rolling hills for miles. With the sun starting to set it was stunningly beautiful. Jeremy took his gloves off and casually rested his hand on my thigh. I looked down, eager for a glimpse of those divine hands, and for the first time noticed his nails. They were painted in a shocking, iridescent purplish-pink color. It was so unexpected. I wasn't sure what to make of it. A wave of concern was brewing and I pulled away slightly. He looked down and noticed.

"Oh my God! I still have the nail polish on! My cousin painted my nails while we were watching a movie the other night and she swore she'd take it off when we got home—which she obviously didn't—and you're freaking out right now!"

"It did require a *little* explanation."

"Wait till we get back. I'm going to give her hell for this!" He started up the bike again and we swiftly made our way down the hill, making time to run over a few more young trees in the process. Once down, Jeremy pulled in and parked next to one of the many guesthouses on the property.

"This is where I stay when I'm here." He helped me off the bike and I followed him inside.

The decor inside the guesthouse was unassuming and contrasted brilliantly with the majesty of the property. It looked like it had been decorated in the 70s and had been preserved in a time warp. There were floral couches and dried flower arrangements and a bright yellow kitchen filled with wooden owls of all sizes displayed on available surfaces. It was quirky and unpretentious.

We could hear people talking in the next room.

"Come and meet everyone."

I followed a few steps behind Jeremy into the cozy living room, where there was a fire raging in the stone fireplace. Jeremy introduced me to his cousins Daphne and Violet, and Daphne's boyfriend, Taylor.

"Hi, Scarlett. Nice to meet you. So glad you could make the trip out," Taylor said as he shook my hand.

Daphne and Violet were both lovely looking girls with long, dark hair and complexions that were ripe with the glow of impossibly rosy futures.

"Hi, Scarlett," Daphne said warmly.

"Hi," said Violet.

Taylor reminded me of a classic New York intellectual—glasses, dark hair and attractive. He was a writer working on a successful television show in Los Angeles and was one of Jeremy's best friends.

"Come and sit down. Tell us what you two have been up to," Daphne said with a touch of mischief.

The girls were remarkably down to earth and didn't appear the least bit snobby. Their small, scruffy Jack Russell terrier came over and parked itself on my lap, which I took as another good sign.

Taylor wasted no time, quickly asking me a stream of questions.

"Where are you from Scarlett?

"I'm from Australia."

"How long have you been in LA?"

"Oh, it feels like forever."

"So . . . you're an Aussie. Do you like rugby and cricket?" Taylor asked.

"That would be no and no."

"So you do makeup for celebrities. Do you ever work on TV shows?" Taylor asked.

"No, I haven't. The very long hours would be hard for me because I have a young child—and I'd never get to see him. Maybe at some point down the road when he's in school . . ."

"Yes, of course. You have a little boy named Oliver," he said, looking very pleased with himself.

I looked over at Jeremy who gave a slightly embarrassed smile. This was evidence he had been talking about me. Another good sign, I hoped.

Then Taylor's questions veered strangely toward my cooking skills and exactly what I prepared for Oliver.

"What are Oliver's favorite foods?"

"Pasta."

"Pasta? What kind of pasta? With sauce or no sauce?" Taylor asked.

"Bow-tie pasta with butter . . . hmm." Taylor was weighing my answers but didn't explain why he could possibly care. It was an odd line of questioning but anything was preferable to the typical dreaded divorce questions.

"What else does he like to eat?"

"He likes chicken fingers, strawberries, bananas, quesadillas, ice cream . . . come on," I said finally, "you can't possibly be interested in any of this."

"No, no, you don't understand. He finds this *fascinating!*" Jeremy said. "You're speaking to a guy who only eats foods that are one color . . . and that's white!"

"That's not true. I eat peas." Taylor stuck out his tongue at Jeremy.

"Yeah . . . you'll eat them, but not if they're on the same plate!" Jeremy roared with laughter. Then a full-scale debate ensued regarding color variances of the foods that were allowed to be on his plate or consumed at the same time.

"Taylor has food issues," Jeremy explained, as if speaking about a child. "He'll only eat white foods, with an occasional odd green thing thrown in."

The good-natured ribbing they gave each other was endearing and their laughter infectious. Soon I was laughing so hard that my sides hurt. I had forgotten how much fun it was to laugh and how much I'd missed it.

Daphne watched with amazement while her dog slept contentedly in my lap. "It's so unusual for Peppy to take such a shine to a new person. He's generally inclined to bite people he doesn't know."

"Yes, he's a very surly boy," said Jeremy, frowning at Peppy. "He's tried to bite me before."

"That's because you're always trying to do rude things to him," said Daphne. "It's an appropriate response."

"*Excuse* me? What *are* you talking about?"

"Remember you tried to do that humping thing in his butt that time?" Daphne was giggling hysterically.

"Daphne!" Jeremy sighed with pure exasperation. "In case it has escaped your notice, I am entertaining a young lady here. I'm doing my best to make a good impression, which you are ruining with your rude insinuations. And by the way, could you please explain to Scarlett exactly *why* I'm wearing pink nail polish!"

"I have no idea what you're talking about," said Daphne, wickedly hanging him out to dry.

"Daphne, come on!"

"I can testify that I did, in fact, *see* Daphne paint Jeremy's nails the other night," said Taylor, finally coming to the rescue.

"Thank you! Good man!" Jeremy bowed toward Taylor, vindicated, and then collapsed heavily onto the couch beside me, dispatching Peppy from his sanctuary in my lap in the process.

Violet, the younger of the two sisters, scoffed at the boys and yawned, apparently tired of the conversation, and walked over to the other side of the living room where she began to put her sylphlike body through a series of stretches and sit-ups. Jeremy observed her for a moment then jumped up to join her.

Daphne turned to me and said matter-of-factly, "Jeremy cannot stand to see anyone exercising. He has to be included. He now has an exercise addiction to replace his smoking addiction."

"I guess that's an improvement." I watched Jeremy contorting himself enthusiastically on the floor next to Violet, doing leg stretches and knee bends.

Jeremy's Aunt Catherine came through on the intercom announcing that she would collect us all for dinner in ten minutes. She suggested eating at a local Chinese restaurant.

"I have plans, Mom. I'm going out with my friends tonight," Violet shouted irritably back at the intercom.

"Okay, sweetie," she said patiently. "Dad's tired and he's not going to be joining us either."

That would leave Catherine chaperoning the two couples.

She picked us up in her black Mercedes. She got out of the car to say hello and shake my hand. The quintessential California woman, she was golden-haired, slim and willowy. Catherine's smile radiated sunny warmth and I was instantly drawn to her.

"Hop in," she said. "I just have to speak to Violet for a moment."

The four of us climbed in as she headed into the house.

Catherine came back to the car and proceeded to drive us into town to the Chinese restaurant. Her demeanor gave nothing away but somehow I got the impression that Violet could be a handful.

We arrived at the restaurant and were seated at a round table. Jeremy started squeezing my hand under it.

Catherine turned to me as we looked at the menus. "Scarlett, they have wonderful vegetarian dishes here, and if you like seafood, their garlic shrimp is not to be missed!"

"Thank you," I said.

Perhaps she sensed that it was a difficult time or maybe she was simply a kind woman but whatever the reason, she went out of her way to make me feel welcome and included me in the conversation.

"You know, Scarlett, you really need to be thinking about school for Oliver. I know he's young but the best places fill up quick." Catherine poured some jasmine tea into a cup and handed it to me.

"Oh, I wouldn't know where to begin to look. He's not even in preschool yet."

"Time flies. Before you know it, he'll be ready for school."

"I'm very keen to see pictures of Oliver, lover of bow-tie pasta with butter. Do you have any?" Taylor asked.

"Yes, of course."

Taylor waited patiently while I rummaged around in my handbag for my phone. Taylor scrolled through the shots—Oliver at the beach, Oliver in his firefighter Halloween costume, Oliver at his first Easter egg hunt. The phone was then sent around the table and everyone had a look. Jeremy had seen some of them on our first date but he gave them a casual glance again.

During dinner, I stole a glance over at Taylor's plate, and indeed, he was eating a medley of very pale-colored food items of an indeterminate nature. Jeremy disdainfully picked at his tofu vegetable entrée.

"Sorry, the food really sucks here," he whispered to me. I offered him some of my chicken but he declined. "Oh, I can't do chicken. I've spent too much time around them to eat them."

Will not eat chicken, but thrilled to run over young trees. He was proving to be an interesting fellow.

We drove back to the 'main' house, and as we got out of the car, Jeremy looked up at the night sky and said, "Oh, look, a full moon . . . I get more handsome in the moonlight, you know!"

"Yes, clearly." I smiled, enjoying the building flirtation.

Everyone retired to the drawing room and Jeremy rushed around getting us all tumblers of caramel-colored liquid on the rocks that he informed me was a "very special rum that you can *only* get in Jamaica."

"That sounds wonderful but I can't drink. I'm driving."

He walked around the table, thrust the rum into my hand, and whispered urgently, "You are absolutely *not* driving back to LA tonight. There are plenty of guest bedrooms here—you don't have to sleep in mine—but under *no* circumstances are you leaving."

I smiled and weighed my options. There was nothing to rush back for since Oliver was with X.

"Let's go back to the guesthouse," Jeremy announced, and corralled everyone out to the driveway.

My car was still sitting outside and was a warmer option than a golf cart, so Daphne, Taylor, and Jeremy piled in for the quick drive across the property. Jeremy took charge of my rum while I drove. The backseat was a complete disaster and I shuddered to think of the crushed grapes, melted chocolate, and other soggy, unsavory items that poor Daphne and Taylor were probably sitting on in the back. They looked hilariously out of place, squashed on either side of the car with Oliver's groovy leopard-print seat as chaperone, insisting on distance between them.

As soon as the car stopped, Taylor and Daphne leapt out and said their good-byes, eager to escape us, or let us have a pivotal moment alone. We sat silently in the car and watched them walk across the path into the guesthouse. Jeremy leaned over as if he were moving in to kiss me, and suddenly grabbed my keys out of the ignition.

"Come on inside." He handed me the rum as he sprung out of the car.

"Isn't it vaguely sluttish if I stay here tonight?" I said, as we negotiated in the moonlight.

"Oh God, I hope so!" he said, flashing that mischievous grin again.

"No, seriously . . . what will your family think? It is only our second date."

He stopped and put his arm around me and squeezed. "They'll think it's great. They really like you. They think you're a huge sport for coming out here and subjecting yourself to all this—*especially* on a second date."

"I've had a wonderful time."

"That's all the more reason for you not to leave."

"All right, I'll stay," I said, unable to keep the smile off my face. I wasn't sure what the implications of staying would be but I was having too much fun for the night to end. I walked back to the car and grabbed the bag containing sweats and my toothbrush that I'd brought just in case.

We walked up the path leading to the guesthouse. He opened the side door, and in one quick move, swept me into his arms and carried me over the threshold and into the living room. After depositing me on the couch, he gave me a quick kiss on the lips and went back outside to collect wood for the fireplace.

Giddy from the kiss and the rum, I leaned back on the flowery green couch and thought about the day's events. It was a bold move to invite me to the ranch, yet it had gone really well. He had given me an intimate glimpse into just how much shit his family gave him. They were not the least bit invested in his looking cool for his date—Daphne had even played the provocateur and done her worst to make him look bad. Exposing this vulnerability made me like him even more. I appreciated the gamble he had taken.

"I've had the best day. Thank you," I said when he returned.

"Me, too."

I nursed my rum and watched as he started to build a fire in the fireplace, purposefully arranging and rearranging the logs into a formation that pleased him. His back was lovely and broad, like an Olympic swimmer. I felt hypnotized watching his large, capable hands working the logs back and forth. He might soon be working me into a pleasing state. I could barely contain my excitement. After igniting the fire, he walked over and sat next to me on the couch. My stomach was doing flips, threatening to override the calming effects of the rum. In an attempt to quiet my nerves, I got up and moved away from him and over to the fireplace.

"Hey . . . are you nervous?" He smiled at this discovery.

"Sort of. I don't remember how all this works." I took a seat at the foot of the fireplace.

"How what works?"

"This whole seduction thing—the fireplace, the warm rum, the handsome man. It's been a while."

"I'll tell you how it works. First, you come back over here and sit next to me right now," he said, patting the couch next to him.

I was only too happy to comply. I walked over to him and as soon as I got within range he pulled me into him, so that we were lying on the couch. He moved the hair away from my face and gave me a long, lingering, tender kiss that sent a current of electricity shooting straight through my body. My legs began to tremble and I struggled to regulate my breath. I couldn't inhale him quickly enough. His mouth was soft and tasted like coconut rum. I wanted every part of him in my mouth all at once. His kisses were igniting small fires all over my body that logic and reason told me I should try to put out. It was dangerous to want somebody this badly.

He stood up and announced, "It's time for bed."

The many other bedrooms on the property he'd offered me earlier were conveniently forgotten as he led me down the hall to his bedroom. The bedroom had a four-poster king-sized bed with a large wooden headboard, and two lemon-colored lamps sat on either side of the bed with wooden owls as bases. Big windows on both sides of the bed looked out into the woods. The moon was streaming in, illuminating the giant pile of clothes spilling out of the suitcase Jeremy had left on the floor.

"Sorry about the mess," he said, and stepped over the mound of clothes. "If you don't mind, I'm going to take a quick shower. I'll be right out." He disappeared into the bathroom and closed the door.

I sat on the bed and rummaged around in my bag trying to figure out what was appropriate to wear for bed. I hadn't seriously considered that I might want to stay over, and was now regretting that lack of forethought. Sweatpants and a T-shirt would have to suffice.

Jeremy walked out of the bathroom wearing only a towel around his waist and casually brushing his teeth. My jaw dropped slightly at the sight of him. With his torso muscular and glistening, he was the very essence of masculine appeal. He noticed my chaste sweats and went over to his suitcase, produced his own T-shirt and sweatpants, and went back into the bathroom.

I got into bed and waited.

He reappeared from the bathroom and jumped into bed next to me.

"Hey, we're twins." I laughed at our near identical ensembles.

"I wanted you to feel comfortable," he said.

"I appreciate that. Thank you."

He slipped under the covers and pulled me in tightly against his chest.

"I do need to be able to breathe now and then." Laughing, I gasped for air. I had forgotten how to be intimate with a man. I had forgotten the choreography involved, all the maneuvering and the breathing in sync.

"Yes, of course. So sorry!" He loosened his grip slightly and then his lips found mine again.

Those lips that I had been relentlessly fantasizing about did not disappoint. They were incredibly soft, yet firm, with purposeful kisses behind them. It was intoxicating to melt into him. We kissed until my lips were numb.

"Let's not have sex," I whispered.

"Hey, who said anything about sex? We're having a sweatpants sleepover party here, lady. I don't know what kind of man you take me for. There won't be any sex happening . . . unless, of course . . . you ask *really* nicely."

He had me in hysterics.

"Okay, I promise I'll try to control myself," I said and kissed him again.

He drifted off but I was too aroused to sleep. It was far too exciting to be lying next to such a strapping young man with his long lanky arms wrapped protectively around me. All six foot two of him curled up tightly against me, as if we were glued together. I didn't want to waste another minute sleeping—who knew when this might happen again? I wanted to stay awake and savor the feeling of being enveloped by him. At one point during the night we disengaged and for a brief moment lay on separate sides of the bed. I lay awake, listening to the coyotes howl outside. Then he stirred, reached over to find me, and swiftly pulled me back into him so that we were enmeshed again.

In the early morning light, he looked much younger than his thirty-four years. I watched him sleep, memorizing every detail of his face, the sharp slant of his nose, the contours of his chin and the small scar on his cheek. It was the first time in years that I'd spent the night with a stranger. I'd forgotten about the excitement in the inherent sense of uncertainty.

When he woke, he looked genuinely delighted to see me.

"Hey . . . you're still here! I was afraid you might disappear into the night."

"Sleep deprived, but still here."

"Why couldn't you sleep?"

"All that kissing made it impossible for me to sleep." I put my jeans and sweater back on.

"Why didn't you wake me up and have sex with me?" he asked, as if he was dumbfounded that the idea hadn't occurred to me.

I raised an eyebrow and gave him a look, even though I'd thought of nothing else all night. I was dying to explore his body and had somehow managed to resist climbing on top of him during the night. I wanted to get to know him better. I liked what I knew so far. I liked his family, plus I was wildly attracted to him. This chemistry was worth cultivating and not squandering. The brief tryst with Dominick had served to highlight what I wanted to avoid. I couldn't afford the letdown after sex with a man I shouldn't have let in to begin with. The longer we could put off sex, the better it would be—at least that was the assumption.

Jeremy leapt out of bed and searched through the mound of clothes exploding out of his suitcase. After a brief hunt, he threw his jeans on, then sat at the edge of the bed and laced his high-top sneakers.

Taylor gave a brief knock on the bedroom door and swung it open quickly before we had a chance to answer.

"Are we up in here?" Taylor asked, his eyes danced over us in swift assessment. It was clear he was trying to gauge what mischief had transpired during the night. Clothed and sitting a reasonable distance apart on the bed, we gave nothing away—other than the fact that I was still there.

"I'm going to run over to the house. Can I interest you two in breakfast?" he inquired, looking disappointed not to have interrupted anything.

"Sure, we're up for it, aren't we, Scarlett?"

"Oh, God, yes! I'm famished!" I said with just enough wickedness to keep Taylor's suspicions afloat.

"Daphne left for the horse show and Catherine's waiting outside for us to join her for breakfast."

We piled into Catherine's car again and she broke into a big smile when she saw me.

"Scarlett, I'm so happy you stayed!"

I blushed. "Me, too. Thank you, Catherine."

Taylor sat up front with Catherine, and Jeremy and I took the backseat. Everyone seemed rather low in the energy department—except Jeremy. He was in a highly excited state. He looked over at me expectantly and gestured toward his crotch. I glanced down and was startled to see one perfectly formed, wrinkly pink testicle hanging out of a strategically placed gaping hole in his jeans.

I gasped then forced myself to abruptly turn and look out the window. The cheeky bugger wasn't about to let me get away from the ranch without at least having a peek at his package. Catherine and Taylor were chatting away in the front and didn't catch what had transpired. Jeremy smiled. I smiled back and shook my head at his antics. I had no idea what to make of him.

Their chef was back from her holiday break. She had prepared a breakfast buffet of scrambled eggs, fresh fruit and oatmeal, and laid it out in the dining room but I was more interested in coffee. The dining table was still decorated for Thanksgiving with a heavy linen tablecloth, silver place settings and several large fall-themed floral arrangements consisting of red and burnt-orange colored flowers. Jeremy's family was so casual and modest that it was easy to forget that they were fabulously wealthy. One look at the formal breakfast setting served as a quick reality check.

Even a huge latte couldn't put a dent in my morning fog. All I could think about was crawling back into bed with Jeremy. Rain looked imminent and I was secretly hoping that it might dash our plans for hiking up the hill. A lazy afternoon spent in bed kissing Jeremy held infinitely more appeal.

Once we were back inside the bedroom, Jeremy grabbed me around the waist and launched us both backward into the air so that we came crashing down on the unmade bed. He playfully rolled over me, smothering me with huge, exaggerated kisses. "Stay with me today. I promise I'll behave!" We both laughed at the likelihood of that.

"I might be persuaded to stay . . ."

After exhausting ourselves with another kissing marathon that threatened to turn into a full-scale romp, we lay side by side on the bed and talked, drifting aimlessly from topic to topic.

"Your extended family is lovely . . . but why don't you spend Thanksgiving with either of your parents?" I asked.

"My parents drive me crazy. As a rule, I don't do the family thing at Thanksgiving—I need to keep my sanity. I usually spend it with one of my best friends and his wife, but they recently split up, so that's why I'm here."

"Oh, I see."

"Tell me how it was being married," he said and propped his head up on a pillow. "It seems to be a really difficult state to live in. Most of the married people I know end up divorcing."

"You know how to kill a mood, don't you?" I laughed.

"Was it that bad?"

"That's what happens if you marry someone and your heart isn't in it."

"Marriage scares the hell out of me."

"You've never come close?"

"Not really. I thought about it once with an ex-girlfriend and we even tried living together. But after we moved in together it all went to shit."

"Oh. That's a shame," I said.

"Since then, I've had dates here and there but nothing serious."

From the sounds of it, he didn't have a terribly lengthy track record with women, but who was I to judge? My own romantic record was less than stellar.

"My parents had such a shitty marriage that I may never recover from the trauma." He laughed.

"How old did you say you were when they split up?"

He stopped smiling and his face clouded over. "I was five when my parents divorced. It sucked . . . I lived with my mom but I'd have to come out here for holidays and it was so forced."

"What was it like growing up with a single mother?"

"After the divorce, she tried too hard to get me to play happy families with my step-father. I hated it. It was such a strain on everybody."

"Oh, that must have been difficult," I said, and noted that I should avoid making the same mistake.

"Enough of that subject. By the way, I don't really understand your dual careers of makeup artist and actress," he said, sweeping a strand of hair out of my face.

"That's okay. I don't understand them either."

"But what do you really like doing? Makeup or acting?" he asked

"Commercials can be great financially, but it isn't reliable work. Makeup is something that I fell into and has been good to me, but it's not the driving force in my life. I'm still trying to figure out what my passions are—other than my son," I said, and hoped that it would suffice. "But right now, I can't be too picky, I just need to work."

By thirty-six, I should have had some plan for what the hell I was doing with my career or life in general.

"I have an idea: why don't you come and work on my movie?" He perked up at the thought.

"That's a lovely offer but I can't leave Oliver. Working outside of LA isn't really an option but I'm very happy that you would even suggest it."

Rain stated to tap loudly against the windowpanes.

He looked up. "I guess we're not going on that hike after all."

"No. I guess we'll have to come up with something else to do." I smiled and gave him a quick kiss. "What made you stop wanting to be an actor?" I asked.

"I remember being at this audition, talking with this guy who was thirty-five and he was so excited about landing a commercial playing a tomato . . . I just said to myself, that's it. I don't ever want to be *that* guy! I don't ever want to be begging to play a tomato in somebody's ketchup commercial. I see what my friends go through and I'm very glad I'm not an actor."

I laughed, but the irony was not lost on me. Auditioning was hoop jumping and I'd spent too much of my life doing it.

"So you turned to producing. That's a smarter choice. There's a lot more power and control on that side of the fence."

"Yes . . . I get this incredible high from seeing a project through from start to finish, putting all the pieces together and conquering all the hundreds of problems that arise. It's the best rush. When I'm on a project, I live and breathe it. I am totally consumed by it—and I haven't even worked with any really good directors yet, but I will and when that happens . . . man, it's just going to put me over the edge."

I found his mouth again and silenced him with a kiss.

Enough talking. It was time to reward him for good behavior.

I needed to taste him.

I lifted up his shirt and traced my finger down his bare stomach, pausing to kiss it, and slowly made my way down to the convenient hole in his pants. I slipped my fingers into the hole and began to stroke him. He arched his back in agreement.

"Wow . . . you certainly know how to get my attention!"

I unbuckled his jeans and freed him from confinement. His cock lunged forth and practically leapt into my mouth. It was his turn to gasp.

"Oh, my God." He gripped the sheets as I teased him, licking up one side of his cock and down the other.

"Oh, my God," he said again.

I took him in my mouth and sucked on him, letting his cock bob and dance to the dictates of my tongue. In this one moment, I completely owned him.

He moaned and exploded into my mouth.

"That was amazing," he said after he caught his breath. "Come here." He grabbed my hand and pulled me into him.

"Thank you for that. You're full of surprises, aren't you?" He kissed me appreciatively as we lay entwined on the bed.

"When are you coming to visit me up north?" He rolled back on top of me and pinned my arms above my head.

"I don't know. That depends. When are you inviting me?"

"I'm formally inviting you right now," he said between planting kisses down my neck. "Can you come back with me tomorrow?"

I laughed, but judging by the look on his face, he was serious. "I can't go tomorrow."

"How about later in the week, then?"

"It will be soon, I hope."

The day was slipping away and it was almost time to go. I collected my things with Jeremy watching from the bed.

"I wish you didn't have to leave," he said.

"It's getting late. I have to pick up Oliver."

Jeremy walked me to the car, and Taylor came out to say good-bye.

"Why don't you pick up your son and come back?" Taylor asked.

I hesitated for a moment. Oliver would have loved all the horses but Jeremy said nothing.

"Thanks but maybe another time."

After Taylor left, Jeremy pressed me up against the car door and kissed me for the umpteenth time.

"Please thank Catherine for her hospitality."

"I will. I had a wonderful time. I'm so glad you stayed. I will be calling you . . . immediately!" He stood in the rain and waved until I was out of sight.

I practically floated back to Los Angeles. Laughter and lots of kissing proved to be an excellent prescription. I couldn't stop smiling. Exhausted but elated, my body felt alive again. I indulged myself in the possibilities of a budding romance. I blasted Stevie Wonder and sang "Boogie On Reggae Woman" down the freeway back to LA.

Despite the rain, traffic was light and I made good time getting to Oliver. I scooped him up in my arms when he rushed out to greet me.

"Hi, Ollie! Did you have a good time with Daddy?"

"Yep . . . look Mama," he said and showed me a small sketchpad of crayon drawings.

"Wow, you've been a very busy boy. Thank you! They're wonderful. We'll have to hang some up!"

I bundled Oliver off into the car and, feeling very generous with the world, even managed to give X a smile and a wave as we left. I hadn't felt adrift in Oliver's absence. I felt calm. Maybe this was the best of both possible worlds. Maybe this was what Susan meant when she said divorced parents learn to like their time off.

—〰—

I didn't have to wait long to hear from Jeremy. He called the next morning at seven forty-five while Oliver and I were making pancakes.

"You're up early on a Sunday morning," I said.

"When are you coming to see me?"

I laughed and tried flipping a pancake, which landed on the floor, eliciting a loud disapproving howl from Oliver.

"Let me look at my schedule and see what we can work out."

"You left your sweater here. I slept with it last night because it smells like you."

"That sounds a bit kinky. I'm not sure I want it back now."

"Yeah, I did wicked things to it all night. I'm holding it hostage until I see you again."

Not only was my sweater being held hostage but he had laid claim to parts of my anatomy, as well. I couldn't wait to be with him again.

Chapter Twelve
Only Kissing?

Emma and I grabbed coffee and took Oliver down to the park. We sat on a bench and rehashed recent developments while he climbed on the jungle gym.

"How was it? Did you have fun with him?"

"Yes! This is *exactly* why I left that lemon marriage; the opportunity to feel like this . . . to feel alive again, to feel a sense of hope about the future."

"And you didn't sleep with him?"

"Not exactly."

"Come on. You didn't have sex?"

"Nope."

"When will you see him again?"

"He wanted me to fly straight back up with him!"

"Wow . . . he scores points with his enthusiasm."

"I have some work with Garrison this week but maybe I could fly up next weekend when Oliver's with X."

"This is what you need, a bit of fun and excitement, something to look forward to. It's all happening at once, isn't it? Work with Garrison, a new man . . . how great is that? Look at where your life is now compared to a year ago!"

She was right. Things were turning around nicely.

We watched a young girl spinning too fast on the merry-go-round until she threw up, which Oliver found wildly entertaining, and then we headed home.

"Mama . . . I can't get the poo out," Oliver said, walking around the living room naked from the waist down, scratching at his bottom.

"That happens sometimes, sweetie. Let's wash your hands and go back and read a story for a while," I said, and attempted to shepherd him back toward the loo.

CeCe was minding her business, having a glass of wine and watching the news.

"Don't look at my butt, CeCe!" Oliver giggled and pranced in front of the couch, so that CeCe was treated to a good show. When he got close enough she leaned out and attempted to pinch his bottom, then he jumped back out of range squealing with delight at the little game they played.

"That's a fine bottom, fine bottom, *fine bottom!*" CeCe sang to him.

"Don't look at my pee-pee, CeCe!" Legs astride, Oliver stood with his hands on his hips, gleefully taunting her.

"Oh, you men are all the same," she said and shooed him away. "If you don't want me to look at it, then stop waving it in my face! Go cover it up!"

Oliver grabbed a pillow from the couch and shielded his butt, confident he'd obscured her view. Still facing her, he was doing a victory dance, unaware that he was, in fact, giving her a full frontal view.

"I've got news for you, sweetheart! You're covering the wrong end! *I can still see it.*" CeCe sang playfully at him.

Oliver shrieked when he realized his mistake and ran back into the bathroom.

It made me think of Jeremy flashing me in the car.

"Men really are the same whether they're three or thirty-three, aren't they?" I laughed and followed him into the bathroom.

"Yes. They never change." CeCe nodded.

Jeremy was determined to lock me down with a date to see him.

It's Tuesday already. If you won't come up, I may be forced to fly down to spend the night with you!

~You'd fly down for one night just to see me?

Of course!

I saved all his texts and looked back over them whenever I needed a boost. A torrent of attention from a sexy fellow can quickly become addicting. I lived for the ping alerting me to a new text.

Thinking of you. Have been doing wicked things to your sweater again.

He made me laugh, which was also becoming addicting. To not have to take things so seriously after the stress of the last year felt like a great gift.

Life was very immediate in Jeremy's world. He was used to making things happen quickly and couldn't quite comprehend my noncompliance. He didn't grasp the responsibilities of having a child and that I couldn't just drop everything, even if I wanted to.

"Well, I can't come up during the week because Oliver is with me. Then on Friday, I'm working with Garrison on more press . . . but I guess it would be possible to fly up on Friday night after work and fly back in time to prep Garrison before his TV appearance on Sunday afternoon. That could work . . ."

"Let's do it!"

I was doing my own countdown. Borrow a cute coat from Susan, get a bikini wax, and tone my entire body in a matter of days.

CeCe couldn't help but notice me beaming.

"Well, this is a marked improvement," she said, watching me tango around the kitchen in my nightgown with Oliver on my hip while he threw his head back and squealed with delight.

"Weee . . . Ollie, let's go dance with the fish!" We danced over to the fish tank and serenaded the goldfish with the *SpongeBob SquarePants* theme song.

Since Oliver was with me all week, that meant no time for yoga. I had to come up with innovative new ways to exercise. A leisurely stroll around the ducky park wasn't going to cut it. Friday was approaching and I needed results fast.

"Mama, you're being silly," Oliver said as I put my body through yoga moves and furious leg kicks on the carpet in front of the television, desperate to firm some of the flab.

"Mama, I can't see," Oliver said with irritation. "I can't see *SpongeBob*!"

Frustrated, he would wander over from his perch on the couch and attempt to shove me out of the way. Fixing his tiny hands on my bottom, he would give a giant grunt and try to roll me away.

"Oh, you want to see *SpongeBob*, do you? Well I bet SpongeBob can't do this!" I flipped Oliver upside down over my stomach and incorporated him into the exercises, giving him a 'flying airplane' ride by balancing his torso on my feet until he roared with laughter.

Oliver came with me as I shopped for makeup items for Garrison at Naimie's, an industry beauty supply store.

Emma liked to tag along on makeup shopping sprees, too, whenever possible. We were both product junkies and loved to play with all the makeup.

She tried on a bronzer and turned to me for approval.

"Uh . . . no. That's turned way too orange!"

"You're right. Yikes. What about this color?" She held up a peachy-pink blush.

I wiped off the orange mess and applied the softer shade.

"There . . . that's much more flattering."

Oliver was having his own fun with the tattoo-concealer display, and was smearing a small sponge into the green camouflage color and rubbing it to his cheeks.

"Nice job, Ollie!" Emma said, laughing hysterically.

I bought some of the eye drops Garrison favored that made his eyes pop, bronzing powder and oil-blotting papers. Then there was that chirping sound that buoyed my day, telling me I had a text message from Jeremy.

What r u doing?
~Buying makeup for Garrison.
Get some for me.

~You don't need any.
I need something. I'm getting so turned on thinking about seeing you.
~Me, too. Can't wait!

Friday arrived and I headed to the Peninsula Hotel to get Garrison ready for his press appearances. Garrison sat in the makeup chair, and I tried to focus on the task at hand.

Garrison told me Jeremy had already called to ask about me.

"Oh, no! You're kidding! He wants a reference? What did you tell him?"

"That you were a cool chick—"

"A cool chick? Thanks! I can't ask for more than that."

"Yeah . . . Jeremy . . . I can see his appeal," said Garrison thoughtfully. "If I were a girl, I'd like him. He really cares about his work and I respect that. He's a good guy."

"I'm flying up to see him later tonight."

"Now listen, Scarlett, you behave yourself," Garrison admonished playfully. "*Only kissing!* Do you hear me?"

I was so thrown by his comment that I let the powder compact slip out of my hand and smash on the floor into a thousand pieces with a loud crash. What did he mean *only kissing*? How long was I supposed to wait? Where was the fun in that?

"Oops . . . sorry about that," I said. "Hardly a cool chick now!" I quickly cleared the mess of shattered glass and powder out of the way using a damp washcloth, and scrambled to find another compact.

While Garrison was doing his first interview, I sat in the back of the room and sent Jeremy a text informing him of Garrison's directive—'*Only kissing*'.

Hmmm . . . depending on where I might be ok with that.

Sexy fucker. He sent a bolt of electricity through my body all over again. I fought to concentrate my thoughts on work and banish him from my head but all I could think about was how many minutes it was until we would kiss again.

If I stopped to think about the radical turn life was taking, it made my head spin. After a crappy year with no romance and little work, life was all of a sudden thrilling. In a few hours, I would be leaving a movie star client at *The Tonight Show* to dash to the airport and fly to San Francisco for a romantic weekend with my marvelous new man. Whose glamorous life had I borrowed? It bore no resemblance to my old one. I had to pinch myself to believe it.

At the end of the day, Garrison gave me a big hug and wished me a great time as I made my mad dash to catch an evening flight out of Burbank airport. It was only when I was seated on the plane and stopped running that I was nervous. We were going to be alone for two nights. Spending the night with him at the ranch had been easy since my car was there in case I needed to make a hasty exit. This time, I felt much more vulnerable, and it wasn't a feeling I particularly enjoyed.

Jeremy was leaning against the wall with his arms crossed, watching me as I came down the escalator to meet him at the airport. His face broke into that infectious smile as I approached. He kissed me and took my bag as we headed for the parking lot.

I prattled on a bit about my day with Garrison and then ran out of things to say. We got to his car and it was completely trashed. The passenger seat was covered in junk, including newspapers, clothing and shoes, and oddly, a pair of water skis.

"Oh, God, I'm so sorry. I didn't have time to clean the car . . . I was afraid I'd be late. Just give me a second here."

I stood back as he cleared the seat and made a laborious attempt to negotiate the skis out of the way. What was he doing with water skis in winter?

The Friday night traffic made the journey slow but it gave us a chance to chat. The cheeky bravado he exhibited in his texts and in our phone calls had vanished. We were just two people unsure about what we were getting ourselves in for and if we were ready for the next step.

Jeremy talked about his new movie and the problems leading up to the beginning of principal photography, which was two days away.

"Our leading lady is a bit of a nightmare. I'm a nervous wreck but hopefully all the pieces will fall into place at the last minute—that's what usually happens."

Movie star tantrums and special effects budget issues were vexing him. Compared to annoying ex-husbands and potty-training setbacks, they sounded like pretty glamorous problems to have.

—◊◊◊—

Jeremy picked a quiet Italian restaurant close to his house and the awkwardness between us began to melt away, helped in part by chardonnay and lots of reassuring kisses that filled any pauses.

"What are you doing sitting all the way over there?" He pulled my chair in as close as he could so that our thighs were touching.

He ordered fettuccine Alfredo and I ordered the roasted chicken but barely touched it. The butterflies in my stomach had successfully abolished any appetite but this time Jeremy didn't notice. Dinner wasn't a lingering affair as Jeremy was keen to get me home and try to separate me from my knickers.

"Let's go home, shall we? I want to show you my house."

"Yes, let's," I said, and the butterflies started up again with a serious jolt.

His house sat at the end of a long drive, nestled in at the base of a small hill. It was a drab off-white color with large windows, and despite being in need of a good paint job, still managed to be rather regal-looking.

"This is the first property I've ever owned," he said proudly, watching me closely for signs of approval. It was a darling property, a bit unkempt but with loads of potential—just like him. There were calla lilies, pink roses and birds-of-paradise haphazardly growing about the garden. It reminded me of my great aunt's home in an old section of Sydney. It was large in stature but not intimidating. Inside it was sparsely furnished with a white couch from Ikea and several plastic chairs surrounding a large wooden coffee table. The old gray curtains that hung in the living room looked like they'd been there for a hundred years but the essence of the house was charming.

"You'll have to excuse the furniture. I've been so busy that I haven't had any time to devote to it. I wish you could see my apartment in LA. Then you might believe I have good taste."

"It's perfect," I said, admiring the impressive stone fireplace and the bundles of logs sitting next to it.

"Let me give you the grand tour," he said with a sly smile.

I followed him up the stairs. He made sure to lean me up against the wall and kiss me ceremoniously in each room along the way. At each stop, he took one article of my clothing off—coat, scarf, and sweater—and kissed any area of skin left exposed.

By the time we reached the master bedroom, I was in such a state that I could hardly find my breath.

He threw me down dramatically on the bed and pounced on top of me. He then dove between my legs and attempted to pry me out of my skirt.

"Wait. Hang on a sec." I stopped the proceedings and sat up. "What are we doing? We haven't really discussed any of this."

"Yes, that's an excellent question. What *are* we doing?" He slipped his head under my skirt and began covering my thighs with a flurry of featherlight kisses. It was a brilliant attempt to squash any protests. How could I possibly stop him when it felt so good?

"Well, we should put off having sex as long as possible, don't you think?" I said, trying to sound more convinced than I felt.

He briefly abandoned his post between my legs.

"That's probably a wise move," he said, and started peeling me out of my camisole and hurled it toward the headboard.

"I'm not quite mentally ready to go there with you yet."

"That's okay, but I'm sure we can find other fun things to do to entertain ourselves." He proceeded to kiss my stomach. "You've already shown me that you're quite creative in that arena."

"Yes, I'm sure that's not an issue . . ."

"I don't mind waiting for sex. I'm not in a hurry," he said, which of course made me want him even more. "But you're crazy if you think I'm not going to return the favor."

"But I—"

"Shhhh. Now, where was I?" He moved back into position between my thighs and began stroking me. His fingers made quick work of the panties that briefly separated us. He moved me up on the bed and as I leaned back, he ran his tongue along the inside of my legs and began eagerly licking me. I wept for him. My legs started to tremble and soon I was writhing from the intense pleasure. I cried out and begged him to stop. I couldn't contain it anymore.

"Stop!"

He shook his head. I longed for him to penetrate me, to claim me. He kissed me until the great rolling waves came through and consumed my body. I moaned and lay there quietly. His head was resting on my thigh, and he was wearing a very big smile.

"You look very pleased with yourself." I laughed.

"I do aim to please," he said.

"Well, you're an overachiever. I did not expect you'd be able to pull that off so quickly."

In spite of my nerves, I had managed to let go and surrender. I hadn't shared that with anyone in a really long time. I hadn't wanted to give a man that power over me.

"Just so you know, I'm fine waiting. We have plenty of time," he said and lay down next to me.

We agreed to skip sex in favor of lots of kissing and fooling around. This meant plenty of canoodling and exploratory expeditions. We kissed until we fell asleep enmeshed in each other's bodies, as we had at the ranch.

The next morning, we got up early and stopped at a nearby coffee shop.

After breakfast, we met his friend George at his boat for a spot of waterskiing. Neither Jeremy nor George thought anything unusual about donning their wetsuits and hitting the water in early December.

"You can try it if you want," he said. "Let's see what you're made of!"

"Uh . . . waterskiing in winter? I think I'll pass," I said, looking at him as if he were nuts.

George happened to be dark-haired and yummy looking. Together the two of them were a sight for sore eyes. Jeremy protectively put two warm ski jackets and a blanket around me and kept asking me if I was okay. I bundled up, sat back, and watched with amusement as they took turns disrobing to change into their wetsuits in the brisk morning air.

"Oh, this is definitely my favorite part of the trip!" I joked, feasting my eyes on their naked male splendor. I didn't bother to avert my gaze. They weren't the least bit shy and if I was going to have to endure freezing temperatures for this adventure, I might as well be rewarded for it.

Both of them turned out to be expert water-skiers, which I could have guessed by their keen interest in winter. They took turns showing off. George could do impressive little flips on the wakeboard while holding the rope casually with one hand, and Jeremy looked insanely sexy out there doing jumps as George put him through his paces. Jeremy was a seductive mixture of power and grace, gliding over the water. My resolve was slipping. I wanted to take him home and rip his clothes off.

After the water-ski adventure, Jeremy and I headed into town for lunch at a quaint little café. The cold weather and the tsunami orgasm had stirred my appetite. I was famished. I ordered mushroom soup and devoured it, along with bread and tons of butter. He looked on in amazement.

"I love that you feel comfortable ordering soup with heavy cream," he said, as if it were something outlandish and daring. I laughed. He seemed shocked to actually see me eat.

Jeremy sat with his thigh pressed tightly against mine in our booth.

"I loved sleeping with you last night," he said while rubbing my thigh. "It's so great to actually want to snuggle with someone."

"Don't you snuggle with most girls you date?" I asked, curiosity getting the better of me.

"No, generally not . . . all that snuggling is not normal behavior for me. I —"

My cell phone rang, interrupting us. Oliver had selected a ringtone that amused him—a hideous meowing cat serenaded by an electric cymbal and drum mix—and I had forgotten to switch it to a less embarrassing one for the weekend. The phone meowed irritably at us, startling me. It could not have been less 'cool chick' but Jeremy howled with laughter.

"Oh, my God! What is that?"

"Oliver picked that ringtone. I'm going to change it right now!"

"I love it. It's hilarious," he said as I answered the call.

"Hello?"

"You didn't pack the SpongeBob pajamas," X barked at me.

"No, because I packed the Bob the Builder pajamas instead . . . is there a problem?"

"Yeah, I need the SpongeBob ones."

"Why is that?"

"Oliver wants them."

"Well, I'm sure he'll be fine with the ones you have. He wears those all the time. I don't see what the problem is."

"We'll drive over and pick them up,"

"The SpongeBob pajamas are not available at the moment," I said evenly. "He'll have to make do with Bob the Builder."

Click. X hung up on me.

"What's the matter with him?" Jeremy asked, completely bewildered by the testy exchange about pajamas.

"There seems to be a pajama emergency but he will have to handle it."

"That seems weird. Do you think he suspects you're away with me? Maybe he's jealous."

"Maybe, but it's none of his business," I said, rubbing his thigh in an attempt to dispel thoughts of annoying ex-husbands.

X rang several times throughout the day. He was determined to disrupt my weekend. Oliver was fine, there was no emergency, but he kept coming up with reasons to call. He'd found an empty wrapper from a chocolate chip cookie snack pack in Oliver's backpack and was pissed off that I'd let him eat sugar. He was also angry that he'd heard I'd let Oliver watch *SpongeBob SquarePants* during the week and not just on the weekend. I stopped picking up and let his calls go to voice mail.

Jeremy was a remarkably good sport about it, saying only, "We need to get that guy a girlfriend!"

We went to a movie starring one of Jeremy's famous friends. Jeremy had a dazzling roster of female celebrity friends and this particular one—Katie Simms—would be 'furious' with him if he didn't see her new film on its opening weekend. The movie was great. Katie gave a very strong performance in a serious drama, but all I could think about during the movie was making love to Jeremy. He kept his hand on my thigh the whole time, rubbing it back and forth and driving me wild with anticipation. I made the decision to seduce Jeremy as soon as we were alone.

In the car on the way home, Jeremy got very quiet. I asked him if everything was okay.

"I'm sad because you're leaving in the morning," he said softly. "We've been having such a good time and I don't want it to end."

I nestled in against his chest and said, "I'm having a good time, too."

When we got back to the house, he still seemed to be in a bit of a funk, so my hot sex plan had to be aborted. I couldn't very well seduce him when he looked ready to cry. Like it or not, sex would have to wait.

Jeremy dropped me off at the airport early on Sunday morning and I flew back to LA in time to prep Garrison for his interviews. By the time I landed, my cell phone was chirping again.

Miss u. Had the best time. Can't wait to taste u again.

I nearly dropped the phone.

~Me, too!

Jeremy was texting again to tell me he missed me. He had put me in a blissful haze, perpetually smiling like a loon, preoccupied with sexy daydreams. It was a delicious, albeit impractical, state to exist in.

"How was your weekend, Scarlett? Were you a good girl?" Garrison asked as soon as he was seated in the makeup chair.

I smiled and nodded.

I thought about asking him if oral still qualified as being a 'good girl' but decided against it. It depended on your definition of sex. Technically, I had made it back to LA without screwing Jeremy, so that should count for something.

"That's a good girl, then. Keep him waiting."

I wasn't about to offer him any more details.

It was not unusual for Garrison to inquire about my romantic life. We were old confidantes. He had surprisingly conservative views when it came to relationships, which I'd discovered accidentally years ago while discussing a breakup I was in the process of. Garrison had been deeply disappointed to learn that I had cohabited with a boyfriend.

"Oh, Scarlett . . . not *you*. Don't tell me that *you* live with guys! Not you!

We can't have that!"

"Well . . . yes. I lived with *a* guy—but what about you, Garrison? I can name at least three actresses you lived with before you got married. That's a bit of a double standard."

"Yes, but that's me, dear. I have higher expectations for you. You're a good girl . . . different standards for you, dear."

Where on earth had he gotten this good-girl idea about me? With a divorce under my belt and past indiscretions, my good-girl status—if not entirely lost—was slipping, to say the least.

Garrison had one interview on Sunday that lasted for less than an hour and then I was free, and had been paid a handsome day rate, to boot. I was feeling so happy I could barely keep the smile off my face. By the afternoon, I was ready to slip back into 'Mommy mode,' as Jeremy called it.

CeCe had picked up Oliver from X for me and they were waiting at home when I finished work.

"Mama!" he said, hurtling his little body at me as soon as I walked in the door. I held him, smoothed the hair away from his face, and covered his cheeks with kisses.

"Hello, sweetheart. I'm so happy to see you!" I bounced him into the air. "Look, I have something for you." I set him down and pulled out the San Francisco snow globe souvenir I'd bought at the airport for him.

"Wow. That's cool, Mommy!" Oliver turned it over and watched the tiny glitter flakes fall and settle on the miniature Golden Gate Bridge. He started to shake it vigorously and ran off to show Sam and Mikki in the bedroom.

"How was X when you got there?" I asked CeCe as she was making her delicious breaded chicken cutlets.

"He was his usual ill-tempered self. Why?"

"He called a lot this weekend for no real reason. It felt weird . . . like he was checking up on me or something."

"It's a bit late for that. He doesn't get to control what you do anymore."

"Thank God."

"I'm making these for Oliver but I have to get ready. I have a date coming in forty-five minutes."

"Oh? Well, let me take over for you," I said, and started flipping the cutlets in the pan while CeCe retreated to the bedroom to prepare for her date. Oliver and I had Sunday night dinner with Mikki and Sam and then I gave him a bath and put him to bed. It was business as usual.

The next day, I splurged and bought two more pairs of SpongeBob pajamas.

Chapter Thirteen
Mating for Beginners

During the week, Susan called and asked if I was free for lunch. It was difficult to schedule time with her, as she was always busy with clients and meetings, so I jumped at the chance.

We met for lunch at La Scala in Beverly Hills. The restaurant was crowded with Beverly Hills socialites, sleek well-kept ladies who lunch, and entertainment executives, but Susan always got a table. Susan's status as a power player in the industry ensured that. All the maître d's in the best restaurants knew who she was. Stylish in her Phillip Lim dress, Susan turned heads as she passed but she was still just Susan to me.

She and I met while taking classes at UCLA. We were there for each other through the romantic trials of our twenties and I'd been there for her during her courtship and marriage. Steadfastly loyal to me during the tests of my own marriage and now through the divorce, we'd covered it all. Married for years with kids, and with a colorful past behind her, Susan usually offered a cool voice of reason to any passion-driven impulses I might entertain, but not this time.

"What do you mean you didn't have sex with him?" she asked over the famous chopped salad.

"We played around but we're waiting," I said, and buttered a piece of their delicious bread.

"What on earth for?"

"For things to develop. I want the whole experience, you know, that blissful state with a lover when your breathing is totally in sync and you feel completely connected. Not just another roll in the hay. There's nothing special about that. Anybody can have that."

Susan looked confused. "What the hell did you do all weekend, then?"

"We had a great time. We fooled around but we kept busy doing other activities. Did you know people water-ski in winter up there?

"In the San Francisco Bay?"

"No, there are all these waterways up there. Anyway, he and his friend are die-hard water-skiers, so they did a bit of that, and we went to a movie and went to restaurants. Plus, his movie just started, so there's a lot going on. We did everything but have sex."

"Just enjoy him. Don't spend too much energy overanalyzing everything. You just got rid of one husband—you don't need another. When will you see him again?"

"Next week, I hope."

"As a person just out of a sexless marriage, aren't you supposed to be swinging from chandeliers or something by now?"

"We'll get there. Trust me."

"All you should be doing at this point is having fun. That's what the kid-free time is for."

"No worries there. He's the poster boy for fun—it just revolves around him. He makes me laugh. He's so tender and affectionate. I don't want to surrender this lovely beginning too quickly."

My phone chirped and I shared the text with Susan.

"Listen to this: 'I'm on a boring conference call thinking about sleeping with you. Over and over. What an exhausting day. We've had sex so many times already. Can't wait to be with you again.' "

"Well at least he's practicing."

"I've been doing exactly the same thing. I can barely think of anything else and I walk around smiling like a loon."

The waiter swept in and placed a piece of tiramisu in front of me.

"Look, he just sent another one! 'I've had a hard-on all day. Can't stop thinking about you!' "

Susan smiled and shook her head. "Charming. By the way, whatever happened to regular phone sex? When did people decide to ditch it for sexting?"

"Oh, we have a bit of phone sex, too!"

"I'm married. We don't do much of any of that anymore."

Susan watched me inhale the tiramisu. "Anything has got to be an improvement on X. Remember when you were pregnant and X wouldn't even let you eat a fortune cookie? He thought they had too much sugar in them and you were polluting *his* child. Ugh, what a nightmare that guy was."

"Yes, I remember it like it was yesterday. He wouldn't even let me watch television, for God's sake!" I shuddered.

"Now, when you look back, isn't it hard to believe you were ever with him?"

"Yes, sometimes it is. But he wasn't as controlling when I first met him. It sort of crept in incrementally until it became suffocating."

"That's usually how it happens," said Susan.

"I know you never liked him."

"He had those eyes like Robert Chambers. Do you remember that guy?

The one who killed the girl in Central Park? They always creeped me out. I could never get past that."

I laughed. "Oh, no! You never told me that."

"What was I going to say? 'Hey, your new boyfriend kind of reminds me of that murderer'?"

"I see your point. But at least we're moving past that now. Someone else can have him."

"Good. By the way, I put in a good word for you with a publicist I ran into this weekend. I gave her your card. She said she'd keep you in mind for some work they have coming up."

"That's fantastic. Thank you. Work has been picking up. Lunch is on me." I grabbed the check and handed the waiter my credit card.

"I'm going to make a quick stop at Barney's before I go back to work. I need a shoe fix. Do you want to come?"

"I can't," I said. "I'm going to get Oliver soon."

Susan and I exchanged a hug.

"You look happy. It's nice to see that," she said.

"Thanks." I smiled.

We turned and headed in different directions.

I felt euphoric. Things were improving on all fronts. Jeremy texted again.

Can you get away next weekend? Come up and see me.

~Let me check but I think I can pull it off.

The next plan was that I would fly up to see him the following weekend. I was counting the days until we were together again and doing massive amounts of sit-ups and Kegel exercises.

A couple of days before I flew up he called.

"Listen, I've just received an invitation to the biggest party of the year. It's the crème de la crème of San Francisco society. I've always wanted to go. It's going to be a blast. Bring something black tie, okay?"

"Oh . . . black tie . . . um, okay," I said, and scrambled to think of what I had that could be considered black tie, other than my wedding dress.

I tried to share his enthusiasm about the party. All I had been able to think about for two weeks was another lazy weekend with my fabulous new man. I didn't feel like sharing him with San Francisco's elite.

"Oh, it'll be fine," Emma said. "It's sexy to be 'in the love bubble' and be out at a party but still be in your own little world, your own love cocoon. There will always be time for bed."

The immediate dilemma was wardrobe. Until recently, I'd been a breastfeeding housewife in the valley—not much call for black tie. Ever. Susan let me try on several of her dresses, but nothing fitted well. I hardly had a black-tie budget but I went hunting in the stores for a new dress and found a black halter dress, which was lovely but it only came down to the knee. I hoped it was dressy enough to make up for the lack of length, although I suspected it might not be. It was really a cocktail dress. With any luck, we would be too preoccupied in bed to be bothered going out to rub elbows with San Francisco's upper crust. Maybe I wouldn't need it.

Dominick, as if sensing I was in a new relationship, resumed his campaign of calls.

"Scarlett, you saucy tart! What are you doing? Come over."

"No. I'm in a relationship and I'm very happy, thank you."

"Who is he?"

"A guy I met. Nobody you know."

"What does he do?"

"He's a producer."

"How old is he?"

"He's a bit younger than me."

"*Younger?*" he asked incredulously.

"Only by a year. Or two."

That was enough information to rattle him.

"Catch you next time then," he said abruptly and hung up.

CeCe had heard about Puppetry of the Penis, a live-performance act contorting their private parts into various configurations, and wanted to know if I would go with her.

"You mean the one with the nude guys having a good wank on stage? I've heard of it."

"All the girls in the office are raving about it. We have to go. They are Australian, after all. It's our national duty to go inspect them—I mean support them." CeCe went online to book tickets for us. "Look—it's 'genitalia spectacular' and there's a show tomorrow night."

"If I want to see that I can watch Oliver in the bath. Isn't that pretty much what all boys do with their private parts?"

"Yes, and these clever bastards have figured out a way to get people to pay them for it."

"In that case, let's go."

The next night, CeCe and I had a necessary glass of wine beforehand and went to the theater for the penis show.

"I've brought my magnifying glasses, just in case." CeCe patted her purse.

"Good thinking. We might need them."

I wondered what kinds of people came to penis shows. Mostly single, I guessed. I could never have imagined being married and telling to X that I was going to go watch some naked guys fondling their penises. But then again, X was pretty busy with his own penis show, so maybe I didn't need to.

The two guys played to a completely full house. There was a drunken bachelorette party that kept heckling them, and lots of horny-housewife types. I wasn't sure what category CeCe and I fitted into. The men were funny and very good sports, which is probably not easy when you're naked and doing weird things to your penis in front of strangers.

It was impossible to keep a straight face as the fellows put their penises through their paces. We were treated to various configurations featuring animal impersonations and windmills and food items.

"The burger is the best one." CeCe clapped enthusiastically.

Jeremy called during the intermission.

"You'll never guess where I am," I told him. "I'm at a penis show! These guys are naked and doing strange origami things with their penises."

"I know all about it. I used to do that act in college and those bastards ripped me off! I do a fantastic cheeseburger. They stole my act."

He gave too many details to be joking.

"Somehow that doesn't surprise me. You are a man of many talents," I said and chuckled.

When we were back in our seats, I leaned over to CeCe and whispered, "Jeremy says they stole his act. He knows how to do all this stuff."

CeCe's eyes widened. "What sort of boy are we dealing with here?" She raised an eyebrow.

I didn't know but I was keen to find out.

Chapter Fourteen
Back in the Saddle

The hot sex countdown was on!

Giddy with anticipation, I caught the three-thirty flight up on Friday afternoon and dashed through the airport to our meeting spot, but this time there was no sign of Jeremy. I tried texting and calling him on his cell but it went straight to voice mail every time. I couldn't imagine what was keeping him. I kept checking my phone but there were no new messages.

An hour later, I was still cooling my heels at the curb, wondering what the hell was going on, when he pulled up.

He leapt out of the car. "Sweetheart, I'm so sorry! I lost my cell phone," he said, and planted a quick kiss on my now frozen lips. An hour waiting in the cold had done nothing for my disposition.

"Where did you lose it?"

"I'm not sure. Maybe I left it at the gym. Come on, let's go!" He tossed my suitcase into the back of his car. This time he had cleaned it out and there was somewhere to sit.

"Can I use your phone? I have to call and have my assistant get me a new one. I need to catch her before she leaves."

"Sure," I said, still a bit miffed.

"I just need to stop by the office for a moment and sign some papers. It's on the way."

He made calls on my cell all the way to the production office—a forty-five minute drive. It was not remotely the reunion I had been fantasizing about. I expected we'd be thrashing about the car and ripping our clothes off by now but he was totally preoccupied.

As if reading my mind, Jeremy swiftly pulled into a parking spot, shut off the engine and turned to me.

"You're finally here and I haven't been showing you the proper attention, but after I deal with this mini-disaster, I'm going to make it up to you."

He wrestled me out of my seat and onto his lap. He nestled his cheek against mine and held me. Close proximity to him somehow managed to both soothe and electrify me. My breathing followed his as his chest rose and fell.

"I'm *very* happy to see you, Scarlett," he said, stroking my thighs. Then he gave me slow sensuous kisses that tingled all the way through my body.

"I'm sorry if I've been a distracted asshole. It's just the worst possible time to lose my phone with production just about to start."

"That's okay as long as it's not your usual state."

"Was I distracted at the ranch?" he asked.

"Not at all. Where's that guy? I don't remember you being on the phone much at all."

"Full disclosure: I don't get cell reception there." He laughed.

"Oh, great. Thanks. Good to know." I smiled and shook my head.

"Hey, I am very happy to see you."

He lifted my head and silenced me with another long, languid kiss.

The frustration I felt earlier evaporated. Everything was all right again. We stopped briefly at his office to pick up some papers.

"Come with me," he said and reached for my hand.

We passed through glass doors and down a hall. It looked like almost everyone had left for the day. We walked through a bank of empty rooms and chatted briefly with an intern and a production assistant at the copy machine.

"This is my office," he said as we came to the end of the hallway. He whipped the door open. "Won't you come in?"

I stepped inside. It was a typical production office—all but stripped of personality, except for a nice large desk.

"This is the desk I sit at and think wicked thoughts of you all day," he said and patted the antique wooden desk.

"Aha. Nice." I ran my hands along the perimeter of it, not taking my eyes off him.

"And this is the chair that I sit in and get massive erections, thinking all those wicked thoughts." He put one hand on the back of the chair.

"Really? Massive erections?" I moved in close enough to inhale him.

"Yes. Massive."

"Sounds awfully impressive." I started to kiss his neck.

"Yes. See?" He took my hand and placed it on his crotch, and indeed he was rock hard.

"We might have to do something about that," I said.

He thrust me up against the wall behind his desk and pressed against me. His lips hungrily found mine while his hands explored my body.

I couldn't wait to have him inside me but I didn't want the first time to be in his office.

I leaned him back against his desk, unzipped his pants and put him in my mouth.

He inhaled deeply. "Oh, my . . ." He gripped my hair and moaned as I went to work and sucked on him until he came in fits that seized and convulsed his whole body.

He leaned his head back and fought to regain his breath.

"I can't speak," he muttered.

It didn't hurt that he would likely flash on that moment each time he was in his office.

Again, as if reading my thoughts, he said, "That's a nice little memory you just gave me. Now I'm really not going to be able to concentrate at work."

"I'm hungry." I realized that it had been hours since I'd eaten anything—other than him.

"Let's go. I know a great sushi place . . ." He grinned.

"Shut up."

He found the papers that had been our reason for the pit stop and we headed off in search of food that wasn't raw.

We settled on another Italian restaurant in town. Jeremy filled me in on various problems he was troubleshooting: a difficult actress, a shrinking budget, and location hassles. I usually loved to hear all about his work but I found it hard to focus on anything other than what I knew was going to happen once we got home. Our thighs kept touching during dinner, sending exquisite shivers through me. Jeremy made my legs tremble. It was a unique response from an experienced woman who was thirty-six and not a teenage girl experiencing a first crush. I couldn't easily explain his effect on me.

Despite how hungry I'd been, I found I wasn't able to finish my pasta. The anticipation of what the rest of the evening held was getting the better of me. Jeremy noticed and used the considerable pauses to lean over and kiss me.

"I can't wait to get you home," he said, with his voice filled with promise.

As much as I was dying to have him consume me physically, I was nervous, too. A good portion of the jitters stemmed from wondering if my body had bounced back after having had a child. Things could be radically different down there since I'd had Oliver—and how would I know? I'd squeezed a good-sized baby out of there almost three years ago and just had to hope that everything had swung back to where it was supposed to be—no low-hanging fruit, thank you very much. I'd had sex with Dominick but that didn't really count because he was always stoned when he had sex, so he wasn't a reliable judge of much of anything.

We drove back to Jeremy's house. He grabbed my suitcase and pulled me up the stairs to the front door.

"What's the hurry?" I laughed, knowing exactly what the rush was.

He'd had his appetizer and was ready for the main course.

Jeremy swung the door open, kicked it closed behind him and carried me up the stairs fireman-style. He threw me onto the bed—which I discovered was becoming his signature move. He then heartily launched himself on top of me, stifling my giggles. There was no time to have a bath or put on a sexy negligee or anything. It was all happening, right then. My skirt and sweater yielded to him and he threw them across the room. He paused for a second when he came to the fabulous Catwoman boots, giving them the respect and reverence that they commanded.

"Ooohh . . . maybe we should leave these on." He caressed the sleek black leather as he lifted one leg onto his shoulder and then the other.

He expertly eased my panties up and over them before deciding that the boots had to go. "I want you completely naked," he said as he kissed his way down my thigh and took them off.

His large hands canvassed my body, careful not to miss an inch.

I felt tiny and delicate in his charge. It felt magical to be touched, as if the heat we generated lit up every part of my body, healing it of past hurts and regrets. In that moment, nothing else mattered. He grabbed my ass, slid me down the bed, and pulled me into his face. He teased and probed me with his tongue. There was no escaping the intense pleasure and I had to surrender. My body eagerly accepted his attentions and wept its approval. He was right there, present and in tune with every signal my body gave him. It was beyond sexy. I tried to resist but quickly came for him. The anticipation had been so sweet that I was on the brink before his mouth met me. As soon as I stopped shuddering, I started laughing.

Jeremy propped himself up on one arm and looked very pleased with himself.

"Well, that wasn't much of a challenge," I said. "I'll have to make it harder for you next time."

"That's my job."

He leaned over to the bedside table drawer and extracted a condom.

"It's not usually that easy," I said, as if I needed to explain.

"Let's give you another one," he said and casually bit the corner of the wrapper.

"Oh, no . . . I can't have more than one."

"Sure you can." He rolled the condom over his cock.

"I mean, I never have had more than one before and sometimes not even one . . ."

He kissed me again. "Let's work on that." He smiled and hovered over me expectantly.

"Um . . . okay."

Jeremy held my hands over my head and started to kiss his way down to my breasts, taking them into his mouth and sucking on them as his attention moved south. He parted my legs with his knee and firmly shifted his way into position. I was already so wet for him that I couldn't bear it as he teased his way back and forth, and I moved my hips up to meet him.

"Do it now," I whispered.

He laced his fingers through mine and eased his way inside me, slowly and steadily at first, and then he began to plunge in with confidence. I gasped. It was completely consuming, the feeling of him filling me up, pressing into me. I wrapped my legs around his waist and arched into him. We melted back and forth into the bed together, our breathing totally in sync. It felt like we were floating. I thought about performing CeCe's Magic Prostate Trick while he was still inside me but I couldn't quite reach the bull's eye. One must need longer arms—or maybe longer fingers—to hit the right spot? And besides, maybe that was a little much straight out of the gate. Much to my surprise, I had another glorious orgasm that shuddered its way through my body in deliciously slow waves. I was completely spent.

He held me tightly against him the whole night and this time neither of us moved. With our similar skin coloring and freckles, we looked like pieces of the same map, wrapped closely together. In my mind, this was further evidence of our compatibility.

We slept well, and by morning I was basking in the afterglow of being thoroughly ravished by Jeremy. Like a cyclone, he had swept through my body, electrifying every cell in the process. I couldn't stop smiling but I still craved more of him.

We went into town for a feast of cheese omelets and chocolate croissants—and I ate every bite. After breakfast, we went to the market. Jeremy had a new round of houseguests arriving the next day, including another famous actress friend making a cameo in his movie, and he needed to stock up.

Even going to the market with Jeremy was fun. He grabbed my hand and said theatrically, "Walk down the aisle with me, my darling!" And then he twirled me down the aisle.

We went back to the house and spent the afternoon napping and making love. I was beginning to dread getting ready for the party. I wished we could skip it and stay home, light a fire and continue our fabulous sex marathon instead.

Jeremy had to finish some work, so I busied myself in the kitchen. I arranged the flowers in anything resembling a vase I could find and put the groceries away. Jeremy had one old photograph of his mother in a frame on the wall in the hallway. She looked to be in her thirties and bore a slight resemblance to me with long blond hair and similar coloring. She was looking away from the camera as if the intimate act of taking her photo made her uncomfortable.

It was time to get ready for the party.

I laid our clothes out on the bed and positioned my dress on top of his tux with our shoes in between each other on the floor. "Look—our clothes are making out on the bed!"

He looked over from his desk and smiled.

Jeremy was insanely gorgeous in his tux. I wanted to tear it off him and throw him back onto the bed. Gone was the disheveled snowboarder or old-jeans-with-holes-in-them look I had begun to associate with him. He'd been transformed into a dapper young society fellow. It was a look that he wore exceptionally well.

The party was the highlight of the San Francisco social calendar—if one cared about such things. The San Francisco socialites planned all year for this. Studying my dress next to his tux, I decided it definitely wasn't black tie. I must have been out of my mind to think it would do, but there wasn't anything I could do about it now. I felt exceedingly dull in my dress next to him. Now, sadly lacking in the jewelry department, there weren't even any diamonds to call upon to jazz up the dress. Any jewelry I had once owned was long gone. My two-hearts necklace was the beginning and end of my jewelry collection.

San Francisco was enchanting at night. We crossed the bridge into the city, made a turn and the houses became very grand indeed. Having never spent time in San Francisco before, I was awestruck at the imperial-looking homes. I was thrilled to have my sexy new man squiring me around town.

"Wow, these houses are really something," I said, marveling at the majestic old mansions.

"Maybe you could marry some rich old guy and you and Oliver could live in one of them." Jeremy said out of left field.

"I don't think so . . ." I was stung by the bluntness of his comment. Why on earth was he trying to marry me off to 'some rich old guy'?

The cars were backed up for a block when we arrived at the party. The home was a grandiose white Pacific Heights mansion, and looked like something out of a movie with tall white pillars and artfully manicured green hedges. I felt a wave of panic as we left the car with the valet. The guests were very, *very* black tie—as I'd feared—with stately looking, bejeweled women handing over their furs to uniformed maids who struggled to keep up with the furious pace. We made our way down the line to greet the host, an older man, portly in stature. He stared at us with pointed distaste.

"Scarlett Spencer and Jeremy Plume. Nice to meet you." Jeremy extended his hand, which the old man shook reluctantly.

The host regarded us with the disdain of someone encountering a wretchedly foul smell. It was such an overtone of disgust that it went well beyond anything we could have possibly merited in the brief encounter. He might as well have shouted, "Out, fucking peasants!"

The evening was not getting off to a good start.

I wished the floor would open up and swallow us.

We stood there, momentarily stunned as the full weight of the affront sank in, then Jeremy snapped into action and directed us past the nasty old bastard. Jeremy looked aghast.

"What a nasty old fuck," I muttered.

It was completely humiliating and neither of us mentioned another word about it.

Maybe when you were as rich as he apparently was, you didn't feel the social burden of feigning politeness, even if it was your own party. I cursed my too-short dress. It must have tipped him off to my peasant status.

"Let's hit the bar," Jeremy said gaily in a valiant attempt to save the rest of the evening.

We clutched our vodka tonics for dear life and Jeremy excused himself to go to the caviar bar for the first of four trips. I tried to focus on the beautiful surroundings and drink in the opulence, the very high ceilings, and the classic artwork on the walls everywhere you looked. It was a private museum; I couldn't believe that anyone actually *lived* there. I turned my attention to the paintings on the walls, many of them depicting old battleships fighting rough seas. I couldn't escape the irony.

"Would you look at those flowers," I said when he returned. "They are insanely beautiful."

"Oh . . . uh, yeah. They're nice," he said, oblivious to how truly spectacular they were.

Decadent flowers—jasmine, lilacs, roses and hyacinths—sat in lavish arrangements several feet high in all corners of the room, filling it with an intoxicatingly sweet aroma. The flower budget alone looked staggering. It was the height of excess. CeCe would have loved it. The flowers alone should have been enough to cheer me, but for some reason I couldn't help wishing I was home cuddling with Oliver watching *SpongeBob*. I looked around at the guests, a sampling of the richest and most glamorous people in San Francisco. What the hell was I doing here? I didn't have the wardrobe for this and had no business rubbing elbows with this lot. And my darling new man seemed currently less than enchanted with me. With nothing else to console me, I sought solace in a second vodka tonic.

Jeremy returned from calming his anxiety with ample servings of caviar and said, "We have to find Frank. He's the one who got us invited to this thing and there's another really happening party he wants us to go to." Jeremy scanned the crowd for the elusive Frank.

Another party? Shit. I would need an ungodly amount of vodka to get me through another of these soirees. I was in no mood for this level of punishment. It was so crowded that we had to inch our way through the endless string of rooms in search of Frank. We were greeted by heaving, heavily perfumed, diamond décolletage at every turn and old men who smelled loudly of gin who pressed against me lasciviously as we made our way through the sea of guests. This was not my idea of a good time. Couldn't we just go home and fuck?

The vodka was thankfully starting to work its magic in my head. The room seemed to swirl a little, which seemed appropriate given the circumstances. Nothing made sense to me. Jeremy refused to hold my hand, which was unlike him—Jeremy *always* held my hand. What was going on?

He ran into a few people he knew and introduced me to a banker and his gorgeous conservationist wife who, unlike me, was dressed appropriately in a floor-length caramel sequined gown. It was so loud that I had difficulty following the conversation. Eventually, they stopped trying to include me.

We finally spotted Frank in one of the three buffet rooms. We worked our way around the people feasting on Kobe beef and lobster. Frank turned out to be delightful. He was a popular interior designer and a hell of a lot nicer than the stuffy wanker types we were drowning in.

"Scarlett, you have to meet my new boyfriend," Frank whispered conspiratorially, and passed me a plate. "He'll be joining us later. He's simply divine." He squeezed my elbow for emphasis.

"I'd love to meet him," I said and heaped lobster salad onto my plate.

Frank evidently knew all the right people in the Bay area. He gossiped to me about all the parties he and Jeremy had been busy attending lately. The plum racy tidbits were lost on me since I was not familiar with all the society movers and shakers whose secrets he was gleefully imparting, but I did my best to look riveted.

Jeremy and Frank were still in the buffet line so I found a table that was empty except for an elegant older lady. She looked beautiful, resplendent in a shade of lavender organza that complimented the lilac hue of her hair. She looked in need of a friendly face, too. I asked if I could join her.

"Yes, you can sit here . . . but I'm saving *this* seat for my husband," she informed me and felt the need to repeat herself three times.

"That's okay," I reassured her. "We'll make sure to save that one for him."

"Do you come to this party every year?" she asked.

"No, it's my first and last time I'm afraid. I don't live in San Francisco." I smiled at her but I wouldn't be coming back again if you paid me—and gave me a proper dress.

"My husband used to be his private pilot," she said, referring to the nasty host. "He's retired now but we still come every year."

"Good for you."

As we talked, I redid her makeup in my head—as I always do with someone whose makeup is completely wrong. I toned everything down—less liner, finer brows, lighter lipstick—and added more blush.

"I'm Darlene."

"I'm Scarlett. Nice to meet you."

We started to chat about the extravaganza we were at. I was happy to sit with her and have my meal.

Jeremy came over, stacked buffet plate in hand, and sat next to me. I introduced him to my new best friend and life preserver.

"I've been talking to your lovely wife," Darlene said and smiled warmly at Jeremy.

Jeremy bolted upright at the mention of the word *wife*. It was as if he'd had a close encounter with a cattle prod.

"Oh, we're not married," I jumped in to correct her. God forbid he thought I was telling strangers we were married. "Technically, I'm still someone else's lovely wife—but I'm divorcing that guy!" I raised my glass in a toast, feeling the effects of the vodka.

Darlene toasted back but looked a bit bewildered by my comment.

With our marital status clarified, Jeremy refocused on devouring his plate of delicacies. The boy had been working up an appetite. The vodka swept in to save me. For a glorious fleeting moment, I didn't care about anything.

Frank joined us at the table. Jeremy chatted with him about the various events they had been attending lately. It sounded like a lot of society benefits and openings but the names were lost on me.

Bored with the conversation, I excused myself to go to the ladies' room, and when I returned there was no sign of Jeremy or Frank. I checked the caviar bar and the buffet rooms again before wandering around the huge house, dodging the lecherous old men, who were at least preferable to the mean ones. The handsome young mayor and his wife were holding court in one room. For a moment I stopped and watched the patrons flitter about the power couple but there was still no sign of Jeremy. Darlene hadn't seen him back at the table either.

Half an hour later Jeremy finally reappeared. I spotted him chatting with a glamorous woman whose shimmering azure dress gloved her body in a way that screamed femme fatale. They made a striking pair. Jeremy was leaning in, listening intently to her, nodding and laughing. They looked so intimate that I had to fight the urge to turn and run the other way. Instead, I took a deep breath and steeled myself in their direction.

As I approached, Jeremy looked up and casually extended his hand to me. He then let his hand drop proprietarily onto my hip—his first friendly gesture of the evening—and introduced us. She was obviously well acquainted with the benefits of a professional blow-dry and makeup application. Her name was Carolyn and we chatted for a few minutes, ignoring Jeremy completely. It turned out that we were both navigating the choppy waters of divorce—except she was in a multimillion-dollar yacht—and I was struggling in a leaky dinghy. I could feel Jeremy staring at me as I talked with her, trying to assess my state. In one of my finest acting moments, I was the very picture of calm assurance and betrayed not a trace of the turmoil that had been churning within.

After Carolyn left, Jeremy said, "I was outside smoking with Frank when it occurred to me that you might be looking for me."

It wasn't exactly the desired response from a man I'd spent the entire weekend making love to, but I brushed it off. And when did he start smoking again?

"That's okay. I've been busy scouting for rich old San Francisco men," I said and winked. Screw him. "I may have found a couple of candidates."

"Okay, I deserved that. Let's get out of here," he said with a laugh. "Let's get your coat."

We got in Jeremy's car and followed Frank over to the other party, which was close by.

"That's an outrageous house. Who do you think lives there?" I asked, overwhelmed by a huge house on the left.

"I don't know but we'll find out because that's where we're going." Jeremy pulled in behind Frank's car at the valet outside.

Taking another deep breath, I got out of the car and prayed they would be a much nicer lot at this party.

Once inside the wrought iron gates, it was instantly apparent that this was a younger, hipper party. Thank God. At least I wouldn't be glaringly underdressed in this crowd. We walked into a huge foyer done completely in black and white to great effect, with a huge chandelier hanging in the center of the room and candles and gardenias on every surface. I watched Jeremy greeting the society hipsters with kisses on both cheeks. They swarmed around him, not bothering to notice he had brought a date. It was painfully apparent that Jeremy had also forgotten he'd brought a date.

Witnessing Jeremy in action was something to behold. He was the center of gravity in any room. It was a social gift. He possessed a keen ability to charm women and they flocked to his side. Everyone was positively taken with him, except perhaps a certain flirty young woman's husband, who kept his distance and didn't seem to share everyone's enthusiasm. Feeling uncomfortable despite the effects of the vodka, I went to find the ladies' room and left him to his coterie.

The bathroom was lit by candlelight and so dark that I didn't notice how much blush I had applied. When I returned, Jeremy looked askance at me.

"What happened to your face? Why is it all red?"

I decided to lie. "I must be having an allergic reaction to something."

He handed me a glass of champagne and I followed him into one of the drawing rooms, trying discreetly to smear the blush off my cheeks. We found a chartreuse velvet antique couch to sit on, and watched the young aristocrats mingling.

"Wow, look at *that* dress," said Jeremy gesturing to a fetchingly beautiful dark-haired girl in a peach silk dress with a mink stole draped provocatively around her. "Now, that's an outfit!" he said, admiringly. "She looks really put together."

"Yes, she does indeed," I said, nodding in agreement, knowing that her level of fabulousness usually required a trust fund and a team of experts to pull off.

The evening seemed interminably long. I had to leave in the morning and begrudged wasting valuable shagging time critiquing the dresses of the myriad of young vixens.

The flirty, young, married woman came back again and perched herself precariously on the arm of the sofa, which was as close as she could get to actually sitting on Jeremy's lap. Her perfectly coifed blond mane barely moved as she laughed and threw her head back. She kept playing with Jeremy's hand, lifting it and dropping it into hers over and over. I couldn't help but notice the huge canary diamond she was wearing. Even for this crowd it was spectacularly big. Her husband drained his scotch and watched closely from the chair opposite us. He looked like he was enduring the same sort of painful evening I was.

Frank lured Jeremy away to introduce him to a local architect and I decided to explore the house on my own. There was only so much punishment I could take. I found a couch in an empty drawing room and sank into it. A stocky, disheveled-looking fellow wearing a brown blazer with a crest on the breast pocket came and sat down next to me. He fixed me with a brazen, unnerving gaze that was completely inappropriate for a total stranger. I had been briefly introduced to him when we came in. I struggled to remember his name and couldn't, but he remembered mine. Creepy Guy began to barrage me with questions.

"Is Jeremy your husband? . . . how long have you been with him? . . . are you happy with the relationship?"

I wanted to say that that depends on which Jeremy shows up—the lovely one or the aloof and distant one.

"Do you live together? . . . can I see you again?" he said with increasing urgently.

Would I consider dating him instead? Creepy Guy kept asking if he had a chance to see me again. Part irritated and part relieved to have someone to talk to, I fielded his questions with detached amusement. From his behavior, he was obviously more than a little inebriated.

"I'm feeling a bit out of it," he said finally. "I ran over a homeless person in the Range Rover on the way over. It startled me a bit, but I'm okay now." He took another sip of his cognac.

He didn't look like he was kidding.

"Did you stop to help?" I asked him.

"Good God, no!" he said with a disquieting grin. "This is San Francisco. What's one less homeless person?"

"There you are, darling!" Frank bounded into the room with perfect timing and intervened. He sat on the other side of me and squeezed my hand, while keeping an eye over my shoulder on Creepy Guy.

"I've been looking for you. I have to leave. I'm going to go track down my errant boy friend he's at another party."

"I'm sorry I didn't get to meet him," I said.

"Next time. I'm glad I got to meet you—you are a lovely thing! Our boy Jeremy is very lucky!" Frank enthused while shooting dirty glances at Creepy Guy.

If he was aiming to dispatch Creepy Guy, it wasn't working. Creepy Guy was in an altered state that rendered him impervious to minor affronts like dirty looks. Frank left, and less than a minute later Jeremy appeared. He came over and kissed me like he meant it for the first time all night.

Creepy Guy grunted and turned his attentions to a woman who had the misfortune to just sit down on the other side of him.

"Frank told me I better get in here *fast*—that you were about to be stolen away from me. That guy is really bad news," he whispered.

"I rather got that impression. He just told me he ran over a homeless man. Do you think he's joking?" I whispered back as he threw an arm protectively around me and ushered me out.

"I don't know but let's go home."

Those were the words I had been dying to hear all night.

We began the drive back to Jeremy's house and started to rehash the evening's events, my encounter with Creepy Guy and his episode with the flirty woman whose husband kept a watchful eye on her.

"Mmm, she's nice and certainly beautiful, but I wonder how smart she really is," he said, as we passed over the Golden Gate Bridge.

"Who cares how smart she is?" I asked. The woman had married into one of the wealthiest families in America. Most people would say she's fucking brilliant. "I don't think we need to worry about her. She seems to be doing just fine."

"Yeah . . . I guess so."

The frost between us began to thaw. He pulled me over and kissed me at the stoplight.

"Why is it that you don't fully open your mouth when you kiss me?" I asked him. "It feels like you're holding back."

"What? What are you talking about? It's not me—it's *you*!" he said, as if it was the funniest thing he'd ever heard.

"Rubbish. You're holding back!"

"Get over here right now and I'll show you who's holding back!"

He reached over and pulled me into him, keeping one eye on the road while furiously thrashing his tongue around in my mouth. We both burst out laughing.

"See, it is you! Damn it, woman, give me your tongue," he demanded dramatically.

I had no choice but to comply.

We kissed all the way back to his house, punctuated by fits of laughter. He turned the stereo up and sang an old K.C. and the Sunshine Band song loudly, "Please don't go . . . don't go. Don't go away . . ." After a chilly evening, the Jeremy I was crazy about was back.

"Okay, I am seriously starting to think you must be bipolar or something. I can't keep up with you."

He shook his head and laughed at the suggestion.

I couldn't figure him out. Maybe he felt overwhelmed by all the togetherness. If that was the issue, I could understand. Sometimes I felt a bit that way, too.

We got into bed and he pulled me in against him. His chest and arms offered a generous smattering of freckles, tiny little constellations I traced with my fingernail, connecting the dots. His chest had just the finest covering of hair in the center.

"I'll be back in LA soon and it will be different. We'll have more time."

He turned my face to him and kissed me.

Amorous Jeremy had returned. Maybe it was the strain of those wretched parties that had put him in a funk. He kissed me with increasing urgency, slipped one hand down between my legs, and parted them. They offered no resistance. When we were in bed, he was present, tender and loving. We made love with the growing confidence of two people learning the maps to each other's bodies, and then fell asleep entwined in each other's arms.

The alarm went off at five thirty in the morning.

"Ugh. This feels absurdly early." I pulled a pillow over my head.

"Not if you want to make your flight. And I have to be on set soon, anyway."

"Tell me again why you have to shoot on Sundays? That producer of yours must be no fun at all."

"Yeah, he's a real asshole. But I'll make sure he makes it up to you."

He rolled over and kissed me, while letting his hands skim my body, fully igniting that tingle in my stomach. His hand found its way down between my legs and he stroked me.

He had skillfully managed to slip on a condom without me noticing—not that difficult to achieve when my head was still buried in the pillow. He squeezed my ass and lifted me onto him and slipped himself inside me one last time before we had to leave.

He laced his fingers through mine. "I'm not sure you should be going anywhere," he said as we began to move together.

"I'm not sure I want to be going."

We didn't have time to luxuriate in a blossoming connection. There was a flight to catch and a movie to be made. He rocked his hips back and forth with mine until he couldn't contain it anymore.

With no time to waste, I hurriedly threw my things back into the suitcase and we hit the road.

"What are you doing for Christmas?" he asked as we drove to the airport.

I wasn't sure if it was a question or an invitation. "We'll be home. What about you?"

"I go to Aspen every year with my family." His voice sounded heavy with obligation. "It's kind of a chore to get through but at least I can snowboard and ski."

"Yes, it doesn't sound all bad." I laughed. Jeremy could make a vacation in Aspen sound dreary.

Jeremy leapt out and wrestled my suitcase from the backseat. He leaned back against the car and wrapped his hands around my waist. "Thank you for coming to see me," he said, and pressed me tightly into him. He lifted my face and gave me a lingering kiss.

"See you soon."

And then in a flash he was gone.

I hurried through the airport, stopping briefly for a chocolate bar from the newsstand and caught my flight home.

By Sunday afternoon, it was back to mommy business as usual. Oliver and I read stories and fixed dinner together while CeCe watched *60 Minutes*.

CeCe came into the kitchen to refill her wine when the strange little cat noises started coming from Sam's room again.

Oliver perked up at them instantly and turned toward Sam's bedroom.

"Oh . . . who *lives* in a pineapple under the sea . . . SpongeBob SquarePants!" I sang loudly while stirring the pasta.

"Yellow and hairy and *horny* is he!" added CeCe with gusto.

"CeCe! Don't sing that. That's the wrong words!" said Oliver indignantly.

"Oh, they're the right words for some people, darling!" She gave his hair a ruffle as she walked past.

The next day, a magnificent floral arrangement arrived. With lilacs, roses and hyacinths spilling out of it, it was a smaller yet impressive replica of the giant floral masterpieces that I had admired at the wretched party. He had been paying attention after all.

The card simply said, 'Miss you. J.'

Once again, he was full of surprises.

It was completely unexpected. Oliver joined me in a victory jig around the living room.

I called Jeremy at the office and his assistant said he was in a meeting, so I texted him instead.

~Thank you for the outrageous flowers. They're breathtaking . . . xoxo

In a meeting. Can't stop thinking about what u did to me on this desk. Haven't heard a single word anyone has said. Can't wait to b inside u again.

~I can't wait either. What have you done to me?

Not half as much as I'm gonna do.

I gasped when I read it. The man had the power to snatch the breath right out of my body. I felt my entire body flush and I couldn't keep the smile off my face.

Chapter Fifteen
Henry the Eighth

It was a week away from Christmas and CeCe, Oliver and I and had been on a decorating frenzy. Making Christmas special for Oliver had given me a new enthusiasm for the holidays that hadn't existed before. Oliver loved all the Christmas traditions. From the selection of the tree, to when I dragged the damn thing up in the elevator on my own, to the proper placement of ornaments, he was thrilled with all of it.

The apartment looked pleasingly festive and happy with red and green candles, poinsettias, and CeCe's famous collection of little Santa miniatures that she named after ex-lovers. They sat jovially all around the place, and Oliver thought they were the best things ever.

"This one's name is Leonard, darling," CeCe said and handed another jolly-looking one to Oliver. "Let's find a spot for him. That old boy liked a bit of mischief and a bit of a smoke, too, so let's put him by the fireplace. He'll be at home there."

It definitely looked like whoever made Leonard had been smoking something. Leonard had a wicked, lopsided grin and was missing a boot.

"Okay, CeCe." Oliver dutifully placed Leonard on the mantelpiece next to 'Chip' and 'Wally'.

CeCe played Eartha Kitt's "Santa Baby" on an almost constant loop. It was a sharp contrast to last Christmas when court appearances and the aftermath of the separation threatened to derail me.

Our own Christmas rituals consisted of a family dinner, and that was about the extent of it. There wasn't a budget for extravagant vacations. No skiing or snowboarding adventures in the cards for us, at least not this year, but I wasn't opposed to the concept.

Not one to be easily dissuaded, Dominick called frequently to see if I had tired of my young suitor yet. When he called, I often sent him straight to voice mail where he would leave his characteristically improper messages.

"What are you doing, you horny tart? When are you going to dump that boy and come get a pounding?"

Once, I had made the mistake of checking my messages while in the car with Jeremy. Dominick's voice came blasting out of my cell phone. "Call me back, you naughty slut."

I shoved the phone back into my purse and held my breath. Jeremy stiffened at the wheel but said nothing. My relationship with Dominick was a little hard to explain.

Not returning Dominick's calls made him more persistent. He caught me in the bath a few days before Christmas and did his best to fan the flames of doubt about Jeremy's level of interest.

"Have you had your finger up anyone's arse lately, nurse?" Dominick said in his mock Australian accent.

"No. It's been a slow week. Have you?"

"Every chance I get. So have you broken up with that joker yet? Are you ready for a real man?"

"Why? Do you know one you want to fix me up with?"

"Ha, ha. Very funny. What are you doing for the holidays?"

"Oliver and I will be here."

"Oh, really? You'll be *here*? Lover boy didn't invite you to spend Christmas with him? Hmm . . . *that's* interesting."

"No, he didn't," I said, doing my best to sound casual. "But it doesn't matter because I'm with Oliver and it's too soon to bring him along, even if he did ask me. This is what his family does every Christmas. We just met, and that's too much pressure."

"I still think it's strange that he wouldn't want to be with you. Why don't you put on your Christmas stockings, get your arse over here, and I'll give you a good holiday spanking!"

"I think I'll pass."

"Well, what's your mother up to? Send her over. Now, there's a real woman."

Oliver and I were finding plenty of things to do to get in the Christmas spirit. In the evenings, he and I would often drive around touring the lavish homes along Sunset Boulevard decked out with extravagant Christmas light displays. During the day, we found things to do to get in the holiday spirit. We visited The Grove shopping mall for pictures with Santa, went to a holiday party at Susan's, watched the tree-lighting ceremony at Rodeo Drive—complete with fake snow—and anything else I could think of to keep busy.

My mind was occupied, but my body was hooked on Jeremy. Like an addict, I was getting shaky and needed another fix. Sex with him made me feel drunk. It was a potent, much needed elixir. My body felt like it was vibrating at a higher frequency when we were lying naked together. On full alert, every part of me was keenly attuned to him. His breathing, the way he smelled, the way he tasted, the way his skin felt beneath my fingertips. When I closed my eyes, I could almost feel his hands on me. The heavy hit of love chemicals was making my head spin. I could only hope that it worked both ways.

Jeremy sent me a text saying how much he was dreading leaving for Aspen. He caught me on the way to yoga and in a flippant mood. I was getting frustrated. We had not made plans to get together again.

~Sounds very dull. Have fun with the boring Aspen fucks!

You're right! They ARE boring. Wish I had a week alone at home with you.

~Me, too.

Can you come up and meet me on New Year's Eve?

~YES!

Call you later and we'll figure it out. Xxx—J.

Hurray! We had a plan.

—m—

On Christmas morning, Oliver woke up and feasted on the gifts under the tree that awaited his approval. Santa left him a little red tricycle—CeCe and Sam had stayed up half the night assembling it because I was useless— books, clothes, and a generous stack of SpongeBob pajamas, assorted toys, and SpongeBob paraphernalia.

The most exciting and unexpected gift came from Sam and Mikki, who presented Oliver with a little brown bunny, whom he christened Henry the Eighth after his favorite song.

Oliver squealed with delight and chased him around the house. This new pet had been an impulse buy and had not been cleared in advance with CeCe, who eyed it disapprovingly as it hopped around the living room leaving a trail of fresh droppings behind it. The tiny turds looked exactly like the beloved capers CeCe sprinkled liberally on her smoked salmon plates—an observation not lost on her.

"I'll never be able to eat a caper again," she said wistfully as I followed him scooping up the droppings in a paper towel.

Oliver played contently all day with the bunny. While I was distracted and chatting to Emma on the phone—which was always a prime opportunity for chaos—Oliver put the bunny on one of Sam's skateboards and was preparing to send him on the ride of his life down the corridor when I rescued him.

"Ollie, now, we have to be very gentle with him. This is not his idea of fun. Bunnies don't ride skateboards."

"This one's a racing bunny!"

"Okay, but he likes to be in control of how fast he goes. Let's not scare him."

I was more concerned about CeCe impaling him on one of her stilettoes —by accident, of course.

Aside from the occasional bunny drama, it was a mellow day. CeCe was busy in the kitchen preparing her traditional Christmas dinner of lamb and roasted potatoes with pavlova for dessert. I wondered how Jeremy was faring with the 'boring Aspen fucks.'

CeCe had invited one of her Internet dates to join us for Christmas dinner —a lanky fellow named Gerald. Gerald was not a spy. He was a Jewish accountant. The spy was unavailable somewhere on a secret mission, so Gerald became the beneficiary of his invitation. It was their second date, and since he had never been to a Christmas dinner, CeCe thought it might be fun for him to endure one with our family. He made little attempt to converse with the rest of us and looked distinctly uncomfortable with his predicament. The poor chap tried to cling to CeCe as she moved about the kitchen, like a child grasping at his mother's apron strings. It was an unsettling sight.

Even more unsettling was not hearing a word from Jeremy. This was a first. Perhaps he was busy on the slopes all day and that was why he hadn't called.

I started Oliver's bedtime rituals of bath and stories but by ten thirty that night, there was still no word from Jeremy.

CeCe and I sat in front of the fireplace after Gerald had left.

"Haven't heard a peep from Jeremy all day," I said gloomily. "Not even a text. Don't you think that's weird? It's Christmas and he calls me every day. If he's going to skip a day, this is sort of a significant one, don't you think?"

"Maybe he doesn't like Christmas."

"You might be right. What was the deal with that guy tonight?"

"Oh, he's nice enough, but I probably won't be seeing him again. He's not 'the One'. He's separated but still living in the same house as his wife."

"He's still in the same house? Oh, no, CeCe. Forget him. I didn't see you two as a match, anyway. Aside from that large obstacle, he seemed a bit needy for you. That would get old very quickly. Besides, all of that living-in-the-same-house nonsense should be an immediate deal-breaker. In the New Year, no straggling wives or girlfriends, or they do not pass go. All candidates must have a clean slate and be available, and that goes for me, too," I said. *Why did I always feel like her mother?*

"Yes. I need a man with a bit more oomph, anyway!" she said with renewed enthusiasm. "The New Year will bring a more promising crop. If I want a big fish, I have to go where the big fish are, and if I want a tiger, I'll have to go where the tigers are."

"Okay, then. Here's to surf and turf, CeCe."

"Cheers." She raised her wineglass and we toasted to hunting and fishing in the New Year.

—⁂—

In the morning, I checked my phone and there was still no word from Jeremy.

Images of him in bed with sexy Aspen snow bunnies flitted across my mind.

"Come on Ollie," I said. "Let's get out of here. Let's go to a movie."

We went to an animated Disney movie at The Grove. We got popcorn, soda, and candy, and enjoyed the show.

By the time the movie was over, Jeremy had surfaced and left a message on my cell phone.

I was thinking about calling him back when he called again.

"Ahh . . . there you are, darling! I've been trying to find you."

He sounded very chipper for a man who had been missing in action for two days.

"And here I am," I said. "How are you?"

"I'm good but I'm *exhausted!* How was your Christmas?"

"It was great, thanks. How was yours?"

"Hectic. I was on the slopes all day and I was going to call you but my cell phone ran out of juice. Then I went to dinner with the family and we ran into some old friends of mine who come here every year, too. A whole group of us went out until about four in the morning . . . so I've just gotten up and the day's almost over!"

"Sounds fun." I tried to sound cheery but I was still pissed.

"Not as fun as being with you. Can't wait to see you on Friday."

"Me, too."

"How's Oliver? Was Santa good to him?"

"Yes, Santa outdid himself this year. Oliver now has a pet bunny."

"A real bunny?"

"Yes, I'm afraid so—which I needed like a hole in the head."

"And who was responsible for this gift?"

"My brother."

Jeremy found this wildly amusing.

"I'm glad you think it's so funny. I'm not sure CeCe's as excited about it. He has been leaving a trail of turds everywhere."

"I can imagine. I can't even deal with a dog."

"You can't have a pet. You travel too much," I said, and then thought about the ramifications of that statement.

"That's true. Listen, sweetheart, I have to run. I'm going to go hit the slopes for some afternoon runs before dinner. Talk to you soon."

"Have fun," I said, even though the guy ran on 'fun' and didn't need my encouragement.

Boring Aspen fucks. But then, Jeremy brought the party with him wherever he went—Jeremy *was* the party. At least our plans were still intact for New Year's.

Chapter Sixteen
A Crash Course in Mating

New Year's Eve arrived. Everything was in place for our reunion that night. X had picked up Oliver, I'd waxed everything that needed waxing, and was counting the minutes until I hopped on that plane to meet him.

I was at the Burbank airport, ready to check in for my flight to San Francisco, when he called.

"Sweetheart, I have bad news. My connecting flight from Colorado is overbooked. There's no hope of getting on."

My heart almost stopped. "What are you saying?"

"I guess I'm stuck here for the night . . . or I could fly back to Aspen and try to fly out again tomorrow . . ."

"Fly back to Aspen? That's a terrible idea."

"You could fly up and stay in the house by yourself and I'll fly home tomorrow."

"That's even worse."

"Well, I'm up for anything but I don't know of any other options. Do you?"

"Maybe there's something I can do from here," I said, doing a quick scan of the long bank of ticket agents. "I'll call you back."

This was a disaster but I was not about to have my romantic New Year's Eve snatched out from under me. I needed to quickly find an airline agent who could work some magic. Powered by sheer determination, I canvassed the airport until I found an available ticket agent at the United counter and threw myself at her mercy.

"Could you please, *please* help me? It's New Year's Eve and my wonderful new man is stuck in Colorado. I have been so looking forward to this reunion and if we don't meet up tonight, I could potentially die from the grief! I've been in divorce hell for the last year, and this man is the most fun that's happened to me in *ages*. So could you please, *please* help us?"

She remained visibly unmoved by my desperate pleas but said, "I'll see what I can do."

Thirty minutes of phone calls followed between the agent and various gate agents in Colorado, with me giving Jeremy the updates.

Finally, she announced, "The flight to San Francisco is a lost cause. There's no way he's getting that one . . . but I *could* possibly get him on a flight to Ontario, California, which is only about an hour from LA. That way you lovebirds could be together for New Year's."

"Oh, thank you so much!" I said and attempted to hug her over the counter. There was the tiniest hint of a smile in the corner of her mouth as she said, "Happy New Year."

I quickly relayed the information to Jeremy and made a mental note to send her a basket of chocolate chip cookies.

After some skillful negotiating between the various ticket agents, it was all worked out. It would require a last-minute sprint to the gate, hampered by his injured knee—a casualty of his wild abandon on the slopes—but if he hurried he could make the flight to Ontario. His luggage, unfortunately, would have to continue on to San Francisco without him.

Maybe it wasn't perfect but it was a hell of a lot better than being apart for New Year's.

I threw the suitcase back into the trunk of my car and drove to the Ontario airport to claim him.

After what felt like an interminable wait, there he was riding down the escalator toward me. My very own disheveled dirty-blond snowboarder.

"Hello, sweetheart," he said, and pulled me in for a hug.

"Listen, what do you think about spending the weekend in Palm Springs? LA is too depressing on New Year's. We could get a reservation at The Parker hotel—I already checked. What do you say?"

Yet another swift turn. This was how quickly things changed in his world.

"Sounds great." I didn't care where we were as long as we were together.

"Let's get out of here!" he said and grabbed my hand.

Once inside the car, he gave me a good and thorough kissing that was worth the wait.

We drove out the freeway and headed toward Palm Springs. My attention drifted over to him, needing to look at his hands and check what he was doing with them, or admiring how handsome he looked in profile while laughing, or noticing how well he managed to fold his long body into my cramped car without complaining, even with a sore knee. It was a constant challenge to redirect the energy that magnetically headed in his direction.

He started pecking at his BlackBerry, checking the hotel address for us.

"My charger was in my suitcase that went to San Francisco, so my phone is going to die soon."

"You can use my phone if you need to." A missing charger? I couldn't have planned that better if I'd tried.

"I did not see how that was all going to work out for us tonight. That was wild."

"Yeah, I had to use a lot of magic on that trick," I said and laughed.

"Magic? What magic do *you* have?" He stopped typing on his BlackBerry and turned toward me to await my answer. I had his full attention.

"Well, if I have to explain it, then clearly it's lost on you."

He laughed. "I see your point."

"Haven't you noticed? I have *vast* amounts of feminine magic!" I teased him. "How else do you think you managed to get back on a totally booked New Year's Eve flight from Colorado?"

His face clouded over and he was very quiet for a moment as he considered what I'd said. It was hard to deny that luck had been with us. It was New Year's Eve and in spite of bad weather in Colorado, overbooked flights and a knee injury—here we were.

"Have you put a spell on me?" he asked earnestly. He seemed bewildered by the concept but nervous enough to be slightly open to it.

"I don't know. You tell me. Is it working?"

He looked unnerved but said nothing.

Jeremy shifted uncomfortably in his seat, considering the evidence I'd presented. He scratched his head.

I couldn't resist taking it a bit further.

"And how do you explain that neat little trick when we e-mail, text or call each other at *precisely* the same second? How do you explain that? And we do it a lot."

Jeremy said nothing but was starting to look a little piqued, so I decided to stop tormenting him.

"Oh, relax! I'm only kidding. I'm a regular girl with a regular amount of magic. It's absolutely nothing to get unnerved about."

The Parker was proving hard to locate. I drove past it twice without realizing. Jeremy generously pretended not to notice when I pulled up a little too closely and the tire jumped the curb.

"I'll go ahead and check us in. Wait here," he said and kissed my cheek.

I wrestled with the unyielding suitcase full of San Francisco sweaters. Packing lightly was a skill that had eluded me thus far in life. A dazzling stroke of foresight had prompted the inclusion of a swimsuit—defying all logic for a San Francisco trip but now seemingly ingenious.

Jeremy reappeared and waved me over.

"It's this way." He turned and hobbled in the opposite direction, disappearing behind a shrub, leaving me to drag the disagreeable bag along the cobbled path behind him. I hurried to catch up with him, which wasn't easy in my magic Catwoman boots.

"Do you need help with that?" he asked in a tone that declared he was not actually offering help.

"Uh, no . . . it's okay," I said, picking up the pace. "You're the one with a sore knee."

The cream-colored woolen beanie I had been wearing in preparation for freezing San Francisco weather was now producing beads of sweat that ran down the sides of my face. I ripped it off and stuffed it into my purse.

Jeremy opened the door, revealing a tiny lemon-colored room housing a queen-sized bed with barely enough room to swing a cat.

He gasped in horror. "Oh, no! No, no, no! This will *not* work," he said, and slammed the door shut. "I'm going back to the front desk right now."

We walked back to the path.

"Wait here. She'll give me a better upgrade if she thinks I'm alone . . . if you know what I mean. I'll be right back."

I knew exactly what he meant. I was getting the distinct impression that Jeremy's life ran a lot smoother if he was unencumbered. I sat on my suitcase in the courtyard and waited until he reappeared again five minutes later.

"Okay, I think it's sorted out now. Sorry about that. Come this way. This one's around the corner."

We negotiated the maze of lemon trees, passed a pool and climbed a flight of stairs. Room 216 was a larger room, stark with everything in creamy white, lots of mirrors everywhere, and two queen-sized beds staring at us expectantly.

"Ah . . . much better," Jeremy proclaimed.

I flung myself on the nearest bed and said, "I'll take this one!"

"Ha, ha! Get over here, right now!" Not waiting for me to comply, he leapt on top of me and collapsed.

"Are you happy to see me?" I asked him.

"I'm very happy to see you but, Jesus . . . what a horrible day it's been. I hope my luggage makes it," he said, and rolled me over so that I was lying on top of him. He smacked his hand to his forehead. "I forgot to cancel our dinner reservations in San Francisco. I'm such an idiot."

"It's barely noticeable," I said, and busied myself by kissing the exposed areas of his stomach while he checked his messages.

It was too late to go anywhere for dinner, and Jeremy wasn't hungry. He picked up the phone and ordered martinis, and chocolate ice cream for me from room service.

He rolled back on top of me and kissed me deeply. Like a hot wave, it rolled deliciously through every part of my body. I became a melted mess beneath him.

"I'm going to take a hot bath. My muscles are killing me. Come join me." He rolled off and then disappeared into the bathroom.

Room service arrived and I brought him a martini, which he happily accepted while I ate the ice cream.

Jeremy was quite a sight. His long legs splayed up on either sides of the small bathtub as he sat in a mound of bubbles, martini in hand. Sitting on the lid of the toilet next to him, I resisted the urge to soap up his hair like I would with Oliver.

"Why are you still dressed?" he demanded. "Get your clothes off this instant and come keep me company."

I had Jeremy's undivided attention as I stood and let my clothes drop to the floor. He held out his hand and helped me into the hot bath. The water was hot but not scalding. I settled my back against his chest and exhaled.

"I have a little Christmas present for you, Scarlett. Have you been good?"

I seemed to be getting that question a lot lately.

"That depends on your definition of *good*. But if memory serves, it's rather a *big* present, isn't it?" I lathered up my arms with citrus body wash.

Jeremy laughed. "There's definitely *that* present," he said and placed my hand on his buoyant, instantly erect member. "But I got you a real present, too."

"Thanks," I said, as he wriggled to position himself so that he was poised to impale me.

"Yeah, I have something for you, all right." He rubbed himself up against me, teasing me.

I turned my head and arched to reach him while his hands wandered down my stomach and found their way into me. His vodka-flavored kisses consumed me. I couldn't wait to have all of him inside me again. I *ached* for him.

"Let's get out," I whispered.

He helped me out, wrapped a bath towel around me, and threw one around himself.

"Come, my sweet," he said and held out his hand.

And I almost did, just hearing those words.

He surprised me and insisted we open Christmas gifts before unwrapping each other.

I made him open his first.

"Wow," he said as he lifted the James Perse sweater out of the box. "Now *that's* a hell of a sweater!" Anytime Jeremy said *hell* it was a high compliment. As in, 'that's a hell of a movie!' or 'that's a hell of an outfit!' It meant he approved.

He threw it on and admired it in the mirror, stroking the chestnut-brown cashmere.

"It looks good on you," I said.

"Here's your present. Thank goodness I put it in my carry-on, otherwise it would be sitting in San Francisco right now. I'm worried you're not going to like it." He handed me a crushed red box tied with gold ribbon.

"Nonsense. I'll love it," I said and opened the box with trepidation. The whole concept of exchanging Christmas presents terrified me. It was ripe with the potential for disaster.

"How cute! A bunny sweater . . . I love it. Thank you." I was a terrible liar.

He pulled it over my head and stepped back to admire it. I tugged at the tiny sweater, trying to encourage it to cover more of my midriff. It looked like I was wearing the top half of a bunny costume. Oliver would think it was hilarious. Maybe Jeremy had been drunk and bought it in the children's section. Perhaps Oliver could wear it.

"Is this in honor of our new bunny?" I asked. It required some explanation.

He nodded and we both cracked up.

We stood in front of the mirror laughing, completely naked except for our new Christmas sweaters.

"Oh, God . . . it's hideous isn't it?" he asked, aghast as the full measure of the pink sweater sunk in. "I think I may have been inebriated at the time." He giggled, confirming my suspicions. "Ugh! Come here. Let's get it off," he said, peeling it off me. He threw it on the floor as if he expected it to burst into flames, and started kissing me.

I slid his new sweater off him and we made rapturous love on top of our discarded Christmas gifts.

At least in that department we were in perfect harmony.

It sounded as if a full-scale Mardi Gras celebration was going on outside our door but we were happily ensconced in bed. Midnight came and went without us leaving the room.

The next morning, exhausted from our nocturnal activities, we strolled hand in hand down one of the main streets in town in search of replenishment. Jeremy was in his new Christmas sweater and I couldn't get the smile off my face. I felt high from the heady lovemaking.

After a decadent breakfast of eggs and crepes with chocolate and hazelnut spread, along with huge bowls of cappuccino, Jeremy was in relaxation mode. Thanks to his missing phone charger, he was forced to disconnect from the outside world. Well-fed and well sexed, he was the picture of contentment. We read the papers, held hands with plenty of kissing breaks —just like a regular couple.

We walked around, looking in the various shops and art galleries and then went back to the hotel to take a nap.

After an afternoon of luxuriating in bed, I decided I would go for a walk. I needed to take a brief break from all the togetherness and regain my balance.

Jeremy lay in bed and turned on the television while I dressed.

"Is there anything you want from the store?"

"No, thanks, I'm fine, but leave me your cell phone and I can catch up on calls. When you get back let's explore the hotel a bit."

"I'll get you a toothbrush while I'm out so you don't have to use mine."

"I don't want another toothbrush. I want to use yours. It makes me feel closer to you."

"You're funny," I said, not sure what to make of him.

He playfully grabbed the cell phone out of my hand and gave me a quick but distracted kiss.

"See you later," he said, already lost to the charms of the phone.

I had been dying to call Emma and give her an update. She still thought I was in San Francisco. But that call would have to wait.

I went for a walk into town on my own, happy to have a moment to catch my breath.

Next door to the pharmacy was a sporting goods store. On an impulse, I went in search of swimming trunks for Jeremy so we could get in the Jacuzzi. The salesgirl steered me over to a very unimpressive and limited selection of men's swimwear. I settled on the least ugly ones I could find: a black and navy pair that looked a little big but might work. With a new toothbrush and swim trunks in hand, I hurried back to the hotel.

"How about we have a swim? Look what I found." I waved the new trunks at him.

"Oh my God! Do you think I'm a huge fatso?" He stretched the offending item out in front of him. "We could both fit in these."

"Oh, for God's sake. Try them on. Who cares if they're a bit big—at least we can have a swim without you frightening the natives."

Jeremy threw off the sheets and tried on the trunks. Much to his amazement, they fit surprisingly well.

"Okay, see . . . all that carrying on for nothing." I shook my head.

The fabric was a bit voluminous and they were hardly the designer fare he was used to, but they would perform their function adequately.

"Wow. That's a shocker. I guess I'm fatter than I thought."

"O ye of little faith," I said with a large exhale. It was like having a second child.

"They're fabulous and I love them!" he said in a sudden change of heart, and grabbed me and smothered me with kisses. "They are my second favorite Christmas gift!"

I slipped on the charcoal crocheted swimsuit Emma had given me for Christmas. It fitted beautifully. She had a natural eye and instinctively knew what worked on any figure—and luckily I'd remembered to bring it.

Jeremy and I threw on bathrobes and found a pool with a Jacuzzi. The drab weather had deterred all but the hardiest of swimmers. There was only a dad with his two young kids playing in the pool.

We tossed off our robes, slipped into the hot tub, and began frolicking in the warm water. Jeremy was still in an amorous mood. Whenever I got out of range for too long he would stretch out, grab my foot and reel me back in again. The hot water made it easy to relax, which seemed a good time to try and pry all sorts of juicy info out of him.

"Why do you think it's been three years since you were in a relationship?" I asked.

"I don't know. It's not by design. There have been a couple of false starts but nothing that felt right."

"Fair enough."

"I'm not a jealous guy and that seems to get me in trouble with girlfriends. I get accused of not being attentive or jealous enough. Girls like it if you're a bit jealous."

"If they are looking for evidence that you care, then yes." I could identify a few areas that needed improving.

"Yeah, I probably need to make more of an effort with that. One time when I was in St. Moritz skiing with my old girlfriend Josephine and her family, Josephine got so mad at me for not noticing that some guy was flirting with her. We almost broke up on that trip."

"Well, you are supposed to notice."

He shared stories about prior girlfriends who were angry with him for not showing displays of jealousy at appropriate moments or not being sufficiently sensitive to their needs. Many of his stories involved sexy skiing backdrops or exotic locales. I also noticed that the girlfriends all seemed to have pretentious, WASP-y sounding names.

"Why is it they all have names like that?"

"Like what?"

"Oh, let's see: Whitney, Josephine, Tinsley and . . . Clementine." I gave an eye roll for emphasis.

Jeremy's eyes grew large. He didn't know I knew about the last one on the list. Clementine was a high-profile actress, and Susan had heard the news from Randall. He couldn't resist sharing the gossip-worthy details of Jeremy's romantic resume. But it was just a fling, apparently.

"Hang on a minute . . . Scarlett's a name like that," he said, recovering nicely. "*You* belong on that list." He followed with the grin that allows him to get away with murder.

"Oh, you think so, do you?"

"Yes. I am a collector of women with names just like yours!" he said, and waded toward me.

"A collector of women—oh, that's charming." I paddled backward and escaped him by jumping into the cold pool.

He quickly followed suit and pounced on me before I could protest. He swept one arm around me, the other under my knees and whipped my feet out from under me and swirled us around in the water.

"Where do you think you're going, young woman whose name *clearly* belongs at the top of that list?"

"Anywhere I want, pretty much."

He pulled me into him. I wrapped my legs around his waist and enjoyed the instant electric charge it produced.

"Let's go back to the room," he said between wet kisses.

Exiting the pool I felt a swelling sag in my crotch. I looked down and noticed to my dismay that the heavy wet crochet material had created a big unfortunate sag in the front of the bikini, giving me the appearance of sporting a rather generous penis. I wondered if Jeremy had noticed my swelling crotch. The little girl on the chaise lounge certainly had and gave me a very rude stare. I glared back at her. She turned to her dad, shook his arm violently and said, "Look daddy! That lady has a wiener!"

I made a mental note to remember to train Oliver not to say rude comments about women with wieners. Not every observation needs to be voiced.

Jeremy smiled at me supportively.

"I seem to have grown an appendage!"

"Ah, but it looks good on you," he said wickedly.

Back in the room, I collapsed on the bed.

"I can't move. I feel like the inside of one of those lava lamps. What have you done to me?" I asked him.

"Not nearly as much as I'm going to do," he said with a huge grin. "I'm just getting warmed up. I am going to fuck any remnants of that stale marriage out of you."

"I see. So that's your plan. It's safe to say that you've accomplished that mission."

"Let's go and get some dinner. How about margaritas and Mexican? Or do you not eat Mexican either?"

"I'll have you know that I have a very healthy appreciation for Mexican food—and margaritas. As long as it doesn't involve raw fish, I'm good."

"Duly noted."

After dinner and another quick stroll we went back to the room, made love and watched a movie. Or at least he watched a movie. I was so exhausted I fell asleep halfway through.

Jeremy surprised me and booked massages at the spa for us for the morning. I couldn't remember the last time I'd had a massage. Jeremy opted for a sports massage and I selected one with heated stones that were placed on my back. It was divine.

The weekend was over too quickly. It was time to disengage and go back to our real lives. I hated for it to end. I wanted to live in that cocoon.

While we were waiting for the valet to bring the car around, Jeremy looped his hands around my waist and pulled me close to him.

"I'll be back soon and it won't be all of this chasing around. It will be a lot calmer," he said and kissed me.

I smiled. I'd only been in his life for two months but the word *calm* had never come to mind. He was pure high-octane energy. Calm was a totally foreign concept.

I dropped Jeremy back at the airport and headed home in a torrential downpour. This winter seemed to be unusually wet and dreary. As usual, Jeremy had left and taken the sunshine with him. It always seemed to be raining whenever we parted.

Jeremy texted me when he got to San Francisco.

It feels weird not having you around. Miss having my mouth all over you.

~Miss you, too.

I was completely, gloriously *spent.*

Back in LA, reality was waiting. I was starting to feel a bit schizophrenic. I had these lusty weekends away with Jeremy but they bore no resemblance to what my real life was actually like. How would this relationship fit in with Oliver? How did Oliver and I fit into his crazy schedule? Did any of it fit at all?

The high from the weekend was starting to wear off but I didn't have time to dwell on it.

All I longed to do was lie about and fantasize but I had a Sunday night meeting with a divorce attorney at the Polo Lounge in The Beverly Hills Hotel.

The divorce was dragging on. If it didn't wrap up soon, the disengagement ran the risk of being longer than the actual marriage. Ironically, our meeting was in the same hotel where X and I were married. When the attorney suggested we meet there, I could have suggested an alternative, but there was something poetic about it, a certain symmetry that pleased me. Meeting a lawyer to map out the end of my marriage—on the same soil it was planted in—stated that I had achieved a certain level of detachment. It was proof that I was moving on with my life, and so did my lusty weekend romp in the desert.

I was officially moving on.

Chapter Seventeen
The Accidental Asshole

The danger of lots of sweet sex after a long dry spell is that it can lull you into a state of dependency. Calls from Jeremy were a little scarce that week.

Back in stay-busy mode, Emma and I went for a hike in Runyon Canyon. Runyon Canyon was located in the heart of Hollywood with incredible vistas of the entire city and a bird's eye view of the expensive homes nestled in the hills. It wasn't unusual to run into movie stars hiking with their dogs or trainers or both. Emma brought her dog, Skip, a German shepherd and chow rescue mutt, to keep us company. Skip was old with a bad hip and couldn't go very fast. Not known for my hiking prowess, Skip's leisurely pace suited me perfectly.

"Skip! Come on, old boy! Let's kick it up a notch!" Emma goaded him. "How am I going to get in shape for pilot season when we're all dragging our sorry asses?"

Skip ignored her pleas and kept plodding along beside us as if he was enduring the longest walk of his life.

"Maybe I should skip men altogether and get a dog. Dogs couldn't give a shit what shape your ass is in. They're always happy to see you. Do you think Jeremy's not calling because my ass is a bit flabby?"

"Oh, sweetie," Emma said in the soothing voice that had launched a thousand commercials. "He just spent an entire weekend with his face buried in that ass! Everything's fine. Your ass is fine. The problem is he sweeps you off your feet—and then he leaves—so it's hard not to feel off balance. Things will be better when he's back in town."

"How dare he get me addicted to all that dreamy sex and then think it's okay to just go off the radar? Why do I always feel like I'll never see him again?"

"Oh, you'll see him again all right. You're not getting rid of him that easily. Forget about him right now. It's a new year. You need some new headshots. You have a commercial running now. Do a mailing to casting directors and put yourself out there, capitalize on the momentum."

"Good idea."

Emma was up for a role-playing a murder victim in a *Lifetime* movie of the week. It was a good part because not only did she get to die in a dramatic fashion—sacrificed at the altar by a crazy cult—but she would also have lots of scenes leading up to her demise.

"What kind of makeup do you think I should wear for the audition?" she asked while pouring some water from her water bottle into Skip's disinterested mouth.

"Definitely a slutty, smeared eye-liner look. That would be my professional opinion. All of those shows depict bad girls wearing slutty makeup, *especially* the dead ones!"

"You're right! I will go all-out slutty! Yippee! Thanks."

Emma referred me to a photographer, and I made an appointment to do a photo shoot with him. I landed a last-minute makeup job with a surly starlet who was very demanding and had me sweating bullets, but I was grateful to have the work and keep my mind occupied. There were a number of ad gigs starting to trickle in.

Back at work and on long boring night shoots, Jeremy returned to his late-night flirty texting mode. We would text until I fell asleep.

Jeremy called at the end of the week and casually dropped that he would be in town for one night the following week to attend the Golden Globes.

"That's great!" I was dying to see him and couldn't believe he hadn't mentioned it earlier. "I can't wait to see you."

"Well, here's the problem: I have to escort my friend Savannah. She's nominated in the best supporting actress category. It's purely business. It's just for one night and I have to fly straight back up in the morning."

"Well, that sucks. Can't you come a day earlier so we can have some time together?"

"I wish I could, love, but it's not possible. I have commitments that weekend."

"I hate for you to be here and not even see you."

"Me, too, sweetheart."

Why had he even bothered telling me? I bit my lip and got off the phone as quickly as possible.

"Can you fucking believe it?" I screeched to Emma as soon as I'd hung up with Jeremy. "For two months we've been flying back and forth, and now he's going to be in town and not even see me!"

"It's not a good sign that he's so cavalier about not seeing you. But it's also not the end of the world. Who is he taking?"

"That Savannah woman." Jeremy's roster of Hollywood's starlets was about the last thing I wanted to contemplate.

"He knows Savannah Bingham?"

"He knows everybody. It's ridiculous."

"Try and forget about it. Pretend he's not even coming."

"Fat chance."

The Golden Globes weekend arrived. Los Angeles was buzzing with one of the biggest events of the year. All over town, parties were being held for the nominees and free swag was being thrown at anybody who remotely resembled a celebrity. The excitement was palpable. All efforts on my part to ignore the event failed dismally. Beverly Hills was wallpapered with large banners heralding 'Hollywood's Favorite Awards Ceremony! The Golden Globes!'

Jeremy called me as soon as his plane landed.

"Come meet me later," he pleaded. "Come on, it'll be really nice."

"What do you mean later? You'll be busy all night."

"I know, but I can leave a key for you and I'll get home as soon as I can." And then he said the magic words, "Come on . . . please? I *need* to see you."

Who was I kidding? Of course, I would see him. *I had to see him.* I couldn't bear to have him in town and not be with him. He had become a full-blown physical addiction.

CeCe and I sat and watched the Golden Globes together.

"Let's get a look at this Jeremy person," CeCe said and put on her glasses to inspect him, in case he appeared on camera.

I darted into the bathroom to do my hair and makeup during the commercial breaks. Oliver didn't share my rapt enthusiasm for the telecast and kept demanding *SpongeBob*. He got Henry the Eighth out of his cage and was feeding him parsley, and then when he tired of that, Oliver disappeared into Sam's room.

"What should I wear?" I asked CeCe.

"Something cute."

"Well, yes . . . but considering that, technically, I'm only meeting him at his apartment and not out to dinner or anything."

"I think you wear evening attire as if you *were* going out. The fact that he may be lucky enough to separate you from your clothes shouldn't be a consideration at all," she said thoughtfully.

"Good point. Thank you." I paused for a second. "Do you think I should be going over there? It's silly, isn't it? I should just make him wait and see me another time. That would be the sensible thing to do."

"Rubbish. Of course you should see him. Why not lunge for every shred of happiness that comes your way? It's silly not to. Plus, you'll just make us miserable all night if you don't."

Sometimes I couldn't decide if CeCe gave the best advice—or the worst.

I tried on various ensembles in the closet for CeCe's approval. Oliver came in, sat on top of the full laundry basket that I'd been avoiding all week, and watched me.

"Put your pajamas on, Mom!" he demanded.

"Not yet, sweetheart. I'm going to see a friend," I said.

"Why?"

"Because I haven't seen my friend in a while and I want to say hello."

"It's nighttime. No playdates at nighttime, Mama."

"Usually we don't, but tonight is an exception."

He watched disapprovingly as I slipped on a pair of CeCe's strappy black heels.

"That bloody bunny has left turds everywhere!" CeCe shrieked from the living room.

"Oh, shit! The bunny!"

"Mama! You said a *bad* word! You owe me a dollar."

"Oliver, we have to remember to put him back in his cage. Come and help me find him."

I scurried around scooping up the turds in a tissue and attempting to corral the errant bunny—which was no small feat in high heels. Oliver and I chased him around the apartment. He disappeared under the couch and CeCe got out the broom. Finally, after another sweaty lap around the living room, we got him back in his cage.

Jeremy's starlet lost to an English actress. I hoped that, in light of her loss, she might want to go home early and let me have my man back. CeCe and I caught a glimpse of him sitting beside her at the table when the camera flashed to her during her category. Happily, he did not look the least bit romantically inclined in her direction, or terribly concerned with her at all, for that matter.

"You look nice, Mama," Oliver said as I kissed him good-bye. He was getting sleepy and leaned his head on CeCe's shoulder.

"Thank you, sweetheart. Have a good time with CeCe. I love you!"

I collected the key from the doorman and let myself into Jeremy's apartment. As I expected, it was very tasteful. Despite the haphazard mix of modern and funky, cool and classic, it meshed well. He had contemporary artwork on display throughout the living room and large beautiful photographs of stately homes. I wondered whose homes they were. Perhaps they belonged to other wealthy relatives? I looked at everything but didn't dare touch a thing. I didn't even pour myself a drink. Two hours alone in a gentleman's apartment could tell you a lot about said gentleman—even without doing any snooping or opening any drawers.

Jeremy's bathroom was devoid of any feminine touches or remnants of girlfriends past. There was only the lovely Molton Brown Naran Ji hand soap, which most likely came from a gift bag from one of the fabulous events he was always busy attending. I loved that he did not seem overly concerned with his appearance. A few token Kiehl's products, but thankfully he was definitely *not* a metrosexual. There's nothing more boring than a man who pays more attention to his upkeep than you do.

Jeremy did, however, care about decorating. The longer I sat there the more it bothered me. His apartment was stylishly cool to the point of being annoying. It seemed to scream at me "This is the home of a Hot, Young Movie Producer! You're way out of your league, lady!"

His kitchen was well stocked with wine and champagne—nothing else—not surprising since he hadn't been home in months. I had only seen him reheat leftovers, and suspected his culinary instincts ranked somewhere around mine. I studied the two lonely photos on the fridge. One was of Jeremy as a child with his father on a beach. Jeremy looked about seven and was wearing his inimitable devilish grin—looking straight into the camera—with his father looking on in repose. His father, even in supposed relaxation mode, wore a stoic expression but still managed to look irritated. From the picture, I surmised that he probably wasn't much fun. I decided I ought to cut Jeremy some slack for a presumably tortured childhood suffered at the hands of a difficult and disapproving father.

The other photo was of Jeremy with friends at a dinner party. No photos of old girlfriends, no visible remnants of prior attachments. So far, so good.

Jeremy sent a text.

Be there soon, darling. Can't wait to ravish you!

His television was impossible to work. The complicated series of remotes refused to comply with my simple request: *Please turn on.* Eventually, I gave up and flopped on his crisp white bedspread. His bedroom bore the same characteristics as his car—clothes strewn everywhere—and as per usual, he had dumped his suitcase onto the floor upon arrival. Also discarded on the floor was his briefcase with a copy of the *New York Times* sticking out of it. I stared at it for a moment, weighing the cost of freeing it from its confines and relieving my boredom. But messing with his briefcase would be invasive—a violation of the no-snooping rule—so I left it alone. Where the hell was he? The Golden Globes had ended hours ago. It was twelve fifty-four a.m. and still no sign of Jeremy.

It occurred to me how many dating rules I was breaking by waiting in a man's apartment—on his *bed*—while said man was out with another woman. He was busy attending parties with a nominee on his arm while I studied the gold leaves in his wallpaper pattern. It was sheer madness. Undeniable proof I had taken leave of my senses.

Finally, at 1:43 a.m. I heard the key in the lock. I lay on the bed, fully dressed and pretended to be asleep.

"Hello, my darling! *Oh my God*! Am I happy to see you!" Jeremy said with his trademark theatrical over-the-top delivery, enhanced by what was probably quite a bit of alcohol. He pounced on me, clad in the tux that I hadn't seen since the painful parties in San Francisco. He struggled to free himself from his jacket, then rolled me over, straddled me and smeared sloppy kisses on me that tasted of vodka. I shamelessly drank them in. It was impossible to be mad at him once our unassailable chemistry kicked into gear.

"I'm sooo happy you waited for me," he slurred, finding my mouth and kissing me for the umpteenth time. "It's sooo good to see you . . ." There was a hint of vulnerability in his tone. The vodka had exposed holes in his usual bravado. "I really *needed* to see you. I missed you, Scarlett." He was drunk but I believed every word he said. Drunk and demonstrative, he was worth the wait. "I was so worried that you weren't going to be here when I got home."

"But not worried enough to escape earlier," I chided. "You had well and truly fulfilled your escort duties a few hours ago, I would imagine."

"I was going to get a cab but it was awkward and she was upset about losing . . ."

He sat me up and attempted to peel my dress over my head, but in doing so, we ended up falling backward against the wall and into the painting that was hanging above the bed. He thrust one long arm upward to prevent it from crashing down on our heads. We both burst out laughing.

"Scarlett. Stop wrecking the place!"

Once he had settled the imminent threat, he planted my hands above my head and went back to lavishing my body with kisses. He pressed his flesh against mine, along with various body parts. He eased his way down my stomach and put his mouth on me, effectively silencing the voices in my head questioning my sanity. He grabbed my ass while his tongue made exploratory excursions into me. I ran my fingers through his hair and seized handfuls of it. Right when he brought me to the edge, he stopped and kissed his way back up to my mouth, looked into my eyes and then plunged his cock into me. Before long he was thrusting vigorously. We began moving together and melting into each other. He couldn't kiss me deeply enough. He was trying to devour me, to impale me and I wanted him to claim me in every possible way. Before long we climaxed in tight shudders and then we fell asleep entwined in our usual spooning position.

The next morning, I woke up early, aware of my seven thirty curfew when Oliver would wake up and my absence would need to be explained. "No overnight playdates, Mommy!"

Jeremy squeezed me and said, "I'm so glad I got to see you. Thank you for coming over. I changed my flight from ten to noon so we could have a little more time together. Let's go get some breakfast and then could you drive me to the airport?"

"Sure, but I have to pick up Oliver on the way." I sat up in search of my clothes.

At this news, Jeremy flopped back on the bed, exhaled dramatically, and covered his face with his hands.

"What's the matter with you?" I rolled over and sat on top of him, attempting to pry his hands away from his face.

He shook his head. "I can't. I can't deal with this today." He looked past me and out the window.

"Deal with what? What are you talking about?"

No answer. Could all this fuss really be over my three-year-old?

"You're kidding, right?"

"I told you . . . I told you about my childhood and the stuff with my mother and my step-father. I can't play happy families."

He still wouldn't look at me.

"Oh my God! Are you serious? Are you telling me you think a twenty-minute drive to the airport with my kid in the car turns us into a happy family?" I laughed at the suggestion. "Listen, I hate to be the one to bring it to your attention, but you wouldn't have *picked* me in the first place if you weren't ready to work through some of that old crap. You knew I had a kid when you met me. You said it wasn't a problem. You can't avoid him forever. He is part of the deal."

He lay there silently for a moment. "I don't have the energy. I can't do it today. I'll get a cab."

"Okay, fine. In that case it's probably better if you get a cab." I gave him a brief kiss, threw on my clothes, and left in a hurry.

I didn't like this immature side of him and I wondered how—or more importantly *if*—that would change when he came home permanently. I wanted to believe it would over time. He would fall in love with Oliver if he met him. Everyone did. But could it be possible that he had no plans of ever meeting Oliver? It was a disquieting thought.

Chapter Eighteen
Know When to Cut Bait

I'm sorry I overreacted. I was a wanker. Forgive me?? Jeremy texted the next day.

I felt a bit better but things were not looking good. I didn't respond.

Let me make it up to you.

I couldn't shake that feeling in the pit of my stomach and it wasn't a fluttery good one.

I told CeCe that Jeremy had balked at the idea of being in the car with Oliver for the ride to the airport.

"Maybe he was too hungover," she said.

"Why are you sticking up for him? You don't even like him."

"I don't *not* like him, I haven't made up my mind yet. Sometimes these things take time. It's not easy. You are a package now, you and Oliver, so you can't rush any of it along just because you're impatient. Look where that got you last time. You've barely unloaded that last asshole."

The next weekend, Jeremy flew down and we spent it at the ranch. It was a very different Jeremy this time around. He was constantly excusing himself to make a phone call, needing to send an e-mail, playing tennis all day—anything to avoid being with me. With Daphne in New York for the weekend, Taylor—ever the gentleman—was often left stuck with me and graciously didn't complain about it, at least not to me.

On Saturday morning, Jeremy, Taylor and I drove into town to the local breakfast café we favored. Going out to breakfast was one of my favorite activities. Having someone make your breakfast for you felt like the height of indulgence. I loved it. For Jeremy it was business as usual. We settled in to a table in the corner of the busy café and ordered our omelets, waffles and lattes.

"Oh, I have to take this call!" Jeremy announced dramatically, shoving his chair away from the table with a loud screech that caused heads to turn in his direction. He dashed out of the café, leaving Taylor and me alone again. Taylor and I were sharing a romantic weekend together, minus the romance.

"I don't know that if I were a woman, I'd go out with Jeremy," Taylor said, as we watched Jeremy outside on his BlackBerry, gesticulating wildly, relishing his conversation with some lucky person.

"That's unfortunate for me since I am rather fond of him," I said. The fact that Taylor felt the need to pointedly warn me made me feel worse.

"He's tolerable if you aren't too interested in him. He's hopeless."

"Hopeless? Really? Why is that?" I pressed Taylor for more information. It was more appealing to see Jeremy as a clumsy accidental womanizer rather than a garden-variety Hollywood lothario. I preferred to think of him as the accidental asshole.

"He's never been very good at women. But he likes to fancy himself as a bit of a player," said Taylor with more than a touch of scorn. "But the truth is he's always had trouble with women. He couldn't get many at school."

"I think he's made up for lost time."

Taylor was the more classically handsome of the two, the dark brooding scholar versus Jeremy's casual good looks. It was easy to see how that rivalry might have played out at school. Taylor was very cerebral and introspective and Jeremy was, well, Jeremy. His appeal was hard to discount. He had an undeniable charm that only husbands of swooning females seemed immune to. Even Taylor would have to begrudgingly admit that.

There is nothing more painful than the waning interest of one's lover. They always want you, until they don't. Jeremy was pulling away and I wasn't sure how to handle it. Emma had booked the slutty murder victim role and was exhausted from shooting at night, so I couldn't get her input. I thought about leaving but we had driven up in his car. I hated feeling trapped. Instead of leaving, I took long walks around the gorgeous grounds and hoped that the sun might melt away my anxiety. Jeremy blew hot and cold. Aloof during the day, his interest heated up as the sun went down. It was like a gong sounded in his head and by bedtime he was white hot and present again. Sex with him didn't seem all that different but something was off. I could feel it.

Jeremy slept soundly next to me while I tossed and turned, ruminating over the state of our affair. The last time we had slept in that bed he couldn't get enough of me, and now his affections were cooling.

As it usually happens, I waited until the worst possible moment to initiate a 'talk' with him. Perhaps it was born out of a desire to blow the whole thing up, but Jeremy was drifting farther and farther away and I couldn't stand it any longer. I needed to slash the moorings and be done with it.

He leapt out of bed on Sunday morning without making love—something completely unheard of for him—like a man in a hurry to catch a bus.

I decided I'd had enough.

"We've never actually talked about what we're doing here," I said, safely ensconced in the big green comforter with only my head peeking out.

"Are you sure you want to do this *now?*" he said with irritation, keeping his focus entirely on the laces of his tennis shoes.

"Yes."

"What is it you need to discuss?" He stood up, his whole body stiffening at the sign of this impending threat to his liberty.

"Well, for starters, I don't even know if we are in an exclusive relationship."

He sighed, dragged himself to the edge of the bed farthest from me, and sat down heavily. "And you're *sure* you want to do this now?" he asked again, more pointedly.

"No, but I hate feeling like I have no idea what's going on. This entire weekend you have been acting like you don't want me to be here."

"Scarlett, I think you're a wonderful woman. I have a great time with you. Since we've been together I have not slept with anybody else . . . but if you're asking me *if* I am going to sleep with anyone else in the future, then that's another question. I have no interest in being in a serious, monogamous relationship right now. I *can't* be in a monogamous relationship right now."

"I see," I said, tightening my grip on the crisp white sheets. It was the ultimate bullshit line. What he meant was he couldn't be in a monogamous relationship *with me*. I struggled to absorb the weight of his words.

"If you want to continue to see me, on a casual basis—maybe once a week or whatever, when I'm in town—if that works for you, then I'm really happy. Of course, I'll understand if it doesn't work for you and respect your decision either way."

I had known it was coming and there it was. By giving me the choice of whether to continue the relationship, he effectively gave himself the out he had been seeking. It was a clever move and let himself off the hook brilliantly.

"So . . ." I said in a very measured tone. "Let me make sure I understand. What you're saying is that you're happy to keep sleeping with *me*, while you're looking around for *other* people you'd like to sleep with?"

"If you need to put it that way—"

"Then, no, I don't think that works for me."

"Okay, I can totally respect that." He paused for a second, unsure what to say next. "Taylor's waiting for me to play tennis. I have to go . . . are you okay?"

"Yes, I'm fine!" I snapped irritably.

"All right," he said, the weight visibly lifting from his shoulders as he was released. "I'll see you later." He grabbed his jacket and closed the bedroom door behind him.

I sat in bed and thought about what had just happened. I had forced everything out into the open. He hadn't been sleeping with anyone else after all. Relief washed over me until I remembered that we had just broken up. I thought about the shitty 'choice' he had given me, that I could settle for whatever crumbs he would throw my way and be happy with that, or not see him at all. It wasn't much of a choice. No self-respecting woman would be okay with that, and he knew it. Not that I had been behaving as a self-respecting woman lately. Waiting in his bed while he was out with another woman was not one of my finer moments. Good sense had checked out as soon as Jeremy checked in between my thighs.

I went into the kitchen and made a cup of tea, which always made me feel better in moments of crisis. Stuck without my car, there was now the significant obstacle of how to get home. A taxi back to Los Angeles would be a fortune.

The morning brightened considerably with the sight of Daphne arriving home from her New York trip. With the boys off playing tennis, we had time to have a hot chocolate and a chat. One glance at my glum countenance and with minimal prompting on her part, it all came tumbling out. I sat on her blue velvet couch, nervously playing with the Indian embroidered pillows while she unpacked her bag. Daphne mulled it over while I sat breathlessly awaiting her insights. She was pale and delicate, so positively lovely that it was hard to imagine her ever being upset by any man. She looked unpolluted by the unpleasantness of life.

"Oh, he probably just needs a bit of space. Leave him alone for a while. Don't you think you're past all that? You've been together for a while now. He must be serious about you. He never brings anyone he's dating here to be with his family. I think all he really wants at the end of the day is someone to be nice to him."

Now I was completely baffled. I couldn't be any nicer to him and that made things worse.

"I'm not sure what to do—if I should call someone to come out and get me, or take a cab—"

"Nonsense. Don't go anywhere. Act as if nothing happened. Be carefree and happy and let him take you home. Trust me, I'm good at this."

I went for one last walk alone around the property, past the horse paddocks and along the oak tree trail. This business with Jeremy was starting to have an old familiar ring to it. He was not available for a relationship, yet I had worked so hard at trying to sustain whatever flimsy scraps he threw my way. Why did I always seem to find myself in this predicament? And why did I feel okay about allowing people to slide into the habit of treating me poorly and then letting them off the hook? I had never even bothered to confront X about his extramarital affairs. It was painful to realize that even after going through so much I was still making the same mistakes.

Taylor and Jeremy arrived back at the house in the late afternoon, exhilarated from hours of tennis. Taylor ran to embrace Daphne and cast a rather forlorn look in my direction from over her shoulder, which I took to mean Jeremy must have told him everything. If by chance Jeremy hadn't told him, Daphne certainly would. Jeremy was pleasant but his tone was decidedly cool. I followed Daphne's advice and pretended nothing was wrong.

"Shall we hit the road soon, then?" Jeremy couldn't look me in the eye.

"Excellent," I said brightly. It was time to go—in more ways than one.

As Jeremy drove us back to LA, we kept the conversation light. My head was buzzing with how to say good-bye. Who needed him and his silly aversion to monogamy? Oliver and I deserved much better.

Jeremy pulled up to my building to drop me off and turned off the engine.

"Wait a moment, will you? I need to go get your sweater that I borrowed last time."

"Oh, don't worry. You can give it to me another time."

"No, if you don't mind, I'd rather do it now. Wait right here," I said and ran upstairs to retrieve his sweater. Since I wouldn't be seeing him again, it was only appropriate to return it. As soon as I put the key in the lock, I could hear Oliver squealing with delight.

"Mommy!" he said triumphantly and barreled toward me.

"Hello, my sweet boy! I missed you! Did you have fun at Daddy's?" I scooped him up, covered him with kisses, and feasted on his magnificence. He was clad in a cream shirt with a large blue dog on the front, a bright fuchsia beanie on his head which belonged to me, and a pair of SpongeBob pajama leggings that clung to his fleshy thighs.

"Oh, you're looking *very* handsome, my boy! I have to run downstairs quickly and give something to my friend."

"I want to come, too, Mama!"

I paused for a second and weighed the implications of bringing him down with me. Jeremy would freak out, which was fine with me. Let him see what he was missing out on.

"All right, then, let's go." I slid Oliver onto my hip and hunted around in the closet for Jeremy's Prada sweater. I felt a strange calm for the first time in ages. Making empowering choices felt good. Screw Jeremy and his allergy to my life and its inherent complications.

Jeremy was pecking away at his BlackBerry, as usual, when we went back downstairs. He looked up at me and then his jaw hit the floor when he discovered Oliver, buoyantly content on my hip. His eyes widened for a second in disbelief and then he scrambled for something to say.

He was speechless. Floored by a three-year-old. His dazzling Ivy-League wit was at a loss for once.

"Oh . . . hi . . . um . . . you must be Oliver. How are you?"

"Oliver, this is my *friend*, Jeremy."

Oliver eyed him coolly, twirling one of the blond curls that peaked out from under the beanie. He made him wait through an excruciatingly long pause before uttering "Hi" with little enthusiasm. It was *perfect.*

"I like your blue dog," he said pointing to Oliver's shirt. "And I especially like your beanie." He worked hard to establish a little repartee.

Oliver was content to say nothing and let him sweat. He stared down at him from his perch on my hip in his groovy outfit, and made Jeremy do all the work. It occurred to me that I ought to be taking lessons from Oliver. He owned his power at the ripe old age of three. The harder people worked for his attention, the more he delighted in depriving them of it.

"Well, here's your sweater," I said and handed it back to him through the car window.

"Thanks," he said, and tossed it onto the seat beside him.

We looked at each other and said nothing for a brief, awkward moment.

With the distinct advantage of having my best man on my hip, I decided to plunge ahead.

"Look, this is the deal." I sounded more confident than I felt. "This is the package. If it doesn't work for you, it doesn't work for you. I have this little man to consider and I'm not going to do this with you and feel like I'm begging for your time or trying to make you into someone you're not. If you need to go explore the dating world for what you might be missing then that's precisely what you should be doing. You should just go and be Mr. Hollywood and fuck around with your starlets and leave the rest of us alone."

"Mom. You said the *bad* word. You owe me a dollar."

"Yes, Ollie, I owe you a dollar."

Jeremy buried his face in his hands.

"Besides isn't it somewhere in the Guy Handbook that you aren't supposed to be a dick to single mothers? Isn't that some sort of mandate?"

Jeremy looked horrified.

Oliver, tiring of the boring adults, broke the silence and said, "Mama, let's go watch *SpongeBob*."

"Good idea! Let's go . . . let's say good-bye to Jeremy, then," I said and turned on my heels. "Let's say *adios*, Jeremy!" I waved my hand in the air as we walked the other way. "Come on Ollie, let's go watch some *SpongeBob* and eat some ice cream like reasonable people."

Jeremy was still sitting in the car when I closed the door to the building.

I hadn't planned to say any of that with Oliver as my witness, but I also wasn't about to stifle it for eternity.

Saying good-bye seemed so trite. What was the proper way to end things with young men you'd given your heart and other juicy parts to? Hours earlier I would have done anything to preserve our connection. But now, watching how uncomfortable Jeremy was with Oliver, it made the decision much easier. Jeremy couldn't handle the package. And the package could do nicely without him.

Chapter Nineteen
At Least You're Not Fat

The bravado I'd felt initially started to fade a bit as the days went by and I started to miss him. My phone had ceased buzzing and chirping to notify me that I had texts and had instantly become far less entertaining. It sat there idly and refused to give me any news at all. It seemed like Jeremy had gone and taken the wave of good work with him. There were no auditions or makeup jobs to be had anywhere.

Oliver was with X, and I was feeling blue. It had been two whole weeks since the Jeremy debacle and my resolve had started to crumble. For some silly reason, I still expected he might call. He might have some sort of brain aneurism and realize that he had to give up his nonsense and be with me. And Oliver.

While I was busy consoling myself with episodes of *Downton Abbey* countless magazines and coffee ice cream, a surprise call came from Kelly Carter. Kelly was an actress I had been friends with for years but hadn't heard from in ages. She and I met when she was dating the best friend of my old boyfriend Grant, and we often double-dated. The romantic relationships didn't last but our friendship had remained.

I hadn't seen Kelly since before my divorce drama began, and in fact, she'd been absent for most of my marriage. Kelly had been living on the east coast when she wasn't busy filming her television show, so I was delighted to hear from her. I was divorcing a husband and Kelly had just acquired a new one. There was much to catch up on.

"Listen, I'm in town and I have to go to one of those silly publicity things tonight, but you can come as my date. We'll make it fun! Pick you up at seven."

An evening out with Kelly would take my mind off everything. I sprang into action and threw on jeans, a peacock-blue silk blouse, and a pair of CeCe's pink strappy sandals.

Kelly picked me up in her blue Corvette and we headed to Fred Segal in

Santa Monica, a chic Westside boutique, for a party in honor of something or other—Kelly couldn't remember what. Although Kelly was as American as apple pie, her long, dark hair and piercing brown eyes gave her the appearance of an exotic Indian goddess. She proceeded to do her makeup in the car on the way, skillfully applying eyeliner, blush, and lip gloss at the red lights we encountered along La Cienega on our way down to the freeway. Kelly exuded more of a rock star vibe than an actress one, which gave her a certain edge, a dangerous sexuality that other actresses were always trying to emulate.

Being in Kelly's presence could be intoxicating and sometimes a little scary. Knowing Kelly, intoxication was almost always on the menu. Kelly was a self-proclaimed master of her own destiny, especially if that immediate destiny consisted of getting to the bar. Kelly owned her power, even when slurring her words, which is a difficult feat to accomplish.

We arrived at the party, and Kelly did the obligatory red carpet posing while I stood off to the side with the other nobodies. I watched her pose provocatively with the promotional Disney characters in front of a Disney backdrop with the paparazzi going crazy, fully aware that they wouldn't be able to use any of the footage. Shots of her with one leg wrapped around Mickey Mouse and humping him while waving an arm in the air rodeo-style wouldn't exactly thrill the conservative Disney executives.

"God, I hate this shit!" she said as soon as she'd finished.

I nodded sympathetically, thinking how dreadful it must be to be paid hundreds of thousands of dollars and have to come to events like this and hump Disney characters. Where did you sign up for jobs like that and *could I please have one?*

We inched our way toward the entrance, through the hordes of people gawking at the celebs arriving. Holding my hand, Kelly negotiated our way through the crowd to the bar, where she proceeded to flirt shamelessly with the handsome young bartender.

"Hello, handsome. What's with the sissy shit?' she said disdainfully, eyeing the martini glasses filled with frothy pink liquid laid out on the bar. "Give me a double vodka, on the rocks!"

The bartender smiled, in full salute to a girl who likes to party, and handed her a serious-looking tumbler. Opting for the sissy shit, I helped myself to one of the pink fruity cocktails while Kelly made quick work of her vodka.

Kelly chatted for a while with a female fan of her show. The woman was in her late forties and was enchanted to make Kelly's acquaintance. Kelly was exceedingly good with her public. The girl knew how to work a room. Kelly had that movie star-politician trick down. She was well versed in the make-everyone-feel-important-for-those-fleeting-moments-in-your-presence trick. She listened intently and nodded as the woman rhapsodized about Kelly's performance on the television show as an alien bounty hunter.

"Oh, sweetie, you're much too kind," she said, squeezing the woman's hand.

I was happy to be invisible beside her for a moment and watch Miley Cyrus trying on hats. It was a veritable smorgasbord of young Disney actresses.

"This is my friend, Scarlett. She's an actress, too!"

My calm was punctured by her unexpected remark. What the hell was she saying? She knew I hadn't had anything resembling a real acting job in years.

The woman turned toward me with renewed interest. "Oh?" she said, searching my face for any hint of familiarity. "What show are *you* on, Scarlett?"

"I'm not actually on a show right now," I said, glaringly aware of how lame it sounded. I thought about listing the commercials I'd been in, but thought better of it. Telling her I was the girl in an anti-diarrheal commercial that ran for two years was not going to knock her socks off.

"Oh." She turned her back on me and resumed her conversation with Kelly until someone more famous caught her eye, and she rushed off.

"So what's the story with this guy you're hung up on?" Kelly slurred at me when we were finally alone.

I proceeded to tell her the details of my romantic travails with Jeremy—how he had been the first big romance and sex-fest since my divorce, and that I had fallen for him, and now it was over. Recounting the events out loud made me feel even more foolish.

"Jesus, Scarlett, you are a disaster magnet! Yeah, I know that guy. I met him at the Chateau years ago. He's cute but he's a total player! *Pa-lay-YAH!*"

My stomach sank and I felt like I was going to start hurling the sickly, sweet drink onto Kelly's sandals.

"Why is it that everybody else could smell it a mile off?" I lamented. "Is my asshole radar really that screwed up? One stinking divorce and I'm rendered clueless? Or have I always been clueless about men?" It was a depressing question to ponder. Maybe my picker mechanism was completely off.

Watching the tears start to spill down my cheeks, she threw her head back and roared with laughter.

"Oh, God, you're gone, aren't you? That's *pathetic*."

I wanted to say, 'Yes, but he used to sleep with my sweater because it smelled like me, and he cried on my shoulder when I had to leave him and fly back to LA, and he used to use my toothbrush, and he used to like to sleep as close to me as physically possible—and he used to text me like *twenty* times a day! He's not an asshole. He *liked* me—I know he liked me. I'm not making this whole thing up but what was the point? She was probably right. The general consensus was that she was right. I must be out of my mind.

"I'm fine, really . . . I'm okay." I was not convincing anyone.

"No, you're not! You're a fucking mess! You might as well own it. At least I own my fucked-up-ness. That's part of what makes me so loveable. Yeah, you had a bad break with your shitty marriage, but you're out of that now. You have an amazing kid. You owe it to him to get your shit together."

"That's what I've been trying to do."

"It's simple. Let me spell it out for you. Number one: You're going to go crazy if you keep living with your mother. Number two: You need a fucking job, which goes hand in hand with number one! Number three: *Forget that asshole.* You need a real man who can handle responsibility and not some hot, Hollywood-player guy who bails at the three-month mark. If you don't watch it, you are in *serious* danger of becoming your mother! You'll just keep bouncing from man to man!"

That was more than enough to throw me over the edge. With that coup de grace, I felt a bolt of pure, white-hot fear shooting down my spine. A full-scale panic attack was brewing. I took another sip of the hideous pink drink and tried to pull it together. For a woman who spent relatively little time in my life, Kelly was able to land crushing emotional blows with Jedi-knight precision.

"Fuck this. This is boring. Let's get out of here! Let's go meet my husband. Let me show you what a real man looks like!"

Kelly said *husband* with the reverie of a new bride, rolling it around in her mouth and savoring its inherent orgasmic quality before releasing it.

She grabbed my hand and once again started to head back through the throngs of people hunting for free swag bags from Fred Segal. She came face to face with a large woman wearing an unflattering black and purple floral-print dress whose considerable girth inadvertently blocked our passage. She turned back to me and said loudly, "Well, things could be worse—at least you're not fat!"

I kept my head down and couldn't bring myself to look up at the woman who must have heard her.

"Did she hear me?" Kelly asked when we'd cleared her.

"Yes, I think so," I said, not daring to turn around and check.

"Oh, well . . . fuck her!" Kelly sang out loudly and headed us toward the exit, extending her arm out to the female attendant at the door who obediently looped two goodie bags over her wrist without skipping a beat.

"We're swag whores!" Kelly told the confused valet attendant, whose slight grasp of the English language likely prevented him from seeing the humor in her comment.

While waiting for Kelly's car to appear, we rooted around in our goodie bags, producing a selection of white, conservative underwear—which Kelly promptly grabbed and tossed in the trash—and the usual assortment of scented candles, lip glosses, T-shirts and chocolates—standard issue goodie-bag loot.

It was going to take a lot more than a cocktail and a goodie bag to improve my disposition. As much as I wanted to dismiss what Kelly had said, I knew she was right. Her bluntness cut right to the core of my most basic fears. My life was a mess and after more than a year, I wasn't any closer to pulling it back together. The even scarier question remained. Was it ever together in the first place? I had to admit the answer was a definitive no. But what was I going to do to fix the mess? My own lousy choices had created these circumstances but that was going to have to change. Oliver had given me a sense of purpose, a pressing need to live up to that and get my act together. I needed to get my career and finances in order and stop focusing on the fact that Jeremy had dumped me or I'd dumped him. Or we'd dumped each other . . . or whatever happened. I still wasn't clear. All I knew was Jeremy was gone and I wasn't happy about it.

I hopped behind the wheel and drove us back into Hollywood to the Whiskey Bar so I could meet the new husband. The last two hadn't done much to impress—or lasted very long—but this one, she assured me, was 'the real deal.' At least this one wasn't a struggling actor or a musician.

We walked through the lobby with Kelly turning all heads in the vicinity. She commanded attention wherever she went and reveled in it. She walked into a room with an almost feline grace. There was a slink in her hips that was subtle, yet at the same time hard to miss. It put any man in the room on alert. Her sexual power was something to behold.

"This is where I met George!" she said with a mischievous giggle. *George* naturally meant George C. Mr. C. had spent *quality time* with almost all of my actress girlfriends. Sadly, I was not on that list.

Once inside, a quick scan of the dark, tiny bar revealed that the *real deal* husband hadn't arrived yet.

"Sweetheart, let's start a tab," she said flicking her platinum credit card across the bar to the instantly attentive bartender. "Give us a couple of vodkas on the rocks. We'll be sitting over there."

"Absolutely." The artfully scruffy bartender leaned toward her, primed for further flirtation, but she turned on her heels and headed for the table nearest the door, leaving him lost in her wake. Nobody was immune to her charm, as evidenced by the cocktail waitress in the tiny black miniskirt who brought our drinks to the table. Even though this was a celebrity watering hole and they were accustomed to serving very famous people, the young girl melted in the warm glow of Kelly's fleeting attention.

"Thank you, darling," she purred, focusing on the girl. "Let's keep that tab *open*." Kelly mouthed the last word in a slow exaggerated motion and finished with a wink. The poor girl nearly dropped her tray.

"Scarlett, we need to find you a *good* man," she said, returning her attention to me. "Maybe my husband knows someone."

"Great," I said feigning enthusiasm. The last thing I needed was more men. Hadn't she just told me not to go from man to man? Now I was supposed to find a new one? We'd just established that I was a train wreck with men. There was nobody I wanted to meet.

I had no business hanging out with these young hipsters. It only made me feel old, lonely and even more depressed.

I excused myself and headed for the ladies room. Maybe Jeremy had felt us talking about him. I whipped my phone out as soon as I was out of sight, and was rewarded with zero calls and zero text messages for the effort.

Back in the bar, Kelly was surrounded by three men. I sighed heavily and hoped that one of them was the new husband so I could meet him and leave. Having a long history with Kelly, I knew better than to leave her unattended. I did not want to be held responsible for any aftermath. At least she was only drinking vodka. The really sloppy nights were the scotch ones.

The new husband, Adam, was tall, lean and looked like a scruffy rocker —black leather pants and a loose shirt—which was just what she liked. He had a nice calm energy about him, which was what she needed. Kelly needed someone to ground her. The best news was that while he looked like a rocker, he actually wasn't one and had a real job at a record label. The two guys with him were pleasant enough but I wasn't up to the task of small talk.

"So you survived the red carpet bullshit," Adam said to me with a grin.

"Yes, barely."

"Adam won't come with me to any event. He *loathes* the whole Hollywood thing." Kelly gazed at him with admiration.

I smiled but said nothing. He'd married the wrong person if he was hoping to avoid it. Kelly lived for publicity of any kind.

We sat down and Kelly began to make a series of toasts to her new husband, the miracle of true love, and all the unborn 'magical love-babies' they were going to be making. After the third round of toasts and all the merriment I could handle, I decided to make my escape.

"I have to go," I said and stood up.

"No, you don't. You can't leave now," she said, leaping to her feet and grabbing both my hands. "We're just getting started."

"I have to pick up Oliver early in the morning." I was lying.

"Don't try to fuckin' bullshit me! I'm a first-class bullshitter!" Kelly slurred, pulling my body in close to hers for a very tight hug, fixing her hands to my ass.

"I'm not bullshitting you. I have to go home," I insisted.

"Fine. Go home. But forget about that loser player guy! Fuck him! You deserve better."

Kelly grabbed my face with her hands and gave me a sloppy kiss on the mouth, extending a flicking, exploratory tongue between my lips. It was not a shock. Kelly would make out with a lamppost if she'd had enough to drink.

"*Okay*, that's enough, honey." Adam pulled one of her arms off me and reeled her back over in his direction.

"Good-night, Adam," I said. "It was nice to meet you."

"Nice to meet you, too, Scarlett." Adam wrapped Kelly's arms around his waist in an effort to contain her.

"Bye, sweetie, I'll call you when I'm back in town." She pried one arm loose and blew me an exaggerated kiss.

I knew this could mean 'you won't hear from me again for a year,' but sometimes a small dose of her was more than enough to sustain me for a year. As far as I was concerned, it made for a good arrangement. I could only handle so much 'Kelly truth' in my life.

I felt bad for Adam. He looked embarrassed that his hot mess of a new wife was trying to make out with someone else in front of his friends. But that was the deal with Kelly. She had a heart of gold, but she was a handful.

"I'll call you soon. Love you!" Kelly called out after me as I left.

The cab driver drove down La Cienega Boulevard toward Beverly Hills. The night was quiet and still. Los Angeles could be incredibly lonely and isolating; all these people driving around in their little boxes without connecting or interacting with anyone.

From the top of the hill, the city below looked like black velvet stretched out as far as the eye could see, adorned with twinkling colored beads. It reminded me of my first plane ride into Los Angeles as a teen. The black velvet city had looked so alive and full of promise, as if anything could happen, and quite often it did, but not the way you thought it would. Back then, I assumed that in time the city would open up and share all her secrets with me. All these years later and I was still waiting.

Going out to take my mind off my life wasn't the answer but, of course, I knew that. When I got home, the apartment was dark and filled with the stillness that I dreaded.

I got out a new canvas and started another painting. This one featured another nude woman but instead of looking bereft and beaten down, this time she was euphoric, lying on a sea of cupcakes and donuts. Large, colorful cupcakes cushioned her like a life raft. The silliness of it was the perfect counter to the evening's adventure. I laughed at the absurdity of it, took an aspirin, and went to bed.

Chapter Twenty
Piss-Off, Depression

Life carried on without a peep from Jeremy. The painful realization that I had meant nothing to him made the humiliation harder to avoid. He wasn't interested in me and perhaps he never had been. I had made a total fool of myself and was supposed to be past that nonsense at this point in my life.

If I didn't have work or auditions lined up, or Oliver was with X, I was in danger of falling into the black hole again. I was intimately acquainted with the black hole after doing the wretched dance with it during my divorce. To avoid this old trap, I would refer to my new mantra: 'Piss-Off, Depression!' or POD for short. This meant that when I was faced with unavoidable downtime, I had to commit to doing fun things such as going to yoga, painting, going to a movie or going for hikes in the park, taking a bath or masturbating—easier said than done in a full house. But whatever I did, I couldn't just sit home and wallow in it. Sometimes the formula was as simple as *just keep moving*. Some days going to the market or going to buy a coffee and having simple interaction with people saved me from the loneliness that threatened to engulf me.

Darcy sent me on a last-minute audition for an antidepressant medication in Hollywood. By now, I was pretty familiar with the actresses who went up for the same commercials, and said hello to the usual suspects. The director of the spot wanted me to look lost and depressed, which didn't seem that much of a stretch, and play with this dreary little doll that was supposed to represent me in my compromised depressed state. It was a 'sudden death' audition, where they eliminate you instantly if you are not what they are looking for, and ask the appropriate candidates to stay— leaving an awkward tension between the ones asked to stay and the ones asked to leave.

"Thanks, Scarlett, you can leave," said the casting assistant cheerily.

As I walked to my car and shook the rejection off, I laughed and took it as a good sign that at least I didn't look miserable enough to book a spot about depression. They should have caught me earlier.

When I got home, Oliver was sitting on the kitchen counter with Mikki and Sam, watching them boiling the teenage delicacy known as ramen noodles. Oliver was obsessed with the junk food noodles. Mikki and Sam subsisted on them, even when the fridge was stocked with suitable healthy alternatives. Sam and Mikki made exactly two things in the kitchen— milkshakes and noodles—and they were happy to include Oliver in their simple dining rituals. X would go ballistic if he thought I was letting Oliver ingest ramen noodles. They were not on his approved organic foods list, and that was part of their appeal.

"Scarlett, did you hear we're moving out?" Mikki called out to me.

No, I had not heard this news. "What do you mean?"

"Our friend Ronny's uncle owns an apartment building and he's going to rent one of them to us."

"Wow!" That would alleviate certain credit check requirements. "That's big news. Does CeCe know?"

"Yes, I told her last night."

I wondered why she hadn't mentioned it.

CeCe was remarkably sanguine about the news when I cornered her.

"Well, he is twenty now. He'll need to chart his own course at some point. I moved out at eighteen."

I was thirty-six and still living with my mother. Even my twenty-year-old brother could get his shit together enough to move out. I took this as evidence that there was something truly wrong with me. I couldn't realistically afford it yet with my erratic income, but aside from that, I was still resistant to the idea. There was comfort in coming home to people and bustling activity, even though sometimes it drove me mad. Oliver and I coming home to a quiet, empty apartment was something I didn't feel ready for. The full weight of my single mother status would be difficult to escape then.

Oliver was sad that Sam and Mikki were moving out, but on the bright side, their exit meant that he could have their room. CeCe loved to decorate and had big plans for Oliver's new room. He was going to get his very own big-boy bed! She wanted to buy him a flashy racecar bed he'd seen at Neiman Marcus, one where the bed sits inside the frame of a wooden racecar. It was very cool, very big boy indeed.

It had been very quiet work-wise, and I was fretting. I looked at extension classes at UCLA and tried to figure out what to do next. The freelance existence required deep wells of faith. It was like swinging on a trapeze and having to trust that when you let go there would be somewhere to swing to and land.

I scoured magazines and read the *LA Times* daily for anything that could lead to a makeup gig or a job lead. As I was browsing the newsstand on South Beverly Drive one day, I looked up and saw a familiar face watching me. His name was Paul Gold, and CeCe had briefly dated his father.

Whenever I saw him, he was wearing the Beverly Hills 'man of leisure' casual uniform of expensive sweats and a hoodie.

"Long time, no see," he said, smiling. His dark eyes darted over me.

"Hi, Paul. It's been forever."

"How is your mother?"

"She's good." I placed the copy of *Allure* back on the rack. "How is your dad?"

"He's doing okay. He's still living in Florida. He loves it there."

"Good for him."

"How are you doing? How's married life?"

"I'm getting divorced," I said with no emotion. What was the point in hiding it?

"Oh, wow . . . I'm sorry."

"I'm not. It's okay. My son and I have been living with my mom since the separation. The divorce process has been dragging out, but otherwise everything's fine. How are things with you?"

"I'm great. Life is great. You can't beat living in the Hills."

"I'm sure."

"If you're free, I'd love to take you to dinner sometime and catch up," he said.

"I'd like that," I said.

He got out his cell phone and programmed my number into it.

"I'll call you very soon. Good to see you," he said, giving me a chaste kiss on the cheek before hopping into his brand new silver Mercedes that was waiting at the curb.

I watched him drive away. There was something empowering about feeling broken-hearted but still accepting a dinner invitation from an attractive man. Screw Jeremy.

CeCe was going to freak when she heard this news. She had always harbored a thing for Paul. She used to rave on about what a lovely face he had, how polite he was, what a gentleman etc., etc. She all but salivated at the sight of him—and she was supposed to be dating his father. I had to admit he was appealing. Paul owned his masculinity. Tall and muscular with very short, cropped dark hair, he had a rough and tumble look, like a Brazilian street fighter—albeit one with a lot of cash. His demeanor was always polite and cordial, yet there was something mysterious about him. His stoic, reserved demeanor told me that those still waters likely ran deep.

CeCe had no clear idea what he did for a living. She and I would run into him in Beverly Hills having lunch or dinner with an assortment of stick-thin model-looking girlfriends. Usually, there was more than one girl at a time, as if his models only traveled in packs. The girls were good at creating commotion and accompanied by the ultimate attention-seeking accessories—small white yapping dogs. Paul always looked a little embarrassed by the spectacle, as if he were in on the joke. He would smile as if to say, 'Here I am with my traveling pack of models and small dogs!'

Paul called the next day and we talked for half an hour. We'd never had a lengthy conversation before. He asked a lot of probing questions. We talked about the disparate courses our lives had taken over the last few years; he had two broken engagements, I'd had one marriage, one kid and was enduring one divorce.

"You've been a busy girl!" he joked.

"What can I say? My finger was on the fast forward button," I said, trying to wrap it up. It was a boring subject.

With two broken engagements, Paul was hardly the poster boy for commitment but one could make the argument that *not* marrying one of his tipsy model friends was a very sound decision. As befitting his man-about-town status, he was busy for the coming weekend, so we made a plan for the following Saturday night.

CeCe thought it was a spectacular turn of events.

"Oh, he's so lovely. I knew one of us had to have him!"

"Keep your pants on, CeCe! It's just dinner."

"We'll see . . . one dinner leads to another."

Chapter Twenty-One
Beverly Hills Man of Mystery

The dearth of work ended when a producer I knew called to hire me for a three-day makeup job on a documentary she was doing. I could make it fit with my schedule with Oliver, and I was thrilled to have work. It was such a joy when everything flowed effortlessly.

The following Saturday, Paul picked me up to take me to Dan Tana's for dinner. He was wearing jeans and a black silk shirt that skimmed his frame beautifully. I caught a hint of his cologne when he opened the door for me. His distinctly masculine presence coupled with an enticing fragrance was a potent cocktail—a juxtaposition of forces. It was a delicate balance to achieve. It had to be the right cologne on the right man, but when it worked, it was a powerful aphrodisiac.

Dan Tana's was packed with short men, tall women in tight dresses, and a token sprinkling of celebrities. It was a local landmark and a favorite old Hollywood haunt that featured fantastic Italian food. The maître d' gave Paul a giant hug and seated us promptly at a prime table.

"Are you from LA originally?" I asked him after we were seated and had ordered drinks.

"Yes, I'm a local. I've been coming to this restaurant since I was a kid with my family. I've forgotten where you're from . . . is it England?"

"Australia."

"Right. Now I remember. What brought you out here?"

"This is where all the magic happens, isn't it?"

He laughed. "I don't know about that."

"When I was growing up in Australia, I was obsessed with all things American: movies, television, music, fashion—you name it. I was determined to get here, one way or another. Luckily, my family ended up moving here. "

"Now that you're here, is it magical?"

"It can be. The other day I was working on a job doing the makeup for musicians appearing in a documentary. We set up the interviews in old recording studios tucked away in Hollywood. It was really cool. Walking the halls where Frank Sinatra and all these other great artists had recorded hits, and feeling the energy in that place, it was such a treat! Marinating for three days in all that creative juice felt like such a privilege. Hollywood is a giant vault filled with places like that. But over the years, living a day-to-day existence here, it's easy to forget how magical the town can be."

"Yeah, I've grown up here and I never think about any of that."

"Exactly," I said, as the waiter came to take our order.

Paul asked me what I wanted.

"The lady will have the New York steak, medium," he said. "And I'll have the lamb chops, rare."

Paul's exceptional attention to detail was a new experience. It was important to him that I was enjoying myself.

"Is the steak to your liking?" he asked after I had taken a few bites.

"It's a bit rare for me," I said.

He instantly summoned the waiter and sent the steak back.

My diet coke tasted suspiciously like real coke, so Paul exchanged that, too. He went to great lengths to ensure I was satisfied in every possible way. I couldn't decide if his focus was refreshing or disarming—or maybe a combination of both.

The backless Diane von Furstenberg dress I was wearing refused to cooperate. It kept slipping off my shoulder, threatening to flash my entire left breast at him. I'd bought it to wear with Jeremy, but we'd broken up before I'd had the chance. Now I was stuck with trying to delicately balance my elbow on the table all night in order to thwart the unwanted exposure. He was aware of it but I didn't catch him looking once. He was the perfect gentleman.

"So . . . have you dated much since your separation?"

"I've had one relationship since the marriage ended," I said.

"Why did it end?"

"He wasn't available for a relationship. I think he was a little freaked out by the fact that I have a kid."

"Didn't you tell him?"

"Yes, of course I did."

"It sounds like that guy had commitment issues."

I laughed. "Commitment issues? That's funny coming from a guy who's had two broken engagements! But you're probably right . . ."

His jaw dropped for a second and then he threw back his head and laughed heartily. "Are you saying *I* have commitment issues?"

"No, I just said it was *funny*—"

"I broke off my engagements because they were both gold-diggers and cheaters," he said, with a tight smile affixed to his lips. "I won't have a problem with committing to the *right* woman."

"Fair enough," I said and decided to leave that subject alone.

"Let's go to The Beverly Hills Hotel for a drink," he said, as we waited for his car at the valet.

I hesitated for a moment. I'd had my one vodka, and was ready to go home and watch *Saturday Night Live*. "It's been a really long week . . ."

"Oh, come on. How about a coffee or tea, or a dessert at least? It's Saturday night. I can't take you home this early. It would be very bad for my reputation."

I smiled. He was working very hard. "Okay, one quick nightcap," I said and he steered the car up toward Sunset Boulevard.

When we arrived at The Beverly Hills Hotel, every valet knew his name and they jumped to attention as he approached. A chorus of "Good evening, Mr. Gold" greeted us at every turn. The maître d' in the Polo Lounge bent over backward to accommodate us, immediately giving us a highly coveted booth in the front, which infuriated the guests who had been waiting. Paul then instructed the maître d' to lower the lighting to his liking. He nodded and said, "Right away, sir."

I ordered tea and Paul ordered bourbon on the rocks.

"I can see you're a regular." I noted how good he was at getting what he wanted.

The waiter swept back in gracefully and deposited our drinks.

"I like it here. Do you come here often?" Paul asked when we were alone.

"I got married at this hotel," I said casually as I poured honey into my mint tea.

"Here? Oh, shit! I'm sorry, sweetheart, I didn't know. Why didn't you say something? I'll take you somewhere else. We could go down to the Peninsula?"

"No . . . it's fine. I *love* this hotel. It can't be held responsible for my lousy marriage. Let's forget about my marriage. Let's talk about your boozy model girlfriends instead. That's a much more interesting subject!"

He laughed. "There's nothing to talk about. They were too young. I'm looking for more in a relationship now. Those girls are fun but after a while, it gets boring. No matter how beautiful they are, it's the same thing over and over. I'm looking for substance—and quality."

He'd been coached on the correct answers: looking for more in a relationship, bored with the fun and frivolity, able to commit to the 'right' woman.

He told me a little more about himself. He talked about his close bond with his siblings. He had two younger brothers and a sister. He spoke about his work, and how he managed the family import-export business with his brothers. Family was very important to him.

He paid the check and on the way out we were serenaded again by choruses of "Good-night, Mr. Gold!" and "Thank you for coming, Mr. Gold!" or "Hope to see you soon, Mr. Gold!" He must have greased a lot of palms over the years to get that kind of hearty reception.

It was almost midnight when he walked me to my front door. His hands were fidgeting in the front pockets of his jacket. For the first time during the entire evening, he seemed a tiny bit unsure of himself. The flash of vulnerability behind the cool, confident exterior made him more interesting.

"Well, should we do this again?" he asked.

"I don't know. What do you think?" I said with a smile, and bounced the ball back into his court.

"I think we will *definitely* be doing this again." He leaned in and gave me another non-imposing kiss on the cheek.

"I'll call you next week. Have a great night," he said brightly as he strolled down the path back to his car.

I smiled. It was a funny thing to say to someone when it was almost midnight.

Emma and I met for breakfast at Urth Café the next morning and rehashed the evening's events over honey-vanilla lattes.

Emma had just been to the gym and attacked her breakfast burrito with gusto.

"So how was it? Do you think you'll see him again?" she asked.

"It was fun. He said he'd call next week. There's something about him that seems a little . . . off. I can't quite put my finger on it," I said, as I tucked into my smoked salmon plate.

"You'll find out what his story is. Besides, what's the harm in a few dates? It'll help you move on from that Jeremy twat."

She was right. It did stop me from obsessing about Jeremy and that had to be a good thing.

Emma was up for a major recurring role on another CSI, so we went back to her house and rehearsed the lines for her audition.

"Detective Harlot, what is going on with this investigation?" I gruffly demanded of her, trying to keep a straight face.

"It's *Harlowe*. Sir, we've identified the leaks in the case and it's being handled." Emma tossed her hair dramatically for effect. We both erupted into giggles. A lot of auditions consisted of trying to say terrible lines with a straight face.

I missed those days when we were hustling to auditions all over town and changing clothes in our cars, never knowing if the next audition could transform everything. I missed the sense of excitement and possibility but I didn't miss the rejection and disappointment. For Emma that sense of promise was still her reality. I predicted it was just a matter of time before someone was smart enough to give her a lead in a series that showcased her talents to full effect.

Sometimes my heart ached a little and I wished that it had worked out that way for me, but mostly I was learning to be okay with it.

Chapter Twenty-Two
Take It Or Leave It

Over the next few weeks, while Paul was busy squiring me to lovely dinners, a funny thing happened—I forgot to think about Jeremy.

We had a flurry of intoxicatingly romantic dinners at the best restaurants in town, which happened to be the only restaurants he was interested in. He wouldn't be caught dead in a little hole-in-the-wall sushi place.

Paul was into what pleases a woman. Exotic floral arrangements of hydrangeas, roses and tuberose started to arrive on a weekly basis.

CeCe was thrilled and a bit envious. "Now this is more like it!" she said with admiration. "This boy's got style!"

We had our first kiss in a dark corner of the bar at The Peninsula. After finishing a long, lingering dinner at The Ivy, we made our way over for a nightcap. Paul was big on nightcaps. He was turning me into a night owl. Only a handful of people were in the bar by the time we got there. We amused ourselves watching a negotiation of sorts between some large German businessmen and two disproportionately attractive women. Paul assured me they were hookers. It seemed a reasonable assumption because the women were so much younger—and hotter—than the fat German men. It made for a riveting diversion.

Paul ordered mojitos.

The mojito was delicious and went down a little too smoothly, belying its potent effects. Paul quickly ordered another round.

We hadn't had anything resembling a real kiss even after a handful of dates. I was getting tired of waiting for him to make his move. I needed to know if it was worth going any further with him or if I should relegate him to the 'friend' category.

"Are you going to get around to kissing me anytime soon?" I asked him, emboldened by the mojito.

He laughed, leaned in, and gave me a tender, breathtaking kiss that completely got my attention. *Holy fuck!* He was an amazing kisser and he smelled divine. He tasted divine, an appealing mixture of breath mints and mojito. His soft, freshly shaven face proved irresistible. I put my hand on his cheek, and pulled his face and lips back into mine. Although I thought we were being discreet, tucked away in a dark corner, the waitress appeared almost instantly at our table.

"Okay, sweethearts . . . that's enough," she said, expertly walking the fine line between admonishing us, which might risk her tip, and fulfilling her duty as proprietress—a wrangler of drunks and inappropriate lovers.

We promised to behave but started kissing again as soon as she was out of sight. Now that our mouths had found each other, they were like two magnets and it was difficult to pry them apart.

"Okay sweethearts, I'm going to have to ask you to leave," she said, presenting Paul with the tab. She stood there waiting as he struggled to find his wallet.

We were being ejected like naughty teenagers—it was *gloriously* wicked.

Paul paid the tab. Since we'd both had a few drinks, we left his car there and took a cab, and proceeded to devour each other in the back seat. I instructed him to drop me at home. I was testing the waters but I was in no hurry to consummate this deal; in fact, I was terrified. Since I'd completely lost my head once I'd slept with Jeremy, I wanted to take my time. Paul seemed happy to go along with the ride and let me control this one part of the equation.

My radar told me he was dangerous. I couldn't pinpoint it exactly, but there was an air about him and it dictated that I move forward cautiously. He was doing the right things and saying the right things but I didn't quite relax with him. Why this radar didn't go off with Jeremy is a mystery. Paul was used to dating a lot of women and I had no interest in becoming just another name on his roster. After all the bullshit with Jeremy, I had transformed into some sort of maverick dating creature—or maybe I just didn't care as much—but things came out of my mouth that I would never have had the nerve to say to a man before. The new bravado extended even after the effects of the mojito wore off. Who was this confident, powerful woman suddenly seizing control of my brain? And where had she been hiding for the last thirty-something years?

We had been dating for almost six weeks. We would end up in bed sometime soon, this much I knew. He was a luscious kisser and I didn't see any point in waiting much longer. Besides, I was keen to have memories of melting with Jeremy out of my system. Every time I closed my eyes at night, I could almost feel Jeremy slipping into me. For self-preservation, if nothing else, I needed to evict him from my body.

Over dinner on Saturday night at Mastro's, I told Paul, point-blank, "Just so we're clear, I have no interest in being one of many women you are possibly screwing."

He paused with his fork in midair, but I was undeterred.

"If you are intimate with other women—or plan on being intimate—don't bother going any further with me," I said, nonchalantly. "We can maintain a friendship but I have *zero* interest in being one of many women in your life —or in your bed. So that's the deal. That's where I'm coming from."

He almost choked on his rib eye steak.

"I can't believe you just said that to me!" he said, laughing and wiping his mouth with his napkin. "No woman has ever said *anything* like that to me before." He looked at me with marked admiration. "Baby, you've got *balls*!"

I couldn't believe I'd said it either.

I sat there silently for a minute, weighing my new balls, afraid of what might fly out of my mouth next. I never would have dared to say anything like it to Jeremy.

Paul studied me for a moment before a sly smile slowly crept its way across his face. "So what you're saying is you want *exclusivity*?" he asked, measuring the words carefully before releasing them.

"Well . . . only if you plan on sleeping with me," I replied calmly.

"I guess I just got myself a girlfriend. Check please!" He flagged the waiter immediately and handed him his black American Express card. "Could you run this for me? We're in a hurry!"

What just happened? I hadn't expected him to say yes quite so quickly. My head was spinning. It certainly seemed a lot easier when you laid it out for them: 'Here's the deal, buddy—take it or leave it.' I'd always been too scared to do that before, scared of looking needy. After walking blindly into a broken heart with Jeremy, I couldn't afford to be an emotional wreck again. Jeremy had kicked my ass but, hopefully, I was a little wiser for it.

We drove straight back to Paul's house in the hills, barely stopping at red lights. I had deliberately avoided taking the tour of his home until now. As I suspected, it was a fabulous house. Spanish-style and draped in bougainvillea, the house was so sexy it almost had a pulse. Most women he brought home would probably slip out of their panties the moment they made it past the front door—and tonight I may or may not be the exception, but at least it would be on my terms.

He helped me out of the car and we made our way up to the house. My heart began to race. The game was on. From the driveway, there were tiny mushroom lights accentuating the way up the steps to the front door, illuminating impressive landscaping on the way. The bewitching scent of night-blooming jasmine greeted us as we made our climb to the entrance. The front door was dark wood with intricate carvings and a bold brass handle. Inside, the décor had an Oriental flavor with large Buddha statues placed around the living room and fuchsia orchids sitting at their feet. The walls displayed artwork that was a cultivated mix: erotic paintings of women in various states of ecstasy, juxtaposed with martial-arts-themed masculine pieces, including one huge oil painting of two bloody boxers in a ring that dominated an entire wall. Women and martial arts: the passionate pursuits in his life.

I stood transfixed in front of an oil painting depicting a woman sitting with a snake between her legs, rising up from who knows where. I studied the intricate detail and the pattern of the snake. There was something hypnotic about it. Then something struck me.

"Hey . . . are you the snake?" I asked and laughed.

"Come upstairs with me and you'll find out," he said as he took my hand. I followed him up the winding steel staircase. Leading the way down the hall toward his bedroom, he had the good sense to joke about his 'Wall of Testosterone'—a series of photographs lining the wall depicting him in various masculine pursuits. There was a photograph of him sitting in the cockpit of a small plane, one of him parachuting out of another plane, one in his karate gear disassembling an opponent, and one of him kayaking in Kauai. I expected the last one to be of him sitting alone, in front of another beautiful backdrop, with large, erect cock in hand—but mercifully it was one of him post-marathon, sweaty and triumphant. It was a bit much, but again, he seemed to be in on the joke.

Everything about Paul seemed primed for seduction, especially his probing questions, wanting instant access to my innermost thoughts. *He wanted to get inside me.* He wanted to know how my mind worked, what turned me on. He approached the act of seduction it as if it were his vocation, his purpose in life—and perhaps it was.

His bedroom was tastefully done in olive and gold, with a few splashes of red for good measure. It screamed *sex*. Large decorative pillows sat in an orderly fashion on the bed. Candles sat expectantly beside the bed, ready to be called into action. Paul walked over and proceeded to light them. There were twin dark wood Chinese medicine cabinets, gold lamps, mirrors and large windows that showcased the twinkling lights of Hollywood below. It was a den of debauchery. I felt queasy, like I might have gotten in over my head. I concentrated on my breathing as he laid me onto the bed, almost losing me in the midst of the massive elaborate pillow configuration, and started kissing me.

"You don't actually make this bed yourself, do you?" I broke away and sat up, eager to slow things down a bit, and swatted the small decorative pillows out of my face. "You must have a housekeeper who makes it."

"No, I make it. Why?"

"No straight man can make a bed this well!" I said, laughing nervously.

He looked at me for a second and laughed. "Sweetheart, do you think I'm *gay*?"

"No! What I meant was I'm impressed that you are such a tasteful, *meticulous* fellow."

He hung his head and shook it in amazement before smiling.

"You're a funny one. Yes, *I* make the bed. My mother always made us make the bed every day. Some habits stick, I guess. Now shhhhhhh!"

Paul pushed me back on the bed and kissed me slowly and deeply. He trailed his way south, pausing to gently kiss and bite my skin. He peeled my panties off and enthusiastically went to town, licking and sucking me. As I suspected, his attention to detail outside the bedroom translated into a very attentive partner in bed.

"Do you like this?" he asked as his tongue made circles on my clit.

"Uh-huh." I moaned.

"How about this?" He moved his tongue up and down me in slow strokes. I swallowed. "Yes. That . . . um . . . that feels very, *very* good."

He pulled my hips into him and wouldn't let me move as he alternated between stroking and circling this tongue dance on me.

After what felt like a really long time, and plenty of prompting on my part, he grabbed a condom and eased it on.

He eased his way on top of me and kissed me again. He pressed my thighs apart and after a few preliminary strokes, he dove into me. This sudden penetration sucked the breath right out of me, but as he moved it started to feel really good.

He was a very proficient lover but there was nothing relaxed or organic about his lovemaking; it just felt like fucking. I couldn't get out of my head. It felt rehearsed and technical, which made me miss the syrupy sweetness of sex with Jeremy. Paul had an orgasm and noticed that I didn't, which bothered him.

"You just need to relax a bit more, baby," he said. "First times are always awkward."

He kissed me good-night and we went to sleep on different sides of the bed—another sharp contrast to Jeremy.

The next morning, we drove to the Beverly Wilshire Hotel to have brunch, after making a quick pit stop so I could change.

Paul referred to me as his girlfriend all day. "Could you please bring some more coffee for my *girlfriend*?"

Being with Paul was indulgent. He knew how to enjoy life. He was only interested in the best of everything and it was fun to be along for the ride. I couldn't discern whether Paul loved women or was just very good with them, but we went back to his house and I surrendered to his attentions in bed all afternoon. This time, I came.

By the end of the day, I was lit up like a Christmas tree. X regarded me quizzically when I picked up Oliver.

"What's up with you?" he asked, not masking his annoyance.

"Nothing. Why?"

"You look . . . different," he said, while checking out my tousled bed-hair.

"Do I? I can't imagine why," I said, trying not to smile. But I did feel different. Officially, I had a boyfriend.

Chapter Twenty-Three
Blow Jobs For Botox

Autumn and I met up during the week at the Korean day spa tucked away on Olympic Boulevard. It was our favorite spot for a little rejuvenation. Autumn had discovered it years ago. Her days as a model had cemented her instinct for finding the best person for *anything* in town. She was the ultimate resource for anything relating to self-care and could tell you where to find the best acupuncturist, manicurist or plastic surgeon, as well as the best beauty bargains and newest skin treatments. She used to joke about trying to trade blowjobs for Botox with one doctor she went to. He declined. After hearing that story, we came up with what we thought was a brilliant business idea: starting an online company of T-shirts and bumper stickers stating naughty things like '*Blow-jobs for Botox.*' But then we decided that idea was probably already taken. Still, I loved the idea of having my own business.

The Korean spa was a little hideaway close to downtown Los Angeles and it offered the best body treatments—decadent massages and body scrubs—along with saunas, steam rooms and a hot tub. Clean and minimalist, it was the best deal in town. During the week it was mostly populated with older Korean women, but on the weekends the hipsters descended. It wasn't such a well-kept secret anymore. A few magazines had done stories about its jade steam rooms and the mugwort hot tea bath that was supposedly very good for your skin, so now everyone was catching on. It wasn't uncommon for me to run into my agent, Darcy Hobbs. Frolicking naked with your agent made for awkward moments.

Autumn and I lay on our tiny white towels in the empty sauna.

"How's it going with your new guy?" Autumn asked, and twisted her long, wet hair into a bun.

"He's been treating me very well. We've been to the best restaurants in town, he calls frequently, and he sends flowers. He uses the same florist Jeremy used. Isn't that funny?"

"Cut to the chase—what's he like in bed?" Autumn poured water onto the rocks, producing a satisfying hiss.

"He's a fantastic lover. He's very attentive . . . maybe a little too attentive, now that I think about it."

"What do you mean?"

"I hate to seem ungrateful, but he insists on going down on me for a *really* long time! After about half an hour everything just feels numb and I'd like to move on, but if I try to sit up he just pushes me back down and keeps going!"

"Oh, yeah, that's a bit excessive. I never much cared for getting head. I like it if we've been fucking for ages and all our juices are mixed together; then I'll let him get down there, get his face in it and get to work."

"That sounds nasty!"

"That's the idea. Oral sex is only good if a guy *really* knows what he's doing. I'll give him a little instruction but if he's not a quick learner, forget it!"

"What kind of instruction?" I asked, intrigued at the thought.

"I pull him up by the ears and say 'You've been watching too many pornos, buddy! That's not how we like it!' " She pantomimed holding the two ears above her crotch and demonstrated the furious licking. We both roared with laughter.

"But it is time someone made it about you, for a change. That part, at least, is a good thing," Autumn said and wiped the sweat from her brow.

"Except that I get the feeling it's not about me at all. He's all about the act of seduction but it doesn't feel personal. Even his house screams sex with all the pillows and candles. It feels shallow. He's very proficient in the sack but I don't feel that I'm connecting with him—and I need that part."

"He sounds like one of those typical LA guys, spoiled by too much time in the candy store. I'm not predicting a long shelf life for this one."

Autumn was probably right but I didn't want to totally squash my new relationship. It was fun being with Paul, and I didn't want to give it up yet.

Paul invited me to attend his sister's birthday party with him. Before the party I wanted to find something cute to wear. Oliver and I went to The Grove for some shopping and spent the afternoon riding the trolley, getting ice cream and reading in the bookstore. My cell rang while we were in Barnes and Noble. It was Paul.

"Hello, baby. How are you today?"

"I'm fine. Oliver and I are shopping at The Grove. We're in the bookstore buying some books."

"Oh, great. Could you do me a favor? There's a book I want to pick up, and since you're there it would save me a lot of time if you'd get it for me."

"Of course. What book is it?"

"It's called *The Rule Book: 100 Things Men Do When They're Cheating.*"

"You're kidding, right?" I laughed at the ludicrous title.

"No. My friend told me about it and said I had to read it."

"Oh?" This didn't sound good at all. Why was he asking me to buy him a book about cheating? Alarm bells were sounding in my head.

"Um . . . okay," I said. "But just one thing, is it for *you* or should I be buying it for me?"

"No, baby!" he said, laughing. "You're so funny! I would never cheat on *you.* You know that! I just want to read the book from a psychological viewpoint."

"What does that mean?" I asked, bewildered by his request.

"You know . . . I like to learn about people and study them."

"How do you know you'd never cheat on me?"

"Because *you* are special, that's why."

It sounded like a crock of shit. "How am I special?"

"Because you are *quality,* baby!"

"Oh," I said wondering what that meant exactly. My stomach dropped, with my mood quickly following suit. "Okay," I said reluctantly. "If they have it, I'll pick it up for you."

"Thanks, baby. I'll call you later."

We hung up and I became wretchedly curious about this cheating book. I hadn't noticed a single book at his house. Why was he now professing a purely "psychological" interest in the book, like he was fucking Freud.

Oliver was sitting on the floor in front of me with a fan of *Dr. Seuss, Dora the Explorer* and *Danny and The Dinosaur* books surrounding him.

"Come on, sweetheart. Mama has to find a book for a friend."

"Mama, can I get this?" Oliver produced a happy-looking green book from another pile for my approval. The title proudly read *The Best Bottom.* We'd read it together earlier. The story featured farm animals vying for the title of *The Best Bottom*—and it was hilarious. CeCe would love it!

"Yep, that's just the book we need right now. Let's go buy it."

We walked to the counter and I asked the clerk if he had heard of some book about cheating called *The Rule Book.*

"Oh, yeah," he said, nodding sympathetically. "The Cheater's Handbook. I know the one you're talking about. It's over here in the self-help section."

The clerk probably thought I was some sad woman whose husband was cheating on her. But I'd already been that woman. Somehow, the idea of correcting him and saying, 'My new boyfriend asked me to buy it for him' sounded even worse.

Oliver and I trailed the clerk through the self-help section and paused behind him while he quickly scanned the shelves. After a moment, he triumphantly thrust a bright orange book into my hands. There it was. A book dedicated to unveiling the top one hundred shitty things men do and say when they're cheating on you. My guts churned as I thanked the clerk.

Oliver and I waited in line to pay and I opened the book. The very first warning in the very first chapter was:

Number One: He says: "I'd never cheat on you."

I gasped. I called Paul right back. "Um . . . hi. I have your book for you

—"

"Great. Thanks, baby. I'll get it from you later."

"Guess what the number one thing is that the cheaters say to their partners?"

"No idea, baby."

"They say, 'I would never cheat on *you*.' Isn't that funny? That's exactly what you just said to me."

He paused slightly, and nervous laughter quickly followed. "Yeah, baby, that's pretty funny!"

"I don't know if you need this book. It sounds like you kinda know the drill."

More nervous laughter followed. "You are *too* funny, baby! You two have a great afternoon and I'll catch up with you later."

We hung up and I paid for the two books: a cheater's handbook for Paul, and a children's book about best bottoms. This time the clerk was careful not to meet my eyes.

Chapter Twenty-Four
What Happens In Vegas

"Damn, baby, you look sexy as fuck!" Paul exclaimed as I dressed for the birthday dinner. Jeans and a lacy black shirt had never met with such an enthusiastic response before, but for Paul it must have hit the right note. In his book 'sexy as fuck' was the height of compliments. It didn't get any better than that.

We drove to Mastro's again to meet his sister and her friends for her birthday dinner. There was a private room reserved in the back and we joined a group of twenty-six for dinner. Paul introduced me to his sister, Kristy, who was turning twenty-eight, and I gave her the fancy candle I'd picked out for her present. Kristy was a stunning blonde with a runner's tight physique, effectively showcased in a chocolate-colored bandage dress.

She looked me over and gave me a warm hug, saying, "Thanks for coming. Paul says great things about you!"

Paul introduced me to his younger brothers, their girlfriends and the rest of Kristy's group of friends.

When we were seated and the dinner commenced, I began to feel self-conscious. Several of the women made eye contact with me but when I smiled back, they looked away. As Paul's new girlfriend, it was understandable that I would meet a certain amount of curiosity, but I thought I detected something more.

"Is it my imagination or do the women here seem to be *really* checking me out? Is my blouse see-through or something?" I whispered to Paul, as our salads were being served.

"Shit . . . are you uncomfortable, baby? I'm sorry. I was going to mention something but I didn't want to freak you out."

"Mention what?"

"Well . . . it's just that . . . I've kind of *dated* a lot of my sister's friends," he said cautiously, keeping his voice low.

"Oh?"

"Not *all* of them . . . but . . . quite a few."

"Which ones?" I asked, scanning the table for likely candidates.

He didn't answer.

"What about this one sitting opposite us?" I asked, referring to an alarmingly skinny girl with curly dark hair and smudged eyeliner who had been throwing attitude at me since we walked in.

"Yeah, that's Nicole. We slept together a few times . . . but it was years ago . . . and it was nothing. Baby, I don't want you to feel uncomfortable. Nobody here meant anything to me the way you do."

I felt ill.

"What about the redhead next to her?"

"I never slept with her . . . but I did go down on her and her blond friend in the ladies' room at a nightclub once . . . but that was in Vegas years ago. What happens in Vegas stays in Vegas, right, baby?"

I decided Paul had some sort of sexual Tourette's syndrome. He compulsively blurted out shocking details, regardless of the impact. He couldn't possibly believe these details helped his cause? He couldn't seem to control this impulse, even when it was in his own best interests.

"I didn't sleep with the heavyset one or the older lady at the end of the table . . ."

"Are you *fucking kidding me*?" I hissed at him. "Why would you bring me here? I feel like an idiot. So you're basically telling me you've screwed all the *cute* ones here?"

"Sweetheart, I'm sorry," he said, shaking his head. "I thought it would be okay and you wouldn't notice. Of course I'm gonna date my sister's friends if they're *cute*—why wouldn't I? I'm a guy! My sister's been a good resource for women over the years—but that was all before I met you. Everything has changed now. I wanted *you* to be here tonight because you're my woman and I'm crazy about you. I want them all to see what a great lady I have and how happy I am."

I didn't know what to say to him.

I knew Paul was a player, but to sit and have dinner face to face with a high number of his conquests was a bit much. I stuck it out through dinner and engaged some of the women in conversation. The way to survive the dinner was to own it.

His sister came up to me after dinner. "I've never seen my brother look this happy. What's the secret?"

I had to admit he did look content.

"I don't know that any one woman can please him for long," I said.

She smiled. "You know him well, then."

"Yes, I'm starting to get the picture."

He was apologetic about subjecting me to the evening and was working hard to make it up to me. While not in his league, I hadn't exactly been a nun either. But I couldn't escape the fact that it changed how I felt about him. All of the information I was getting about him made me want to run as fast as I could. We were very different people with very different values and that was becoming increasingly apparent. I also had developed a stomachache that never seemed to go away when I was with him. It was obvious that his hedonistic package wasn't going to work for Oliver and me.

Quietly seething, I managed to hold it together for the duration of the dinner.

I was relieved when it was time to leave.

We waited silently at the valet. I collected my thoughts and contemplated how to do what had to be done.

As soon as we were in the car, I took a deep breath and jumped in.

"Could you take me home, please?"

"What do you mean? It's Saturday night?"

"I've come to an important realization," I said, as he looked puzzled.

"Oh, really, baby? What's that?"

"That I'm done with this arrangement," I said, throwing my arms up in the air in resignation. "I'm done with you telling me inappropriate tales from your fucking boudoir! And I'm done with hearing how you need *me* to buy you some book on *cheating!* Seriously, what the fuck is that about? I'm quite sure you could be *writing the damn book yourself!*"

"Now, sweetheart. I said I was sorry about all that."

"I don't care to hear about all the women you've screwed in Vegas—or anywhere else for that matter. And I certainly don't care to have dinner with *a whole fucking slew of them!*"

"Okay, now, baby . . . you need to calm down. Are you feeling jealous? Is that the problem? You're acting really unstable right now," he said in a calm and condescending voice that made me want to dig my nails into the seat and tear up his upholstery.

"No, I am feeling quite stable," I said between clenched teeth.

"What are you really upset about, sweetheart?"

"Don't patronize me. We're *done.* You can do what you like. It's not my problem what—or who—you screw anymore. Save it for the next girl."

"Are you trying to get me to break up with you, baby? Because you're really testing me with this bullshit!" He was starting to get annoyed, and for some reason, that seemed to calm me.

"I'm not *trying* to break up with you. I *am* breaking up with you," I said, firmly and evenly.

"Oh, really? You think you can break up with me? Nobody breaks up with me. I was going to break up with *you!*"

He slammed his foot onto the accelerator and I held on.

"Just take me home, please."

"Gladly."

We flew down Burton Way and he maneuvered the car through the side streets until we came to mine.

I looked at him for a moment but he was too angry to speak.

I put my hand on the door.

"Get out," he said, as if I needed encouragement.

I got out and slammed the door for emphasis.

That went well, I thought as I watched him peel up the street, leaving a trail of burnt rubber behind him.

One of our neighbors, Mrs. Whitaker, was walking her dog, and looked over and smiled sympathetically at me.

"Everything okay?" she inquired.

"Yes, never better. Thank you," I said and hurried inside.

Being with Paul was starting to make me feel dirty—and not in a good way. It was like layers of dirt were starting to accumulate on my skin and I needed to scrub them off.

I wasn't sure how I'd break the news to CeCe but everyone else in my circle was going to be ecstatic.

I texted Emma to give her the update.

~Depending on your perspective, dinner was a great success. Broke up with Paul. It turns out he'd slept with most of the women at the party! Not kidding.

Congratulations! Good move. R U OK?

~Strangely, yes.

Good riddance! So over the man-whores!

At least I had cut bait early on. Perhaps it would have been better if I'd skipped him altogether but sometimes progress is made in small steps.

I made a cup of tea, pulled out a new canvas and got to work. Another nude woman, but instead of lost and lonely looking, this time she was adrift on a sea of penises. Big ones, small ones, limp ones, erect ones—a smorgasbord of cocks in all shades and sizes. I laughed as it recalled memories of X's screen-saver collection.

CeCe came home from her date, heard me chuckling in the dining room and came to look over my shoulder.

"How was your date?" I asked.

"It was okay. Nothing special. Why are you home?"

"I felt like coming home."

"I see things are looking up," she announced brightly, examining the penises closely for anatomical correctness. "Oh, I rather like this one!" she said, pointing to a robust pink one.

"I think I'll call this painting 'The Sea of Dicks,' " I said, painting a few precisely placed pubic hairs on one pair of testicles.

"This could be your best work! Maybe we should hang it over the couch in the living room?"

"Do you really think Oliver's not going to notice a bunch of dicks on the wall?" I asked, shocked at the suggestion. My nocturnal painting efforts were for therapy and amusement, not for public consumption—and certainly not for my kid to see.

"Well, we can tell him they're oysters or exotic seashells or something!"

CeCe said, enjoying the prospect. "He won't know what they are."

"CeCe, Oliver is a boy. He actually has a penis—and he's pretty sharp. I'm positive he'd figure it out. But besides the Oliver issue, it would take a lot of explaining to your dates. Don't you think it might be intimidating for someone to pick you up and find penises on display on the wall . . . like trophies of cocks?"

"I don't know . . . I think it's a conversation piece." CeCe mulled the words over in her mouth.

"You seem irritable," she said accurately.

"I am. The party didn't go very well."

"Oh? Why is that?"

I was going to have to deliver the disappointing news at some point, and decided the best approach was to dive right in.

"It didn't work out with Paul. We broke up." I said

"What do you mean? I thought it was going really well."

"Well, it hasn't been." I said, wiping the brushes and putting them away. "He's got some big issues. He's not the right match for us. There were a lot of things that bothered me about him. He kept mentioning cheating and then had me buy him some cheater's manual and I never really recovered from that bizarre incident. We were at very different places in our lives. I couldn't see how in the world it could go anywhere, and so I broke up with him," I said, sounding more sensible than I felt.

"But why would you want to go and do that? Paul is a very nice man. He's a man of means and he has *such* a lovely face—"

"Yes, *Mother*, Paul has a lovely face, but *you* try going to a party with him and discovering that half the women there have had the pleasure of sitting on that lovely face! That's exactly what happened tonight at his sister's dinner. He'd slept with half of them! And the other half, the ones he hasn't *technically* screwed—not counting the one large woman and the old lady—the remaining women have given him head in the bathroom! Let's see how *lovely* you find all that."

"Well, that boy knows how to have a good time!" CeCe snickered.

Her amusement further enraged me. Why couldn't she be supportive?

"Yes, that's my point. He does know how to have a good time. It is his entire focus in life, aside from sitting around and counting how much money he has. Paul is 'Mr. Good Time Guy', not to be confused with 'Mr. Come-Raise-My-Kid-With-Me Guy'."

"Well, yes, perhaps that's true but people can change. Whatever you do, don't go back to that silly Jeremy boy again. Jeremy jerked you around and he'll only do it again. Don't make another big mistake, Scarlett."

"Since when has going back to Jeremy been an option? But Paul isn't a viable option either. I'm sorry if that disappoints you. Obviously I'm lousy at choosing men, and nobody is more frustrated than me about that, but that's not exactly a news flash. I'm sick of the whole bloody lot of them!"

"Oliver is disappointed, too, don't forget," she said, and effectively torpedoed any good feelings I had achieved by dumping Paul.

"Well, I'm figuring things out a bit quicker, at least."

CeCe sighed heavily. She went into the bedroom and closed the door behind her.

Chapter Twenty-Five
The Flick

Work was starting to be a little more regular. Handing out my business card to everyone I met, on every set I worked on, seemed to be paying off. I was getting more calls for jobs. I could almost get ahead if I didn't have to write big fat checks to the divorce lawyer every month.

"Mama—look!" Oliver pointed to the television. My fabric softener commercial was starting to air. Oliver ran over and grabbed a dishtowel and waved it in the air, like I was doing in the ad. We recorded it and he played it over and over. We'd dance around the living room, giggling and getting our laundry groove on.

Having free days with Oliver was a treat but it was time for him to be in preschool. X and I had not been able to reach an agreement; he wanted a location next to him, and I wanted one on my side of town. We had been locked in an impasse for months, trying to find something close to the halfway point. If we weren't able to sort it out amicably between ourselves soon, the court would decide for us.

Finding the right preschool was put at the forefront of the agenda.

I was not remotely prepared for the hell that calls itself 'preschool admission'. If the divorce litigation process came as a rude shock, the preschool nightmare came in as a close second.

"Do you mean you haven't registered your son *anywhere*?" That was the polite, but bewildered response from the schools I called. They acted as if I was the most ill-prepared mother in Los Angeles, which I began to think was entirely possible. Jeremy's aunt had tried to warn me that I needed to be on top of the whole early childhood education system but I hadn't quite realized the depth of what I was going to be facing.

Could it be true that some people preregister their children before they are even born? What happens to people without perfectly ordered lives? What if you were in just-get-through mode?

—W—

Luckily, I had a press junket with Garrison on Friday to save me from dwelling on it and needed to prep for it. I needed time to organize and clean my kit and go to the beauty supply store to restock.

Garrison had a huge action movie coming out called *The AfterZone,* and I was called upon to do his makeup for two days of press interviews leading up to the premiere. He was having an incredible year.

It would be the first time we'd seen each other since everything happened with Jeremy.

I removed all thoughts of the Paul debacle from my head—rather easily, I might add—and got into work mode, if you could call hanging out with a handsome movie star all day *work.* Sometimes I felt so lucky I had to pinch myself.

I arrived at The Peninsula Hotel twenty minutes early and cooled my heels in the lobby before calling up to the publicity suite. The hotel was buzzing with journalists and publicists from the studio releasing the film. Hair and makeup squads for Garrison's various costars arrived, and assistants carried back trays of coffees from Starbucks. Bellboys were whisking carts of luggage past me and glamorous-looking tourists followed behind them. I watched the activity from a seat in the lobby and drank my latte, which should have been decaf. My nerves always acted up with Garrison's sexy-movie-star-right-next-to-me factor—and a serious jolt of caffeine didn't help. As warm and gracious as he was in person, I never quite got over his enormous presence. The man was a walking Greek god, for Christ's sake.

At precisely nine in the morning, I knocked on the door of the suite and one of the junior publicists answered. Garrison hadn't arrived yet so she was flitting about the suite making sure the coffee was hot, the breakfast buffet was in order, and giving instructions for Garrison's lunch—grilled salmon, Caesar salad and beer.

I set out my supplies in the bathroom, arranging then rearranging them on the towel I'd brought in my kit.

Finally, Garrison arrived.

"How are you, dear?" he asked, leaning down to give me a big bear hug before settling into the makeup chair.

"Good, thanks." I commanded myself not to look into his eyes for too long. *Feign immunity from his dazzling charisma!*

"How's your little guy?"

"He's fine, thanks, Garrison. How's your family?"

"Good . . . yep. Everyone's good, *Scarlett.*" Just the way he said my name made me weak in the knees.

I started prepping his face and attempted to master the task of looking at him without really looking at him and risking getting sucked into the throes of that charisma. It was a fine dance.

"So, Scarlett, you don't see Jeremy anymore?" he asked.

"Um, no. It didn't work out with Jeremy," I said, and focused on putting a dab of concealer on his chin.

"Oh, that's too bad. I always liked the idea of the two of you together," he said, and straightened slightly in the chair.

"Yes . . . so did I," I said softly.

"I might be doing a movie with him. We're trying to work something out."

"That's great."

I resisted the urge to ask Garrison questions about Jeremy and if he was dating anyone. Just being around Garrison made me think of Jeremy; they were now irrevocably linked in my mind.

"Have you met anyone else, then?"

"I had been seeing someone else briefly but that wasn't going to work out."

"That's too bad," he said. "Make sure you don't settle, Scarlett."

"That's good advice. Thank you."

The day ran smoothly, and at the end, Garrison asked his Los Angeles hairdresser, Suzy, and I to join him downstairs in the hotel bar for a drink.

We sat at a table in the corner, and waited for Garrison's agent to join us.

"Sitting in those interviews all day is really killing my back." Garrison gave his lower back a rub. "I need to remember to do some stretches before or something."

"You ought to try some yoga," I suggested.

Garrison laughed heartily until it gave way into a deep smoker's cough.

"That's right. I remember you were really into yoga. We've talked about it before."

"It helps with a lot of things and it's great with relieving stress. I love it."

"They don't have big guys like me doing yoga, do they? It's a bit dainty."

"You'd be surprised."

"I remember you saying you were really into dance as a kid or something?"

"Yes, I can't believe you remember that! I was heavily into dance. Now most of the dancing I do is around the living room with my son. But doing yoga helps me keep that mind-body connection going. It's not dance but it feels similar somehow."

"I'd like to meet your son, Scarlett. I bet he's a terrific little guy."

"I like to think so." I smiled.

I wanted to tell him that Jeremy didn't have the balls to deal with my 'terrific little guy' but what would be the point? It was water under the bridge.

Garrison turned to Suzy. "And tell us all about your engagement news."

Part of Garrison's appeal was that, unlike a lot of celebrities I'd met, he had a genuine interest in other people's lives. He wasn't so wrapped up in his own existence that he didn't care about anyone else.

To the contrary; he adored a good chat with normal people.

"Darren and I just announced our engagement, so that has been really exciting. Now everyone wants to know when we're getting married. It's been a bit of a whirlwind but we're very happy," Suzy said.

"Congratulations!" I said.

"That's terrific, sweetie. Let's get some wine and toast to your engagement." Garrison ordered a bottle of red wine and some appetizers. We sat and discussed love and marriage and what prompted men to take that step.

"As the lone single and divorced person here, I had better shut up now," I joked.

It was glaringly obvious I had nothing to contribute to the conversation. I was on quite a lousy roll. I didn't know much about making a relationship work but I seemed to be figuring out the breaking up part pretty well.

"Don't be hard on yourself," Garrison said kindly. "None of it's easy, right, Suzy?"

"Nothing was easy until I met Darren. I'm just happy to have found my soul mate," Suzy said, as she sipped her Cabernet.

"Soul mates . . . the idea sounds romantic but it's mostly about timing for men," Garrison said, squashing any grandiose feminine fantasies under his foot in the process.

"Timing? So that's it?" Suzy said a tad wistfully. "No, no, I'd prefer to think he's my soul mate and we were destined to be together."

"But that's life, sweetheart. It's all about timing and readiness," said Garrison, sensibly. "It's the luck of the draw who you meet and when you meet them. If you're not ready, it's not going to happen. You're not going to meet *that* person."

Garrison's agent arrived to take him to his next meeting.

He turned to us and rubbed his hands together. "I'll see you at the premiere, right?"

I nodded but Suzy was not going to be able to make it.

"Thanks for all your hard work today putting me together!" he said as he took the last swig of his wine. "See you soon, my ladies." Garrison gave us both a big hug before he rushed off to a dinner meeting with a studio head.

Suzy and I exchanged info and said good-bye before she headed home to her fiancé.

I waited by the valet for my car to arrive. The excitement of the day had all but wound down. It was Saturday night and I was in no hurry to go home. Oliver was with X and CeCe would be out on a date. There was nobody to rush home for, nobody to share my day with and nobody whose clothes I was longing to tear off.

The valet attendant brought my car; I put my makeup kit into the back and tipped him.

I drove down through Beverly Hills and thought about the events of the week. I drove past Maestro's and replayed the messy breakup with Paul in my head. I felt relief but also a wave of sadness at the general state of affairs in my love life.

It's about time I made some changes, I thought. I seemed to end up picking all the wrong men, but at a certain point, I had to acknowledge the problem was with me. I was the one constant in the equation.

On Sunday morning, I hauled myself to an early yoga class. I felt melancholy when Steve, the yoga instructor, played Alicia Keys's "Like You'll Never See Me Again." It made me think of Jeremy and how fun and promising it had been in the beginning and how poorly it had ended. Nothing felt resolved about it. Letting go of it seemed to only happen incrementally.

On the way out, I was startled to run into Frank, Jeremy's designer friend from San Francisco. I almost didn't recognize him in sweaty workout gear.

"Frank! What are you doing in a yoga class in LA?"

"I'm with my boyfriend. He's working here and I'm visiting. Gotta get my yoga fix."

"I can understand that. This is a different look than the tux you were wearing last time I saw you."

"Listen, I'm glad I ran into you. I hope you are doing okay. I want you to know that I got really mad at Jeremy for the way he treated you. We had a fight about it, and I told him I thought he was being a total asshole."

"You did? Wow. Thanks. I'm surprised he mentioned anything about us."

"Oh, no . . . you were a very big deal for him."

"Really?" I had assumed I had only been a blip on his radar.

"Yeah. He's only ever had one girlfriend since I've known him, and that was a total disaster. When he met you, he called me and said 'Oh my God! I've just met the woman I'm going to *marry!*' Trust me; it was a very big deal for him."

That news hit hard. Tears started to pool in my eyes.

Frank looked horrified. "Oh, fuck . . . I'm sorry. I guess maybe I shouldn't have told you that."

"No, it's okay," I said, wiping the tears away. "It was a disappointment. I really liked him. I'm glad you told me. It's nice to know he felt that way . . . at least initially."

"You take care of yourself, you hear?"

"You, too. Nice to see you."

We gave each other a sweaty post-yoga hug and went in separate directions.

As I headed to my car, still smearing tears away from my cheeks, I hurried around the corner and walked right into Dominick. My towel, yoga mat and water bottle all hit the ground in spectacular fashion.

"Hey, what's the rush, sexy pants?"

I wasn't in the mood to explain any of it. I scurried to pick up the bottle as it started to roll away.

"Are you okay? Is that teenage boyfriend giving you a hard time?" He leaned over and picked up my mat.

I didn't answer and I couldn't look him in the eye.

"I have to go . . ." I said.

He handed the mat back to me.

"You know I'm here for you if you need a friend, right? I can stop being a dick for five minutes and be a good listener. Try me."

"Thanks," I said, touched by the flicker of concern he'd shown. "See you later."

There wasn't much I wanted to reveal about what had happened with the 'teenage boyfriend.' I shared myself with him and he'd freaked out, or so I'd thought. But maybe it wasn't that simple. Not every love story has a happy ending.

The confirmation that Jeremy had romantic aspirations for our relationship—at least in the beginning—made me happy and sad at the same time. He was a complicated creature, but then, he'd always been full of surprises—good and bad.

Chapter Twenty-Six
Detective Harlot Saves the Day

Emma picked me up the next night and we drove together to Hollywood for Garrison's premiere. *The AfterZone* was a popcorn movie with lots of explosions and car chases. It was standard summer fare, but was getting excellent reviews. It was déjà vu—Emma and I driving to another premiere of Garrison's after I'd worked on the press junket.

We pulled into the parking garage at Hollywood and Highland and headed for the legendary Chinese Theatre. My stomach was roiling. The prospect of running into Jeremy had my body on high alert.

"Do I look okay?" I asked while pulling at my blouse so that it draped properly over my shoulders. It was my new favorite shirt, a sheer filmy blouse worn over a peach silk camisole. The blouse was a pale seafoam color and had a demure sprinkling of tiny transparent fish-scale-looking sequins that caught the light at just the right angle.

"Yes. That top is killer. I hope we do run into Jeremy so he can eat his heart out!"

Emma looked particularly foxy in a Black Halo dress that emphasized her svelte physique. Emma had just finished a three-episode arc on *CSI* as "Detective Harlow"—or *Detective Harlot,* as we referred to her character—and was in the mood to celebrate.

We were too late for Emma to walk the red carpet, so we took our seats in the already packed theater. I looked around at the sea of faces. I had the distinct feeling that Jeremy was sitting somewhere behind us in the dark watching it, too.

After the movie ended, we made our way to the after-party held at a restaurant a couple of blocks away. Emma scanned the crowd, which was filled with the usual suspects—agents and producers in their uniform of power suits, and actors attempting to look cool.

"Same old, same old. Let's get a drink!" she said and steered me over to one of the standing bars in the large dining room. The restaurant was decorated in a postapocalyptic theme to promote the movie. With black leather couches and silver streamers hanging from the ceiling it looked like the unfortunate aftermath of a bawdy Vegas New Year's Eve party—which made me think fleetingly of Paul.

Emma handed me a glass of red wine. My hand shook visibly as I took a sip, which Emma picked up on right away.

"Jesus! Are you all right?"

"I haven't eaten all day. I'm a nervous wreck at the prospect of running into Jeremy."

"Jeremy might not even be here. You need to relax. Go tell Garrison how fabulous he was in the movie."

"You're right. Jeremy's probably not even here. Surely he has other things to do than go to all of Garrison's premieres." I put up a good front but my body could almost sense his presence in the building. "Let's go find our leading man."

I took a large gulp of red wine and did a quick scan of the room for Garrison. He was usually easy to spot because he was almost always the tallest guy in the room. I spotted him in the VIP section and watched for a moment before it registered who was standing next to him. Chatting with Garrison and his agent was *Jeremy!*

"I think he saw me!"

Emma grabbed my elbow and pulled me in the other direction. "Let's go sit for a minute." We did a swift about-face and made our way toward the large black velvet couches in the middle of the room.

Before we had a chance to make it to the relative safety of the couch, that familiar gravelly voice called out from behind us, "Scarlett . . . hi!"

Holy shit. Jeremy must have done a pole vault from the VIP section to have caught up with us so quickly.

Emma and I turned around slowly and feigned full composure.

Finally, we were face to face. Jeremy was smiling his killer smile, his hair disheveled as usual. He looked ridiculously handsome in his dark blue suit coupled with a pale gray shirt. It was criminal that he thought it was okay to go around looking like that, straining every ounce of willpower that I could summon. *Mercy.*

"Oh, no, not *you* again!" said Emma playfully.

"How are you, Jeremy?" I said a little too quickly.

"Hello, ladies." Jeremy kissed both of us on the cheek.

Emma wasted no time in working him over. "Is life a bit rough these days, darling? You look like you've been pulled through a bush backward! Those actresses giving you hell?"

Jeremy graciously fielded her insults. "Oh, no! Do I, really? I guess I do need a haircut." He laughed, while self-consciously smoothing his hair back.

Why did he have to be such a good sport? How dare he callously flaunt his best traits in front of me like that? *Bastard.*

"Yes, you could use a haircut, darling," Emma said, not letting up. It was the same wicked treatment she had given him on the night we met in the art gallery.

I stood there not trusting myself to speak. There was nothing to say other than *'standing this close to you without touching you is killing me.'* Which I thought was better left unsaid.

"It's nice to see you," he said turning to me, his voice softening. "I've been thinking about you."

Fuck, he really is torturing me. "Is that right?" That was all I could manage.

"Yes. It is. How are you? How's Oliver?"

"Oliver's great, thanks." At least he remembered my kid's name. "How are you doing?"

"I'm starting a new movie next month," he said. "It looks like Garrison's going to be in it."

"Yes, I heard. Good for you," I said with as much nonchalance as I could muster.

There was a brief awkward pause and then Emma took her cue. "*Okay* . . . I think I'll go check out the dessert table. You two behave yourselves. Try not to get into any trouble before I get back."

I thought about stopping her, but there was nothing I wanted more than a moment alone with Jeremy. It was silly to pretend otherwise.

"Let's sit down," he said, gesturing to one of the oversized black leather seats that looked suspiciously like a giant bed. The formerly vacant seats had quickly filled with men in suits and women wearing revealing dresses. There was room enough for one person but we squeezed in together, our thighs firmly locked next to each other. A familiar bolt of electricity charged through my body, making my legs feel weak again, just like old times.

"So, are you still with that guy? Garrison told me something about a boyfriend."

"We broke up." Why did I have to be so transparent? It really was such an annoying trait. Why couldn't I lie and tell him that Paul was madly in love with me and on the verge of proposing? Jeremy's influence extended to my brain. I couldn't even fib in his presence to look good.

"In that case, can I steal you away to come have a drink with me?"

"And what makes you think I want to have a drink with you?" I asked, trying hard not to smile. It was very difficult to keep my armor up in his presence. Something about him just made my insides melt.

"Because I still like you, and you still like me—that's why. We have unfinished business between us, and you know it."

My heart was pounding and threatened to burst through my blouse.

"You really messed with me last time I saw you," he said and shook his head.

"I messed with you? What are you talking about? You messed with me!"

"Well, you balled me out in front of your kid. I was a wreck for a week."

"Really?" I started to laugh. "I guess I did. I wasn't planning on it but it just happened."

"I was afraid to call you again."

"I figured that part out."

"Did this recent ex meet Oliver?" Jeremy asked.

"Yes, he met him briefly. After my experience with you, I wasn't about to risk another relationship with a guy who was afraid of my kid."

"See, I was good for something." He gave another good-humored laugh. "So how did it go with Oliver? Did he pass the test?"

"They were okay with each other, but there were other issues."

"Tell me everything!"

"Even if we got past the other stuff, I doubt he could be faithful. He had me buy this 'cheater's handbook' for him. "

"What? *What* are you talking about? A cheater's handbook?! What the hell is that and why haven't I heard about it?" Jeremy prided himself on having read all those women's dating manuals. He liked to know what the opposite sex was up to—not that it looked like it helped much.

"It was this book about what men say and do when they're cheating on you. He had me buy it for him. When we started dating, he kept telling me 'I would never cheat on you'—which I thought was a bit weird—and can you guess what the very first thing in the book is? The number one thing the cheaters say is 'I would never cheat on you'!"

"Oh, my God!" Jeremy slapped his knee to demonstrate his outrage. "You're kidding."

"No, I'm not kidding. I didn't think it was very funny. It was creepy. Anyway, he's history."

"He sounds worse than me!" Jeremy said gleefully.

"Much worse."

"Thank God you got rid of him. He was not a good guy for you. I hope you yelled at him with Oliver again. That's very effective."

"So . . . what's happening with you?" I asked, turning the tables. "I'm sure you've been dating. What's your story these days?"

"Well, I was seeing this one girl but . . . it's over."

"What happened?"

"Well, it was going really well in the beginning . . . then we slept together and the sex was . . . not great. Actually, it was awful. It made me really miss you."

I laughed. "Oh, that is a bit of a problem," I said, unable to wipe the grin off my face.

"Yes, I thought you'd be happy about that."

"I'm ecstatic! What was so terrible about the sex? I didn't think there was such a thing as bad sex for men."

"No there is, trust me," he said, swirling the ice in his drink and studying it for a moment. "It just wasn't going to work out. The chemistry wasn't there."

"Chemistry is a finicky thing," I said.

"Yes, it is. That's why I'm taking you home with me right now!" he said, brightening at the prospect.

"I can't go home with you. I suppose you're going to tell me that you've changed and now you're good for me?"

"I don't know if I'm good for you, but I *know* I'm not bad for you."

He leaned in, holding my face in his beautiful big hands, and kissed me. It felt like slow motion as his lips massaged mine.

"Why did you get another boyfriend so quickly?" he asked.

"I don't know. I was trying to get over you."

"What do you want a serious relationship for right now, anyway? You just got divorced. You need to be having fun—with *me*."

"That's the thing, Jeremy. You are the epitome of fun—and I had a great time with you—but I do have to think about the consequences. I have to be smart about my choices. That's how I got into that marriage in the first place. I wasn't thinking."

"Scarlett, you're so serious. Why must everything be so serious all the time?"

I looked directly at him. "That's easy for you to say. You're not a single parent. You don't have a little person relying on you to make good decisions."

He held my gaze but didn't have a witty comeback for that one.

The wine on an empty stomach was wreaking havoc in my brain. *Would it be so bad if I had just one drink with him? Would it be so bad if I went home with him?* Only yesterday, Frank was telling me that he had thought he was going to marry me. Didn't that merit a roll in the hay, for old times' sake?

Emma came back with a plate laden with mini-cheesecakes, truffles and crème puffs for us to feast on.

"I'll be stealing Scarlett for a drink," Jeremy said cheerfully as Emma perched on the edge of the coffee table in front of us.

I looked over at him and our eyes locked. He waited to see if I would correct him. But I didn't.

"Oh, God help us . . . I was gone for three minutes," said Emma with mock exasperation.

"I might have to have one of those," he said, sweeping a crème puff off her plate and into his mouth.

We sat there for few minutes while Emma filled Jeremy in on her recent stint as Detective Harlot and he told us about the new low-budget film he was doing that had a phenomenal script.

"Ladies, have we had enough fun here? Shall we head out?" asked Jeremy, keen to commence the next segment of the evening's activities.

"I need to congratulate Garrison," I said.

"Yes, *let's* go congratulate Garrison on how rich this movie is going to make him. He better not expect that kind of return on our little movie!"

Jeremy led us through the crowd and up to the VIP section where Garrison was now seated. The bouncer gave us a nod and granted us entrée into the roped-off area. Garrison did a double take when he saw us together, and leapt to his feet. I introduced Emma, and Garrison gave her the sort of hug I knew it would take her a week to recover from.

"What a fantastic job, Garrison. Well done!" I said, and received my own generous hug.

"You liked it?" Garrison searched my face. He could always tell if I was fibbing. The movie wasn't exactly my cup of tea but he was solid in it.

"You were exceptional," I said with conviction.

"Good. I'm glad you liked it," Garrison said, satisfied.

"Well, we're going to get out of here and go somewhere for a drink. Any chance you want to join us later?" Jeremy said.

"Oh . . . wish I could but I'm stuck here for a while. You kids have fun. Catch you next time," Garrison said and gave me a squeeze.

Jeremy linked his arms through Emma's and mine and said, "Let's go get a drink, ladies." We walked down the stairs toward the valet.

Emma quickly declined. "Oh, no thanks. I'm ready to go roll into bed and jump on the husband."

"Lucky man!" said Jeremy.

Jeremy took Emma's claim ticket and headed to the valet.

"Okay . . . *what the fuck, Scarlett*?!" Emma hissed at me as soon as Jeremy was out of earshot. "Are you seriously going for a drink with him? What the fuck for? Are you sure you know what you're doing?"

"No," I said, watching him peel off bills to pay the valet. "I'm not sure about anything." My head was spinning. "It just feels so natural to be around him again."

"Are you sure you can cover this tab?" Emma asked.

"What do you mean?"

"It's a sugar high. You'll feel great tonight and tomorrow the withdrawals will start all over again, and you'll be back to square one. Do you think he's changed at all?"

"I doubt it . . ."

She was right. At best, I'd have a night of fun in bed with Jeremy and then feel like shit all over again as soon as my feet hit the floor, if not before.

"Is he the type of guy who's going to get out of bed in the middle of the night and go get Oliver medicine if you need him to? I mean, look at him. He wouldn't know baby Tylenol from hemorrhoid cream."

We both started to laugh.

I looked over at Jeremy tapping away at his BlackBerry and knew in my heart that no matter how much I longed for him, I wasn't up for another round of allowing my emotions to be played with.

"This is ridiculous. I'm laughing and crying," I said, flicking away a tear that had started to snake down my cheek. "I don't know what to do."

Seizing on this moment of indecision, she pushed further. "Go home, Scarlett. You know where this road takes you, and it leads nowhere. Let me take you home."

"You're right. Let me just go and say good-bye." I took a deep breath and walked toward him.

He looked up from his phone and assessed the state I was in. The smile quickly drained from his face.

"Sweetheart, what's wrong?" he asked with genuine concern.

"Nothing. When I see you, I just want to drop whatever I'm doing and be with you again. But nothing has changed between us and I can't do this again with you—as much as I might want to—*I can't.*"

"Oh, okay . . . I didn't mean to upset you," he said and looked alarmed. If he hadn't known his impact on me before, he certainly knew now. "I'm really sorry if I hurt you, Scarlett."

And I believed him.

Emma's car pulled up, and I jumped in before I had a chance to change my mind.

She rubbed my shoulder and let me cry as we drove back through Hollywood.

"That was hard," I said quietly.

"Well done. This is a huge step. You don't need him. This isn't about him. You know that. CeCe may have done a number on your self-esteem but you don't need a man. You're just fine without one."

"I might not need one but I especially liked that one."

"I know. But you don't need any of these jokers. You deserve so much better. And so does Oliver."

This made me cry harder.

"I've got to figure out why I pick all the wrong ones," I said as we wound our way along Sunset Boulevard back toward Beverly Hills and the impossibly quiet apartment that was waiting for me.

We turned down Doheny and pulled up outside my building.

"Thanks, Detective Harlot," I said as I gave her a hug. "Another case solved. Another disaster averted."

"Just doing my job, ma'am," she said as I got out of the car. "I'm dedicated to keeping Los Angeles women safe from players!" We both laughed.

She waited until I got to the door and then drove off.

The apartment was quiet and still as I put my key in the lock. No sign of CeCe. I felt better, cleansed after a good cry.

I was famished. It was a deep well of hunger that couldn't be satisfied by food alone. I made a grilled cheese and thought about the week I'd had. I had told Paul to bugger off and I was okay. I had turned Jeremy down with Emma's assistance. I felt shaky about it, but I was still okay. As much as I wanted to, I hadn't gone home with him. I had to admit it did make me feel stronger.

Chapter Twenty-Seven
Divorced (✓)

The next important step in straightening out my life was sorting out the divorce.

Nobody could believe we were still mired in proceedings since there was no property to be shared and no marital assets to be dispersed. Haggling over details of Oliver's custody agreement and who got any tax or financial benefits were the remaining issues. There had been many needless delays but our trial date was approaching.

I didn't have the money for a trial. My lawyer wasn't going to go forward without another ten thousand dollars. I couldn't come up with that amount, nor could I afford to accrue more charges on top of the already staggering bill.

"What if I just settle with him?" I asked my attorney.

"He's not about to give you anything you want. That's why this has taken so long. He won't budge on the tax credit. You won't be able to claim Oliver as a dependent or write off childcare or anything. You'll be responsible for your own legal fees—"

"I know. But I just can't keep fighting anymore. I need to move on, and right now I'm still shackled to that man."

"As your attorney, I have to advise you that it's a bad decision. You'd have a better shot with the judge."

This is what I'd been told happens in divorce. It often drags on until one party can't bear it any longer. Apparently, I was the party worn down and waving the white flag.

I agonized over how to proceed. Reaching out to X seemed like the only solution.

I called him.

"In the spirit of moving on, let's just get this done. It's got to be better than wasting money we don't have on lawyers. And then there's the emotional toll. Please think about it. It's bad for Oliver, and we need to learn how to make decisions together—outside of a courtroom."

He paused for what felt like eternity. "I'll think about it," he said.

Three days before the trial portion of our divorce was about to commence, X agreed to meet. We spent a long day locked away in a room with our respective lawyers and hammered out our own shitty agreement.

It was a lousy and lopsided agreement, in keeping with the marriage that inspired it. I had given him virtually everything he asked for.

"You don't have to do this," my lawyer said. "You could do better in court, most likely. But then again, with a new judge like this one, it could go either way."

"Either way, I'd still owe you more money. I'm ready to be done with this whole thing. Let him have what he wants."

It was the price of my freedom, I reasoned. At least it was done and we wouldn't have to fight over every little detail.

Instead of feeling over the moon, I felt numb. All this time and my life still wasn't where I wanted it to be. I felt as if I should be doing more but I just didn't know what.

"Maybe you should try an antidepressant for a while," Emma suggested as we hiked in Franklin Canyon. Emma had taken psychology classes in school and fancied herself as a bit of an expert in these matters. And she would have made a damn fine shrink if the acting career hadn't taken off.

"I'll think about it," I said and sat on the dusty bench by the pond. I watched as a turtle swam over toward me expectantly, looking for food.

"I tried one for a while." Emma sat next to me and tied her shoelace. "But it made me put on weight, and I didn't want to have anything to do with Chris's penis for months. He threatened to divorce me."

"Now there's a ringing endorsement!" I laughed. "I already have one nice handful of post-baby fat around my middle, thank you very much. Who needs that kind of help? If you weren't depressed enough before, that'd really give you something to be blue about. Actually, now that I think about it, a lower sex drive might be a good thing for me. Maybe I'd get into less trouble that way."

"It might give you a little boost, and maybe that's what you need."

"It might, but I think it's situational. Who wouldn't be struggling with the mess I've made of everything? But I'll turn it around. You watch. Just when you think I'm down for the count, I spring back up!"

I watched as a mother duck swam in front of us with her little ducklings lined up behind her. It was a profoundly comforting sight.

"See . . . the ducks are all lining up in a row," Emma said, brightly. "It's a good sign."

And I agreed that it was.

We walked back to our cars, and I drove to pick up Oliver.

Ollie and I caught a fleeting glimpse of CeCe when we got home.

"Hello and good-bye, darlings," she said as she swept by us and planted a kiss on Oliver's forehead.

"Where are you off to?" I asked, taking in how great she looked.

"I'm off to have a date with *The One*," she said dramatically.

"*The One*? That sounds exciting. Oliver and I are about to do some painting, aren't we, Oliver?"

"Stay and paint with us, CeCe!" he implored. "No dates, CeCe."

"Oh, darling, I'd love to, but I can't. Wait . . . where did I put my keys?" She dashed past us to the bedroom. "Ta-ta, loves!" she said and then waltzed out the door leaving a cloud of Chanel No.5 behind her.

"Have fun!" I called after her, although I doubted she needed my encouragement.

I put some pasta on the stove and Oliver and I sat on the floor. We let Henry the Eighth run around for a bit. We were hoping he'd pose for our paintings, but he didn't quite grasp the concept of posing and ignored the plate of treats we'd placed on the floor in an attempt to get him to stay put. He hopped happily around the room enjoying his freedom. I had to admit that a healthy dose of freedom had a very fine ring to it. Sometimes you just have to accept whatever the bargain is in order to preserve that freedom. I couldn't live within the walls of my marriage and I was going to pay for that in other ways, but at least I was free.

Chapter Twenty-Eight
Just Dinner

The Fourth of July holiday weekend was approaching and I had no plans. Oliver would be with X, and CeCe was off somewhere with her new mystery man. Things had been somewhat strained between CeCe and me after the whole Paul debacle and, sensing a bleak weekend, I attempted to fill it up with activities.

On Saturday morning, I went to yoga. As I was sitting on my mat waiting for class to start, Dominick strolled in and surveyed the day's offerings. He spotted me and immediately headed over. There was nothing like a friendly deviant to improve one's disposition.

"Hello sexy-pants," he said with a grin. "Why the long face? I can tell you haven't been laid in a while. Isn't that pansy doing his job?"

"I'm happy to say that I'm pansy-free," I said, and moved over so he could put his mat next to mine.

"Serves him right. That'll teach him not to give a horny tart like you a long leash!"

"Oh, bugger off!" I said and swatted at his leg.

"Ah, come on. I'm kidding with you. Come out to the beach and have dinner with me tonight. I'll make you forget about that idiot."

"Make that, *idiots*, plural."

"What?"

"Nothing."

Dinner at the beach was the best offer I was going to get.

"I'll have dinner with you. But *just* dinner, that's it . . . and you have to keep your pants on—*the whole time*. Okay?"

"If you insist," he said. "Jeez, you've gotten so boring—"

"On second thought, I'll meet you at a restaurant. They have strictly enforced pants codes, even in Malibu."

"Fine," he said, amiably. "You're a very demanding woman. It's kind of a turn-on."

After class, Dominick suggested we get lunch as well as dinner.

I balked at this.

"Come on, you have to eat," he said. "What else do you have to do today?"

He totally nailed me on the pathetic emptiness of my schedule.

"Jesus, you are turning into an old softie," I teased him. "Since when have you ever wanted to have lunch *and* dinner with me on the same day?"

"My tolerance of you must have improved with age," he said as we walked down the street to A Votre Sante, a popular restaurant specializing in healthy, vegetarian-themed dishes.

"Maybe we should see how lunch goes before we commit to dinner," I said, not trusting how much we could endure of each other.

Over the Trainer's Special plate of eggs, veggie sausages and whole-wheat pancakes, we discussed our romantic travails.

Dominick and I had somehow managed to shift gears and evolve from lovers to having an unusual friendship. He made a much better friend than he did a boyfriend.

"What happened with the pansy?"

"Which one?"

"There's more than one? Wow . . . making up for lost time, are we?"

"Wasting time might be more accurate. I think it's time to stay away from men altogether. I suck at those games you guys play."

"I've counseled you on this before. It's not that difficult. Play hard to get. Men respond to that."

"I can't do that, unless I'm genuinely not interested in them. And then that gets the wrong ones all excited. I am not a game player."

"I know. It's not in your nature. Most men aren't going to understand you, Scarlett. You're a complicated creature . . . not for amateurs. You probably scare the shit out of a lot of guys."

"Great. Where does that leave me?"

"It leaves you coming out to the beach to play with me." He smiled.

"Been there and done that! *Playing with you* isn't on the menu anymore. We've done away with that seasonal special. Finished. Nada. So tell me what's going on with *you*? Are you seeing anyone special at the moment?"

"Not really. It all gets to be too complicated. You go out with a woman a few times, sleep with her, and then she gets all serious about everything."

This was starting to feel very familiar. He sounded just like Jeremy.

"Women bond when they have sex. It's a little late in the day for you to be just figuring that out now," I said, and shook my head. He was possibly worse off than I was.

"Not all women," he said. "But the problem is I'm not attracted to the ones that don't."

"That's a problem, then."

"Women are so different now. They hunt me at yoga. It makes me uncomfortable. I used to like to hunt them, but I can't now cause they're always beating me to it."

"How do they hunt you?" I asked, intrigued.

"There's this one chick up the front of the class with this 'body of life' and she's always eyeballing me. Then, all of a sudden the other day, she's right up in my face, aggressively flirting with me . . ."

"Body of life? Never heard that one before. Go on," I say, riveted.

"Yeah, this chick is insanely hot—and I would have been interested—but the trouble with this scenario is that it has deprived me of any sense of mystery or fantasy about this woman. When I met you at my party, I had a chance to talk to you a little, fantasize about you, wonder what you were like in bed, so by the time I ran into you at the next party I had already developed a 'thing' for you. It really got me going."

"Yeah, I remember that 'thing' well, and how you tried to mount me on the garbage can."

"Those were the days!" he said and laughed.

I can see where he's going with this. Men are hunters, after all, and having the sheep walk right up to the wolf and collapse at his feet might take a bit of the thrill out of the hunt. But it's confusing because women are taught that sometimes we have to show men that we are interested. It becomes a fine line between signaling interest and stalking.

"What about that voluptuous girl I saw you talking to after class?"

This particular woman's presence in class was hard to miss. She was so buxom that her gravity-defying balancing acts left the men around her barely able to focus. Her boobs strained the limits of her exercise bra, and threatened to snap free at any moment and propel her forward into the next row. Dominick had been interested in her for a while, although the last time I asked him, he admitted he was 'not man enough to go there.' This time, he lit up at the prospect.

"Oh, yeah . . . I have to date her. We haven't gone out yet but we will. What *do you do* with those gargantuan boobs? Do you cup them one at a time? Or rub your face in between them like a towel?" He demonstrated rubbing his face vigorously between his hands. "For the sake of anthropology, if nothing else, I *have* to know."

"Weren't you dating someone else? What happened to that spinning instructor?"

"I wouldn't spend money on her. She's a 'stairwell candidate.' "

"A what?"

"A *stairwell candidate*—meaning I could bang her on the back stairwell after class if I wanted to. No need to take her out on a date."

"You're such an asshole!"

"Yes, I am," he said proudly. "But at least I'm in touch with my baseness. That stairwell comes in handy. There was this one chick I was dating that was really nasty. She used to love it when I'd bang her in her sweaty ass right after spinning."

"That's charming. But what about any woman you're legitimately interested in? What happens with the ones that aren't *stairwell candidates*?"

He became quiet for a moment, lowered his voice and leaned in, as if imparting a great secret. "My standard tactic is when there's a woman I'm interested in, I wait a long time before making a move. I never come on strong. Flirt with them a little and then let them go nuts wondering what's happening, if they're misreading the signals. I need to let their interest *percolate*. When I feel the timing is right and they are ripe for the picking, I make my move."

A glimpse into the inner workings of the male brain, while fascinating, could also be repellant. It confirmed my worst fears.

"I've never thought about it before but you're a hard-core misogynist, aren't you?"

"Absolutely not, I love women. That's why I can't commit to just one."

The check came and I reached for my purse.

"Don't be silly, I've got it." He waved me off.

"You don't have to do that."

"A deviant can still be a gentleman," he said and gave the waitress his credit card.

—⋙—

Later that afternoon, I headed out to Malibu for dinner with Dominick. The drive was one of my very favorites—it was one of the most glorious stretches of coastline in California—and was breathtakingly beautiful. Lush patches of marigold-yellow and electric-purple wildflowers spilled down the hillsides, reaching out like colorful long fingers inching toward the beach. I was early, so I pulled over by the side of the road to drink in the beauty of the ocean.

Economically blessed Malibu folk were winding down the day. I watched as a small girl ran around in the sand, squealing gleefully as her mother chased her. The dad and the older boy packed up the toys and towels after a day in the sun. The mother grabbed the errant tyke and twirled her in the air —happy times on the beach, just like the milk commercial I didn't get. Their life looked perfect next to my own mess. The best thing I'd ever done was have an incredible little boy—and now I got to see him fifty percent of the time, so I'd managed to screw that up, too. A lot of things hadn't turned out the way I thought they would. Oliver was having his own holiday weekend adventures somewhere with X and whatever date he brought along. My chest tightened at the thought. I had no say in whom X picked for a partner. All I could hope for was someone who would be good to Oliver.

Watching the woman living in her own picturesque Malibu postcard, I longed to ask her about her perfect-looking life. How had she managed to create it? Perhaps she knew some secrets that I didn't. Was she propped up by a surfeit of pharmaceuticals or had she slogged her way through romantic lessons to get to this point? After cutting my own swath through the dating world, it didn't look like I had learned much. One amusing dead-end relationship followed another. And now they all seemed dishearteningly similar.

It felt like I'd somehow lost myself in the promise and phony swirl of Los Angeles, where everything looks real but very little actually is. I had invested too much time in men who weren't ever going to treat me well. Sometimes my loneliness felt overwhelming, and at other times, if I dove into it, I found that it was bearable. The good news was that I could continue to make changes for the future. There was still time.

Dominick was waiting at Nobu when I arrived. It was packed with Malibu locals satisfying their cravings for sushi and black cod miso. This time I could order something cooked from the menu. We sat at the bar so he could keep an eye on the door, lest he miss an opportunity. We didn't linger over dinner. He'd told me most of his naughty stories at lunch, and he knew there weren't going to be any after-dinner treats.

Luckily, we ran into a couple of girls he knew. He stayed to have a drink with them and I cut out. I was happy not to be one of those young girls falling prey to his charm and good looks. They had their own romantic lessons to learn.

Driving home from Malibu in the moonlight, I felt calm, peaceful. I'd been able to enjoy Dominick's company and his wit but I was also thrilled to leave him with his young fillies. I wouldn't have to deal with any emotional aftermath. Sometimes it was just easier not to. It felt empowering, like staring at a chocolate cupcake and then deciding not to eat it. What a novel concept. I'd never had anything resembling willpower before. I always ate the cupcake.

Chapter Twenty-Nine
The Man Diet

I hadn't seen or heard anything from CeCe in days. This was not entirely unusual if she was in the throes of a hot romance but it seemed a bit cruel when she knew that I would worry. I tried her cell again. No response.

My cell rang back almost immediately but the screen said *Emma*. I answered.

"Hi. Listen, I just got back into town. I've been invited to this party today at the home of a top female producer—you have to be my plus one! She has an amazing house in Bel Air. It will be so fun."

"I'd love to."

"I'll pick you up at three."

"It's not black tie, is it?" I joked.

"Haha. Hell, no. It's Fourth of July. Casual is fine. You can wear a bikini if you want."

"Yeah, that's not happening. By the way, CeCe is MIA again. At what point am I supposed to call in a missing person's report? I hate it when she does this. She keeps mentioning some Phillip person but how do we know he hasn't offed her or something sinister?"

"If there's anyone who can take care of themselves, it's CeCe. You don't have to be her mother. She'll surface again. If there's any sinister business happening you can be sure she's in on it, and probably having a ball—or two."

"Good point."

Emma picked me up and we drove up to Bel Air. We wound our way up on Bellagio and then onto Bel Air Road, and climbed our way higher and higher into the hills. Breathtaking beauty greeted us at every turn. Stunning isolated mansions sat behind imposing gates, some offering only a glimpse or hint of the grandeur contained inside. We came to the home of Holly Fielding, an A-list movie producer. Huge wooden gates lay open, exposing a narrow road up to the house. Valet attendants were scampering about, trying to keep up with the pace of cars delivering guests.

"What's Holly like?" I asked while we were waiting for our turn in line.

"She's a hoot! You'll love her. Keep an open mind. She's into some eclectic stuff."

"What do you mean?"

"She's on a spiritual quest. She's always going to Peru to see some shaman or holding Indian puja ceremonies at her home . . . you know, all of that wacky LA stuff."

"Sounds intriguing." I said as the valet opened my door.

We walked through the gates and up to the house.

"Whatever she's into, it must be working. Look at this place,' I whispered as we were suddenly transported into a Zen Buddhist garden complete with a pond, lush emerald-green foliage, and fuchsia flowers.

"Holy shit."

I looked at all the beautiful serene stone statues of goddesses in various states of repose. I couldn't imagine how it felt to wake up surrounded by such beauty every day. I inhaled deeply and took it all in.

"I know, right? Amazing." Emma said. "But the really cool part is that she created this all on her own. She didn't inherit any of this."

"I love her already," I said.

We made our way up the steps to the open front door and went inside. The house was filled with "seekers," as Emma referred to them. Young artist types sipped cocktails with Hollywood heavyweights and, as usual, a generous sprinkling of famous actors and musicians.

"Emma!" We both turned to see an attractive woman in her fifties heading toward us with arms outstretched.

"Holly!" Emma disappeared into the folds of Holly's flowery aqua gown as she embraced her.

"How are you, honey?"

"I'm great. This is my best friend, Scarlett."

"Hello, honey. Welcome," she said. I extended my hand to her and she grasped it with both of hers.

"Thank you. You have a beautiful home."

"Honey, this is what twenty-five years of toiling in the movie business can bring you."

"Not a bad deal," I responded.

She smiled. "You girls must go and have a session with Karolina. She's in the guesthouse in the back. She'll only see people for a little while otherwise she gets overstimulated, so get in there quick."

"Who's Karolina?" Emma asked.

"*Honey*, she's only the best psychic I have *ever* been to—and you know that is saying a lot! I have been to damn near every psychic worth his or her salt on the planet!"

"Wow," I said in awe.

"And she means it," Emma said to me.

"That's just how I am. I never make a move without consulting my shrink and my psychic!" Holly laughed heartily. "I have all my bases covered. Go enjoy the party," she said, and kissed us both on the cheek.

"Cameron!" she called out over Emma's shoulder to the actress Cameron Diaz who had just walked in behind us.

"What do you say we get out there now?" I nudged Emma in the direction of the guesthouse. "I'm fascinated."

"You go. I'll mingle for a bit and meet you there in a minute. Psychics are so *not* my thing. Now, if she had her shrink here, that would be a different story!" Emma laughed. "I'd be first in line."

"Fair enough. See you in a bit."

I walked out past the pool and the stylish couples lounging by the hot tub. I followed a small stone path overgrown with lavender and rose bushes that led to the guesthouse.

A woman hurried by me and whispered "she's amazing" in an aside as she swept by.

The glass doors to the guesthouse were wide open and filmy white curtains curled out into the doorway.

"Hello?" I knocked on the glass door.

"Come in," a soft feminine voice responded.

"Hi, I'm Scarlett. I was wondering if you were available for a session?"

I peered in and saw a figure moving about the dimly lit room. I squinted to adjust to the low light. A slim figure in a long white backless dress wafted incense around the room. Finally, she came into focus. She was much younger than I had expected, and carried herself with an aura of quiet dignity. This was not a Venice Beach twenty-dollar psychic, and that was instantly clear. She had a dancer's body and a natural grace. I guessed that she was in her mid-thirties. Her long, thick dark hair cascaded down her back and she had layers of wooden and gold bangles that jangled on her arms as she waved the incense with a peacock feather.

I waited for further instruction.

"Sit down, love." She gestured toward one of the chairs at the table in the middle of the room. "I'll be with you in a minute."

I sat down, and tried not to feel nervous.

She lit several more of the tall candles in the room and took a sip of her tea before turning her attention to me. She swept her long dress out to the side of her and sat down opposite me.

I looked into her green catlike eyes. They were lined in a simple black liner, to great effect. I mentally made a note to try and copy it later. She looked like she'd been cast in the part of a high priestess—a hip, young goddess in waiting.

"How can I help you, love?" she asked with a calm assurance that told me I was in good hands.

"Well, I'm not sure exactly. My life has been all kinds of screwed up lately—and by lately I mean ever since I can remember—and I'm not sure what I can or should be doing about it at this point. I feel lost . . ."

"Okay, sweetheart. I understand. Hold my hands." She held her open hands out across the table and I placed mine into hers, as instructed.

She closed her eyes and breathed in deeply several times, and said nothing. I looked down at her perfectly manicured smoky-gray nails and all the rings that adorned her fingers. A platinum snake wrapped itself around her ring finger with a lone diamond for an eye.

"You have a young son," she said after several long silent minutes.

I gasped. "Yes, I do," I said, although she didn't pose it as a question. Another few moments of silence followed.

"Sweetheart, I have to tell you, he is the one good male energy in your life."

I laughed. "I guess that's not a surprise."

"You have had a lot of other males in your life, and they've been jamming up your frequency."

"That's one way of putting it . . ."

It was her turn to laugh.

"These men have really polluted your energy. You need to cleanse yourself of them and any negativity that's been lingering. We need to clear your channels, so to speak."

"How do I clear my channels? Do you mean a colonic? My friend Autumn raves about them—"

"No, I didn't mean literally, but knock yourself out. What I meant is that you need to go home and cleanse your aura, your energy field. Clear it of the men who have been weighing you down, and your constant focus on them. What you focus on gets larger in your life, so if you focus on dating guys who are wrong for you, you will continue to manifest exactly that."

"Wow. That makes total sense," I said. "How do I do that?"

"Here, I have something for you." She got up and went over to her gray suede purse, and rooted around in it for a moment before coming back to the table.

"This will help. It's a first step." She presented me with a bundle of dried leaves wrapped in a purple ribbon.

"What do I do with this?" I asked.

"It's white sage incense. It's a smudge stick for cleansing and purifying negative energy. I want you to go home, light it and make sure you let the smoke touch all the corners of your home. Then I want you to have a friend sage you."

"Um . . . okay. How do we do that?"

"Get naked and have her swirl the smoke around your entire body."

"Even . . . down there?"

"Especially down there," she said matter-of-factly. "Where do you think that energy gets in?"

"Ooohhh . . . got it. Okay, and what happens then?"

"Then, after you have thoroughly cleansed your aura, I want you to go on a man diet."

"A what?"

"That means no men. For at least six months. No dates, no sex. That will do a psychic reboot on your choices, which I can see have not been good so far."

"Got it."

"Then, after the layers of all of their vibrational connections to you are severed, you will have a better idea of how to proceed in your life. Follow your passions . . . and not men."

"Whoa . . . that's deep."

"Yes. But it will be really beneficial for you and your son. That's all I can tell you for right now. All of your focus has been outward. You are called on now to change that."

"Thank you so much!" I went to shake her hand but instead she clasped her hands around mine and looked into my eyes.

"Good luck," she said, and smiled.

"What do I owe you for the session?"

"Today is my gift to you. If you'd like to do another session, you may call me." She handed me a card that said simply *Karolina* in a fancy cursive, and a phone number.

"Thank you." I gingerly tucked the bundle of leaves away in my purse and skipped out into the garden, feeling high as a kite.

I looked around for Emma and found her on a chaise in the garden, sipping a margarita.

"There you are," she said. "I was wondering what happened to you. You've been gone for an hour."

"Really? It was that long? She must have put me in a trance or something. I thought it was five minutes."

"Well, how did it go? Did she transform your life?"

"She's about to. I'll tell you all about it later. She gave me very explicit instructions, and there's a special part for you in it."

"I can hardly wait," Emma said dryly.

—⚹—

On the way home, I broke the news to Emma that she couldn't just drop me off. She was going to have to come upstairs for a task that could only be trusted to a best friend.

"Hmmm." She regarded me quizzically. "Is there alcohol involved?"

"Absolutely. Why not? And there will be some smoking, too."

"Okay, but I'm not helping you wax your bikini line again. That was a disaster."

"That's not it exactly . . . but you're not that far off."

I let us in to the quiet apartment, grateful that CeCe had not surfaced yet.

"You're going to need a drink for this. Do you want wine or something stronger?" I disappeared into the kitchen, trying to hurry before she changed her mind.

"You're making me nervous. Wine is fine."

"Have a seat in the living room. I'll be right there."

"Do you want to tell me what we're doing?"

"In a minute," I said as I struggled with the wine opener. It gave a satisfying but gentle pop as the cork released. I poured it into a glass and headed in to give it to Emma. She was sitting on the couch, watching me expectantly.

"Okay, let's hear it," she said as I gave her the wine.

"Now, I need you to keep an open mind here and suspend disbelief along with all your years of psychology training. Think of it as an experiment. Are you with me?"

"So far . . ."

"Okay, so Karolina told me I need to cleanse all the negative energy from the guys I've dated, and the best way to do that is to do a ceremonial clearing . . . a ritual. It's an Indian thing or something."

"I'm still waiting for the punch line."

"It's coming. So now I'm going to sage the place with incense to purify it, and then you're going to sage me."

Emma laughed. "Okay, I'm here for duty. Go for it."

"I'll be right back." I ran into the bedroom, took my dress off, and stripped down to my panties.

I tossed my dress onto the couch, took the bundle out of my purse, and walked over to the fireplace. This was so out of my comfort zone, but at this point, I was willing to do just about anything to get my life on track.

"Hello!" Emma yelped when she saw me. "Don't you think you should close the curtains? Unless you want this documented on You Tube or something."

"Good point." She helped me close the drapes, obscuring the view for the building across the street.

I took the large matches off the mantelpiece and lit the tip of the bundle until it ignited. Once it was well lit, I blew out the flame, leaving just the glowing embers, and started waving it back and forth like I had seen Karolina doing with her incense.

"She said something about all the corners of the house," I said as I moved around, making sure to waft a heavy dose of smoke into each nook I came to. Emma followed behind me, taking it all in. After I finished the entire apartment, I turned to her and said, "Are you ready for the fun part?"

"I don't know. Am I? Let me have another sip of wine," she said, and gulped the rest of the glass.

"I have to be naked for this part." I wriggled out of my underwear, still holding the sage stick.

"You know I love you, but not in that way." Emma giggled.

"Don't worry. It's not that experimental. I just need you to waft this thing around me to let the smoke cleanse me."

I handed the stick to her and stood with my arms and legs outstretched and eyes closed.

"Okay, here goes," she started walking around me with the sage, fanning it into me. "Is this how you do it?"

Huge plumes of smoke began to rise as she waved the stick back and forth.

"I think so. That's good," I said between coughing fits. "Now waft it in between my legs." I helpfully lifted one up in the air and then the other. "Careful not to start any 'bush' fires with that thing."

"I'll try." She started giggling again. "You look like a drunken Irishman."

"That's good! It must be working! Let's get rid of all those guys, drunk or otherwise. All the ones I've dated—or married," I said, exploding into giggles punctuated by coughs.

Just then the smoke detectors went off. Impossibly loud, screeching bleats filled the apartment.

"Oh, fuck," I said, and ran to open the balcony door. Still naked, I grabbed my dress and started frantically flapping it at the smoke, trying to encourage it to go out the door.

Emma dissolved into a fit of hysterics. "I think I'm going to wet my pants!" she yelled over the din of the smoke alarm.

"Help me before the fire department comes. Open some windows!"

Emma pulled the curtains back and opened all the windows. I grabbed a towel and wrapped it around me. After what felt like five interminable minutes, the alarms stopped.

Emma and I collapsed on the couch.

"That went well. Let's hope to God it worked." I coughed.

"Thank you for the most memorable Fourth of July ever!" she said, and buried her head into my shoulder, laughing.

Chapter Thirty
What Do You Mean No Men?

The next morning, I sprang out of bed with renewed energy. I grabbed a latte and went to collect Oliver from X.

"Ollie, let's go to the ducky park and do some sketches. I brought a picnic lunch for us."

Ollie nodded his consent and we headed for the park.

I had woken up full of vim and vigor, eager to capture some sketches on paper. Images of dancing animals in vibrantly colorful costumes had haunted me while I slept. A comical circus of dancing animals—a Cirque du Soleil of forest dwellers—had been parading through my mind in the night. I didn't have any choice but to follow that creative stream. I wondered if it had anything to do with all the incense burning business. Perhaps it had lit some creative fires within?

CeCe was getting ready for a date when we got home.

"Darling, it smells a bit . . . funky in here. What have you been up to?"

"You wouldn't believe me if I told you."

"Try me. One of the neighbors accosted me in the lobby. Something about a smoke alarm late at night."

"Yes, there was that unfortunate incident but it was short-lived."

"It doesn't smell short-lived."

"Oh, well, I burned a bit of incense and it was stronger than I realized. No big deal. So what have you been up to? I feel like I haven't seen you in ages." I was keen to change the subject. Telling her a psychic to the stars had told me to smoke the place out to exorcise all the deadbeat boyfriends out of my crotch might not go over terribly well. "Where have you been, CeCe?"

"Phillip surprised me and took me to San Francisco for the weekend! He had a meeting this afternoon but he'll be back to pick me up for dinner."

"Wow. So it's going well, then?"

"He's utterly fabulous, darling. You'll adore him."

I made myself a cup of Earl Grey tea, sat on the edge of the bath, and watched her applying her makeup—just like I had done as a child—but these days my opinion was a little more valuable.

"Is that too much eyeliner?" she asked as she applied a second coat of her Dior mascara.

"No, it's perfect. Maybe a tad less blush, though."

"Thanks, darling," she said, and softened it with a powder brush.

"I've recently had an epiphany. I have a new plan of action."

"Really?"

"Yes. I'm going to do something that I think will help me. I'm going on a 'man diet'—"

"Meaning what? All you eat is men?" CeCe chortled at her own joke. "I like the sound of that."

"No, quite the opposite. I'm not going to have another date for six months —or maybe even longer!"

"Not go on any dates? What's the point of that? I can't think of anything more dull or dreary," CeCe said incredulously. "You'll bore yourself to tears and be back to square one."

"The *purpose*, CeCe, is for me to shift focus. I always leap headfirst into new romances to squash the pain from my last romantic train wreck. I keep making the same lousy choices in men, so it's time for a break. It's time for some clarity and a reboot. It's time I got my shit together. I don't want to have to worry about what some guy is thinking or doing or why they're not calling me. I've always been like that. This is a great plan. It'll be good for me."

CeCe looked at me as if I'd totally lost the plot.

"Well, darling . . . it's very nice for you to 'get your shit together' but I don't see why you have to be quite so drastic about it. Six months is an awfully long time to waste."

"It makes perfect sense to me. It's just like going on a fast after you've been pigging out. Just imagine that it's Lent and I'm giving up men instead of chocolate. A sort of long, protracted Lent."

CeCe recoiled from such a notion.

"Well, whatever works for you, Scarlett," she said with a large exhale, and went back to applying her shimmery petunia-pink Chanel lip gloss.

"Not all of us have the ability to leap from man to man completely unscathed," I said, feeling my irritation rising. "I'm trying to recover from the last thirty-six years of crappy choices—mine and yours."

"I'm so glad you can finally meet Phillip. He's picking me up in half an hour," she said, choosing to ignore my inflammatory statement. She had changed the subject and sounded excited again.

"Great." I was less than enthusiastic.

I went into the kitchen and grabbed an apple for Oliver. Slicing into it, I thought about CeCe's comments. I wasn't sure why I bothered telling her. I should have known better than to look to CeCe for support for abstaining from men. Men were the very lifeblood of her existence. To her, a life without men would be like life without sunshine, without dessert or wine with dinner—a dry, brittle life without flavor or reward, pointless.

This new Phillip character was suddenly all she wanted to talk about. Any topic of conversation would quickly revert back to something witty Phillip had said, or his love of opera or how well traveled he was or how he liked tea from Morocco.

I gave Oliver the plate of sliced apple and sat next to him on the couch.

"Hi, Mom." He climbed into my lap, dumping Henry the Eighth onto the seat beside him.

"Hi, my love." I stroked his head and kissed him. Karolina was right; he was the best man in my life and always had been. We ate apple and watched *SpongeBob* together.

The doorbell rang and I answered it. A tall, silver-haired fellow with a fresh haircut stood there eying me. He was smartly dressed in a gray suit with a light blue shirt, brandishing an impressive bouquet of pink peonies —CeCe's favorite. No wonder she fancied him; this was exactly what she fell for.

"Hello. You must be Scarlett. I've heard so much about you. I'm Phillip —the lucky man who's squiring your mother to dinner this evening," he said extending his hand for me to shake.

"Nice to meet you. Come in. What lovely flowers! Shall I put those in water for you?"

"Thank you, but I'd better present them to her first. Make sure I get the points, if you know what I mean," he said with a wink.

"Got it."

I got the feeling Phillip was busy accruing a lot of points. He seemed to have a sense of humor about him—as if he understood that his position was not guaranteed—and that he needed to work at it. This behavior would make CeCe very happy. Nothing pleased her more than a fellow working hard to earn her favors.

"Would you like something to drink, Phillip?"

"No, thank you." He walked into the living room. "Well, hello there young man," he said when he saw Oliver engrossed in his show.

"This is my son, Oliver. Oliver, this is CeCe's friend, Phillip."

"Hi," Oliver said softly.

"Good show?"

Oliver nodded.

"That's a nice rabbit."

"Except when he poos everywhere. Then CeCe gets *really* mad at him." Oliver was not one to leave out juicy details.

"I can understand that," Phillip said. "Pets can be messy."

From the way he turned up his nose, Phillip didn't look like he had much tolerance for mess of any kind. He strolled around the apartment, taking a long look at the family photos sitting in silver frames on top of the piano.

I had to admit that he looked like he belonged with CeCe. *'He presents well,'* was how CeCe described him, and he did. He was well dressed, well spoken, with a good head of hair, and he was at least six feet tall. CeCe didn't tolerate short men well. A short stature wouldn't rule out a potential suitor completely, but it would be a strike against him that he would have to work very hard to counter. CeCe had certain standards that needed to be met. She had zero interest in bald men. Hair and height were in the must-have column. CeCe had learned her own painful lessons from relaxing those standards in the past and seemed to be making bold new choices. For a man to capture her interest these days, he would have to be politically aware, educated, cultured, and well traveled, but most importantly, he would have to have *bread*. CeCe was not into roughing it. She had endured plenty of challenging years as a single mother and had dated her share of men who were broke, but was now at a point in her life where she didn't have time to waste. Being a *sugar-mama* was of less than zero interest to her.

That didn't look like it was an issue with Phillip. He exuded an air of confidence. A man in charge of his life who knew what he wanted. He looked quite at home, as if meeting his date's daughter was the most natural thing in the world. It was usually tiresome and taxing to have to make small talk with CeCe's suitors, but there was something different about this one. I strained to remember the details she had divulged about him. Was he a banker, a lawyer, a doctor? He carried himself as a professional, someone whose time was valuable, but I couldn't remember what his story was. My brain didn't have enough storage room for all the info about her myriad of dates. It refused to absorb needless data, choosing to commit data to memory if it looked like the candidate was going to be around for a while.

"Do you have any kids, Phillip?"

"Yes, I have a son, Allan. He lives in New York. He's thirty-five. He works in publishing."

"That's interesting. What does he publish?"

"You name it. It's a large publishing house with many divisions," he said.

"That sounds like a great job."

I stifled the urge to ask him what his intentions were with my mother or quiz him about any hidden wives or girlfriends he might have hanging around his life.

CeCe appeared in the hallway to save us from more awkward attempts at conversation. She looked gorgeous in her sleek black pants and gunmetal-gray silk blouse, adorned with tiny iridescent beads along the neckline. Upon seeing each other, their faces lit up. CeCe blushed, something I'd never witnessed before, and then she got very quiet.

"Miss CeCe, you look very lovely this evening." Phillip walked over to her, took her hand and gave her a kiss on the cheek. CeCe basked under the glow of his attentions. They were clearly smitten with each other. I couldn't recall CeCe ever looking this happy. This chap was a serious contender.

After they left, I cooked some pasta for us and gave Ollie a bath. I put Henry the Eighth back in his cage and sat down for a date with my beloved Tivo. There were a few episodes of Kelly's show waiting for me to watch. She was deep into filming her show again and the most I could expect from her was a random phone message here or there, but if I needed a Kelly fix, I could watch her in skimpy outfits battling with the evil aliens. I had also recorded Emma's appearances on her episodes of *CSI*.

I flicked through some of the latest paintings. There was one where I had improvised and made a circle of bunnies dancing. It was silly but it made me laugh. Who says that bunnies don't have their own secret dance parties? I put a tux on one of the bunnies to dress him up and a couple of tutus on the others. On one majestic-looking deer, I placed a royal purple masquerade mask, as if they were all attending a ball in the woods.

We were starting to accrue a lot of sketches and paintings. Looking at them cheered me tremendously. I loved the row of ladybugs doing a cancan around the pond. Maybe there was something to be made from them. If they cheered me, maybe other people might enjoy them. What was that fairy tale about the maiden in the woods spinning straw into gold? I vaguely remembered a childhood fable about a young woman spinning something out of nothing. This was precisely the feat I needed to accomplish. I'd mastered the nothing part; now if only I could create something out of it.

Chapter Thirty-One
She Comes First

While I was embarking on a journey *sans* men, romance was blossoming around me. CeCe and Phillip's relationship was thriving.

"CeCe, do you want to see that play with me at the Geffen this Friday?"

"Oh, no, I can't darling. Phillip and I will be in Santa Barbara for the weekend."

"Away again?"

"Oh, yes! You have to come and see the house. It's fabulous! You know, it is almost as if he designed it with me in mind. It's filled with wisteria and white roses, which are my very favorites, and a koi pond! Can you believe that? Is he not the most perfect man?"

"I'll take your word for it, CeCe. Might we be expecting wedding bells anytime soon?"

"Oh. I don't know about that," she said, and quickly changed the subject, leading me to believe that indeed there might be.

Emma and I ate salads at the fashionable Country Mart after yoga. The Country Mart was a very upscale cluster of boutiques and restaurants located on the Westside and housed one of my favorite bookstores

"Still date-free?" Emma inquired, digging into her 'Beach Body Salad'.

"Yes. Totally."

"Good, because I'm not purifying your coochie again."

"Don't worry. We're done with all of that. But there's one male I can't get rid of—X. Even a damn divorce can't dispatch him, and I can't smoke him out either. I'm tethered to that joker. We have years and years of co-parenting ahead."

"How has he been lately?"

"A lot better, actually. He seems to have calmed down a lot since there isn't any male interference in my life. There's a lot less hostility. He's even started telling me about all these women he dates."

"Oh, God. That's tacky."

"Actually, it's sort of amusing. I guess I'm just grateful for any improvement."

"You've come a long way. Remember how he used to call you an evil cunt and scream at you in the hallways at the courthouse?"

"Yeah, that's what I mean by improvement! I'm glad that's behind us. This about-face is a bit drastic, though. He now drops more details about his liaisons than perhaps one ought to share with an ex-wife. It's as if he's forgotten that we were once married and he speaks to me as if I'm his best friend, spilling details about his active sex life."

"In that respect, you could say you married your mother!" Emma howled at her astute observation.

"You're right. What a terrifying thought! I've never looked at it like that."

"Oversexed, overly detailed-sharing habits . . . I'm just saying . . ."

"Oh, God, please don't! I can't bear any more parallels between them!"

"What does he tell you?"

"He tells me intimate details about his dates. When he sleeps with them, how he sleeps with them."

"You're kidding." She nearly dropped her fork.

"Nope. He is definitely keeping his end up, so to speak. There have been awkward run-ins with him and his latest fine young thing—usually in her twenties."

"Ewww. What do they want with him?"

"Who knows?"

"Does he introduce you?"

"If I run into them, then yes. There was the *really* young girl from Starbucks, a couple of girls from yoga, and some mystery ones I never saw in person but heard about when Oliver mentioned them. He plays the hapless single dad card, toting Oliver around to parties with him, and reels them all in. It drives me mad, but what can I do about it? I can't yell at him and tell him not to use our kid as a chick magnet. He'll only do it more to spite me. Oliver is always a big hit with the ladies."

"Well, at least they will be relatively short-lived flings. After they get a glimpse of his famous penis photo collection, they'll run for the hills."

"We have another interview and tour for a preschool tomorrow. Maybe he'll bring them for show and tell."

—⚉—

X and I were doing our part and dutifully trotting out for interviews with a handful of preschools. They weren't the coveted ones because those schools had laughed and hung up on me, so we were left with a smaller, more obscure selection. If you weren't well moneyed or well connected in this town, you might as well throw in the towel. It was proving to be an uphill battle.

The interview process forced X and I to deal with each other and at least pretend that we could get along, which we found we could—for brief periods.

All the benches were taken when we arrived for the latest tour, so X and I sat on the swings in the neatly manicured playground, waiting with other prospective parents.

"I'm glad you broke up with that Paul guy," X said, kicking at the sand beneath him.

"Oh?" I adjusted the strap of my purse. It wasn't a subject I wanted to get into with X. I didn't care if he spilled details about his love life but this was not going to be a quid pro quo situation. I wasn't aware he even knew I was dating Paul. Maybe he'd heard from Oliver.

"Yeah, I know people who know him. I heard all about him. He was a bad dude."

"Well, he's long gone," I said, abruptly concluding the conversation.

"Good."

"They're calling us in now."

We got up and joined the tail end of the tour.

Once inside one of the viewing classrooms, we were startled to observe the children engaged in such abnormally quiet 'play' that they almost appeared to be anaesthetized. It was creepy. Children make noise when they're playing in groups—whether you like it or not—so it was unnerving to see the kids building with wooden blocks and playing dress-up, all without making a sound. Their attendants—two women dressed as pilgrims —sat at small tables and sliced vegetables for soup with *very* sharp knives, while humming quietly. X and I looked at each other, made our excuses and made a mad dash for the door.

"That was truly bizarre," I said once we were out of the school.

"That was like a freaky *Twilight Zone* episode in there." X was laughing and shaking his head.

"I think we can safely veto that one as an option. What's next?"

After an exhaustive search and six interviews, we finally found a preschool that focused on art and music. X had found a new place to live in Santa Monica and this school was much closer to X's than mine, but considering how long it took to find a suitable one, I agreed to the long drive in rush-hour traffic without hesitation. We felt confident that Oliver would thrive there but then had to campaign to convince the school that we, as parents, were worthy applicants. The selection process seemed to be more about the parents than the kid. We needed to volunteer our talents, reveal all possible avenues of contribution to the school, and basically seduce the admissions officer into accepting us. We jumped through every set of hoops for them. We were so grateful to have found a school that we both agreed on. We labored over the application, paid fees in advance, brought baskets filled with CDs and cookies, and displayed our very best courting behavior.

Once Oliver was accepted, it became a process of celebrating and getting him excited about going to school, making it a very special activity—and a notable step into becoming a 'big boy.'

Oliver and I made a little book together and filled it with painted pictures of his colorful new school, along with new friends waiting to learn and have fun with him. He was already very social and warmed to the idea brilliantly. Thanks to our custody plan, Oliver was accustomed to separating from his parents. Unlike some other kids who had meltdowns when faced with separation anxiety, he had already met that challenge.

Oliver started with a three half-day program that would eventually extend to five. They also offered the option of after-school care until five thirty in the evening—which would be perfect if I was working.

Parent participation at the school was stressed and you were billed if you didn't meet your monthly allotment of volunteer hours. When I didn't have work scheduled, I helped out at the school, volunteering in the classroom, sewing costumes for the upcoming school productions, and other duties I felt equally unqualified for. The reward was witnessing Oliver thriving among his new friends, and engaged in his new structured school life.

"That's my mom," I would hear Oliver telling his classmates when he would pass me painting sets in the playground.

The mothers at the preschool were a mix of artistic 'Earth Mamas' and hip, young Westsiders. Almost every time a mom bent over to pick up their kid, a flash of an exotic tattoo would be exposed from beneath the back of their jeans. Butterflies, unicorns and dolphins danced over exposed skin on bottoms and ankles everywhere you looked. Oliver soon became fixated with tattoos.

"Ooh, Mom . . . look! She has a tattoo on her butt!"

One of the mothers at the school stood out. Originally from Russia, she had twin boys and was very involved in putting together the school productions. She went out of her way to talk to me whenever she saw me. We often found ourselves working together on projects or painting scenery. Despite her overtly friendly nature, my interactions with her left me feeling vaguely unsettled, if not downright insulted.

"Oh, Scar-lett, for makeup artist, you *not* good painter! *Ha, ha, ha.* Maybe you need find new job? *Ha, ha, ha.* Don't vorry, I jus' kid you!"

She said everything with a big smile, a toss of her long, glossy mane, and punctuated by fits of giggles. I wrote off her behavior to quirky cultural differences that perhaps didn't translate well. Other parents at the school seemed to tolerate her jokes; she was very popular.

Soon after Oliver started school, X began a tumultuous relationship with a redhead. She was the first one X labeled 'serious' and introduced me to. The redhead—or 'Workout Girl' as I dubbed her—was a personal trainer with a fierce body. There was nothing relaxed about her, with her finely chiseled physique and meticulous attention to her appearance. She had such an edgy, hard look about her that I couldn't help softening her harsh eyeliner in my head each time I saw her. I wanted to get a sponge and wipe it all off. One look at her could tell you she was a major control freak and he was in for some big-time ass kicking. Go, Workout Girl!

I couldn't have been happier.

X had always been keen on exercise but with her, he became a devout gym rat, working out for hours a day and then bringing Oliver along with them on hikes and other athletic excursions.

X also looked like he was having his turn riding the emotional rollercoaster. He was euphoric and glassy-eyed when I saw him at the exchanges—or wrung out and spent. It reminded me of my experience with Jeremy. It was a relief to feel grounded and not swept away by anyone else's moods. The man diet had benefits.

One Sunday afternoon when I went to pick up Oliver, X opened the door, nodded in the direction of where he was napping in X's bedroom, and went back to his phone conversation. He shuffled off into the kitchen hoping for some privacy but I could tell by the hushed, urgent tone and the way he was nervously pulling at strands of his hair that he and Workout Girl weren't getting along. It sounded like he was doing damage control. I knew all of his signals, and simultaneous hair coiling and tugging were not good signs.

"I didn't say that . . . that's *not* what I said," he kept repeating.

I went into the bedroom and sat down next to Oliver on the bed. It was the first time I had been allowed into the inner sanctum of his new house. Oliver was sound asleep on top of X's thick, navy bedspread and didn't stir as I kissed his cheek and smoothed the hair off his face. I looked at X's crisp new bedding with its black geometric pattern and struggled to recall what we'd had at the old house. Like pain at childbirth, those memories had been erased. Sharing a bed with X felt like another lifetime ago. Even if I strained, I couldn't recall what it had been like to be intimate with him. The very notion seemed unfathomable. But there, sleeping in front of me, was a toddler who was the living evidence that we'd had sex once upon a time—at least once.

I glanced over at the bedside table and the stack of books resting there. Sitting on top of the pile was a book titled *She Comes First—The Sensitive Man's Guide to Pleasuring a Woman*. The title was too outrageous to resist and I grabbed it. The book was filled with tips on performing oral sex and other handy techniques designed to enhance a woman's sexual satisfaction. X was arming himself with powerful new skills for his single adventures. Why didn't he care about new oral sex techniques during our marriage? I glanced out into the hallway but there was still no sign of him. Had he not been so preoccupied with Workout Girl on the phone, he would never have granted me access to his bedroom unsupervised—and for good reason. I returned the book to its preferred position on top of the stack.

X, as if sensing I might have uncovered something, hurried into the bedroom. He stared blankly at me for a moment, waiting for me to say something.

"I hope that isn't your idea of a bedtime story," I said, gesturing to the book. "The illustrations might be a bit hard to explain."

"Oh, yeah . . . I forgot about that." He quickly slipped it into the drawer. "Somebody gave it to me," he said, as if he needed me to know he didn't purchase it himself.

The idea that somebody felt the need to give it to him somehow struck me as worse.

The next day X called to announce that Workout Girl had dumped him and he was depressed.

"She just couldn't accept me. She kept pressuring me to take testosterone and all this other stuff," he said, sounding miserable.

"I'm sorry to hear that," I said, unsure of what the appropriate response should be. Anyone could see that one coming.

"You'll find someone else. Go have some fun with Oliver today. Take him to the park. Go ride your bikes or something. It'll get your mind off it."

"Thanks. Good idea."

It was still unclear what miracle had occurred to transform me from reviled ex-wife into confidante and shoulder to cry on. None of the divorce books mentioned anything about dispensing dating advice to your moping ex-husband. Ours was a truly modern divorce.

Chapter Thirty-Two
The Penis Flytrap

The next week on my way to yoga, I noticed a couple leaning against a car, locked in a lusty embrace. The absence of romantic affection in my life made public displays of passion seem much more foreign and intriguing. How glorious that some people were unfettered by social constraints and stuck their tongues down each other's throats wherever they felt the urge. I could vaguely remember that deliciously urgent need to have Jeremy . . . anywhere and everywhere.

As I got closer, it was amusing to note that rather than engaging, the man was struggling to *disengage*. The woman was petite but what she lacked in size she made up for in enthusiasm. As soon as he succeeded in prying off one of her arms from around his waist, she would instantly replace it. A slinky little octopus with long glossy black hair, she was not easily contained. As I approached, the man's wavy hair looked strangely familiar. His posture and lanky frame were instantly recognizable. *It was X!*

He looked up in my direction, and turned ashen when he saw me but didn't let on to the woman that they had been discovered. He recovered and, not one to miss an opportunity, gave a slight shrug as if to say, 'What can I do? She finds me irresistible.'

I rolled my eyes and kept walking.

Who was the woman? It wasn't the redhead. It was unlike him—in this divulge-everything mode—not to have mentioned a new one. At first, I thought it might be the young girl from the coffee bar, and as I turned the corner I couldn't resist looking again. This time I recognized her right away. She was the Russian woman from Oliver's preschool! Now her odd behavior at school was starting to make sense.

That was quick work; Oliver hadn't been at the school for very long.

As soon as I left yoga class, my cell phone was ringing. It was X.

"Um, hi," he said awkwardly. "Sorry you had to see that. You didn't see us making out in the coffee place, too, did you?"

He didn't sound sorry; he sounded almost giddy.

"No, I missed that performance," I said. "What the *fuck* are you doing? Why are you fooling around with married mothers? Have you completely lost it? I don't think that's what the school meant by parent socializing. You might want to be a bit more discreet. I mean, you guys were making out in the street!"

"Yeah, but I can't keep her off me. She's so hot it's insane."

"I need to point out that insane is the key word in that sentence."

"She's nuts. How did you know? She calls me all the time and keeps asking to come over to my place, but I don't want her to know where I live or I have a feeling I'll never be rid of her!"

"Have you seen the husband? He's huge. What if he finds out and wants to beat your ass? Have you thought any of this through?"

"They have an arrangement," he said.

"Oh, right. The 'arrangement' is probably that he doesn't have a clue about her extracurricular activities. We had such a hard time finding a school for Oliver and if you screw this up for him because you need to bang a few MILFs *I'm going to be pissed.*"

"I know! I know! I'm trying to break it off with her. I can't understand a word she says, there's kind of a language barrier, but she's just so . . . sexy."

"Try telling that to her husband."

He'd lost his mind. Workout Girl must have really done a number on his head to send him reeling in this direction. With each romantic disappointment he encountered, his meter seemed to reset in a radically new direction. He needed to try his own diet and stay away from women for a while.

The next week when I picked up Oliver from his house, we sat on the garden steps while Oliver collected the books he wanted to take with him.

"I broke it off with her," he said, out of nowhere.

"Who? The Russian woman?"

"Yeah . . . we finally did it and the sex wasn't great. I wanted to try all my new moves from the sex book on her. But when I went down on her, each time I looked up, she was either staring at the ceiling or checking her nails. It was such a bummer. She wasn't into it at all."

"Okay, I don't think I need *all* the details . . ."

I couldn't figure out why he wanted to share this unsexy story.

"I decided I can't see someone who's married, no matter how hot she is."

"I think you can only claim points for that if you decide *before* you sleep with her."

It was a bit silly for him to be playing the morality card after the fact.

I plucked one of the lush gardenias from the bush next to me and inhaled its sweet fragrance.

"Well, better to end it now before it got ugly."

"Yeah, but now she's stalking me. She's calling me all night. How do I get her to leave me alone?"

"She's pissed because you slept with her and then broke it off! Just wait it out. She'll be onto someone else soon enough."

X's affair with the Russian minx was aborted and her calls eventually dropped off, but her curiosity about me didn't abate with the end of their affair. Her fixation with X seemed to shift strangely in my direction.

"Scarlett . . . vhy you haff no boyfriend? . . . Vhere you buy dat dress?"

She fired lots of questions in my direction. What did I do on the weekend? Where did I go to eat? Her tone was very irreverent and condescending for a woman who had been screwing my ex-husband. I was endlessly amusing to her. It drove me nuts, all the giggling and faux friendliness. Her twin boys were in Oliver's class, so avoiding her wasn't easy. As fate would have it, her son, Tommy, was one of Oliver's best friends.

She managed to corner me at a birthday party for one of Oliver's classmates.

"How are you, Scaar-lett?" She giggled at me in her uniquely annoying fashion. "You still sick? You still haff stomach flu?"

Oliver had not learned the finer points of discretion and told everyone in class anything he deemed newsworthy. Unfortunately, this included if Mommy wasn't feeling well.

"I'm fine. Thank you."

"See, Oliver tell Tommy *everything!* Hee, hee, hee. Oliver tell Tommy *all* stories about *you!* Then Tommy tells me *everything!* Hee, hee, hee. First you get a food poison, then stomach flu . . . vhat vrong vit you, Scaaar-lett? Hee, hee, hee." She picked up a spaghetti noodle from her Cinderella paper plate with her long, fuchsia fingernails and dangled it into her mouth, muffling the giggling briefly.

I'd had enough of the silly cow.

"Yes, that's very funny," I said evenly. "Tommy tells you everything— and Oliver's *dad* tells *me* everything! So I guess we both hear . . . *everything!* Hee, hee, hee! We both hear *all* of the stories around here!" I added another goofy giggle for good measure.

Her eyes widened as the impact of my words sank in. She doubled over, emitting loud coughing and choking noises, and it looked like she might spray noodles all over the freshly manicured lawn. She didn't look quite so smug anymore. The color drained from her face. With her hand covering her mouth, she hurried over to the drink table and downed a cup of orange soda to recover. For the rest of the party, she stayed far away from me and applied her cling-on grip to her own husband, for a change.

The Russian minx was conspicuously absent from school the following week.

"You'll never believe what the old X has been up to," I said as soon as I could catch a moment with CeCe. "He's been sleeping with this Russian woman at Oliver's school . . . and she's married! He's lost his mind since Workout Girl ditched him."

"Oh, you know, I read about those Russian temptresses. They go to classes and learn tricks they can do with their vaginas to catch the billionaires! I read all about it in *Marie Claire* magazine. They have some magic Venus flytraps down there—or *penis flytraps,* as the case may be." CeCe chuckled.

"Well, she's wasting her *penis flytrap* on him. He's nobody's billionaire."

The school recital was approaching. The costumes had been made, the sets painted, and the kids had been rehearsing every day. As a creative preschool, they put a lot of effort into their productions and this performance was the highlight of their season. The Russian minx was in charge of many aspects of the production, including the costumes. Oliver was very excited about his class's number and had bad been practicing "All You Need Is Love." They were to wear black tights with colored T-shirts proclaiming the name of a planet. Oliver was Venus and had a special part with Tommy in the number.

CeCe, Sam, Mikki and I sat in our seats in the theater eagerly awaiting Oliver's number. Sam was videotaping the show for me. X sat in the row across from us with one of his yoga tarts. The Russian minx was sitting in the front row with her husband, and kept turning around and smiling at me in a disconcerting fashion. She looked very pleased about something.

"All you need is Love" started playing and Oliver's class came out onto the stage singing. All the girls were dressed as little stars and I noticed that another boy was wearing the Venus shirt. When Oliver finally strutted out into the middle of the stage, he was proudly sporting a yellow T-shirt that said 'U-R—ANUS' in a very pronounced bold print.

It was so unexpected that I gasped.

Why the sudden switch? What the hell happened to the Venus shirt? 'U-R- ANUS' didn't have such a nice ring to it and the font was far more exaggerated than the other shirts. Oliver started his routine with Tommy, who was wearing a inoffensive Pluto shirt. The Russian minx was sending us a not-so-subtle message.

Sam leaned over and said, "Nice costume."

CeCe chuckled and whispered, "At least Oliver doesn't know what it says."

We cheered as Oliver executed his jumps and turns before joining hands with Tommy to make a bridge while all the girls skipped by underneath. At the end of the performance all the kids joined hands and the boys took center stage for final bows. I looked over to gauge X's reaction but he was staring at the stage in stunned silence. The Russian minx had cleverly exacted her revenge.

School was on spring break, so happily I didn't have to deal with the gloating minx for a while. This gave Oliver and me time for painting. Oliver asked me if we could make more books like the one we did for preschool.

Creating storybooks together had become one of our favorite things to do.

We began by taking simple experiences—like going to the park and feeding the ducks or looking for ladybugs and froggy friends—and then weaving stories out of them. The first efforts were simple but gradually became more detailed. We worked on the illustrations together, creating booklets that we bound together with colored ribbon from CeCe's extensive collection. They were fun and uniquely ours. One of the characters we created was an unpopular toad named Harry. Harry was a toad that sprouted hair and thus all the other toads shunned him, calling him Hairy Scary Harry.

CeCe found this detail objectionable. "You can't have a hairy toad. Toads are not hairy."

"First of all it's called make-believe, so we can create whatever we want. And secondly, I've kissed enough toads in my life and I can assure you that some of them can be pretty bloody hairy!"

"Well, if you put it that way . . ." CeCe couldn't argue with that.

Our most ambitious book we named *India and the Ladybug Circus*— about a little girl named India who makes friends in the forest with a troupe of athletic ladybugs—with the sequel, *India and the Ladybug Ballet*. It was Oliver's idea to make the lead character a girl—probably a consequence of watching too many *Dora the Explorer* episodes—and we named her India after a little girl at school. We painted the ladybugs, added a few sequins and modeled what dance positions they needed to have—a challenging transition to the page, since ladybugs are not naturally the lithest of insects. We took artistic license and gave them longer legs, making them more limber and pliable creatures, which served our purposes. Ladybugs need long limbs when they are doing an arabesque. Contorting ladybugs was a funny concept. We couldn't look at the pages without laughing.

Emma thought we should try to publish them. "They're cute and very commercial. I think you should do something with them."

The idea seemed far-fetched at first, but as a parent of an avid young reader, I knew there was a market for this sort of thing. It was something to look into. We certainly knew a lot about kids' books from the sheer number of them we read. The idea stirred me and, as it marinated, I began to get excited about it.

—⟨⟨⟩⟩—

For my thirty-seventh birthday, Oliver and CeCe invited Susan and Emma over for Chinese takeout from Mandarette.

"Where is Autumn?" CeCe asked. "Why isn't she here?"

"She's off the radar. I haven't heard from her in a while. She just disappears like that sometimes without a word, like some other people I know." CeCe smirked but said nothing.

"Oh-oh . . . Chinese food. Watch out for Mommy's farties!" Oliver warned the group and pinched his nose for effect.

"Thanks for the heads-up, Ollie!" Emma howled.

"It's the baddest smell *ever*," he stated with a wicked little grin.

"Hey, Oliver, that's not a nice thing to say," I said. "There's no need to tell everybody that!"

"*Okay,*" he said, turning to me with a deeply pained look on his face. "I guess it smells kind of . . ." His face was scrunched up like a cat's puckered ass as he struggled to find something less offensive to say. "It smells kind of . . . *nice*," he said, grimacing to express the great effort involved.

"You don't have to say *that* either!" I laughed. "But if someone's tummy is having a bad time, we don't always have to mention it."

"There goes my appetite," CeCe said as she put a platter of spinach and glass noodles on the table.

"You need to promise us you'll go out on the balcony if you're going to have any episodes." Susan teased me.

"Yes, don't worry; I'll quarantine myself if it gets out of hand."

Oliver and CeCe had made me a wonderful birthday cake with coconut icing—my favorite. Oliver gave me a special 'Happy birthday, Mommy' booklet he'd made all on his own with happy colorful drawings of us going to the park together. I was deeply touched by the effort he'd taken.

"Thank you, my sweet boy. That is a beautiful book." I kissed him and wrapped my arm around him. "And while I'm at it, I need to thank each and every one of you for pulling me through some interesting times lately. I am very aware how lucky I am to have you all in my life. Thank you for spending this birthday with me. It's going to be a really good year. I can feel it."

Chapter Thirty-Three
Wedding Number Four

CeCe had big news brewing. Ever the romantic optimist, she and Phillip had decided to tie the knot.

It did not come as a surprise. They had been exclusive for seven months and had barely come up for air. Their lives had become entwined to the degree that the idea of separating them at any point looked unlikely.

CeCe's engagement provided the perfect illustration of the marked differences in our lives. CeCe was getting married and I was divorced and on a man diet.

A true testament to the powers of manifestation, Phillip had presented her with a stunning emerald-cut ring from Harry Winston's—the exact one from the clipping that had been sitting on her refrigerator on her 'wish board.' She had clipped it from a magazine and had left it sitting there for years. It had taken a while but it had worked its magic. Judging from the small amount of time they spent in her apartment, Phillip had remarkable powers of observation.

When I asked her why they were in such a hurry, she smiled and said, "When you meet the man you want to be with forever, you want forever to begin right now!"

It was a romantic notion for someone about to embark on marriage number four, but regardless of my cynicism, I did think how lovely it must be to feel that way about someone and have your feelings returned. I'd never experienced that; at least not in any lasting way. In relationships, after the initial sizzle and bang, things always seemed to go south rapidly. Marriage hadn't been a romantic experience for me but CeCe kept taking the plunge, so there must be something to it that I was missing.

Marriage appeared to be an enigma, rarely letting you in on its secret when it worked, but clobbering you over the head loudly when it didn't.

CeCe focused on planning her wedding and I focused on putting my non-romantic plans into effect. I decided that I wanted to have my own business. Once the idea of getting our storybooks out there took hold, things began to click into place. After taking the classes at UCLA, I felt charged up and stimulated. Ideas began to bubble up in my brain, demanding to be addressed. Oliver and I spent more time at the library and local bookstores exploring the competition and noting what worked. After considerable research, I decided to take the rest of my commercial money and invest it in self-publishing. I plunged in and printed one thousand copies of *India and the Ladybug Circus,* which seemed to have the most commercial appeal of our book series.

Writing the checks to fund this adventure made my stomach feel weak but when I picked up the first box filled with our little book treasures, it was like opening the best Christmas present ever.

Oliver howled with glee.

"Oh, my! Ollie, look, our very own books!" I inhaled the smell of the freshly printed pages.

Seeing our names in print for the first time on the pristine new books sent a tingle all through my body. It was another unique thrill to have a tingle run through my body that wasn't driven by a man. This was all our own.

Oliver got such a kick out of seeing our very own insect creations transformed into real stories in real books that real people could read.

It was the best magic.

"Mommy, look! Our stories! How cool!" Oliver pressed his face against the pages.

"Yes, isn't it great? Now we can share them with everybody."

"What on earth are you planning to do with all of those books?" CeCe asked as she watched me pile the boxes on top of each other in the closet.

"The idea is to sell them."

"Well, that's a bit lofty, isn't it?"

"I wouldn't have invested all this time and all of my money if I didn't think people might buy them," I said flatly.

"If nobody buys them, I guess you can always give them away as birthday presents . . . or to hospitals or shelters or something. They're not picky. You could get a tax write-off at least that way."

"Thanks, CeCe. That's very supportive."

In CeCe's opinion, this was another ill-conceived, harebrained idea, just like my man diet, but I couldn't afford to indulge any negative thinking. Forging ahead was the only option.

I kept boxes of books in the back of the car, and Oliver and I traveled to book fairs and expos, farmers' markets, small bookstores for readings, and anywhere else I could talk our way into. The children's reading groups around town that we had frequented before Oliver started preschool became our first targets. They even agreed to sell our books at the yoga studio.

Other opportunities presented themselves. We rented a stall at the Santa Monica Farmers' Market from nine to one on Sundays and started a children's reading group. Once CeCe saw that I was serious about our books and making things happen, she became more supportive. If she was in town for the weekend, she would stop by with chocolate croissants.

We needed more stock to sell so I ordered a thousand copies of *Harry the Hairy Scary Frog,* our story about a misunderstood frog with serious grooming issues. It was Oliver's favorite of our series and to commemorate the second printing, Autumn with her fashion connections, helped me print up some T-shirts bearing the titles and lead characters of our two books. Desperate for product to sell, I even sold some of my nature paintings from our ducky park adventures. Sometimes Emma would lend us her charisma and come and do a guest reading. Before long we had a nice little following.

When they were available, I hired Sam and Mikki to help run the stall, drop off, and pick up orders. Through the farmers' market we met some local preschool teachers who invited me to come to their classrooms and do readings. Emma referred me to someone to help get a website up and running. Our little business venture suddenly had legs.

Residuals and makeup work were still the main source of my income, and paying off lawyers ensured that there wasn't much left, but there was a swell of goodwill that was generated with our books that developed a life of its own. They were cheery little books and people seemed genuinely happy to help us.

Susan called with an interesting proposition. "Listen, what would you think about me submitting the book series to Nickelodeon and Noggin? They are always looking for children's programming. I could see if they're interested."

"Oh, wow . . ." I felt a flood of anxiety about it at first. What if they didn't like the books? Could I endure another failure? Yes, I'd be fine. "Yes. That would be amazing. Go for it! We've got nothing to lose. Send them anywhere you want. Thank you!"

Oliver and I would be just fine if our books didn't take off but it was crazy not to ride the tide of opportunities and be open to them. We'd come this far.

It was almost effortless the way opportunities presented themselves. I could feel the momentum building. The steps began unfolding in front of me and all I had to do was breathe and put one foot in front of the other. It made me think of Karolina and how she had said if I stayed away from men for a while, a lot of things would simply fall into place. It certainly seemed that way now.

Having a stall at the market on a regular basis was like having a window into the world. Everybody I knew floated by at some point or another.

X was amused with my latest undertaking. He had a lovely young Brazilian girlfriend named Isabella, whom he introduced to me at the market. She understood very little English, which no doubt worked in his favor. She was very sweet and Oliver seemed to like her. At least she looked too young to be hiding any husbands anywhere—a marked improvement.

A solid six months on the man diet hadn't erased *all* of my instincts. In the sea of attractive Westsiders who strolled by our stall, I couldn't help but notice an attractive man in his forties who came by each week with his daughters. I also noticed that he didn't wear a wedding ring. He told me his name was Patrick. He had short sandy hair—couldn't I be attracted to anything else?—and startlingly blue eyes which became enchanting when he smiled. And he smiled a lot. His girls—Sophie and Marissa—were eight and nine, which was a little older than our target demographic but they stopped by to say hello and play with Oliver when he was with me.

Patrick began a little ritual of bringing a latte for me, and chocolate-chip cookies for Oliver when they stopped by. We would attempt to steal a moment of conversation while the kids played. His girls would smile and look embarrassed.

"He likes you," Emma said one morning after they left.

"I'm on a man diet, remember? We smoked them all out!"

"Don't be an idiot. He seems great—and he has adorable little girls. He is exactly the kind of guy you should be going out with . . . for once. He *is* the prototype. You turn him down and I will have to ring your neck."

"Well, I can't turn him down because he hasn't asked me anything yet," I said, and busied myself rearranging the books for the third time.

"Are you going to tell me you think he brings you a latte and cookies because he has nothing else to do with his Sunday mornings? Trust me. He's going to ask you out!"

"I don't want to think about it because I don't want to be disappointed if he doesn't."

"Okay, that's reasonable. He's probably shy in front of his girls, but I'm betting he will get around to it."

"We'll see . . ." I didn't want to devote any time thinking about it, but I was hoping he would.

I had more immediate concerns. CeCe was going to be putting her apartment on the market soon and I had to get my finances in order. Oliver and I would be moving out. I had no choice but to make this venture a success. Distractions were not part of the deal.

Chapter Thirty-Four
Fancy A Quickie Wedding?

With the wedding only a couple of weeks away, CeCe's unadulterated enthusiasm for this fourth venture down the aisle was infectious. It was impossible to begrudge her this happiness. She deserved it. She'd kissed enough toads in her day—hairy or otherwise.

The nuptials were to be held at Phillip's Santa Barbara home, and he had given CeCe carte blanche. She was getting to plan her own spectacular affair and have the wedding she had always wanted—after three smaller-scale 'rehearsals', as she preferred to call them.

CeCe hired the uber-wedding planner Missy White to oversee every detail. From the pictures she showed me, the Santa Barbara house looked like it had been designed for a wedding—it was something straight out of *Architectural Digest* magazine or *Elle Décor*. It had a large sprawling lawn perfect for a tent and a dance floor, and large oak trees to hang chandeliers from. Sam was tapped to walk her down the aisle, Oliver was going to be the ring bearer, and everything was swiftly falling into place. CeCe had never looked so happy.

She had chosen a slate-blue silk cocktail-length dress that swept over one shoulder and left the other one exposed. The length highlighted her spectacular legs. There had been some debate about showcasing "the boobs or legs, but never both," as CeCe had put it—and the legs had won out.

"Not bad for an old bird, eh?" she joked as she modeled the slinky number for me at her fitting at Neiman Marcus.

"You look stunning, CeCe. It's gorgeous!" I said, impressed that she could still stop traffic in her sixties.

"Good. I think it'll do the job!"

CeCe insisted I try on a cream strapless dress.

"Don't you think this style and color looks too much like a bride?" I sucked in my stomach and looked at it in the mirror. It was dreamy and skimmed my body in a tasteful, yet highly effective manner, which was suitably reflected in its price tag.

"Maybe I should wear that dusty-rose-colored dress instead. That looks more like a traditional maid-of-honor color," I said, and indicated a much more drab-looking option that was still on the hanger.

"Nonsense," said CeCe. "Dusty-rose is boring. It's for tired old tarts, not for you, my darling. You've still got a lot of game left in you. This is the one!"

"Game-free would be more like it but I'll wear it if you like it," I said, feeling a well of excitement brewing inside me. There was something magical about the dress. I felt *different* in it.

"Great! Let's take it," said CeCe triumphantly.

The flush of wedding planning activities brought back memories of my own wedding. Under CeCe's direction, it had been a lavish, overblown affair. It was an auspicious beginning for a marriage that soon fell as flat as a pancake. CeCe had often lamented that *if only* her wedding planning duties had extended to selecting the groom.

We sat at the bar on the fourth floor of Neiman's and sipped Kir Royales to celebrate selecting the dresses and to toast her upcoming nuptials.

"Are you okay that I don't have a date for your wedding?" I asked, as we sipped the champagne and watched the well-heeled Neiman's shoppers parading by.

"That's fine, darling. It's still better than being stuck married to that cretin," she said with a chortle.

"Marriage isn't my forte," I said, although it didn't need stating.

"Oh, sweetheart, some marriages aren't meant to last," she said. "And it's a mistake to try and give them a longer shelf life than they have any right to expect. Oliver was the great gift to come out of that, and we're all grateful for that perfect child."

CeCe raised her glass to toast again.

"To Oliver . . . bless his heart."

"To Oliver, cheers." I took a sip. "It was a beautiful wedding you gave me, CeCe. Thank you. I'm sorry that the union didn't justify the send-off."

"Of course, darling. It's been years now. You can stop thanking me for that. You've got to get past that. We all knew *that* marriage wasn't going to last, but I wanted you to have the best wedding because that is what you deserved. I couldn't do anything about the ding-dong husband but at least I could give you a spectacular send-off. But you've got to move past that now. That marriage is *over!*"

"I'm very lucky to have you in my corner." I leaned over and rested my head on her shoulder briefly.

This was as close as I got to telling CeCe that I loved her—not because I didn't, but it just wasn't ever verbally expressed. Warm and fuzzy was not something we cultivated. It was only when we moved to America that I thought anything of this restraint. American people seemed quite casual about saying *I love you*. They ended conversations with *I love you* and tossed it around like confetti. This was the very opposite of how I had been raised. *I love you* was very hard to earn and not to be bandied about at the drop of a hat. CeCe attributed her reserved nature to her own mother and her colonial stiff-upper-lip upbringing, claiming that physical or verbal affection just wasn't done in her house. CeCe might not have been the most conventional Mother of the Year but her heart was always in the right place.

It was possible that CeCe might have inspired a dose of wedding fever because whirlwind weddings were popping up all over. Autumn had been missing in action again, this time for over a month. But when she surfaced, she had her own big news. She'd dumped her long-time boyfriend for a lawyer named Peter who kept her on a very short leash, and they'd had an impromptu seaside wedding in Cabo San Lucas.

It seemed like an odd match—an ultraconservative guy with an exotic, untamed creature like Autumn—but in a way it made perfect sense. She said he wouldn't tolerate any of what he termed her 'unacceptable behavior.' He laid down the contract—she would have to commit to him and only him—and amazingly, she agreed. Autumn was the last person I thought would succumb to marriage, let alone to such a traditional man, but she did. They would be making their first official appearance as husband and wife at CeCe's wedding. If even die-hard commitment-phobes like Autumn were taking the plunge, there was hope for everyone.

Autumn met me for dinner at Katsuya in Brentwood to give me all the details. Her hair was a subdued brown hue that I'd never seen before. I had to do a double take to make sure it was her. Radiant and gorgeous in one of her drop-dead foxy outfits—funky heels and a sleek shift dress—she was a glowing example of newly wedded bliss.

"Okay, what on earth made you decide it was him?" I asked her, puzzled by the sudden about-face. "You always said that marriage was boring and for wimps. Now you've surrendered and joined the enemy camp! What happened?"

"Part of it was timing," she said, playing with her new simple gold wedding band. "I would go out to bars and look around, and to my amazement—and *abject terror*—I discovered that I wasn't always the hottest woman in the room anymore. All these young beautiful girls everywhere . . . *where the fuck did they come from?* It was getting harder and harder to compete. Sooner or later, I guess we all have to hang up our dancing shoes."

"Jeez, that's a depressing answer." I laughed. "Tell me about Peter. What's he like?"

"He's normal, just a normal guy. He's straight as a fucking arrow. He doesn't take my shit, likes very normal, traditional sex, and I dig that about him. He doesn't need a lot of bells and whistles."

"But you're the bells and whistle girl, for crying out loud. Since when have you been interested in traditional sex, or traditional anything, for that matter? What made you decide to marry him so quickly?" I asked.

"I decided it was time I grew up."
I couldn't argue with that. We all had to grow up sometime.
Some of us just needed a man diet and an Indian cleansing ritual first.
I drove home and mulled over what she had said about growing up. It sounded so simple but I knew it wasn't or everyone who got married would 'grow up' and stay that way. My failure at marriage had inspired me to discover what made other people successful at it. What made people feel comfortable taking that step?
It became a question I posed to all my married friends.
Emma gave the most revealing response one evening over drinks in the lobby bar at L'Hermitage.
"Listen," she said. "I knew I wanted to marry Chris because he had seen me at my best, but more importantly, he'd also seen me in my deepest, darkest moments of self-loathing. And he still wanted to be with me. He wasn't scared off by my emotions or all the crazy shit that lies under the surface. I never have to pretend with him. He sees me, he gets me and he likes the whole package. None of it fazes him."
"You mean you actually *let* him see all that self-loathing business?" I asked, floored by the concept.
"Oh, yeah. Believe me, honey . . . he's seen it *all*." Emma laughed heartily.
"Wait a minute, aren't you supposed to keep all that crap under the hood?"
"You don't have to let it all hang out on a first date," she said. "But I have never hidden anything from Chris. No game playing. I was myself with him—the good, the bad and the ugly."
"That sounds so brave," I said, absorbing what she'd said. "I could never do that."
"Yes, you could—and you have to." Emma grabbed a handful of nuts out of the bowl and started eating them.
"I'm so afraid of . . ." I paused, took a sip of Cabernet and struggled to come up with the right word. "Seeming needy? Showing who I really am? I don't know exactly. CeCe's philosophy is never let them see your hand, but she also thinks life isn't any fun if you're not with a man, so you can see why the subject of love is mystifying to me."
"I think you're avoiding intimacy. You've been dating unavailable men as long as I've known you. That's probably so that you don't have to risk dealing with true intimacy. It is a scary thing but I can promise you it is worth the risk. Don't you want to take that chance?"
"I think not having a father in my life wreaked some havoc. It feels like it left a big hole in my heart that I've been trying to fill ever since. I've watched CeCe's revolving door of men for years and now I realize that, subconsciously, I have been repeating the pattern. I end up picking ones that it will never work out with. It's terrifying to think that I could be destined to be in this loop forever."

"You can change that any time you want."

"Do you think so?" I said, feeling a surge of hope.

"Sure, pain is a great motivator. Haven't you had quite enough shitty relationships? When you realize that you are enough without a man, having one can be a beautiful thing . . . and you will have one again someday, when you're ready."

"My whole life I've tried to fill up this sense of longing. And getting lost in men only made that ache worse."

"Yeah, men . . . they have to be used in small doses, as directed. They're not the solution."

"The only thing that seems to help combat that feeling of emptiness is when I get lost in a painting or when I'm doing someone's makeup and I get caught up in that swell of creation. There's a freedom there."

"I know just what you mean. When I'm acting and it just flows . . . it's magic. 'The only way for a woman to find herself, to *know* herself as a person, is by creative work of her own. There is no other way'—Betty Friedan."

"Wow, that's brilliant and so true! Why don't they teach us that in school? Why don't they make movies where the woman saves herself? Where are the fairy tales that teach us to get our shit together first before you expect the prince to appear? It might save a lot of heartache looking in the wrong places. I wish I could have back some of those lost years pining for idiot wankers when I should have been focused on my own life!"

"Keep working on your creativity and you can't go wrong. Look at how well you're doing with your books. People are gobbling them up and that's something you have created on your own. Your brains and your drive made this happen. Who needs a man for that? You're doing great!"

"Yes, that's true. I'm on my own and I'm rather enjoying the simplicity of life without a man. I like not having to work so hard."

"It's been good for you but don't use it as an excuse to hide out, either. You have to get good at negotiating the balance."

"Aren't you the sage one tonight?" I said with admiration. "I think CeCe getting married again has brought up a lot of memories."

"That makes sense," Emma said, picking up another handful of nuts.

"You know what I remember most from my childhood? I remember feeling so relieved every time CeCe found a husband or a serious boyfriend because that meant I didn't have to worry about her anymore. Somebody else could have that job. It was so exhausting."

"She's your mother. You're not supposed to be worrying about her. It's supposed to be the other way around."

"Yes, but I'm not sure CeCe knows she's the mother. She's never really acted like a mother. Maybe it was a consequence of having me when she was so young."

"I don't know if it's about age," Emma said, tentatively. "She left you like a piece of luggage in different countries around the world and took off. I love CeCe, but that's *not* what mothers are supposed to do. Think about it. Would you dump Oliver in another country with relatives and go off on adventures?"

"I can't imagine doing that," I said softly.

"You need to accept CeCe for being CeCe. Accept the wonderful things about her—and there are a ton of great things—but also accept her limitations. You're a very different person and you're a very different type of parent. Look at what you've been through and you're dealing with all of it well now. A lot of people are content to stay in bad marriages. Sometimes it's just easier."

"Staying in that marriage wasn't an option. I was suffocating. I'm not a perfect mother by any means. It's a hard job and I see that now. Being a parent is such a huge responsibility. It's quite daunting when you think about it. The ramifications are huge. Oliver is so sweet and innocent. I keep thinking, 'I hope I'm not screwing this up!' "

"Oliver's fine. But at least you're aware. My parents were clueless and I bet I'd be just as bad at it—that's why I'm not sure if I want kids. If it happens, it happens. I like my life. I like being able to work out when I want, or work on location and travel. What can I say? I *enjoy* being selfish." She laughed at the admission.

The waitress came by and collected our empty glasses.

"Nobody gets through childhood unscathed and that's just life, I guess," Emma said after she'd gone. "Do you know a single person who's not pissed at one or both of their parents?"

"No, I don't," I said, after a quick scan of the memory banks. "Everybody's pissed at their parents at one point or another."

"Yep. Nobody gets through childhood—or life—without baggage. It's what you do with that baggage that counts."

"Well, it's not too late to turn mine into a charming set of Louis Vuittons!"

I felt more on track than I ever had before, so that was an improvement. Something had shifted. I was working toward something and making plans for Oliver and me. I was happier and productive and not looking to other people to distract me—or fix me. I had my flaws but in the grand scheme of things, I was doing okay. I was opting for my own version of the modern fairy tale. I was working on myself, and letting everything else fall into place.

Chapter Thirty-Five
The Drought Is Over

The following Sunday, amid the sea of families enjoying their morning perusing the stands of colorful fruits and vegetables, I spotted Patrick walking toward me. This time, he was alone.

"Hi, Scarlett," he said with what looked like the tiniest hint of a flush to his cheeks.

"Hey, Patrick. Flying solo today? How are the girls?" I asked.

He looked especially handsome and had a fresh haircut to boot. I wondered what he did for a living. He had "professional-hair," as CeCe always called it, meaning that someone didn't look like a dropkick loser; that he likely had a job.

"The girls are fine, thanks, but I wanted to come on my own today. Would you like to have dinner with me sometime?" He blurted this all out in quick succession, as if the words might expire if he didn't expel them in time.

"Oh, I'd love to," I said, feeling myself blush.

"How about Tuesday?" he said, beaming a smile filled with relief.

"Sounds great," I said. We exchanged numbers and put them into our respective cell phones.

I watched him walk away, enjoying the way his jeans afforded me a very nice view of his beautiful thick thighs striding away purposefully.

As soon as he was out of earshot, I called Emma.

"You're not going to believe this. Patrick asked me out. We're having dinner on Tuesday. *You called it!*"

"See! I'm not at all surprised!" Emma laughed.

"Do you think it's a real date, or do you think he wants to have a chat about kid things?"

"Okay, now I *do* think you're losing it. Don't be silly, of course it's a date!"

"Am I ready to break my man diet? I've been getting along very well without a man. I'm terrified about losing myself again. What about all the

Synchronized Breathing

good work I've done in the man-free zone?"

"You'll be fine. It doesn't vanish. Just go slowly, that's all."

"You're right. Go slow. I'll have to test it at some point, anyway. I didn't commit to being a hermit forever."

"As if. You have CeCe's genes, for God's sake. Let's not forget that genetic mandate."

—∽—

Patrick chose The Little Door restaurant in Hollywood, which thrilled me as it was romantic and signified that this was indeed a date. I was no longer in trying-to-impress-a-man mode and selected a navy DVF wrap dress that looked feminine but didn't have all the bells and whistles going at once. It was understated. For this date, I wanted to feel comfortable and be myself.

I checked my e-mail before leaving. Susan had been sending my proposals out. I needed to be on top of all her correspondence. Things were moving quickly.

There in the in-box was a message from Jeremy.

It said *Whassup?* in the subject heading.

I gasped. What could he possibly have to say? Hadn't we covered everything?

After the initial shock wore off, I sat there looking at it for a moment, wondering whether to open it. Then the sweetest calm came over me and I discovered I really didn't care what he might have to say. *Whassup* really said it all, and I wasn't interested.

I hit delete and logged off.

—∽—

Walking into the restaurant to meet Patrick, I had butterflies in my stomach. The nerves went away as soon as I spotted him. He was leaning against the wall, looking at his phone. When he looked up and saw me, he gave a broad smile and put his phone away.

"Hello, Scarlett," he said, and gave me a kiss on the cheek.

He looked far dressier than I'd seen him at the market—and sexier. He wasn't in casual dad mode. He was in date mode—for me. He was wearing dark jeans with a crisp white linen shirt, to mesmerizing effect. I felt my knees go a little weak. My hormones were kicking in.

"You look lovely," he said with that smile still etched to his face.

"Thank you," I said, feeling shy all of a sudden.

The hostess showed us to a table in the courtyard and Patrick ordered us glasses of pinot noir. It was the first time we'd been alone and could finish a sentence without being interrupted.

"So how are you, Miss Scarlett?" he said and focused his attention on me.

"I'm exceptionally well, thank you," I said, blushing. "How is it being a divorced dad?"

"It's a lot of pressure. You feel like you can't afford to drop the ball, you've already screwed up once and you've got these little people depending on you."

"I know that feeling." I nodded.

Patrick talked about his girls and how important they were to him. His eyes lit up when he spoke of attending every dance recital, of rearranging his work schedule so that his girls were the priority. It was clear that he was very serious about his role as a father. I got the impression he wasn't busy banging married moms at school. There was nothing boyish about him. He was a man. He was an adult and it was profoundly attractive.

"Between the girls and work, it gets pretty hectic but it's sort of an organized chaos. At least that's what I'm aiming for."

"What sort of work do you do, Patrick?" I held my breath and hoped that he wasn't going to say he was a musician or, God forbid, a movie producer.

"I am an architect," he said between bites of salad. "I've loved building things since I was a little kid—and now I just build bigger things." He laughed.

He was hypnotizing me with the way he lightly stroked the stem of his wineglass. I noted that he had beautifully thick fingers as a delicious bolt of electricity ran down my spine. It was nice to know that the machinery still worked.

"I love what you're doing with your books. They're fun and upbeat, and as an artist, I respect that you're putting your work out there. I admire that. It isn't easy."

"Thank you," I said, and felt myself blush again.

"Have you been doing this for long?" he asked.

I laughed. "I guess you could say I have suffered from a bit of career ADD. I've been an actress and a makeup artist, and now I'm peddling children's books." My patchwork quilt of a career made me sound nuts.

"Well, I think it's terrific," he said and held my gaze.

Patrick was a great storyteller with an infectious, hearty laugh. He told me about moving out from Chicago and how he should have taken a course in 'how to deal with the flaky people' in Los Angeles.

"How do you not lose yourself out here?" he asked.

"That's an excellent question," I said. "There's a reason they call it La-La land."

He laughed.

"You have to be conscious of it and work very hard to remember what's important," I said.

"There are so many things in life that interest me, but I have to say that being a father is the most important one right now. I just try to do the best for my girls and enjoy my time with them."

"That's admirable," I said, trying not to slip off my chair onto the floor. He was such a different type of man than I'd ever encountered. It was so refreshing.

"How is Oliver faring with your divorce? He seems like a great kid."

"He is the most amazing kid. I'm so fortunate. He seems to be adjusting well, which is probably because he was so young when the split happened, but I still worry about him. You always feel a sense of guilt, that you've put them through this ordeal."

"Yes, you do. But you also have to trust that kids are resilient," he said.

"Thank God for that!"

"And how are you faring, Scarlett? How do you feel about where your life is at, after your divorce?"

I was disarmed by the question. Kids I could talk about all day long, but now he wanted to know my feelings, too? It was scary territory.

"Well, I can tell you it's heading in a lot better direction than it was, so I am happy about that. It requires faith and a lot of hard work. And how far along are you in this whole process?" I asked.

"It takes at least three years to get your bearings, I've found. But I'm getting there," he said with a hint of a smile.

"I can tell you have sisters," I said. "You're a good listener and you ask the right questions."

He laughed at this. "Yes, I have two sisters. Is it that obvious? I thought the heel marks had faded from my forehead by now." He brushed at imaginary marks on his face.

We both laughed and then we stopped, and there was a moment where we just looked at each other, full of anticipation.

Just breathe.

"I haven't had a date in a long time." I made my confession apropos of nothing and then wondered why I was compelled to announce that. Rule number one: *Don't bring up your crappy dating history.*

"Really? That surprises me." He smiled.

There was something about Patrick that made me feel comfortable. Eating didn't seem to be an issue around him either. I polished off my steak, plus half the olive bread without any problem.

"Tell me about your divorce," I asked, turning the tables.

"It turns out she was sleeping with my best friend—among others."

"Oh, wow. That sucks. I'm so sorry."

"Yeah, it was humiliating. You think you know someone and then you find out that while you're at work, they're sleeping with trainers at the gym. She had this whole other life with secret cell phones and would meet these guys in hotel rooms. It was pretty unbelievable."

"That is beyond awful."

"Yeah, she would leave the kids at dance class and forget to pick them up. I would get a call at work saying 'Your kids have been sitting here for three hours. Is anyone coming to pick them up?' "

"That must have been so painful for all of you. You didn't deserve that."

Her antics made X seem stately by comparison.

"She cared so much about how everything looked, that we appeared to have the model family, but it wasn't real. It was rotten to the core."

"I'm sorry to hear that."

I was impressed that he was able to share that ugly information with me. We had both been through a lot but there was a huge difference: Patrick's life had always looked perfect from the outside before it imploded, and my life had never looked even remotely perfect. Patrick was a salt-of-the-earth type of guy who believed in commitment. When he married he thought it was forever. He never dreamed he'd find himself divorced with two lovely girls. Somehow finding myself divorced and a single mother had not come as a huge shock.

"You know, I consider myself lucky to not be in a sham of a marriage anymore thinking I had it all. What a fool I was, but now if I can make things as good as they can be for the girls, then I have to be happy with that. I count my blessings."

"That's a commendable attitude."

"There's no other choice, really. I tried sitting around feeling sorry for myself, and that wasn't much fun."

"Yeah, I did that, too. It gets old. Not to mention dull."

Three hours flew by. We ordered coffee and dessert. Our waiter—irritated that we had monopolized his table all evening—became hard to ignore.

"Can I get you *anything* else?" he said for the fourth time.

"Are you sure you don't want another dessert?" Patrick asked, after watching me all but lick the tiramisu off the plate.

"Oh, no! Don't encourage me!" I shrieked.

"I think it's very sexy that you like to eat, Scarlett. You'd be surprised how many women in this town don't, and I find that so boring. They order a salad with dressing on the side and then don't even finish it."

"Oh, I'm very good at eating," I said. "No issue there."

"I guess we have been camping out. I better leave him a big tip," said Patrick, laughing as he paid the check.

We walked out to the street through the late night crowd that was starting to gather at the bar.

"Thank you, Patrick. That was lovely. The restaurant was wonderful."

"I'm glad you liked it. I asked my buddy at work where I should take you. He always knows all the cool spots and I have no clue," Patrick said, quite comfortable with this admission, which was a distinct turn-on.

It was so sexy to be in the company of a man who was comfortable in his own skin and didn't have anything to prove.

"My car is over there," I said, and pointed down the street.

"Let me walk you, then," he said, and we started to walk toward it.

"Listen, the girls are with their mother this weekend. Would you like to have dinner with me on Saturday?"

"Oh, I'd love to, but this Saturday I can't—it's my mother's wedding!"

"Wow, your mother's getting married? That's great. You didn't mention it."

Stories about CeCe opened the door to questions about CeCe, and that sort of information was definitely not on the approved program for date number one, *or four*.

"Yep, she's tying the knot . . . again."

"Do you have anyone escorting you to the wedding?"

"No. Well, Oliver's my escort."

"Did you want to take a date?" he asked and then gestured to himself as if to say *Ta-dah!*

"You're kidding, right?" I asked. "You'd sign up for that?" I stopped and looked at him with utter amazement.

"Sure, why not?"

"I can give you plenty of reasons: my family's a little nutty, the wedding's in Santa Barbara—two and a half hours away—and I'll have Oliver with me, and so I'll be a bit preoccupied and you hardly know me . . . and you won't know anybody there." I rattled off my list of deterrents but he was unfazed.

"Sounds great to me," he said, amiably. "I can make all of that work."

I looked at him like he was mad. "So let me get this straight . . . you'd be willing to come as my date to a wedding? Aren't weddings in the 'don't-even-think-about-it-for-the-first-six-months' section of the dating rule book?"

"Oh, I don't believe in those rules," he said and laughed.

"Well, then, yes . . . I'd like you to be my date for the wedding. You are a brave man!" I said with admiration, and linked my arm through his.

We strolled up the street toward my car, neither of us in a hurry to end the evening.

"Would you like to go and get another drink or a coffee?' Patrick asked as we approached my car.

I smiled. He was trying to prolong the date. "Thank you, but it's getting a little late. I'd better get home."

I followed an impulse and kissed him good-night on the cheek. It may have been my imagination but I thought he blushed.

"I had a wonderful time," I said, before hopping into my car.

"Me, too." His broad smile was still affixed to his lips. "I'll be seeing you very soon, Miss Scarlett."

—m—

As soon as I got home, I called Emma.

"Are you kidding me?" She shrieked. "He's coming to the wedding? Oh my God, I love this guy already!"

"Can you believe he's fine with immersing himself in wedding craziness this early in the game? He gets major points for that."

"He doesn't scare easily, that's for sure. He has kids; maybe that helps."

"Yes, the kid factor helps. He's already met Oliver and we've met his girls. So all those cards are on the table."

"He sounds like a good guy. CeCe is going to shit herself."

"I know. I haven't even told her that I was breaking my man diet."

"That's the best damn wedding present you could get her. This guy is a mother's wet dream!"

Chapter Thirty-Six
Synchronized Breathing

"CeCe, sit still!" I admonished her as she wriggled on the barstool. "These false eyelashes will look very drag-queen-*ish* if I don't get them on properly." Using the edge of a skinny liner brush, I pressed the lashes firmly against her lash line.

"I'm too excited to sit still!" She shrieked. "I'm getting married today!"

"I know. It's very exciting. Now let me finish your makeup so you can get down there and marry that wonderful man of yours!"

We sat upstairs in the master bedroom with the balcony doors open and the Pacific Ocean shimmering in the distance. It was a glorious day for a wedding. Andy LeCompte had just finished blowing out CeCe's hair, giving her the sleek, glossy mane that was her trademark. She looked fabulous. Even in her bathrobe. Missy White nodded approvingly. She walked over to me when I was finished and said, "Scarlett, you did a lovely job. You know, I have weddings virtually every weekend—you should come and work with me. We could use you. Why don't you call my office next week and we'll get all your info and get you on our books."

"That sounds great. I love doing brides—even ones I'm not related to. Thank you, Missy."

I couldn't keep the smile off my face. Good news was springing up all over CeCe's wedding. Regular work meant regular paychecks—which I would need to pay the rent when Oliver and I found our apartment.

"I'm so excited you brought a date, Scarlett! You're going to be next up for this wedding business, you know! I can feel it," CeCe said.

"Okay, settle down there. Let's not put the cart before the horse. I've had one date with the guy! Let's focus on one wedding at a time," I said, and applied a crème blush to the apples of her cheeks.

"Phillip's son is here from New York and wants to see your books. He's in publishing, you know."

"I'd love to show them to him but let's get you married first, so then we

Tara Ellison

can work the nepotism angle!"

Oliver darted in, with Sam trailing behind him. Oliver was wearing his suave new tuxedo that CeCe had selected to match Sam's, and the two of them looked ridiculously handsome together. I kissed Oliver and smoothed his hair behind his ears. It was getting too long but I loved the way the curls sat at the nape of his neck and was hesitant to cut it.

Oliver produced a crumpled napkin from his pocket bearing a handful of melted chocolate truffles and proceeded to eat them. I waited for CeCe to start shrieking but she didn't.

"Let's wash those hands, sweetie," I said, and started to walk him to the bathroom.

"Oliver, darling! You look smashing, my boy! Come and give me a lucky wedding kiss."

He walked over and licked his fingers while CeCe covered his cheeks with kisses. CeCe was bubbling over with affection—a rare sight, given that it was not a natural inclination for her. Even Sam was treated to uncharacteristic pats and smooches. Sam had been cultivating long sideburns, which made him look much older. He cut a handsome figure in his tux to give his mother away at her fairy tale wedding. CeCe rested her head against his broad shoulder while I took pictures.

Mikki was nursing a glass of champagne in her own chic wedding ensemble—a slip dress in the uncharacteristic shade of soft pink, with her standard super-high black booties. Her makeup was still on the heavy side with dramatic metallic-gray eye shadow, thick black eyeliner and bubble-gum pink lipstick but she looked beautiful. I couldn't help but completely redo her makeup in my head, as I always did when conversing with her.

"Mikki, darling, you look lovely!" CeCe said as soon as she saw her, and gave her a hug.

Mikki looked stunned. You could have knocked her over with a feather. CeCe didn't dole out hugs.

Sam took Oliver's hand and everyone cleared out as I helped CeCe into her dress.

"I don't need the *something old* part since that would be *me!*" she said gaily.

"Old? Hardly! Don't be ridiculous," I said. "You're covered with the something blue—with your dress—and you have new shoes, but you need something *borrowed* . . . I don't have any jewelry you'd be interested in but I found grandmother's old jewelry box with some potentials. Here, take a look." I produced the little treasures I'd found when I cleaned out the closet. "There's nothing too fancy but there are some fabulous costume earrings, and there's a delicate diamond bracelet here, too. That might be more your style."

"They're very pretty, darling, but what I'd rather like to wear—if you're okay with it—is your heart necklace. That way I can carry a bit of you and Oliver with me. That would mean more to me."

"CeCe, what a lovely gesture. Of course you can have it. I'd be delighted if you wore it." I was touched. "Here, you go." Fighting back tears, I unclasped it from my neck and slipped it around hers.

We both looked in the mirror. She looked radiant and was getting misty, too.

"There . . . that's perfect." I said. "Now you're ready to go and claim your man. Don't you *dare* cry or you'll ruin your makeup and I'll be very upset with you!"

"No time for tears—I've got a wonderful man to marry! And it took me a lifetime to find him!"

"Let's not keep him waiting another moment."

I presented her with her bouquet of lilies of the valley and we walked downstairs, arm in arm.

"Here we go!" she said triumphantly.

"Yes, this is it. Here we go." I gave her a big, lingering hug—for perhaps the first time ever. CeCe whimpered softly and held onto me for dear life. The silence was heavy with unsaid apologies, on both parts. After an extended moment, she exhaled deeply and released me. I blotted the tears from her eyes and then my own. "Okay, let's do this," I said.

Oliver waved to us from where he was waiting with Mikki. "Hurry up, CeCe!" he said with all the cheek a four-year-old boy could muster. We waved back and Missy White gave Oliver his cue to walk down the aisle. Sam stepped in between us to take over. We both held Sam's arms for a moment, and then I slipped ahead of them and made my way down to the front, which was carpeted in pink and white rose petals.

I tried to maintain my composure as I walked down the aisle. I *loathed* this part, hated the attention and the weight of everyone's eyes on you, however briefly.

I spotted Susan, and Autumn with her new husband Peter, sitting next to the aisle. She smiled and waved as I passed. Peter, who wore a smart-looking suit, looked straight as an arrow, which was exactly how she'd described him. He was about as far as you could get from the broke, artsy types she used to favor. I smiled and waved back, trying not to let my heel catch in the grass and launch me indelicately into the front row.

Patrick was in the third row, next to Emma and Chris. Emma gave a thumbs-up gesture behind Patrick's back, and Patrick smiled as I approached.

Everyone rose as Sam walked CeCe down the aisle, which was just the sort of reception she relished.

I took my place off to the side and turned to see CeCe beaming with joy, arm-in-arm with her handsome young son.

Once they got to Phillip, Sam joked, "Take my mother . . . *please!*" Everyone laughed, although some of us knew it was not a joke.

CeCe and Phillip were married on a platform inside a huge hanging heart made of fresh pink and red roses—to startling effect. They took the plunge in front of one hundred of their closest friends, with the air heavy with the scent of gardenias and roses, just as she dreamed it would be. It was perfection.

After the ceremony, Patrick joined us and we sat at the head table with Oliver between us. I tried not to think about how sexy Patrick looked in his suit, eating shrimp cocktail and having a casual conversation with Oliver about school and Henry the Eighth. Watching Patrick with Oliver, treating him as a grown-up boy and having a chat about things that grown-up boys like, was a huge turn-on, and I watched with awe. They discovered they had a mutual affection for *SpongeBob* and took turns asking each other SpongeBob trivia questions.

Oliver seemed to genuinely enjoy Patrick—and Oliver was a hard sell.

"Oliver, would you like to have dinner with me and the girls sometime? You and your mom could pick the restaurant."

Oliver considered the invitation for a moment before answering. "Okay, but *not* Chinese food. My mom does really *bad* Chinese farts when she eats that. Pee-ew," he said, and pinched his nose to make his point.

"Oliver!" I gasped. "That's very rude! What a hideous thing to say!" I was horrified.

Patrick laughed and winked at Oliver. "I think I can handle it."

He didn't scare easily. I could say that much for the man.

I excused myself and got up from the table to say hello to Autumn and meet Peter.

I glanced back over at our table and watched as Patrick had taken the forks off the table and was constructing a building with the silverware. Oliver sat mesmerized as Patrick showed him how he did it. It was a beautiful, unrehearsed moment between them.

I watched Patrick with him and thought *maybe, just maybe . . .*

Susan marched up to me after I'd gone over to say hi to Autumn and Peter.

"And why the hell aren't you answering your messages, missy? Or your e-mails?" she demanded.

"Oh, shit. Sorry. It's been crazy with all this," I said, and waved a hand in the air at the ensuing extravaganza.

"You have a meeting with Nickelodeon Networks on Tuesday! I've been trying to find you since yesterday but you don't pick up your damn phone. I had to drive all the way to Santa *fucking* Barbara to find you. Thanks a lot!"

"*Holy shit!* Are you serious?" This was as golden an opportunity as you could ever hope to find in Hollywood.

"Yes, they want you to pitch them a series based on the books. You better work your ass off on the pitch this weekend. You get one shot with them."

"Wow . . . yes, yes! I'll get Emma to help me rehearse a pitch. Thank you! That is beyond amazing!"

I was bursting with excitement and wanted to grab the microphone and scream out the news to the entire gathering, but instead I nursed it like a newborn chick. This was CeCe's day.

I also just wanted to sit with this glorious development and enjoy it on my own for a little bit.

CeCe's wedding was a huge success. It was the magical affair she had always longed for. She and Phillip were deep in the love cocoon and it was lovely to watch them—husband and wife—making the rounds and chatting with their guests. CeCe couldn't stop smiling and Phillip looked very proud. I noticed that he couldn't keep his hand off her bum, and kept giving her pinches, as if testing fruit at the market. They were made for each other.

After dinner, I spotted Sam standing by himself at the bar, sipping champagne. He looked like a bona fide adult standing alone in his fabulous tux. I excused myself, left the boys to amuse themselves and walked across the manicured lawn to join him.

"So how are you doing?" I asked as I helped myself to some well-earned bubbly.

"I'm relieved," he said with the wisdom of someone well beyond his years.

"Oh, God, it is a huge bloody relief, isn't it?" I exhaled as if all the air had collapsed right out of me.

We both laughed.

"Yeah. Now I don't have to worry about her all the time," he said and his face flickered with emotion for a brief second. I caught it and it suddenly hit me. I had been so wrapped up in my own problems that I hadn't considered how the CeCe Effect manifested for him. He was her kid, too. What a lousy sister I'd been.

"I know just what you mean. That must have been very difficult for you, worrying about her for all those years. It's a lot of energy having to worry about your mother—it's supposed to be the other way around. I escaped for a while but you were stuck there, in the trenches. I'm sorry that I wasn't more of a help to you, and I hope you're not too worse for wear."

"Nah . . . she's a handful, but she's happy now, so it was all worth it." His face brightened at the thought.

"Wow, Sam, you've really grown up. You've become a very fine young man and I'm so proud of you. Here's to you, Sam." I felt the tears welling up again.

"Thanks. Cheers," he said, as we clinked glasses.

"What are we drinking to?" Mikki asked as she joined us.

"We're drinking to the unloading of our dear mother!" I glanced back over at the table. Patrick was holding his own chatting with CeCe and Oliver. He hadn't run screaming from the party. He'd passed that particular test. It was a good beginning.

Patrick must have sensed me looking at him because he glanced up and smiled. I smiled back.

"Let me add something else," I said to Sam and Mikki. "Here's to knowing when to get out of your own way!"

The End

About the Author

Tara Ellison was born in London and raised between Sydney and Hong Kong before coming to the United States. After moving to Los Angeles for a career in acting, Tara realized she was a better author than actor. *Synchronized Breathing* is her first novel.

Acknowledgments

I owe a huge debt of thanks to my friends and family for putting up with me during this book's unreasonably long gestation period.

To my husband who has shared all the ups and downs of this journey and somehow still managed to like me.

To Steph who has simply been the best confidant, advisor and super-glue-wielding friend I could ever have asked for.

To Karen Deitsch for an impossibly long list of good deeds and the kick in the derriere I needed to finally take the leap and make this happen.

A big thanks to UCLA Extension writing community.

A huge thank you to Margaret for tirelessly propping me up and insisting that I had something to say. Thanks to Louise, Steph (again), Pamela, Deb, Brooke, Tanya Woolcott, Charlie Peters and all the wonderful people who have given me editorial feedback.

To Allison Cohen for being such a stellar agent and champion of this book.

To Amanda and everyone at TWCS – thank you for your faith in this story. A great many thanks to my editor Wendy and her team for shepherding me through this process. Thanks also to Christa and Jenny for their unflagging enthusiasm for this project.

To Nina Hunter for the beautiful cover.

Thank you to my mother and my brothers for their continued support. And a huge nod to Bannar for being such a Renaisance woman, a creative force and inspiration in my life – you were way ahead of your time. But most of all, thank you to my daughter for believing in this book and me. (Not that you are ever allowed to read it.)

CPSIA information can be obtained at www.ICGtesting.com
Printed in the USA
LVOW10s0826101013

356126LV00007B/33/P